dancing the river lightly

r. h. sheldon

booth
&bohn
press

dancing the river lightly
second edition

r. h. sheldon

ISBN-13: 978-0-9910741-0-5
Library of Congress Control Number: 2013918755

Cover photo by R. H. Sheldon

Booth & Bohn Press
Seattle, USA

For my parents, my sister, and my brothers—
whose love and support have shown me that a
worm can indeed be on the other foot.

Sunday Afternoon

And God Said...

Paul Kazinski's spiritual quest began with a dream, a dream in which God told him that it might not be a bad idea to take a little trip. God also mentioned—as an afterthought—that Paul should consider using this time to settle down a bit, take a breather from his busy schedule. "Whatever sounds good to you," God said, "just don't make too big a deal out of the whole thing."

Paul took God at his word, even though he had no proof this guy really was anyone with divine connections. His ungodly attire—blue jeans, rainbow suspenders, white T-shirt, and baseball cap, hardly raiment of splendor—did little to confirm his identity. And his gray hair and short stubby body and ample beer gut only added to his less-than-heavenly presence. Still, there was something expansive about him, something wide and deep, like an ancient river. He spoke with confidence and authority, yet maintained a certain distance and nonchalance. Then there was the ease of his tone, the deep resonance, melodious and charismatic. Paul was convinced that this man, this being, had to be God. He sensed it somehow, felt it with a clear knowledge. After all, who else would have taken such pains to visit Paul?

What especially fascinated Paul was the way God considered each of Paul's questions before answering, as though thinking about them for the first time, which was quite surprising, what with the eternal nature of God and all that omniscient stuff. But even when Paul asked about such mundane issues as diets and eating properly, God pondered the questions with a sort of wonder, as though such ideas were being posed for the first time. And when God finally answered, he spoke with a matter-of-fact, almost indifferent tone, never quite suggesting that the issue was unimportant, but certainly striking a manner that delegated the subject to lesser realms, a celestial shrug sort of attitude.

"You know," God said after one of his thoughtful pauses, "a healthy diet is probably a good idea—taking care of the body, eating decent food. Yes, that might be the way to go, makes growing old a little easier, I should think." Then God pointed to a distant valley shoved up against a bluish mountain, where Moses toiled in his garden, tilling his field or raking leaves. "But don't go overboard like Moses or the others," God said. "They insist on turning everything into a religion."

Paul wasn't certain whether his meeting with God would qualify as a dream or a vision. In much the same way that he couldn't attest to the true identity of the guy he thought was God, Paul was also a little foggy about how he would describe his surreal encounter. Not much earlier, he had eaten a substantial quantity of psilocybin mushrooms, enough to make the idea of serious movement inconceivable. Even attempts at negotiating light switches and window blinds proved to be tasks too Herculean for Paul. In fact, the mushrooms warranted little more than lying in bed on his back, buried beneath a pile of blankets with his head nestled between two stacks of pillows to keep his face pointed toward the ceiling. His bedroom, dark in spite of a sunny summer afternoon, provided womblike comfort and safety against the risky world of consciousness.

So it was, within this state of heightened senses, where his atoms vibrated with a daring assault against common awareness, that Paul closed his eyes to shut in his ecstatic visions and shut out reminders of the physical, the mundane—the stains of everyday life. And in his dreamlike, vision-like reverie, he soared to magical, sunlit heights of super-charged, unrestrained, universal consciousness, as though he had plugged into the most cosmic of all outlets and the collective juice pulsated through him. And it was here, after God spoke to him about healthy eating and dogmatic prophets, he mentioned that Paul should consider a journey, a pleasant little holiday someplace nice.

"It will do you good," God said as he looked past Moses to the mountainous backdrop. "And you might want to lighten up on the hallucinogenics. You're thirty-eight now, and you don't have a lot of time to waste."

Paul awoke from his prophetic bout of awareness and stared at a slit of yellow light that filtered through the top of the window shade. Angels the size of dust particles danced in a stream of light, rejoicing at such a perfect and harmonious day.

Paul stared giddily at the performing heavenly creatures as patterns of circles and ovals and spirals wove in and out of the sparkling stream. The celestial beings pirouetted to a vibrating orchestra, an ecstatic hum that transcended sound, that pierced his soul with a steady sensation, beyond touch, beyond sight. Then the light faded to green, iridescent, glowing, sparkling. The light took on the shape of the forests, the green landscape of a lush and wild mountainside, like the forests of the Cascades, outside Seattle, away from the mad rush of flesh and concrete and steel and shouting and honking horns and carbon monoxide.

"The mountains," he thought, "that's where I shall begin my journey!"

And so it was, with little more than a suggestion, that Paul decided to set out for the dense forests of the Cascades, convinced that he now embarked on a journey of universal significance, that he was Siddhartha, striking out against convention and tradition to embark on a quest of the spirit, a crusade of the soul. He, Paul Kazinski, had been touched by the hand of God, directed into the wilderness, relying on faith alone—along with an REI backpack stuffed with REI lightweight, high-tech, back-to-nature camping equipment—to provide him with the comfort he would need in the challenging times ahead.

Monday Afternoon/Evening

The Green, Green Grass of Home

Rebecca Randall kneeled before the tomato plants in her abundant garden, tugging at the stray weeds that sprouted between the thick healthy plants. Early this morning, Benjamin, her husband, had left for the San Juan islands on business and would be gone for a couple of days. She knew little about the nature of his trip, which was not surprising, given that Benjamin, a real estate developer, rarely spoke to her about anything related to business, whether it had to do with maintaining the office, managing investments, or running the house. In the past, she had tried to question him about such matters, but she was met with curt answers and icy stares, so she gave up quickly and asked few questions.

But none of that mattered right now. She seldom had a full day to herself. Either she was tending to Benjamin or to her Church duties. Even when he needed to stay at their condo in the city, he would insist that she accompany him, in part to feed him and to make sure that he had cleaned and pressed clothes, but also because he liked having her around, at least that's what he told her. She never quite figured out why. It wasn't as though they talked a great deal or shared in activities, but her presence must have provided some sort of comfort, and she was happy enough to go along, though she certainly looked forward to these occasional opportunities to be alone.

Benjamin had left at five o'clock that morning. Despite the early hour, she had felt giddy, smiling and humming and sweeping around the house as though she had just won the lottery. Of course, she didn't play the lottery—that would never be allowed—but if she had bought a ticket and if she had won and if she had all that money to call her own, this was exactly how she would have felt. She celebrated by eating breakfast in front of the TV. She savored her corn flakes, knowing she could eat without having to interrupt her breakfast to wait on him, and she could watch what she wanted to watch. In fact, she had not even put on make-up this morning. And if the truth be known, she wasn't even wearing her garments. Frankly, she never understood why the

Church required that they wear garments, especially in summer. It was like wearing long underwear except with short sleeves and legs. And with as warm as it was going to be today and with as much as she wanted to get done, garments would have been bulkier and hotter than ever. She just hoped no one from the Church, or Benjamin for that matter, ever found out. But today, she had no Church activities, no planned visitors, and no one demanding her time. Today she was free of the many demands on her life, and she intended to savor every moment.

It wasn't so much that she minded the responsibilities that went with being a wife or a member of the Church. It was just that there were times when she would have given anything for a few moments of not answering to anyone, not being responsible or accountable. When she was not taking care of Benjamin, running errands, cleaning, or cooking, her time was filled with Church obligations, which could include anything from preparing meals to escorting children on outings to participating in prayer meetings. And living in the country and having a gigantic house kept her that much busier, and when Benjamin worked at home, which happened often, he was always needing to tell her something or have her do something.

They lived about a mile outside of Index—a tiny town in the mountains of central Washington—on a plot of land next to the North Fork of the Skykomish River. Their land, about three acres, was mostly a square chunk of treeless sod, surrounded on one side by the Index-Galena Road, on the opposite side by the river, and the other two sides by towering red cedar, silver fir, and western hemlock. When they had moved into the house a number of years earlier, Benjamin had insisted that they clear most of the trees, leaving only enough to line the road and give the illusion of forests. "Make a lot of clean open space," he said. "Let the sun shine down on us." Benjamin sold the trees for enough money to pay for the finest sod, a John Deere gas lawn mower, and an extensive sprinkling system to keep the lawn green during the hottest and driest of summers.

At the center of this expanse of pedigree lawn, on a slight upsweep of land, sat the house that Benjamin's grandfather had erected, a monolithic, multi-tiered brick home, complete with six bedrooms, a family room, a living room, a dining room, a wilderness of a kitchen, and several other rooms of varying sizes and shapes to accommodate the Mormon sensibilities of a proud, tithing, church-going family. Of course, they didn't have a family when they moved into the house, and as it turned out, they never would. But even when hopes had run high for

r. h. sheldon

a multitude of children, Rebecca had remained unenthused about the size of the house, often suggesting that they sell it and look for something else, that they think about the upkeep. She knew, of course, that she would be the one who would be expected to clean the house and keep it tidy. But Benjamin insisted that, with the onslaught of expected children, the house would be the perfect fortress. So they remodeled and cleaned and removed trash and painted and transformed the home into a modern structure big enough to house a family of twenty.

Closer to the road and off to the side of this giant structure, which looked surprisingly similar to the plain Mormon churches that dot the landscape across the Western states—even the dull brown brick was the same—sat a large barnlike workshop, also brick, that housed a variety of tools and equipment to handle everything from carpentry to plumbing to painting to auto repair. Ladders hung from the wall, a hoist dangled from the ceiling, cans of chemicals and paint adorned the layers of shelves, and a workbench spanned most of the back wall. The John Deere lawn mower, when not in use, was parked in a far corner, away from the door.

The garden lay behind the workshop, out of sight of the house. The bright green of early summer plants—sweet corn, summer squash, cucumbers, peppers, wax beans, and tomatoes—filled the straight rows. Rebecca knelt by the tomato plants, where they were bunched together in the far corner, and pulled weeds from between the bushy stems, stacking the plants into a neat pile next to her side. She wore a wide-brimmed straw hat, a bright green gardener's apron, rubber boots, and a dirty pair of flowered cotton gloves, all of which Benjamin had given her on her last birthday, probably the best gift she had ever received from him.

She pulled each weed with a delighted satisfaction. She liked her garden tidy, free from the intruders that sucked nutrients from the soil and crowded the neat rows of vegetables. She prided herself on an orderly garden, each row a straight line running parallel to the garden's edge. The plants looked like little soldiers standing at attention, spaced out in formation in exact proportion to the expected growth of that variety: tomato plants thirty inches apart, corn twelve, beans two. She maintained the geometric lines with a fierce tenacity, refusing to allow even the tiniest leaf to be out of place.

She cleared the soil in front of her and moved to the right. One of the weeds was larger than the others, thick and leafy. She was surprised that she hadn't noticed it before and had let it get this bad. She tugged hard on this one, but it didn't give, its pulpy tentacles clinging to clumps of rocks and twigs as it twisted through the roots of the tomato plants. She pushed away some of the soil from around its stem, digging down into the moist dirt. The fresh earth filled her head with its rich fragrance. She breathed deeply. It smelled wet, musty, filling her with thoughts of childhood, of a little girl escaping her brothers and sisters and playing in the willow bushes in her family's yard. Their home had sat on the banks of the Snake River in southern Idaho. The ground there was always muddy after the spring floods, and it would often take weeks after the river dropped for some areas to dry out. She liked to play in her bare feet, much to her mother's disdain, and let the mud gush through her toes and splash up on her legs, staining her white skin with dark gray spots.

Her thoughts returned to the gargantuan weed. She grabbed it with both hands, wrapping her fingers around the bottom of the stem so her thumbs dug into the soil. Tightening her fists, she pulled as hard as she could, but it wouldn't give. She tried again. Nothing.

She let go and removed more dirt from around the stem. She rose up off her knees, stood for a moment, and then crouched down so she could use the strength of her legs to pull. She moved into position and grabbed the thick stalk. She sucked in a deep breath and yanked as hard as she could, her arms jerking at their sockets. The weed still did not give.

She tensed her shoulders and back and pulled harder. The muscles in her legs strained against the earth, the souls of her rubber boots digging into the rocky soil. The weed loosened its hold only slightly, as though it dug its claws into the ground, struggling against her abortive attempts. Rebecca pulled. Her attack was decisive. Sweat beaded on her forehead. Her arms tightened into long wiry bands. The muscles in her back and shoulders stiffened into thick knots.

She stared unblinking. The weed had ceded a little more ground, but its roots still clung to the soil. She gritted her teeth and sucked in a deep breath. With one great heave, she yanked at the weed. It popped out of the ground, and she flew backwards and landed on her back. She gulped in air and stared at the sky until her panting subsided and her muscles relaxed.

She sat up slowly. Her head spun in a bright dizzy arc. She waited for a minute and then pushed herself to her feet. She walked over to where the plant had landed, near the pile of the other dead weeds. The long, sinewy roots were a mottled yellow and gnarled with dirt and small rocks. The leaves were a dull green. Several flies hovered above the weed, like vultures circling their next meal, as an ashen gray settled on the plant.

Rebecca shivered. The hot sun and warm air did little to fend off this chill. She kicked the weed into the pile with the others, hesitant to touch it even with her boots. She would deal with it later, after she had calmed down.

She took off her flowered gloves and headed toward the house. Then she heard a voice, calling out from behind her, from off in the trees.

She spun and looked toward the edge of their property, not far from the garden. The forest looked dark and cool in the afternoon glare. She saw no movement, heard no sound, other than a breeze sweeping over the top of the trees.

She stared for several seconds and then heard it again, the same voice, the same words.

"I'm here," the shout erupted. "I'm here!"

The Long Goodbye

Paul removed his backpack and leaned it against an old fat cedar. A canopy of green blocked all but the most persistent of sunlight, which splashed in small pools on the soft composting earth. The air was filled with the scents of summer—leaves baking in the sun, soil drying out. Twenty feet away, the North Fork of the Skykomish River gurgled and popped in long currents that swirled around boulders and emitted a steady hum. Upriver the water ran more swiftly, washing over giant rocks in a loud roar. He would camp near the quieter part of the river, overlooking the deep currents. This seemed fitting somehow, in keeping with the spiritual nature of his journey.

He sat on the ground next to the pack and looked up through the branches, smiling gleefully at the spots of blue sky he saw through the tangles. He had made it. In less than twenty-four hours he had packed his gear, loaded his antique Volvo, bought supplies, quit his job, and driven to the mountains. Of course, he had to first ride out the explosive rush of mushrooms and the gentle down slope of a mellow afterglow. But shortly thereafter, fortified by a quick nap, a bowl of granola, and a few blades of wheat grass, he had descended the three flights of stairs down to his storage locker and carried back up—in several trips—his camping gear and anything else he wanted to salvage for his new life. Preparation for his holy mission had begun.

Paul had assembled everything he deemed essential for his trek into the wilderness—backpack, tent, sleeping pad, rain fly, cooking gear, flashlights, candles, clothes, and whatever else he could squeeze into his pack. Then he searched his cupboards for any dehydrated and instant kinds of food that would travel well. He pulled out powdered milk, ramen, instant soup, dried fruit, and a large supply of granola, which he had made a few days earlier. When he finished, he wrote down what he would need to buy the next morning.

Paul then packed his car with his camping gear and a few other possessions—extra clothes, books, blankets, sheets, kitchen supplies, nonperishable food: whatever would fit into the camper shell—and waited out the rest of the night. It was only a little past midnight.

Paul slept little. The excitement of his blessed mission filled his head with replays from his earlier conversations with God. He was ready. Ready for change. Ready for a new life. He had not felt this kind of excitement in years, not since he lived in New Mexico, when he dreamt that he should move to the Northwest. Even then, he felt directed somehow, certain that a path lay waiting for him and that one day this path would be clear. He was meant to do something important, something great and wonderful.

Back then he had lived in a small dusty house outside Santa Fe, doing whatever odd jobs he could find until he came up with a plan, a direction that would lead him to his unknown destination. In his dream—a normal dream, not the hallucinogenic variety—he visited lush green lands filled with snow-tipped mountains and surrounded by deep blue oceans. It was not the content of the dream that was so remarkable, but the intensity with which he experienced it, as though some deep longing had been exposed. He woke from the dream exhilarated, convinced that he had been directed from the brown hills of New Mexico to the glorious green forests of the Northwest.

And now Paul was ready to move again, ready to ascend the pristine Cascade wilderness. It was six o'clock. The sun poked into his window. He loaded the front seat of his car with a few books and files that he wanted to drop off in his storage locker before he left town. He was ready to go.

He locked his apartment and walked down the hall to the row of tenant mailboxes. He pulled an envelope out of his pocket and shoved it into the manager's mail slot. The envelope contained the keys to his apartment and a note that said, "I'm leaving on my life's journey and will not be returning. I suggest you donate any furniture and personal belongings to your favorite charity—and any deposit I have coming."

Paul drove to the storage facility where he rented a small unit. He had not been here since he moved into his apartment. The unit still contained many of the items that he had meant to bring to the apartment, but never did. He now dropped off the few things he had brought with him and then headed across Lake Washington to his place of work, a megalithic software empire set in the Seattle suburbs. Once inside his office, he logged onto his computer and sent an e-mail to his manager. The message read, "I'm leaving on my life's journey and will not be returning to this office. Good luck with your career." Then he grabbed the few things that belonged to him—a box of granola bars, a book on Zen poetry, and a topographical map of the area surrounding the town of Index, a place he had visited many times. The town seemed the perfect starting point for his journey, a stepping-stone into the wilderness. He would spend a couple days camping in the area, preparing himself emotionally and spiritually for his trek into the deeper bowels of the forests.

Paul left the office and headed toward Index. He followed Highway 2 up the Skykomish Valley. In Sultan, he stopped at the Red Apple to pick up supplies, then continued driving east until he reached the Index-Galena Road, which passed by Index as it stretched into the mountains. As he neared the town, he could feel his excitement mount, a sense of anticipation that had been dormant for far too long. He felt a giddy sense of awe and wonder at the sights and sounds of the jagged peaks and stark rock walls and endless acres of lush green forests.

He bypassed the town itself—and the bridge that led into town—and traveled about another mile, until he reached the gate of an abandoned campground, a place where he had camped on many occasions. He figured that this would be a safe place to leave his car when he embarked on his journey.

The gate, of course, was locked, but there was a way around it, through the trees. A small chain with a sign that said "Keep Out" blocked the illegal entrance. He pulled the chain off the tree and drove through the narrow opening. Rock scraped the car's bottom as branches screeched against the windows and the side of the car. He cared little—the car having long ago faded into the *older model* category—and continued to drive forward, until his rear bumper cleared the last rock. He put the chain back into place and parked his car in an area that was low and off to the side, a place hidden by the thick branches of blackberry and huckleberry bushes. Unless someone stumbled onto the sedan, it would remain unseen until the fall.

Paul climbed out of the car. The door clunked, squeaked. The air was clear and still in the dense thicket. Giant cedars towered around him, surrounding him in a womb of comfort and peace. The air was filled with the smells of the forest, the layers of decay on the forest floor, the new growths on thousands of plants, the musty smells of moss, the fresh wild scent of a hot sun on spots of moist earth. Everywhere he looked was green: bright green, yellow green, gray green, dark green, more shades than could be imagined. A magical landscape—straight out of yesterday's vision.

r. h. sheldon

He spun in a circle, giggling with pure joy at the sights and sounds of the forest.

"I'm here," he shouted. "I'm here!"

The River Runs Deep

The Rainbow Campground was a twenty-acre stretch of land squeezed between the Index-Galena Road and the North Fork of the Skykomish River. The pristine forests, gentle terrain, and easy river access provided the perfect setting for Northwest urbanites to flee their concrete confines and relax in the gentle lap of nature. Every Friday night—from Labor Day to Memorial Day—would-be campers arrived with carloads of beer and food and stereos and lawn chairs and anything else to guarantee a comfortable stay. Some brought pot, others brought poppers. Many carried with them the medications necessary to their survival—AZT, ddC, Ganciclovir, Interferon, or any of the many available anti-nausea drugs to counter the effects of on-going HIV therapy. Ecstasy often made the scene, as did LSD. And few arrived without the preparations needed for a weekend of multiple adventures, their bags filled with condoms, lube, dildos, butt plugs, tit clamps, cock rings, and an assortment of any other paraphernalia that would fit each person's particular needs. A campsite or two might include a sling hanging from the lower tree branches or ropes tied expertly around the trunks.

When Paul first moved to Seattle, he camped at Rainbow regularly, although he preferred the quiet weekdays to the party atmosphere of the weekends. In his mind, there seemed little reason to leave the city if you were going to take the city with you. Still, he appreciated the idea of a rural place where gays and lesbians, usually more men than women, could gather, where they could be free of the stigma of redneck America. He had lived in enough rural areas to know how difficult it could be. When the options often seemed to be narrowed down to two—being stigmatized or being ghettoized—a place like Rainbow Campground offered a tolerable alternative, despite the weekend eruptions of liquor, drugs, loud music, and a whole lot of attitude.

Paul had little time over the last year to go camping or do much of anything else, spending many of his weekends barricaded behind the concrete walls of the corporate compound, convinced that life no longer held meaning other than to answer and send as many e-mails as possible every day of the week. He believed that bonus points must have been awarded to anyone whose mail was time-stamped with late PM hours or weekend dates. Early in his software career, he tried to get up to the campground on Saturdays or Sundays to lie naked by the river and soak up the warm summer sun. But even that was halted, not only by the demands of his job and his self-imposed commitment over the past twelve months, but also by the fact that the campground, three years earlier, had closed its gate forever.

The Rainbow Campground Association had, for sixteen years, leased the land from the state of Washington. At the end of the last lease, the state concluded that, because the campground was operated exclusively for the use of gays and lesbians, the RCA violated certain nondiscrimination laws that apparently were put into place to protect the rights of all citizens. The campground would have to go. The fact that these rights were seldom invoked on behalf of the people they were used against appeared lost on the bewildered faces of the state's petty bureaucratic minions.

But Paul had not been too affected by the camp's demise. In fact, in some ways it had worked to his favor. About a year before the shutdown, Paul had met Aaron, a tall, lean, handsome cowboy from Montana. Paul fell hard, convinced that they were destined for a life together. Within six months, Paul and Aaron moved in together. Within six months of that, they adopted a rambunctious yellow lab named Sarah. Timing could not have been better. The abandoned campground provided Paul and Aaron with a twenty-acre parcel of deserted woods that proved an ideal setting in which to let Sarah run wild without concern for what she trampled, where she shit, and how much she barked. A canine paradise.

Paul now sat against the tree and watched the river curve past him. It was low, long past its spring prime. Stretches of rocks where the water no longer ran lined the banks. Only the deeper channels flowed with the clear silvery currents of melted snow. But upriver, it still ran rapid, where white-tipped waves roared over the boulders. He could smell it in the air, the misty froth of cascading water—a clear bright fragrance, penetrating and sweet. The sound of the river soothed his spirit, refreshed his soul.

He looked around at the trees. The forest had reclaimed much of the trails and campsites with fallen trees and branches, the spread of leafy brush, the tall ferns and widening bushes. Remnants of old campsites were scattered throughout the trees like ruins from an ancient civilization. Flooding, rain, snow, and disuse had eroded the impermanent sites into little more than stacks of rocks where campfires once blazed.

Paul thought about the afternoon he had met Aaron. It was here at the campground. Paul had driven up late one morning, a weekday just before the Sunday of the Gay Pride Parade.

He had walked around the campground, his feeling of awe for the place long since diminished. The word campground must have been used by default, because the only thing that it had in common with camping were the trees. Beyond that, everything took on the surreal quality of a fantasy adventure, where nothing appeared as it seemed.

Campsites were taken over by groups of men and women who, each summer, staked out a site for the season and proceeded to erect, arrange, cut, haul, drag, decorate, and primp the space and its contents until sparkling homesteads manifested in the micro-wilderness. Campsites included everything from sinks to tents. Many had kitchen cabinets, some had sofas, one had a spinet piano, and another, a pool table. The entrances to many of the sites displayed welcome signs and some welcome mats. Flags and banners were draped from tree to tree. Plastic tarps hung in high branches. Lanterns lined the stone walkways.

On the day he had met Aaron, Paul had headed toward the river and staked out a little sand bar on which to lie in the sun. Aaron lay on a white beach towel on the other side of a fallen tree. The large log bowed upward, leaving a gap beneath the trunk that provided a perfect line of sight between the two men. Within minutes, glances became stares, stares became smiles, smiles became introductions. Paul fell in love instantly. In some ways, Aaron had seemed as equally in love with Paul. Yet there was always a hesitation on his part, a fear of committing too much of himself, of being too responsible.

Paul smiled a little sadly as he thought about Aaron. When Aaron had announced that he wanted to split up, Paul was devastated, falling into a dark cavern of depression, afraid that he would never pull out. So he threw himself into his work more than ever, confined to a corporate prison, where solace was found in hard labor, long hours, and constant exhaustion.

Paul now watched the river churn and gurgle. The deep currents bathed him, cleansed him. He listened to its soft musical tones. At first it sounded like a hum, low and melodic, the deep soothing tones of an oboe. But then it brightened into a brisk chant and melted into the sweet harmonies of a majestic choir. Soon a voice awoke amidst

r. h. sheldon

the melodious overtures—a man's voice, low and soothing, almost a chant—barely audible above the choir of voices, but the sound cleared like a lifting fog, and his tones crystallized into words strong and gentle, and he sounded like the voice Paul had heard in his vision. He sounded like the voice of God.

"Watch for the ones who follow," he said. "Watch and learn." And then his voice disappeared back into the choir, lost in the peaceful harmonies.

Paul listened for a long time, but the river told him nothing more.

Sleep Tight

Rebecca fell exhausted into her bed. She couldn't understand how a little weeding could have worn her out so completely, as though she had labored under a great burden, broken by the heavy circumstances of life. This was the kind of tired she felt after a long day of being with her husband. After waiting on him, cleaning up after him, listening to him. But her exhaustion now was deeper, more complete, as if all her years of responsibility and duty suddenly fell heavy upon her, leaving her broken, defeated.

She thought about the large weed, the monster weed, with its tangled, twisted stem. She shivered again, trying to erase from her mind the mangled plant lying on the grass.

She closed her eyes and whispered a prayer—one she had learned when she was a little girl:

> *O God, who lives on Kolob,*
> *In a galaxy far from here,*
> *Where you dwell with your wives and children,*
> *In a land where there is no fear.*
> *Show me now your mercy*
> *And protect me through the night.*
> *Reward me with prosperity,*
> *So that I may know what's right.*

She fell asleep repeating the prayer over and over, her lips moving with each syllable, though sound no longer blew from her lips. Soon her breath deepened into long, uneasy sighs.

As she slept, Rebecca dreamt of a giant weed whipping against the house, trying to break through the walls to attack and destroy her. She lay in her bed, terrified that it would crack through. But then she floated up from the flowered spread and hovered near the ceiling. After a minute, she popped through the roof and drifted above the house. She watched the weed snap its fat root against the building, hitting against the brick with a loud blast, like the sound of a cannon. The weed at-

r. h. sheldon

tacked without mercy, spinning and screaming in a wild frenzy. How could the house stand such an assault?

With one final snap, the weed sprang away from the wall and fell to the ground near the edge of the garden, then it began to change color, like a chameleon shifting disguises, except that these colors were the bright tones of a rainbow. Each hue spread across the weed and was then replaced by the next. And soon the weed was no longer a weed, but the rainbow itself, the source of color, the prism that filtered the light into bright shades.

The rainbow grew and spread, not in an arc of light, but in a straight line that disappeared into the trees next to the garden, as though entering the forests through a doorway. And then it was gone, imploding into a pinpoint of bright, searing light.

Rebecca woke and stared at the ceiling. She felt confused by her surroundings, almost a stranger, like she did when they visited Benjamin's parents, waking in the middle of the night, forgetting where she was. She looked at the clock. It was already six. She had slept for almost four hours.

Rebecca stared out the bedroom window. She could see the roof of the workshop and the upper branches of the trees that lay beyond the garden. That was the area where the rainbow had pointed to in her dream, where the shining hues had disappeared into the dense thickets.

Rebecca and Benjamin never ventured into the woods in that direction. When they had moved into the house, the campground had already been established. A filthy, contaminated place. Had they been aware of the type of campground it was, they would have never kept the house, never have clear-cut their three acres and bulldozed the snarled trunks and roots. They would have taken their satellite dish and gas barbecue and lawn furniture and settled in an area more family-oriented.

But once they discovered the atrocity that resided next door, it was too late. The work on the house had been completed, the trees removed, the junk cleaned out, and the satellite dish installed. So they had to live with it, until they were ready to sell their house and move. In the meantime, they would do their best to ignore the campground's presence, taking refuge in the fact that it was only a few months out of the year. But those were trying, despicable months. Some of the homosexual men, on more than one occasion, would wander downriver just enough so that if she sat on the edge of the water she could see where they stood on the banks. The men would take off their clothes, without shame, without thought of who might see them, and lay naked on the giant boulders, smoking cigarettes, drinking beer. Her husband would complain to local officials, but this did little good. The town liked the revenue generated by the campground.

A few years ago, when she was down by the river, two of those men wandered down to the edge of the campground, further downriver than usual. One of them lay face down on the rock, his white buttocks wiggling in the sun, bright and shiny, as though he dared her to say something, to take action against his evil. And then another man lay on top of him, mounting him like a man would a woman, except with the woman turned backwards. She watched in horror as they committed sodomy right there on the rock, in the full light of day, outside in front of her, God, and anyone else who might be watching.

Rebecca could not believe what she saw. Such audacity, such disregard for the natural order of things, for what was right and wrong. She was convinced that she had witnessed pure evil, evil of such great proportion that she would never be able to tell anyone what she saw, never describe the horror of the two sweaty bodies, naked in the sun, doing what God could never forgive any man for doing.

As soon as she saw them, she ran from the river to her garden and began to tear weeds from between the broccoli plants. She ripped at them with bare hands, pulling weed after weed until her fingers were raw. That night, as she lay in bed, she prayed for guidance, prayed to have this abominable vision erased from her memory, to be free from the sinners next door.

And God must have heard her prayers because several days later she was told that the camp would be closing and those people would no longer be her neighbors. She nearly cried with relief, inwardly thanking God for release from the heathens.

Rebecca now decided that she was ready to enter the forbidden land, to see what the deserted campground was like. She would go in only a little way to look around, and that would be it. She locked up the house and walked across the yard past the workshop and garden. The weed no longer looked fearful or foreboding, and she wondered how she had let herself get so carried away. It must have been the hot sun and the strain of pulling it out. Still, she stepped wide around the pile of weeds as she walked by.

She stood before the trees at the edge of their property. Thickets of blackberry bushes guarded the entrance. She shoved herself in between the tangle of branches. They scratched at her arms and face, but she continued to push her way though until she was standing on the other side. She brushed herself off as she looked around. It took a moment for her eyes to adjust to the darkness, to see more than just the diffused shadows of an early-evening sun. The smell of a musty forest floor filled her head. The air was cool and damp. The tip of the trees moved slightly in the high breeze. When she looked down, she realized that, straight before her, an overgrown trail wove in and out of the fallen trees.

She took a step, descending into the forbidden world that she had so long tried to deny.

Getting Into the Spirit

S tanley Dickel never considered himself a religious man. For him, spirit was something packaged in a bottle, accessible at a whim, effective immediately. He would rather step into dog shit than step into a church. If he showed homage to anyone or anything, it was to George Dickel and his famous Tennessee whiskey. Stanley was convinced that his lineage led directly to the distillery's founder, at least that is what he used to tell people. The fact that Stanley was born in the Northwest was a mere quirk of fate, an indicator that some wayward relative had fled his Tennessee home in search of fame and fortune. Stanley saw it as his duty to remain loyal to his family name, faithful to the man who brought honor to his heritage.

Despite Stanley's aversion to religion, he had felt obligated to enter a church on several occasions, usually for a funeral or wedding, nearly the same thing in his mind. A church seemed little more than a convenient gathering place for people to tell lies. Lies about eternal bliss. Lies about the holy state of matrimony. Lies about the innate goodness and beauty in all of God's creations. When people die, they should simply be stuck in the ground and let the friends and family deal with it in their own way. And if they insisted on getting married, well, Stanley saw little cause for celebration.

But there had been one time when Stanley walked willingly into a church. When he was sixteen, more than ready to test the vaginal waters, he met secretly with the pastor's daughter. She carried with her a spare key to the town's only church, a Methodist house of worship that was little more than a tiny box with a short steeple and a tin roof. It was here that the two teenagers tasted the forbidden fruits, it was here, at the foot of the altar, where he pulled his pants down to his ankles and made awkward attempts at penetration, and it was here that the girl's father, coming in to practice his Sunday sermon, which, coincidentally enough, condemned the sins of the flesh and threatened biblical ramifications, found them prostrate beneath the cross, entwined in a biblical embrace that left even the verbose parson momentarily speechless.

r. h. sheldon

Stanley was no fool. Taking advantage of the reverend's stunned gaze, he leapt up from the floor, pulled up his pants, and ran out the church. He jumped into his father's pickup and drove out to the ranch, where he busied himself with mindless chores, waiting for his dad to hear the news, which he was certain was merely a matter of time. That night at dinner, expecting the worst, Stanley slunk into the house and sat at the table. All through dinner, his dad said nothing, so Stanley wasn't sure he knew what happened. Finally, after his brother went upstairs and his mom went into the kitchen, his dad stood up, slapped his son on the back, and said, "Hope it was all worth it, son. But let me tell you, pussy and trouble go hand in hand." Then he chuckled and walked out the room.

That was well over sixty years ago. Stanley had long since buried his father, his mother, and his wife. His brother, Everett, was also dead. Shortly after he and his wife moved to Nevada they were killed in a car accident, not long after Stanley had returned from the army. The only living relative that Stanley now had was his daughter. She lived somewhere in Oregon and rarely visited, and Stanley wasn't one for writing letters or talking on the phone. They did exchange Christmas cards, but that was pretty much it.

Stanley now lived alone in a small house in Gold Bar, a town just west of Index. His house sat a couple blocks off the highway, far enough not to have to deal with the noise and congestion from the traffic. The house was paid for, easy to keep up, and central to the only things he needed: a grocery store, a liquor store, and a place to fish.

Not much else interested Stanley these days other than going fishing and sipping on a flask of his favorite spirits. He liked to drive up past Index, on the North Fork of the Skykomish River. His favorite time was early in the evening, when the summer sun fell behind the mountains. He would stand in the river and watch the fish jump around him. Sometimes that was enough, just standing there, listening to the hum of insects, the flow of the river. The shadows would grow long and the sky turn gold as cool air drifted off the mountain and pushed away the smells of the warm forest.

This evening was especially calm, like the peaceful edge of an approaching storm. He stood in knee-deep water, his waders squeezing against the varicose veins in his calves and shins. An unlit cigarette dangled from his mouth. He wore his favorite hat, an old, beat-up baseball cap with a black emblem that read "George Dickel Tennessee Whisky." He cast his line into the water and shoved his pole beneath his arm to free his hands. He pulled out the flask from inside his jacket and drew a long swig of whiskey, without disturbing the cigarette. The liquor burned, and heat spread across his chest, warding off the evening chill.

He held the pole for several minutes as he watched where the line disappeared into the water. Then he reeled in slowly, feeling the gentle tug of the current. He might have come a little too early. With the days so long, the fish remained disinterested until late evening. Even the long shadows of the mountains were not enough to persuade them to surface.

Yet Stanley wasn't all that worried about actually catching fish. He had more than enough in his freezer, and the ones he did catch, he usually let go. But it gave him something to do, something other than watching TV or reading. Fishing, he thought, was the only thing that kept him alive.

He decided to walk downriver a bit, by the old campground where the deep pools often held the largest and most elusive fish. He used to fish that part of the river many years ago, before the queers took it over. What an odd thing that was—a bunch of homos trying to camp. And a waste of some great fishing. Yet he didn't mind the queers so much. To him, they were merely one more sign of progress, one more reminder of how civilized—and crowded—this area had become. Too bad he had to sell the ranch when he did. A few more years, it would have been worth a fortune, and he could have made enough to buy a big chunk of land on the river.

Stanley first fished what he now called the Queer Zone when he was a little boy. His dad used to bring him and his brother there. It was one of the few father and son kinds of activities they did together. They would pack enough food to last all day, and there they would hang by the edge of the river or wade into the shallow pools. His dad would even get playful at times, splashing the boys, teasing them about their fish.

One time they sat on the bank, eating their lunch. Their dad started talking about what it had been like when he had been a boy, how little they had, how mean his father had been, how he drank, threw tantrums, beat up his wife. He was always angry, always ready to explode.

It was rare for Stanley's dad to open up like that. Usually he just grumbled or yelled. Sometimes, when he was pissed off at one of his kids, he would grab the leather strap and whip them until they couldn't sit or lie on their backs. But once the strap caught Stanley across the

r. h. sheldon

face. His left eye swelled and a red welt creased his cheek. He told kids at school that he fell down a hill and was scraped up from the rocks. That was the last time his dad ever hit him.

But despite their whippings, his dad hadn't been as bad as a lot of the other men in that area. He never hit his mom and never got so drunk that he would hurt someone. And by the time Stanley got back from the army, his dad had mellowed a lot. Everett had already got married and moved away and his mom was already feeling sick. It wasn't long after that she died and not long after that Everett was killed, leaving only Stanley to take care of his dad and the ranch.

Stanley followed the river along the rocky shore, just beneath the steep banks. Now that the queers had packed up and gone, he could fish the area once more. The best part was that few people were aware that this area existed. There was nothing he hated more than to be in the river, enjoying the quiet, and having some big-mouthed tourist try to make small talk. Stanley used to try to be polite, but now he just reeled in his line and moved somewhere else. That was the nice part about fishing the Queer Zone. The tourists didn't know about it. Ever since the homos got kicked out, the area has remained unused. No doubt the state would eventually do something with it—turn it into a park, sell the timber—but until then, it was a quiet haven.

Stanley reached the part of the river that cascaded rapidly over and between the boulders. The river roared past him, a sustained thunder, white and foaming. Giant eddies whirled at the base of the boulders. The air was filled with a cold mist from the spraying water. He climbed from rock to rock. With each step his muscles shook, his body swayed. He inched forward, steadying himself with one hand while grasping the fishing pole with the other. The mountain shadows distorted the size and shape of rocks, and he would often have to use his feet to feel for his footholds because he couldn't see where he stepped.

He crept along steadily, until he reached a large boulder whose lower edge was nearly invisible. He reached his leg forward but misjudged the edge of a stone and wedged his foot into a crevice. His ankle twisted and he stumbled forward, dropping his pole as he reached to break his fall. He slammed against a boulder and knocked the wind out of his lungs. His foot popped out from between the rocks, and he banged his knee and head.

He leaned against the rock as he tried to catch his breath. The stone felt rough and slimy. Water poured through a crack in the boulder, just inches from his head. Cold drops splashed against his face and hands.

He pushed himself away from the boulder and climbed to his left. He reached down for his pole. His joints creaked and cracked. A twinge shot up the back of his legs and into his lower back. He continued down river, each step slow and painful. His ankle throbbed, but not too bad, not bad enough to make him think that he had broken anything or caused any damage too permanent. Merely another reminder of being old.

When he reached the calmer part of the river, he sat on a log and took a large gulp from his flask. He rested for several minutes, watching the current bend and twist through the rocky bank. He tried to look downriver, but it was difficult to see much once the sun dropped down behind the mountains. When he was younger, he could have found his way around these rocks in the middle of the night, but not anymore.

He stood slowly, his muscles stiff and tired. He decided not to fish any more that evening, a soft chair in front of the TV sounding very nice to him right now. If he headed downriver just a bit further, he could catch the trail directly back toward the road and then walk up to his truck. But the river twisted back toward the bank, so he would have to wade along its edge.

He stepped into the water, hugging the steep bank on his left. He had to stay within a few inches of the bank because the water dropped off into a deep pool to the right, but he had maneuvered places much tighter than this and figured he was pretty safe. Overall, this was a hell of a lot easier than rock climbing back up the river. Quiet pools were better suited to an old man.

The river was shallow along the bank. Stanley stepped confidently until he was within a few feet of dry land. The water grew a little deeper here. He stopped and adjusted the pole in his hand. He took a step. His foot landed on the edge of a rock and he twisted his injured ankle. He fell to his side, into the deepest part of the river. His baseball cap flew off his head. The icy current washed over his shoulders, and his waders filled with water.

He thought he screamed or called for help before his head went under, but maybe he said nothing as the freezing river dragged him to the bottom.

r. h. sheldon

An Evening's Stroll

Rebecca wound through the trees, trying to follow a trail that in many places was nonexistent. She squeezed past tree trunks, ducked beneath branches, and climbed over fallen limbs. She was surprised at how normal the place looked. If she hadn't been aware that a group of homosexuals had once camped here, she would never have guessed it. In fact, if it were not for the occasional outhouse and scattered remains of fire pits, she would have hardly known that it had been a campground. The forest had reclaimed the area with vehemence, swallowing almost all traces of past visitors, as though there had only been rumors of a camping area, substantiated by the few reckless piles of rock. Yet memory told her otherwise—memory of boys' rear ends saluting her with arrogant disdain.

She walked faster. The leaves of a wide fern snagged her shoelace. She pulled her foot back, stretching the stalk of leaves. The plant shimmered in the pale light. For a second she thought that it struggled against her, daring her to fight. She reached down and untangled the lace. The leaves popped back, sending a quiver throughout the fern. She stood for a moment and stared at the plant.

When Rebecca was young, her mother had a fern in the living room, but their houseplant never looked this full and green. Plagued by dry air and lack of constant attention, the plant always looked near death. Many of the leaves were crispy brown with stems dry and brittle. But out here, the fern grew healthy and bright, its leaves moist and pliant like fresh sprigs of grass.

Yet despite its beauty—and the beauty of so many of these plants—Rebecca felt intimidated by the forest. Being in the middle of all these trees, trees that towered at staggering distances above her head, made her uneasy. She couldn't recall ever having stood by herself within such a massive cluster of trees. The place was wild, out of control, lacking order and purpose. Limbs cluttered the ground. Ivy weaved uncontrollably up trunks and through branches. Blackberry bushes grew into spiny walls. Each plant reached into the next, stretching into a tangled mass of thorns and leaves and branches. A desire swept over her to clean up the mess. She imagined herself pulling out brambles, trimming bushes, cutting ivy. She would clear out the dead branches and leaves and get rid of most of this undergrowth. Perhaps a few trails and foot bridges would be nice. She could rest easier in here if there were not so much disorder.

The mountains and forests here were so unlike southern Idaho, where space was open and you could see forever. In the Cascades, she felt closed in, almost claustrophobic. She yearned for the wide expanse of the desert, for the crisp dry air, for that sense of endless horizons that opened her imagination to thoughts of homesteads and pioneers and a West not quite won.

Rebecca first came to the Northwest when she was twenty-one, which was how old women had to be before going on a mission for the Church. Her parents had not been very enthusiastic about their daughter going, believing that this was the domain of young men, not unmarried women. They also believed that it was time for her to find a husband and settle down. But Rebecca persisted, and soon she left for the Missionaries Training Center in Provo, Utah, where missionaries-to-be were chiseled and polished and sent off to places around the world to spread the word of Joseph Smith, as it had been reinterpreted again and again over the last century. The men, whose minimum age was eighteen, might be sent anywhere from Sweden to Mexico to Hong Kong. The women, on the other hand, were seldom permitted such exotic adventures and usually found themselves leading tours through Temple Square in Salt Lake City or sitting at information booths in local temples.

Rebecca's assignment was more mundane than most. She was shipped off to Bellevue, Washington, just outside of Seattle, where she welcomed newcomers, tourists, and curiosity seekers to the temple grounds. It wasn't quite what she had envisioned when she signed up, yet because of her sense of responsibility to the Church, she served her time enthusiastically, bearing testimony whenever the opportunity presented itself.

It was here, on a Saturday afternoon, that she met Benjamin, a devout member who had come to the temple with his parents. When Rebecca was introduced to him, something stirred within her, something mystical and romantic. He represented everything the Church stood for—a model member who easily embraced the clearly defined roles, respect for prosperity, and support for tradition and family. Rebecca saw in him all that was decent and righteous, someone who would bring her good fortune and security into her old age.

Benjamin and Rebecca were married six months after her mission ended. They lived in Bellevue for several years, until after the death of his grandfather. Bellevue was a bustling affluent arm of Seattle, the perfect setting for a Mormon stronghold. Benjamin's business took him all over the Puget Sound area, although much of the development he was involved with was in Snohomish County, where his grandfather had made his mark. After his grandfather died, Benjamin had the house in Index updated and remodeled. When it was ready, they moved up there, and Rebecca did her best to make their home a comfortable, respectable, Mormon household.

When Rebecca thought about all this now, she could feel her chest tighten. She had always done everything right, always followed the rules and performed as she was expected to, always trying to be the obedient Mormon daughter and Mormon wife. If they'd had children, she would have done whatever was necessary to be the perfect Mormon mother. The rules had always been spelled out, and she seldom had reason to question them. She had slipped only once, back before she and Benjamin were married, when Benjamin visited her at her parents' home in Twin Falls. The fiancées tried to resist but failed, giving in to the premarital temptations one afternoon when they unexpectedly found themselves alone in the house. But the exhilaration of discovery did not last, and Rebecca succumbed to feelings of guilt and self-loathing and spoke to the bishop of her ward about what she had done.

The bishop's judgment was swift and just. A temple ceremony was denied to the tainted couple until they had been married for a full year and proved that they understood the sanctity of marriage. As a result, they were married in her parents' living room, overlooking the Snake River, surrounded by family and friends, faithful Church members and their offspring who, it was assumed, would carry on the Mormon tradition.

But throughout the celebration, Rebecca's siblings and their spouses remained a bit standoffish. They believed that Christian charity did not apply to such blatant disregard for God's laws. Her sister-in-law summed it up well when, after the ceremony, she approached Rebecca and said, "Our children had always looked up to you, and then you go and do this."

One year later, Benjamin and Rebecca were granted a temple ceremony, legitimizing their marriage in the eyes of God and the Church. And now, after sixteen years of faithful duty to her marriage and the Church, no one seemed concerned about the whole affair, especially in light of Benjamin's acquired wealth and Church prestige.

Rebecca tried to find her way to the river to escape the suffocating woods. She sought out breaks in the dense undergrowth, pushing toward the water. She twisted past moss-covered trunks of lumbering fir, climbed over the bent branches of vine maple, squeezed through the leafy brush of salmonberry bushes. The razor thorns of blackberry scratched her face, her arms. All the while, she felt continually pushed back by a series of dead-ends that always directed her toward the heart of the forest.

She continued her struggle against the wall of green, determined to find a way to the water. She sweated nervously. It stung the scratches on her arms and face and dripped into her eyes until they burned. The panic swelled inside her chest. Her breath grew rapid and shallow. Her heart pounded in quick fierce beats.

Rebecca found a small hole in a tangle of huckleberry and dove through. The branches tore at her clothes and ripped her blouse. Berries bombarded her in a barrage of bloody pulp, staining her clothes and skin with streaks of red juice.

She tumbled out the other side and landed face down in the damp soil. Berry juice covered the pale skin of her hands and feet. Dirt and bits of dried leaves clung to her clothes. She stood and wiped mud from around her eyes and tried to brush the filth off her clothes. She felt violated somehow, betrayed by an unseen force, as though a thousand ants crawled over her skin. She brushed harder, her hands moving in desperate jerks. But then she grew aware of a steady noise behind her, a long muffled hum. She spun around. It was the river, glistening through the trees. She could see the silvery trail twist through the rocks, the liquid flow of the melodious currents. She began to move toward the water, slowly at first, as though she could not trust what she was seeing, but then she quickened her pace, honing in on the cooling oasis.

She climbed down the bank and jumped into a knee-deep pool. She splashed herself with the cool water, relishing its healing touch.

r. h. sheldon

She poured water over her arms and face. She let it splash her clothes, freeze her body. She felt childlike, playful, rejoicing in the dark pool, the flowing currents.

She spun in a circle and kicked water into the air, then scooped it up in waves and tossed it over her head. It splashed down on her head, pasting the long blond strands to her shoulders. Not since she was a little girl has she had so much fun in water, when she used to play in the Snake River with her brothers. They would chase her and toss her like a toy, and then she would giggle and kick and jump around. It was glorious, like it was now.

Rebecca danced around with her hands in the air, spinning in a wide circle. She kicked up her legs and clapped her hands. And then she saw him—an old man wading along the river. She stopped. He walked along the edge of the water, carrying something in his hand, like a long stick. She watched as he moved steadily along a deep pool, his steps slow, careful.

Then he seemed to tilt sideways, slowly at first, building up speed as gravity sucked him down to the water. He fell with a splash, and the water buried him to his shoulders. He shouted for help before his head went under. She ran toward him, leaping from rock to rock as fast as she could.

A Rude Awakening

Paul lit his pipe and inhaled. This was the first weed he had smoked today. He had wanted his head clear to get out of town and start his journey. He had already set up his tent and gathered wood for a fire later tonight. He had also set up an altar of sorts, a flat rock on which he placed a candle, a small bundle of dried sage, and three feathers tied together with a cord made of hemp. Now he needed only to sit back and savor the calm, quiet evening.

He held the smoke in his lungs, until his head felt light, his body numb. He watched the river as he exhaled slowly. He felt as though he glowed, his soul full and alive. With each puff, his spirit soared above the treetops and floated in the evening breeze. The forest seemed to vibrate, settling into a wonderland of magic and spirit.

The river was silver and gray in the mountain shadows. The currents whispered a steady hum, and he listened carefully for the voice of the river. What had he meant by "watch for the ones who follow"? Would guides be sent to lead him forward, to direct him on his journey?

He studied the river, waiting for an answer. Nothing happened. No new messages. He looked upriver, his sight unfocused. Then he spotted an old man sitting on a log next to the water, drinking from a silver flask. He wore waders, a flannel shirt, and an off-white baseball cap that was tilted sideways on his head. A fishing pole sat next to him. Paul wondered if this were a vision, and if so, what it meant. The rock, the pole, the flask—all meaningful symbols.

He knew he would be sent another message, if he waited long enough, if he was patient. And then the sound of splashing penetrated his thoughts. He looked downriver and saw a woman standing in the water, playing like a little girl. She spun around in large circles and kicked her legs into the air, throwing water out before her in a fat arc. She seemed one with the river, rejoicing in its cool bounty. She moved like a dancer, full of life and vigor.

What did this all mean? The man on one side, the woman on the other. Him sitting, her standing. Him contemplating, her rejoicing.

r. h. sheldon

Were they real? A part of his imagination? A type of seeing? These must be powerful symbols indeed, packed with significance and meaning.

As he watched her wonderful celebration, he heard a yell for help. He turned toward the old man, just in time to see him disappear into the dark pool, his baseball cap floating down the river.

Monday Evening

The Age of Desire

The invitation said quite simply, "You have been scheduled for a complementary massage at Richards Spa at seven o'clock this evening. Please notify the Spa if you are not able to attend." The invitation had been printed with dark brown ink on a small ivory card and placed into a matching envelope. At the bottom of the invitation was the Richards imprint, a large R with a swooping, exaggerated stem. It had been slipped under the door to his room during the morning meetings.

Benjamin Randall had never received a massage before. He envisioned a burly man in a gray sweatshirt kneading him like bread dough. He wasn't particularly excited about the prospects, but he assumed that the massage was a present from the Council's board members, the sponsors of this week's events. The massage was no doubt one more special gift to welcome him to their elite fold. He had received several such tokens already—the basket of fruit, the plate of French pastries, the royal blue, terry-cloth robe embroidered with his initials.

So when Benjamin read the invitation, he felt it was his duty to take the board up on their offer. It seemed fitting that he learn to indulge himself in this way as he moved into the upper echelons of the Mormon business community. He might need to change some of his habits to conform to the behavior of the other members of the Council. He would watch how they acted, learn from them, imitate them. He was, at long last, where he belonged, and this was where he planned to stay.

Membership in the Council wasn't an easy thing to gain. Made up of the most prosperous and influential businessmen in the Church, the Council selected only those individuals whose position and influence could benefit the Council itself and the Church as a whole, and if individual members increased their own prosperity as a result of their privileged alliance, so much the better.

But what if the massage was not a welcoming gift? He certainly wouldn't want to participate in any activity that could be perceived as questionable, and a massage might fall into that category, especially if it meant missing tonight's meeting. Yet he couldn't contact board members to ask if they had provided the gift. These were not men you simply called up and chatted with. And he couldn't ask other members. There was a general expectation that members didn't discuss the gifts they received or the exchanges they had with other members. Discretion was the keyword in their organization. Besides, he wouldn't want to seem naïve or ill-suited for membership. He wondered how his grandfather would have handled a situation like this. Benjamin supposed that the old man would never have gotten involved with an organization like the Council, yet Benjamin was sure that if his grandfather were still alive, he could have convinced him of the strategic advantages of being part of this organization and would have received his blessings.

But his grandfather had been dead for many years, and now Benjamin was on his own to figure out how to proceed. The first place to start would be with the resort itself. Perhaps they had arranged the massage, as part of the room. Although this didn't seem likely, he called the front desk and asked about the various room packages and whether any of them included a complimentary massage. He was assured that a massage always cost extra and that if he did receive one, it was because it had been arranged for him by a third party. He also noticed that the Richards logo on the invitation didn't quite match the imprint on the stationery in his room, which he believed offered further proof that the invitation didn't originate with the resort. That was all he needed to know. He was sure his benefactors had sent him the massage as one more way to welcome him to the fold. Where else could it have come from? The only other person who knew he was here was Rebecca, and she could never have arranged something like this.

The Richards Spa was located in the basement of the resort's main building, which sat on the edge of a tiny inlet at Orcas Island. At three minutes before seven, Benjamin opened the door and walked inside to the spa's gift shop and registration desk. He was assaulted by the smell of incense and soaps and body lotions, the room filled with the heavy odors of lavender and rose and lemon and orange and cinnamon and an assortment of other fruits and flowers and spices. The store looked like something he would see in a large shopping mall in the Seattle suburbs, a sort of New Age look, trendy and exclusive. Yet even these attempts at contemporary conformity could not erase the historic presence of the original structure. Ceramic tile, laid in a mosaic of patterns, spread beneath the massive concrete arches that supported the building above. The tile was worn from years of traffic, the colors dull, muted. The arches were painted bright white and covered with prints of ocean settings and playful whales. Benjamin had read in the resort's brochure that the basement had once housed several bowling lanes. Although these had not survived the renovations, the swimming pool was still intact. But the rest of the lower level had been transformed into a not quite upscale spa replete with a whirlpool, sauna, aerobics room, and of course, the tiny New Age store in which Benjamin now stood.

He approached the front desk and announced to the woman at the counter that he had an appointment for a massage at seven. She pointed toward a doorway without looking up from her book and said that it was the third room on the right. She offered no additional information.

He exited the store and found what he thought was the massage room. A long high table sat in the center of the room, covered with an ivory-colored flannel sheet. He supposed he was to lie on it, but he couldn't be certain. Instead he sat on the edge of the table, waiting for further instructions.

A woman walked into the room. She wore khaki shorts and a pale blue golf shirt that matched her eyes.

"Mr. Randall?" Her voice was low, strong.

"Yes."

"Ready for your massage?"

Benjamin stared. She was a rugged sort of woman, a no-nonsense type. She stood a little taller than he did and had thick strawberry blond hair that barely touched her shoulders. Her long athletic legs were tanned and freckled, not like someone who lay on sandy beaches or lounged in soft patio chairs, but someone who worked and played in the sun, someone who met the outdoors with a natural enthusiasm. Her face, also freckled, was free of make-up, free of the careful pampering that most of the women he knew indulged in.

"Yes, I'm ready," he finally answered. "Do you know where he is? My massage guy, that is. Do you know when he'll be arriving?

She smiled. "I'm your massage guy, Mr. Randall."

"But I thought...I mean, I was expecting—"

She seemed to be trying not to smile. "Relax, Mr. Randall. I've been doing this a long time. My name is Jo." She reached out her hand to shake his. He was confused at first and didn't know how to react. When he realized what she wanted, he returned the shake. Her grip was strong, almost masculine. Her hand felt calloused, yet it wasn't scratchy and rough like skin can become from hard physical work.

"Um, maybe there's…well, you know, maybe there's someone else who can…"

"Mr. Randall, I assure you that I am a complete professional. And there's no one else available right now. If, however, you would rather not receive a massage, the decision is yours."

Benjamin considered this. He thought of her touching him, rubbing him. It didn't seem right somehow. What if word were to get out about this? How would it affect his standing in the Church? Or how he conducted business? And this was no ordinary woman, not the kind he was used to. She seemed a little too pushy, perhaps a little mannish. Yet he had to consider his hosts. They were gracious enough to provide him with this service, and he dare not insult them, especially after just being accepted into their ranks. And certainly they would never have put him in this position if they didn't feel it would be okay.

"No," he said, "this will be fine. I was just a bit surprised, that's all."

"Life's full of surprises." She smiled. "Now get yourself ready. I'll step out while you undress."

"Undress!"

"Yes, of course. How else can I give you a massage?"

"I can't get undressed. I can't be undressed in front of you."

"Mr. Randall, have you ever received a massage before?"

"Well, no, but that doesn't mean—"

"I'm sorry. I hadn't realized that this was your first time. I should have asked you sooner. For some reason, I thought I had seen you here before, perhaps waiting for one of the other massage therapists."

He looked away. "No, this is the first time…I've never…" He felt awkward, embarrassed.

"Normally, people remove their clothes and lie beneath a sheet while I work on them. I uncover only the body part that I'm working on, while trying to respect their privacy at all times. Some men are more comfortable wearing their briefs, in which case I work around them as best I can."

"But why…why do I need to remove my clothes?"

She explained to him how important it was to feel the muscles and bone structure, to see exactly what was working on and watch how he reacted.

r. h. sheldon

"But why *all* my clothes?" he asked. "What parts of the body do you massage?" Again she looked as though she were trying to keep from laughing.

"Generally, I give people full body massages, which includes their backs, chests, stomachs, arms, legs, buttocks, and head—the full body. If, however, someone would like a specific area worked, I'll do that."

He wasn't sure what to do. He would rather have been somewhere else, anywhere else, but he couldn't just leave, couldn't just forget the whole thing. Not only would he be concerned about slighting members of the board, he would feel in some ways like a failure, as though he had run away because he was scared.

"The idea is to make you comfortable, to feel better," she said. "If taking off your clothes is going to make you so tense that you can't relax, then the massage will be a waste. Massage is meant to be a healing process, and the more you're willing to participate in that process, the more effective the massage will be. However, if it helps, you can start by taking off your shirt and letting me work on your back, and then you can tell me how that feels. Does that sound reasonable to you?"

No, it didn't sound reasonable, and it was concession that he didn't want to make. Still, he was open to compromise. In the world of business, compromise was a way of life. "Okay," he said. "What do I do?"

"You can start by taking off your shirt and lying on the table." She pointed to the table.

"Should I take off my shoes?"

"You would probably be more comfortable." Her mouth drew tight from trying not to smirk, and the dimples in her cheek grew deeper. She said, "I'll be right back. Make yourself comfortable." Then she swept out of the room, leaving him staring at the door. He took off his shoes and socks slowly. He pulled his wallet out of his pocket and stuffed it in one of the shoes, then shoved in his socks to cover it up. Finally, he unbuttoned his shirt, pulled it off, and hung it carefully on a hook so it wouldn't wrinkle. He hadn't worn his garments this evening, thinking they would interfere with the massage. He had no idea he would have taken them off anyway.

He looked around the room to ensure he wasn't being watched, climbed onto the table, and lay facedown. He tapped his fingers against the flannel sheet as he waited her arrival, wishing he could get the ordeal behind him as soon as possible. This woman, this *Jo*, was not at all what he had expected. He wasn't used to women who spoke so authoritatively to a man, who could behave so confidently. There was something unnatural about this, something not right. Yet he couldn't help but notice those strong thighs, the full breasts, the thick wild hair, and those eyes, like the pale blue waters near the island's shores, sparkling, iridescent, unfathomable.

He pushed against the table's cushions and repositioned himself. The flannel brushed against his bare chest. It was soft, warm, as though the cushions themselves were heated.

The door opened. He twisted his head around and watched Jo enter the room. Her breasts swung freely beneath her shirt, her nipples poking the material and stretching it into tight points.

"Ready?"

"Sure." He wasn't sure what he was ready for.

She tapped the bottoms of his feet. "Scoot up so your head hangs over. You want your face sitting in that little cradle in front there."

He scooted forward, slightly relieved by her professional tone, yet slightly resentful about being told what to do. He stuck his face into the cradle, which blinded him to anything around him.

"Normally, I would cover you with a sheet, but since you have most of your clothes on, that's probably not necessary. What do you think?"

"No, this is fine. I don't need it."

He heard a squirt and then felt warm liquid drip on his back. He jerked back.

"What was that?"

She touched his shoulder. "It's okay, Mr. Randall. It's massage oil, warmed up so it wouldn't be too cold when it hit your skin. I should have warned you."

"Is that necessary?"

"I'm afraid it is. Without oil, it's difficult to massage deep and hard enough without the skin getting pinched. *Most* people think it feels good."

"Okay." He sighed and stuck his head back into the cradle. Another concession.

She touched his back with her warm hands. He tensed.

"Try to relax, Mr. Randall. You're about the tensest person I've ever met."

She said this so matter-of-factly that she probably had no idea of how disturbing this was to him. He wasn't used to criticism, especially spoken so lightly. He would never put up with this kind of behavior from his wife.

r. h. sheldon

Jo spread her hands wide and pressed into his flesh, sweeping her fingers up from his lower back toward his shoulders. Her touch was strong, controlled. She moved with slow precision, as though sensing how much pressure to use, where to lay her hands. She dug her thumbs into the tight bands of muscles that supported his back, each stroke firm, deep. She rotated sides, first right, then left. He followed the movement each time it climbed up his spine. Her thumbs squeezed his flesh into his back, creating deep pockets that inched toward his head. She stabbed the tense muscles, ice picks into his flesh. Yet he wouldn't admit pain.

His mind began to cloud with the sweet fragrance of lavender oil, the quiet of the room, the steady rhythm of Jo's breath, and he grew less concerned about the situation and the uncertainty and began to think more of the long, deep strokes, the loosening muscles, the sense of release. Her thumbs no longer knifed through his skin, but were transformed, just as he felt transformed. He eased into her soothing assurance, each movement directed, each stroke full of intent, purpose. Her touch relaxed, weakened, healed.

She spread her hands and dragged her fingertips along his flesh. She pushed in with the heels of her hands. She glided along the contours of bone and joint and muscle. She worked the edges of his shoulder blades, the arch of his neck, the base of his skull. She kneaded and stretched and squeezed every muscle, every tendon, every ligament. She wrapped her strong fingers around his arm, squeezing above his elbow, below. She dug her thumbs into his hands, stretched his fingers, worked each tiny muscle.

He was enraptured, giddy with lightness. He never felt so satisfied, so complete. He could only imagine what it would be like to have her massage other parts of his body, his chest, his legs.

"Jo?" He felt as though he spoke from a dream.

"Yes, Mr. Randall?"

"My legs...that would be good...I could take off my pants."

"If that would make you comfortable."

He sat up slowly. His body felt as though it vibrated. He sat for a moment, then took off his pants, but left on his boxer shorts and climbed back on the table.

Just as Jo was about to start again, the door swung open and banged against the wall, like the pop of a gun. Benjamin jerked up his head and twisted it around. A squat pudgy pink man squeezed into the room. He wore a Hawaiian shirt and straw hat. His face was flushed and covered with sweat. He held a video camera in his left hand, squeezed close to his shoulder.

"Can I help you?" Jo asked.

The man spun around with a befuddled gaze. "Is this the whirl-pool?" He spoke in a sort of gasp, his voice confused and tired.

Benjamin's heart pounded. His muscles tensed. He tried to push himself up, but Jo held him down with the pressure of her hands.

"You're in the wrong room," she said.

Looking more confused than before, he spun in a slow circle, mumbled an apology, and stumbled out of the room, slamming the door closed.

Benjamin jumped up from the table and pulled on his pants. He couldn't believe someone saw him like this.

"Are you okay, Mr. Randall?"

"I, ah, I better keep these on."

She seemed unperturbed. "Whatever makes you comfortable."

He climbed back on the table and stuck his face into the little saddle. She began working on his back, as though her rhythm had never been disrupted.

His heart slowed, his breath deepened. He soon forgot the intruder and fell back into the deep relaxation and excitement of her touch. He again felt light, clear, as he sunk deeper into the massage. He felt as though he drifted into an unknown dimension, lost in time and space, his reality shifting out of its normal state of control and certainty. He rarely knew such release, rarely lost the sense of place in which he set himself, defined himself. With each deep stroke, time became irrelevant, worry unknown.

She moved around the table to the top of his head. Her thigh brushed his hair. He smelled a faint odor of sweat and opened his eyes. He stretched his eyes upward, without moving his head, and glimpsed the khaki shorts. Her legs shot out toward the floor. He wanted to reach out and touch the freckles on her knee, bury his face in her strong thighs and let the tanned flesh smother him.

She reached over his head and ran her thumbs along his spine. He imagined what she looked like leaning over him, her breast dangling low, swaying with each stroke. She pushed harder, pulling his lower back away from his head. He felt the soft tip of her nipple brush his back. It was so light, so brief, that she must not have noticed. Or perhaps didn't care. But if her nipple had touched him, the massage oil would have stained her shirt. There would be a spot, a dark circle that

r. h. sheldon

would not evaporate. He would know after she had finished. He would check for himself. He would be subtle about it. Glance at her breast, but not stare. Just to be sure.

She lay her hands wide on his side and slowly pulled toward his head. Her fingers reached beneath his belly and chest, just a bit— enough to tug on the hairs and stretch the muscles along his ribs. She sparked the nerves throughout his body. Each stroke fired off a million cells. He thought of her body wrapped around him, her strong thighs squeezing, her touch on every inch of his skin, sending him into a frenzied spiral of climatic joy.

His penis swelled against the table, held tight to his body by his jeans. He was so hard that he ached. The blood surged through the shaft, its head ready to burst. He felt the pre-cum seep into his pants, warm against the flesh near his waist.

Then she started to rub the top of his head. Her fingertips vibrated against his scalp, twisting through his hair, kneading his skin. She moved faster, harder, his hair a mass of dancing tangles. She massaged every bit of scalp, leaving no part unmolested. He was ready to explode. He wanted to grab her, penetrate her, take from her what was rightfully his, but he dared not move, dared not give himself away.

Her rhythm slowed and finally stopped. Then she reached around him and lightly touched his exposed skin with the tips of her fingers, as though she brushed him with feathers. She floated along the curves of his back, around his shoulders, down his arms. When she finished, she patted him gently on the shoulder. "All done," she whispered. "Lay here for a while, until you're ready to get up."

He would not do anything until his erection subsided.

"I'll be back," she said.

The door opened and closed. He tried to think of business, of home, of church, but all he could think of was Jo and her beautiful freckled thighs and sparkling blue eyes. He stared at the floor, counting the chipped tiles that swirled around the table.

After several minutes she returned. His arousal had subsided enough for him to be able to sit up. He looked at her. She wore a different shirt.

"You seemed to have finally relaxed. How did you like your first massage?"

He couldn't speak at first, didn't want to speak. Finally he said in almost a whisper, "Great. It was really great."

He should have said more, he should have expressed his gratitude, but talking too much would have ruined it somehow, made it less real, less wonderful.

"You okay?" she asked.

"Yeah, I'm fine. Guess I wasn't prepared for enjoying it as much as I did."

"Sometimes it takes a while to get back. Just take your time. There's no hurry."

He got up slowly and reached for his shirt. Jo stood in the corner, wiping off the small table where the massage oil sat. He could not prevent his eyes from darting toward her. There was a natural heartiness about her, healthy and strong. Underlying all this was a deep sexuality, an oozing of raw feminine energy. So unlike what he had grown to expect as feminine—those anorexic frames, the molded hair, the layers of cosmetics, the gallons of perfume. This woman was none of these. Yet she stirred within him a desire he had never felt before, a yearning for a lost part of himself that only she could help to reclaim.

He started to tuck his shirt into his pants but discovered a wet spot on his jeans. He jerked his head up to see if she was looking at him. She was still turned away, but he didn't know whether she had noticed it before. He buttoned his shirt quickly, leaving the tail hanging out—something he would never do normally. He looked down at the massage table. A small wet spot stained the sheet where his fluid had soaked through the jeans.

"Uh, Jo, ummm, could I help somehow. Maybe I can get this sheet for you."

That's okay, I can—"

He grabbed it off the table. The sheet snagged on one of the table's corners. He felt a slight tear. He unhooked the snagged material and bunched it in a ball. He didn't think she heard the ripping sound.

"You're certainly feeling helpful," she said.

"Where would you like this?"

She pointed to a basket in the corner. "Right there would be fine."

He stuffed the sheet in. "Anything else I can help you with?"

"No, Mr. Randall, that will be fine. I'm just about done here."

"Benjamin," he said.

"Benjamin?"

"Yes. Benjamin. That's my name. Benjamin. You can call me Benjamin, not Mr. Randall."

"Okay, Benjamin. I'm finished here. So if there's not anything else..."

r. h. sheldon

"No. I mean yes, there is. That is, I just wanted to thank you for the massage. It was terrific."

"I'm glad you liked it." She reached for the door. "Grab a business card, if you like, off the table over there. You can make an appointment at that number, or just come in here and make one at the front desk." He obediently picked up a card. He noticed that the Richards logo matched the one on his invitation. The color of the card and ink were the same as well.

He shoved the card in his pocket. Jo began to walk out of the room.

"Wait."

She turned.

"I thought…I was thinking that…well, maybe I could buy you a soda or something—you know, to thank you for the massage. To show my appreciation…"

"The last of the big spenders, huh?"

"I didn't mean—I just thought maybe, you know, a coke or something…"

"I'd rather a beer."

"A beer?"

"You're familiar with beer, aren't you?"

"Well, yes, I mean, but I don't…"

"Okay then. Thanks anyway. We'll see you another time."

"Wait, please. A beer would be great. Let's get you a beer."

"A quick beer. But then I have to be going. I need to grab my things. Why don't I meet you upstairs in the lounge."

She walked out of the room without waiting for an answer. Benjamin finished dressing and exited the spa. He was surprised to see how dark it had grown. He was in the spa for nearly two hours. The sky was dark except off to the east where a full moon was beginning to edge up over the mountains and light up the rim of the clouds. A storm was moving in from the west, erasing any glow from the setting sun or any stars that might have been out. The water in the harbor twinkled with the lights of boats that had anchored in the calm waters. He could smell the approaching storm, the air dense with ozone. It stirred a sense of excitement in him, the thrill of being in a strange place, facing the unknown alone.

He entered the front door of the main building and went into the lounge. The concrete walls with the galley-type lighting and dark woodwork made the room take on the aura of a massive luxury liner.

Yet there were still enough features, such as the giant fireplace and wood-block floors, to remind visitors of their land-locked status.

Benjamin sat at one of the tables near the fireplace and ordered a root beer and waited for Jo's arrival. He looked around the lounge. He hadn't been in anything like this before, nothing that would qualify as a real lounge. He knew there wasn't anything really wrong with being here, because he would never dare drink anything with alcohol, but still he had to be vigilant against doing anything that even appeared evil. His actions, regardless of their motivation, must seem to be founded on nothing but the purest intent, directed by faith and duty. He doubted that any of his colleagues would see him sitting in there because they were gathering and none of them would likely come into a place that served alcohol. Still he was a little concerned that they would find out about this. He glanced around nervously, just to make sure he saw no one from the Council.

Jo walked into the lounge and headed for the bar. She ordered a beer, carried it back to the table, and sat down. "Made it," she said with a smile. She lifted the beer in a mock toast and took a drink.

The tourist who had interrupted his massage walked into the lounge. His cheeks were puffed out as he gasped for breath. He still held his camera poised, always ready to capture the unforgettable. The man looked over at Jo and Benjamin. He acted confused, lost. He wandered slowly through the lounge and toward the other door, stopping and turning periodically to look at the various features of the room, his camera swinging around with him like an appendage permanently fused to his shoulder.

When he left, Jo laughed. "That's an odd one," she said. "I doubt he even recognized us. Especially you with all your clothes on." She chuckled as Benjamin looked at the floor. He felt his cheeks flush.

"Not a drinker, huh?" she asked.

"No, I'm not, I—"

"What happened? Get drunk and shoot somebody?"

"No, it's just that—"

"Then you must be a Mormon. Are you a Mormon?" She grinned.

He hesitated. "I am as a matter of fact, but I don't think…"

"You are? It all makes sense now." She smiled broadly. She had large teeth, a little crooked. "So how many kids you got, twenty?"

"None." He squirmed.

"No kids? What's the matter with you?" She smiled. "What about wives, then—how many of them?"

r. h. sheldon

"Mormons don't have—I mean, not any more, that was a long time ago—one wife. I have one wife."

"And I have one husband, so I guess that makes us even." She gulped her beer.

He noticed for the first time the ring on her finger. He had not expected this. He had assumed that she was single. Hoped that she was single. He was surprised by the extent of his disappointment, as though her being unattached made a difference somehow, presented endless possibilities.

"I see," he said, "well, um…" What sort of man would let his wife do this kind of work?

"Don't look so glum, Benjamin. Just 'cause I'm married doesn't mean I'm dead." She winked at him and swallowed half her beer.

A Walk on the Beach

Nathan and Jo lived in a small log cabin outside the town of Eastsound, near the north shore of Orcas Island. Their house stood on an acre of wooded, rocky land at the end of Hemlock Street. In the winter, when the deciduous growth was stripped of its foliage, they could glimpse the calm waters surrounding the island and fantasize what it would be like to own waterfront property. Often they would take their dog, Gabbie, a sixty-pound yellow lab, down to the beach and toss sticks into the gentle surf, which Gabbie would fetch endlessly, if someone were willing to toss them. And she was more than willing to provide her own sticks, searching the shores for pieces of driftwood and then insistently dropping them at the feet of would-be participants.

Nathan and Gabbie now walked along the water. She carried a stick in her mouth, periodically poking Nathan in the leg to remind him of what she would like to be doing. Nathan, accustomed to how pushy she could be, ignored her efforts and kept walking.

The evening had darkened quickly. A front had pushed a mass of clouds over the Sound, blocking out the last bit of sunlight. A soft golden haze had briefly settled on the water and then gave way to the blackness of night. When the front had moved through, it had stirred up the water into a frothy dark pool of blue and green, but now it was black and smooth. Small islands cracked the surface, not as black as the water, like shadows, distant and surreal. Some were spotted with lights, testaments to the summer visitors camping or staying in their seldom-used cabins. Sometimes in the winter, Nathan would come down here at night and see blackness everywhere, when the winters were icy cold and too rough for the small boats of vacationers. Light mists would lap up against the shore, erasing distances, civilization. Occasionally the lights of a tanker would penetrate the thick night, but they would disappear quickly as the ship headed toward Vancouver.

Nathan loved the long days of summer, even if times were a little rough right now. Ever since the accident at work, when the scaffolding

r. h. sheldon

fell apart, he's had trouble finding work. This left him plenty of time to do what he wanted, but little money to do it with. Even so, the only thing he really should be doing was looking for a job.

Nathan stood before the water and looked at Sucia Island. He hated all the tourists who came here, all the fat rich Americans with too much money and too little common sense. They came to the islands in packs, transforming them into mini-versions of their urban lives. Rich and arrogant, they treated island residents like second-class citizens, white trash who could make nothing out of their lives and who lived here for the sole purpose of waiting on the visitors.

He imagined what it must have been like here a hundred years ago, when it was nothing but a few settlers, no weekend visitors, no city folk spending their money, trying to buy up the land and make it impossible for locals to afford living there. He would have owned a huge spread of land. Lots of trees, bordered by a long stretch of shore. He would have been able to hunt deer from his front door, fish salmon that swam up one of his streams. No one would be telling him what to do, when to do it. No one would be nearby.

He stared out toward the water. Gabbie was convinced this meant he wanted to play. She shoved the stick into his hand, pushing it around until he took hold of it. When he did, she leaped off the ground and barked. He waved the stick over her head a few times and then threw it into the water, not too far or she wouldn't have been able to find it. The dog jumped into the water and swam toward the stick. She bit into it and swam back, ran out of the water, dropped the stick near Nathan's feet, and shook, spraying him with icy drops.

"Gabbie!" he yelled, but laughed and picked up the stick.

She barked.

He threw it out again and she swam after it. She found the stick, swam back, leaped out of the water, dropped the stick, and shook. Nathan obediently picked it up and then threw it out. The process repeated several more times.

At one point, Nathan grabbed the stick and said, "Once more, Gabbie. Then it's time to head in."

He threw it out further than before. She jumped in after it. As soon as she swam a few feet, he ran up the beach, toward their house. When he got about thirty yards, he dropped behind a large piece of driftwood and waited. Gabbie soon came running after him, with the stick still in her mouth. After she passed where he was hidden, she stopped and looked around, her eyes bright, alert. Then she spun around and headed the other way. He waited until she was a good twenty yards away and then called for her, but he stayed hidden. She ran back toward him, but when she passed him this time, he jumped out from behind the log and yelled, "Boo!"

Gabbie leaped up and spun around. When she saw Nathan, she wagged her tail so hard her hind end shook in a big circle, but she still didn't let go of the stick.

Nathan grabbed her head and rubbed the top, working his way down to her ears.

"That's it, Gabbie. You need to dry off some before we head back to the house." He sat on the log. She dropped her stick at his feet and sat down next to him, looking mournfully at the ground.

Nathan stared out at the water. There was an eerie calm about it, as though the darkness opened into something more than unseen horizons, something strange and unnatural. It must have been the same type of feeling that early explorers knew when their ships moved through uncharted waters, when night enfolded them and they sailed toward unknown fates. He sat there now, feeling that same sense of uncertainty, as though expecting something to happen, something to change.

He heard a noise out in the water, a sound separate from the soft lapping of waves, almost indistinguishable at first, but then it grew, until he could hear the flapping of wings, and he realized that a bird flew out there in the darkness, soaring low over the water. He thought he caught movement to his right, and he turned his head just as an eagle swooped down toward the shore and landed on a rocky outcrop near the bank. Nathan could barely make out its form in the dim light from the road, but he could tell that it sat watching him. And then the bird flapped its wings and squawked in a high screech, and all Nathan could see was a flurry of shadow, but then, for a brief moment, he thought he saw a man, next to the rocks, but it wasn't really a man, but a man's body, with the head of the eagle, standing naked, proud, but in an instant he was gone, disappearing in another flurry of gray, and out of the darkness emerged the bird, soaring effortlessly up into the night, until he could see it no more. He looked back toward the rocks. No one was there.

"Gabbie, did you see that?"

She barked.

He rubbed his eyes and blinked several times. "Man, this darkness can play some weird tricks on your eyes."

r. h. sheldon

She barked again.

"Come on, girl, let's go home. Your mom will be back soon—and I better lie down."

They walked up to the house and stood in front of the porch.

"Okay, drop the stick and shake."

She let it fall near several other sticks about the same size. Then she started wiggling her body.

"No," Nathan said, "shake."

She let her body gyrate wildly as water flew off her fur.

"Good girl."

They entered the house and he wiped her down with a towel, which he then hung on the front porch. As he stepped back in, the phone rang, He figured it was Jo, otherwise he wouldn't have answered it.

"Hello."

"Nathan?" A man's voice, rough and low.

"Yes."

"Beardsley here."

"Beardsley?"

"Yeah, from the bar. I met you a last week."

Nathan vaguely remembered talking to this man. He should never have drunk so much that night. "Oh yeah."

"I've got the photos."

"The photos?"

"Yeah, the pictures you wanted." And then it came back—the conversation, the plan, the photographs that Beardsley was going to take for Nathan. He held the phone away from his ear and sat down. Now what had Nathan gotten himself into?

The Impossible Dream

Benjamin walked Jo across the dimly lit parking lot to her Honda CRX, an ancient red beater dented and rusted and layered with road dust and grime. The left front bumper hung loose, and a long crack split the windshield.

He reached to open the door, but instinctively pulled back, repulsed by the greasy smears of dirt and mud. She said nothing, but reached around and opened the door. A dim yellow light popped on. The car was littered with pop cans, papers, candy wrappers, and a few beer bottles. The back windows were smudged gray and smeared with dirt. Clumps of dog hair floated along the edges of the seats. A tattered greasy blanket was bunched up against the back of the driver's seat. The car reeked of wet dog.

"Well," she said, "this is it, my giant dog kennel."

"What?"

"My car. A big dog house. Our dog loves to go for rides." She pointed to the smeared windows. "I always mean to clean it out, but…" She shrugged. "Anyway, thanks for the beer, maybe I'll see you around sometime."

He wanted to answer, suggest that they get together sometime—another massage perhaps. Or even just a beer. But instead he watched her drive away, the dust from the road puffing out from beneath her tires.

He stood in the parking lot until her lights disappeared up the road and through the wall of trees. Then he walked down toward the water and followed the sidewalk along the harbor. The clouds now erased the moon and stars. Even the silhouette of mountains had disappeared. A breeze stirred the waters of the bay and blew steady over the shore. The twinkling of lights from the boats bounced on the dark waters like an enclave of intoxicated fairies.

He climbed the steps to his room and went inside. The room seemed emptier than before, more sterile and lonely. He dropped into bed, surprised at his deep weariness. It reminded him of his college days—sleepless nights reading and trying to grasp the material. The

r. h. sheldon

principles of business came easy enough, the manipulating of resources, the understanding of the market, but rote memorization was never his strongest trait, so when it came to taking his exams, he struggled with every bit of determination he could muster to get through, pulling at resources so deep within him that when he was finished he felt drained of all energy and emotion.

The wind had picked up and now gusted off the water and slammed against the glass sliding doors to the balcony. Rain soon spit against the windows like the rapid fire of pellet guns. He lay unmoving for another hour, thinking of this beautiful woman, of this extraordinary night—of his life back home. And with these thoughts, he fell into a dark sleep, a sleep packed with the images of his wife, of his house on the North Fork of the Skykomish River, of his church and his fellow Mormons. And emerging from the center of these thoughts, like lava flowing from a volcano, the image of his grandfather oozed out of the ground and stood before him, wearing the same old suit he'd worn every day and holding the Book of Mormon. And in a voice like the rumble of the quaking earth, he said, "Way to go, boy, now you're catching on."

The Road Home

Jo slipped on her seatbelt and drove out of the Richards Resort parking lot and headed up the steep road to Horseshoe Highway, turned left, and sped toward Eastsound, the largest town on Orcas Island. The road was quiet. Most of the tourists were tucked away in their condominiums and lodges and hotels. The rest squeezed into the few densely populated camp sites where wall-to-wall RVs pumped out the high-fidelity sounds of nostalgic rhythms dating back to the '40s, '50s, and—in the case of wealthy baby boomers who struck it big in high-tech enterprises—the '60s and '70s. The cacophony of stereos was disrupted only by the screeching sounds of videos and televisions that cast a blue haze across the catatonic faces of the intrepid campers.

The Honda sped through the night like a train winding through a black tunnel. The only light was from her headlights, the only sound, the whine of the small Japanese engine. She glanced into her rear-view mirror, but she could barely see through the nose prints in the back window. Perhaps Benjamin would follow her, carried away by his mad passion. He had fallen fast and hard. She could see it in his eyes, the way he stared, anxious, almost panicky. When he talked, he leaned toward her, close enough for her to smell his sweat, his nervousness.

Jo usually found men like him repulsive. They had all the depth of a cardboard box, and often the character to match. And Benjamin was no different. Yet something about him intrigued her, something almost familiar. Maybe it was just sexual. Maybe with the way things were going at home, she was feeling more receptive. And Benjamin wasn't too hard to look at. Nice body. Handsome face. And a great butt! But that was it. His life was his business, his home, his church. Everything else was an extension of these topics.

"I work a lot with the boys at our church," he had said. "I talk to them about responsibility, about community, but I also try to teach them more practical things, like how to work on cars, do repairs around the house."

"That must be fascinating for them."

r. h. sheldon

He failed to note her cynicism and persisted. "It's important for a boy to learn these things."

"Important for whom?"

"Important for them. Who do you think? So they turn out like men—real men, not some dainty little momma's boys who don't know the difference between a girl and a boy, if you know what I mean."

Jo knew exactly what he meant. "I'm not sure what you mean." This guy was so pathetic.

Benjamin lowered his voice. "You know, those homosexuals."

The car hummed along a quiet stretch of highway. The gentle motion soothed Jo's tension. She had always found movement comforting. The idea of being propelled though space, where everything outside was impermanent, moving off to the horizon, was inspiring yet peaceful. Always going toward something, away from something else. Cars, trains, planes, boats—it was all the same, all giant cradles that rocked her gently, securely.

She sank willingly into her reverie, the night's exhaustion settling on her like dew on a grassy field. She had driven this highway a thousand times. She knew every curve, every intersection. She had watched the giant oaks in front of the farmhouses swell with life every spring, dry up each fall. She saw these same farms deteriorate, the land divided into mini-suburban projects, the trees bulldozed, roads paved, fences built. Sometimes people from Seattle would come up and buy these old farmhouses, turn them into bed-and-breakfasts, their stab at getting away from it all. But soon the realities of island life would set in. Winter business would be too slow, too unexciting, and they would be off again to their urban havens, selling their investments to the next set of unsuspecting romanticists looking for a better life.

The night erased all this now. She stared absently at the highway, her gaze aimed at the car's lights. She was guided by memory, by the familiar.

Stands of Douglas fir would snatch at the edges of the highway, looming walls that confined the lights to the narrow road. Then the trees would vanish, replaced by the dark meadows that stretched toward the mountains.

She thought about Benjamin, thought about his oddities, his stuffiness. Can't be much in bed, she decided. Still it might be fun to find out. She let the idea drift around in her mind, toying with the notion of her and Benjamin. Something she would never do, of course, especially a client. She always sought to maintain a professional relationship. But tonight, she let herself slip, extending her massage a little longer than usual, her strokes a little more tender, perhaps more probing. She even had a beer with him, for crissakes, something she had never done.

Still, he was the kind of guy she could not be around for very long. Not that he seemed all that bad, and it was kind of cute seeing how nervous he was, how polite he acted, but there was something a bit empty about him, and she doubted a conversation would ever include anything other than his own narrow world. And he sure as hell wouldn't be much fun at a party. Of course, she could say the same thing about her own husband. But there was a difference. Where Benjamin stood firmly in this cultural hierarchy, grabbing control with a sense of inheritance and pride, without questioning the role in which he had been placed, Nathan positioned himself away from the center, toward the fringes of the cultural order. He would happily cast away all ties to civilization, all claims that placed him—by societal default—at the top of the pecking order.

Jo had not even met Nathan's family. All she knew was that he was raised in Seattle. His parents retired somewhere in Arizona, and his brother lived somewhere in Snohomish County. But that was about all she knew about them. Nathan occasionally received letters and cards from his parents, but he rarely wrote back, rarely called. Nathan didn't speak about his past, and when she asked about it, he would shut down, visibly cringing at her questions. If not for Jo, he would slip into the wilderness, never to search for re-entry. How their marriage had managed this long remained a mystery to her.

The highway wound around a small hill and curved toward the bay. The water was black ink, dotted with whitecaps. The storm moved in quickly. The eerie calm had passed. Those kinds of calms, before the actual storm hit, made Jo uneasy. She preferred the raging wind, the screaming skies. She would rather see the face of her enemy.

The road twisted to the right. The wind whipped off the water and buffeted against the side of the car. She glanced again at the water, the cresting whitecaps, dull sparks against a black horizon. She tried to watch the water and the road at the same time, stealing glances over her left shoulder. Rain began to fall, almost a mist at first, but then giant drops smacked against the windshield, like jellied amoebae sprawled across the glass. She switched on the wipers and tried to watch the road

r. h. sheldon

through the muddy semi-circles. The rain stained the asphalt and bled into small oily pools that splashed against the bottom of the car.

She caught movement far ahead, off to the right. She eased off the gas. Suddenly a deer leaped from the shoulder. She slammed on the brakes. The car skidded to the left, slowly at first, the headlights spraying out like a beacon, then spun in a circle, headed toward the left embankment, bounced, and banged against rock. Tires squealed, metal screeched. She slammed into the steering wheel and door and ceiling. The car rolled over, knocked into a boulder, bounced off, slammed into a tree, and stopped, landing upright. The wind howled through the cracked window next to her head. Rain pounded against the roof. The engine hissed. She tried to stare out, but the light blurred, fell to red. Blood trickled down her face. She felt twisted, crushed. Breath merely a whisper. Then blackness.

Monday Night

Hot Chocolate and Sympathy

Rebecca stood over her industrial-styled gas range and stirred the pan of hot chocolate. It was the only warm drink she had to offer her guest. After a minute, she turned off the gas and expertly filled two mugs. She dropped several brightly colored miniature marshmallows into the chocolate and placed both cups on a tray. Then she reached into a cabinet beneath the counter, burying her arm beneath a stack of enamel cookware, and pulled out a half-filled bag of Oreo cookies.

She always kept some sort of treat hidden in the kitchen. She couldn't say for sure why she did this. Benjamin wasn't much of a dessert eater, and he seldom rummaged around the kitchen, and it wasn't likely anyone else would be looking around in here. Whenever they entertained friends or Benjamin's business associates, Rebecca managed the cooking and the kitchen—no matter who offered their help—and she always provided some sort of dessert for her guests, whether they were there for dinner or for a more informal visit. Yet she felt driven to keep a separate treat hidden, a private stash that only she knew about, a way to satisfy her desires while keeping a part of her life private. And her hidden treats always contained chocolate. One week cookies, the next, candy bars. Sometimes she would sneak home a small chocolate cake, thick with creamy chocolate icing that smothered the top and sides and split the cake into rich, savory layers.

She craved chocolate now, anxious to take her first sip of cocoa, bite into her first Oreo. She filled a plate with cookies and returned the bag to its hiding spot. Then she carried the tray into the living room, where Paul sat close to the gas fireplace, staring at the steady red and orange flame. He wore a shirt and pair of pants that belonged to Benjamin. But Benjamin was a little bulkier and shorter, so the clothes hung limply across his shoulders and around his waist and came up short in the arms and legs. He looked like one of those homeless people she saw when she went into Seattle. The beard did little to dispel this image.

She moved cautiously toward him. Everything had happened so quickly, pulling the old man out of the river, carrying him home, calling the ambulance. And when the ambulance arrived, the paramedics were in and out so fast it hardly seemed real. And then she was there with only Paul, both of them wet, cold. She had no time to stop and think about the implications of being alone with a strange man. What if he were a criminal or crazy or violent? What if he tried to do something to her? And what would Benjamin say when he heard about this? He would be furious. How could she tell him what happened— that she was walking alone through the campground, through *that* campground. And that this stranger now wore her husband's clothes! No matter what the circumstances were, the result was that she was alone in the house with a man she had just met, and if anyone from the Church found out, she would be under suspicion for the rest of her life—and Benjamin would never forgive her.

She placed the tray on the table. Steam curled out of the mugs and twisted toward the ceiling.

"It's so real," Paul said.

Rebecca looked at him half-aware. "Real?"

"The fire, the logs. They all look so real. If you hadn't told me, if I hadn't watched you turn on the gas, I don't think I would have guessed it was fake."

"Except it never changes. You would have guessed by that, by the sameness of it."

She sat down, weary, confused.

"Yeah, I suppose you're right."

"But it's neat. No ash, no burnt logs, no soot..."

"No smoke, no smell of burning wood, no crackling and popping... more like a hiss really."

She shifted in her chair. "Help yourself to some hot chocolate. And some cookies. There's plenty."

"Gee, I don't know...I've been trying to clean up my act, lay off junk food and all..." He hesitated. "But this has been such a strange evening, a really wild evening, that maybe—yeah, I guess. But after tonight, then I'm back to good food only. This is it."

He grabbed a cup of the hot chocolate and a cookie.

"If you would rather something else, I could make you—"

"No, this is fine. Thanks. I plan to savor my last descent into the black well of chocolate and sugar." He looked into the mug. "Look at these little marshmallows. I haven't seen them since I was a kid." He

r. h. sheldon

studied the marshmallows as he bit into a cookie. After a moment, he said, "You think that guy's going to be okay?"

She looked away. "I don't know. I mean, I hope so. He was breathing and everything. But that water was so cold, and it took us a few minutes to get him out of there. And he was pretty old. I just don't know." She shook. She could feel the tears well up in her eyes, the pressure in her temples, the heat spread across her face. She clenched her jaw.

Paul put down his mug and spoke softly. "At least the ambulance was able to get here quickly…maybe we could call the hospital or something and check in on him." He looked at Rebecca with a sort of expectation.

"Yes, maybe. At least we would know." She stared out the window, at the blackness of night. The soft whooshing sound of the river seeped into the house. "How's your hot chocolate?" she asked without looking at him.

"Yummy. Thanks. And I'm feeling a lot warmer now."

They said nothing for several minutes. He sipped his hot chocolate as he watched the gas flames. Then he began looking around the room, straining to see through doorways, into other rooms and halls.

"This place is huge," he announced. "How many people live here? A hundred?"

She grabbed the arm of the chair. "Just us," she said. "Me and my husband. Nobody else."

"Just the two of you? Wow. You could probably go days without seeing each other. But he must not be around. Surely he would have noticed the ambulance."

Why all the questions? "My husband…he's…I expect him home at any time."

"Oh."

What did that mean? Could he tell she was lying? He seemed suspicious somehow, as though he could tell the truth by looking at her. His face was dark, wild. She stared out the window, wondering what to do with him, how to get him out of the house. What if he wouldn't leave?

She nibbled at the cookie. Even the chocolate failed to calm her.

"Ummm, Paul—it's Paul, right? You said your name was Paul?"

He turned toward her. His eyes, a pale green, were set deeply beneath dark brown eyebrows. The light on the fire glowed across his cheeks, his forehead—but only the parts not covered by the thick shock of hair atop his head and the dark heavy beard. He looked evil in this light, as though he planned something diabolical, his thoughts churning out images of her destruction.

"Yes, that's right," he said.

She spoke slowly, hesitantly, "Your clothes should be dried soon. Just a few more minutes, I should think. They're in the dryer. So it won't be long."

"Great," he said. "That will be great."

"So, ah, do you have far to go?" She looked, toward the floor, the ceiling, anywhere but into his eyes. "I mean, where do you go from here?"

"From here? I'm not sure I understand…"

Her cookie snapped and black crumbs sprinkled across her white blouse.

"I mean, do you live around here? Are you staying up here somewhere?"

She felt confused, unfocused, more alone then ever, the way she felt when Benjamin was upset about something and she didn't know how to respond. The way he got when he was feeling impatient with her, like the time he tried to teach her how to park the lawn mower so it fit exactly in the little spot in the corner of the workshop. He showed her how to back it in, then made her try, despite her protests. Each time she would cut the corner too sharply or not turn sharply enough, and the mower would end up in the wrong place. The more she goofed up, the more frustrated Benjamin got. And the more frustrated he got, the more nervous she got. And the more nervous she got, the worse she would goof up. After about the fifth or sixth try, he threw up his arms in a fit of anger and announced, "Just forget it! I don't know why I even bother."

Why indeed.

Her father had said the same thing to her, on more than one occasion. No matter how hard she tried, she could not please him, not live up to his strict expectations. His stern, unforgiving attitude made it impossible to ever be comfortable around him. And now all men made her uneasy, made her feel slightly ashamed, always inferior, always inadequate.

"Are you okay?"

Paul's interruption sucked her back into the room. "What?"

"You asked me a question, then drifted off somewhere. I was just checking if you were okay."

She bit her lower lip, then looked at him. "Yes, I'm okay. I was just—I'm fine, really…"

He looked at her carefully. Her face flushed and scalp grew hot.

"Anyway," he said. "I'm camping in the campground next to here, near where the old man fell into the water."

She jerked her head back toward him. "The campground? But I thought it was closed. I thought nobody came there anymore. I thought—"

She felt as if she were choking, her stomach thick and knotted. She tried to hide her panic, to remain calm, but she knew he could see through her, his eyes narrow, suspicious, penetrating. An icy shiver raced up her spine.

"Yeah," he said, "it's closed—at least as far as I know." His voice was low, even, calm against her terror.

Of course it's still closed, she thought. It must be. This man certainly was not one of them. He wasn't like *that.*

Paul continued. "I decided to get away for a while, to spend some quiet time, by myself."

"And you're camping there?"

"I arrived today."

"Is that legal, I mean, if it's closed, you probably shouldn't be…well, you know. What if you get caught?"

He seemed to consider this. "Well, I can't imagine anyone is checking, and if they are, the worst that could happen is I get kicked off. What are they going to do anyway?"

He was probably right. Still, Rebecca was not one to break laws—or rules of any kind. She always obeyed, did as she was told. At least she tried to. Sure, she made mistakes, like she made before she got married, when she and Benjamin got carried away in her parents' house. But she made up for that, paid her dues. Now the worst thing she ever did was to sneak her chocolate treats into the house. It wasn't like disobeying rules, like consciously breaking the law. A person who didn't worry about doing something illegal might be capable of anything. As the bishop of her ward had said on many occasions, "If you're willing to cross the line once, you're willing to do it again and again."

"Anyway," Paul said, "I'm planning to stay only a few days. I doubt anyone will notice." He smiled. Rebecca tried to smile back but she was sure that it must have looked more like a snarl, like a look she would have given Benjamin when his back was turned.

A ding echoed from the kitchen. She jumped up and looked around nervously. "Oh," she said, realizing the source of the sound, "that's the dryer. Your clothes are probably done." She took a step. "I'll be right back."

Paul stood. "Should I come with you?"

"No!" She looked over her shoulder. "I mean, ah, no, let me check them, make sure they're done. They were pretty wet."

She walked out of the room and through the kitchen, to a small room near the back of the house. She opened the dryer and felt the jeans. They were still damp.

Just get done, she thought. Get done so he can get out of here.

She shoved the jeans back into the dryer and turned it on. The motor whirled as the zipper snapped against the sides of the steel drum.

She returned to the living room. Paul once more stared at the fire.

"They're still not dry, but will be soon. Very soon. And then you can get back to your campsite."

"Thanks," he said. "But don't worry on my account. I'm in no hurry."

She looked out the window. "I wonder where he is…my husband. I wonder when he'll be here. I expect him at any minute."

She sat down and shoved another cookie in her mouth. Neither said anything. Rebecca hated this silence. It was more frightening than trying to speak.

"So, Paul, ah, how did you end up here? I mean, of all places you could have camped, why here?"

"You mean here in Index or here at the campground?"

"Well, the campground. Why did you pick that spot?"

He shrugged. "I don't know. A lot of memories, I guess."

"Memories?" Her voice squeaked. She felt like a mouse.

"Yeah, the campground reminds me of old friends, old times. I used to come here when it was open, before the state closed it down. And even after that sometimes"

"You used to camp here? You? But I thought—" She looked at the floor, the ceiling, praying for this day to end.

He seemed amused. "You thought?"

"What I meant is—I don't know, I just imagined…" She didn't know what she thought anymore, what she imagined. Damn these men, they always did this to her, even this one, even one of *them*.

Paul chuckled. "So I figured it would be good to spend a couple days here, a good place to start."

She only half heard him, answering out of habit more than anything else.

"Start?"

"Yes. Start my journey. I've taken a sabbatical of sorts. I quit my job, moved out of my apartment, left most of my possessions behind—all today. The start of a new life."

"You quit your job?"

"Yep. Walked out this morning, without notice. Just up and left. It felt glorious, the best thing I've ever done."

"And your home, your apartment—you gave that up?"

"Yeah, moved out this morning, right before I went to work. Guess I'm jobless and homeless—and plan to stay that way for a while."

"But how are you going to live? What are you going to do?" This was too much. Here she was with this stranger—a man—alone with him in their house. No job, no home, and worse yet, one of them, one of those *homosexuals!*

What would Benjamin say?

"Oh, I'll be fine," Paul said. "I've got some money saved, and I plan to spend the summer camping—so it will cost me practically nothing to live. It's quite exciting, really."

Rebecca couldn't grasp the idea of someone tossing everything away like this—to behave so irresponsibly, so contrary to how she was taught to live, where hard work and sacrifice led to a life of prosperity and an eternity of salvation. She didn't know how to respond to Paul's decision, especially considering how enthused he appeared, delighted to be running away from life's responsibilities. Maybe she should expect behavior like this. Maybe this was typical of homosexuals. After all, if he chose to live such an immoral and unnatural lifestyle, it wasn't surprising that he would willingly throw away his job and his home just to take off and play all summer. But it wasn't right somehow, not in keeping with the teachings of the Church. This man was an affront to her beliefs and her way of life. He represented everything that was wrong in this world, everything unholy.

Rebecca finally spoke. "But why? Why would you do this?"

Paul smiled. "I've begun my life's journey," he said. "I've heard the voice of God."

Her mouth opened, but she said nothing. She grabbed a cookie and shoved it in, then stared out the window toward the invisible river.

The dryer sounded its haunting ding.

An Ounce of Prevention

Stanley sat up on a gurney with a nasal cannula strapped to his face by tiny elastic bands that wrapped around his head. The green tubing delivered a steady flow of oxygen through his nostrils and into his lungs, a great system if the patient breathed through his nose in a somewhat consistent manner, which Stanley did not. He breathed through his mouth for the most part, something he had done for quite a while now. Perhaps it was the unlit cigarette that usually dangled from his lips and his constant attempts to puff out bits of cigarette paper and tobacco that accumulated along his gums. Or maybe it was the shortness of breath from the early stages of emphysema that had developed as a result of the many years when he actually lit those cigarettes. Whatever the reason, his mouth was often open as a sort of mumbled breath pushed out his lungs and through the brown edges of his teeth.

But the cannula didn't matter much to Stanley. He ignored it with a sort of philosophic indifference, knowing that the medical personnel who raced around the emergency room needed to feel that they were doing their jobs despite his inward knowledge that he was fine, considering his age, his health before he stepped into the river, and the fact that the glow of the whiskey had worn off completely. The truth was, he didn't remember what happened after he hit the water, and not until he woke up in the ambulance on the way to the hospital, still shivering from his spill, was he aware of what was going on. Yet that was of little concern because now he felt as good as he could possibly feel at this point in his life, and he was content to sit back to watch and listen to the buzz of the ER.

In addition to the nasal cannula stuck to his nose, an IV delivered clear fluid into a tired vein in his left arm at a rate of not much more than a few drops a minute. "Just to keep the line open," the nurse had told him, whatever the hell that meant. The tubing ran from his arm to a plastic bag that hung from a silver pole next to his bed. The bag said "0.9% Sodium Chloride." Clear fluid dripped into a small chamber beneath the bag and then ran down the clear plastic line, where it

r. h. sheldon

disappeared beneath a pile of gauze and tape on the inside of his elbow. He had to lay with his arm straight, which added to the discomfort of being pinned to the bed.

But all in all, the IV and oxygen were not too bad, and he could pretty much ignore them. But the heart monitor—and its dozen wires that snapped to small adhesive circles glued to various parts of his chest and legs—were far more annoying. The squeaking beat of the monitor and the green glow of the display with its jagged lines and pulsating rhythm and the tangle of wires that kept him sprawled out like a bug in a spider's web, all conspired to remind him of his mortality, to calculate with an executioner's precision the broken pieces of his heart, the tiny weaknesses that would lead to his inevitable demise.

Stanley, for the most part, operated with the belief that what he didn't know didn't hurt him. He was not a fan of doctors or the medical industry as a whole. He placed little faith in these men and women in their starched white coats who walked around with their arrogant smiles and feigned interest. He knew that he was no more than a scientific experiment to them, an old guy who should not be, by all reckoning, still alive.

Yet he persisted, despite years of drinking and smoking. He'd been in fights, fallen off roofs, and was even run over one time—at least almost run over. It was more like being knocked out of the way. The tumble down the embankment hurt a hell of a lot more than the car, which ended up with a big dent in its side. He worked hard all his life, too. He worked the ranch, logged up in the mountains, built houses, tore down barns, poured cement. He never let sickness stop him either. No matter what the weather, no matter how hard the work, he never missed a day just because he was too sick to get out of bed. Even the hangovers didn't stop him—and he had a few that would turn even the staunchest of men into stumbling sick dogs who would have rather been dead than feel as shitty as they did.

And through it all, he rarely walked into a doctor's office, except maybe to have a broken bone set or a cut stitched up that was too deep to hold together with tape. And now he was stuck here in this hospital, with wires and tubes going in all directions, as if they could save him from the inevitable, prolong what was merely a waiting period, a countdown till his entire system shut down and he was no more than a bag of gas.

When Stanley had been brought into the emergency room, he had been told that he was at Westside Hospital, which was located in Seattle. Stanley wasn't fond of hospitals or of being in Seattle. He could never understand how a place that had once been so beautiful could have been reduced to such a maze of roadways and congestion.

Seattle, like Rome, had been built on seven hills. The sweeping tree-studded landscape, once the peaceful domain of hunting and fishing villagers, was transformed into stripped hillsides of concrete and asphalt that were now dotted with towers of steel and glass, rather than the elaborate stands of ancient forests. Hemlock gave way to highways. Cedar to sidewalks. Cottonwood to condos. Even one of the seven hills, the one that had edged what was now the central business district, had been mowed down to create an area known as the Denny Regrade, an industrialized slope surrounded by Queen Anne Hill, Capitol Hill, and First Hill.

First Hill was a small medical-centric mountain just to the east of downtown Seattle. It was here on First Hill—also referred to as Pill Hill—that many of western Washington's major medical facilities were located. In addition to these facilities one of the more minor medical establishments—Westside Hospital—sat prominently on the edge of Pill Hill, overlooking the downtown area and the sometimes glistening, often gray, waters of Puget Sound.

Westside Hospital tended to receive only the less critical types of injuries and illnesses from around the region, unless the trauma centers grew too crowded to accommodate all the serious patients. Accident victims from around the state might be diverted to Westside, when space was at a premium and injuries were not quite as life-threatening as those requiring immediate intervention.

Even though Westside wasn't a first-class trauma center, it nonetheless bustled with activity this evening, its ER beds nearly filled to capacity. Stanley watched the staff scurry from patient to patient as they tried to manage the influx of broken, bleeding, and ailing humanity. The patients would moan, scream, shout, cry, their voices erupting from behind the curtained cubicles in an international outcry: Asian, Russian, Mexican, American. Patients were rolled in, others rolled out. Efficient secretaries chased gurneys with their clipboards and forms, waving their pens as they tried to protect the hospital from legal and financial liability. Nurses and technicians juggled the influx of patients, administered medication, IV therapies, shots. Plugged wires into monitors, adjusted the flow of oxygen, checked blood pressure, pulses, as doctors strolled from patient to patient, paying brief visits, listening halfheartedly to the nurses' reports as they read charts and evaluated patients through distant gazes.

Despite his reluctance to be here, Stanley was amazed at everything he witnessed. Never had he beheld such a swarming mass of confusion, of near chaos, yet everyone seemed to have a place, to serve a purpose within this endless cycle of pain and suffering—as though they each reached for the same goal: to turn the extraordinary into the ordinary, the unpredictable into the predictable, the abnormal into the norm. Their target seemed always moving, a step beyond their reach, yet they somehow managed to escape the inevitable descent into the chaos, to maintain a sort of order that prevented their structure from tumbling down around them.

Stanley watched as two paramedics—one man and one woman, both dressed in navy blue jumpsuits—rolled a patient into the slot next to his. All Stanley could see emerging from the gray wool blanket was a tangle of reddish-blond hair that lay knotted and gnarled against the backboard on which the patient lay. A nurse from the center desk followed them into the cubicle and asked how the patient was doing. As she spoke, she pulled the curtain partially closed so that Stanley could no longer see them.

"Still no response," Stanley heard one of them say. "Her vitals have remained stable, breathing fine, lungs sound clear, abdomen soft, color good, motion in her extremities—a few minor cuts and a little bruising around her right temple. We didn't feel or see anything too strange—except for the bruise. Here's the trip ticket."

The nurse sounded as though she read from a chart. "Pulse, seventy-eight. Blood pressure, one-thirty over seventy-two. Almost no fluctuation since you picked her up. How were her vitals at the scene and in the ambulance?"

"About the same. And nothing changed during the entire flight over."

"Was she wearing a seat belt?"

"Appears to have been. Her car rolled over—at least once, and then she hit a tree."

"Any signs of alcohol, drugs?"

"There were a couple beer bottles in her car, but we didn't smell anything on her."

"Okay, let's see what we've got."

Stanley listened as equipment was rolled in, machines hummed, questions were asked. No doubt she was being plugged into the same assortment of tubes and wires that now held him captive. He wondered how she had had the accident, how her car had rolled over. He had been in several accidents, most of them minor fender benders that were more inconvenient than anything else. He and the boys would get kind of crazy when they were out drinking, sometimes taking their cars into places and at speeds that were probably not the smartest. But that was a long time ago. He'd never do anything like that now. He no longer had anyone to do that kind of thing with. Life had become a safe routine, a cautious process of survival.

The busy hum quieted in the next stall. The nurse said that they should get some pictures right away. He assumed that meant X-rays. The nurse walked to the station in the middle of the room. Two other staff members slipped from behind the curtain and walked in opposite directions. He heard no other sounds from the cubicle, at least nothing distinguishable from the clicks and beeps in the rest of the ER.

He waited. He could do nothing else.

After several minutes, he heard movement from her bed, a rustling about. Then a low moan, followed by a crash—the loud clang of steel against the cold tiled floor. And then she shouted—almost a scream, "Where the hell am I?" she yelled. "What the hell is going on?"

r. h. sheldon

On the Road Again

Nathan left Gabbie in the house and closed the front door. Her face immediately appeared in the nearest window, her wet nose flattened against the glass. She looked out with eyes dark and sad, her rejection measured in the way her face sagged as she watched with despair his impending departure. Nathan had thought Jo would be home by now, but she probably stopped at a friend's, or maybe she went into town for a beer, assuming that he was already in bed, bored into early sleep. At any rate, she was sure to have left from work by now. She never stayed longer than necessary. She didn't mind rubbing the backs and shoulders of the resort's guests, but she seldom rubbed elbows.

At least with Jo gone, he could slip out of the house without having to say anything. If she had been there when he received the call, he would have had to tell her all about it, or make something up. But now he could slip out comfortably, without having to admit anything or, worse yet, lie, something he was never good at, especially with Jo.

The rain fell through the trees, caught by limbs and needles and gathered into golf ball drops that hit against the wood steps in heavy clunks. Water poured from the brim of his hat, dripped onto his denim jacket, down the back of his neck. He ran to the truck and climbed in. Gabbie continued to stare, her abandonment now complete. Nathan would have taken her but he didn't want her making a lot of noise or getting in the way. He wanted this to be over as quickly as possible.

He pulled out of the driveway and onto Hemlock Street. As soon as he drove out from beneath the trees, the rain pelted the truck with rapid blasts, like a machine gun popping off a continuous round. He followed side streets until he reached the highway, where he turned left, toward Richards Resort. He steadily increased his speed as he strained to see through the smeared window and down the darkened road. He felt the anxiety twist his guts, like a rope pulled into a tight knot. His heart raced. His breath grew shallow. "Just settle down," he told himself. For several minutes, he took long, deep breaths and let out slow exhalations while he counted to himself. But the feeling of excitement persisted, an anxious anticipation, and his breath again grew short and his heart stomped against his chest. He held the wheel with white knuckles, pushed the gas pedal to the floor. The rain banged against the roof of the cab. The wipers rattled and squeaked, smearing a murky film across the windshield.

He drove for several miles like this. Then ahead, far down the road, he made out the dim flash of lights. Red. Blue. He squeezed the steering wheel and eased up on the gas. It looked like a couple cop cars, maybe a tow truck. He slowed more. The lights flashed their silent warning. His truck crawled. He leaned toward the windshield, but could make out only a blur of lights, the details wiped out with each stroke of the blade.

Hazard flares glowed at the edge of the road. As he crept closer, he could see a tow truck off to the side, its winch pointing toward the embankment. The cop cars were parked on the shoulders, one on either side. Someone had no doubt gone off.

He eased past the red and blue lights. Each flash flooded his truck with a stark glare and turned his hands a deathly gray.

Once beyond the cop cars, he pulled away slowly, burrowing into a dark stand of trees. The road curved to the left, and the lights disappeared from his mirror. He pushed on the gas pedal and let out a long heavy sigh. He had barely breathed as he passed the cars, an unconscious act that was as instinctual as eating and drinking.

He had reacted that way to tense situations for as long as he could remember, since he was a little kid and had to put up with an older brother who was always criticizing him, demeaning him in front of his family. Nathan was the one who always got into trouble, the one who never fit in. And his brother, with his good grades and even better behavior, served as a constant reminder to Nathan's own inadequacies, always lurking nearby, ready to lash out with his sharp criticism. Growing up had been marked by the panic that he felt whenever his brother was close at hand. And just like now, his heart would pound, his breathing quicken. The coldness, the pain in his guts, the fear— they had all stayed with him.

After driving a few more miles, Nathan turned off the highway. He followed the narrow road as it wound down toward Richards and emptied into the resort's parking lot. The rain looked denser in the dim light, giving depth to a downpour that erased all but the nearest of objects. He drove slowly around the lot. The asphalt was spotted with deep puddles. Oily water sprayed to the sides, against the bottom of the truck. He felt the wash vibrate through the metal floor.

He first wanted to be sure that Jo had left. The last thing he needed was for her to learn of his involvement in all this. He drove around until he was satisfied her car wasn't there. Then he went to the far end of the lot, the point nearest the bay, and parked next to an old green Chevy van that shimmered in the eerie glow of a streetlamp.

Nathan turned off his lights and waited. The engine moaned uneasily as it strained to maintain the low idle. He needed a new truck. This one would probably not last another year without a major rebuild. His whole life was like that—everything ready to fall apart.

A knock on the passenger's window snapped him out of his reverie. The door flew open and a gust of wind and rain whirled inside the cab. A large balding man climbed into the truck and slammed the door. He wore a Hawaiian shirt, pasted by the rain to his rolls of flesh, and carried a plastic grocery bag, which he set on the floor near the wet skin of his legs. Water dripped from his head and arms and soaked the worn sheepskin seat cover. His breath spurted out in hot puffs of air, a panting sigh that steamed the windows and filled the truck with the smell of garlic and onions.

"Any problems?" Nathan's voice felt thin, weak.

"Like a dream." He chuckled, a low rumbling noise, the earth moving, groaning with strain.

Nathan shifted in his seat. He couldn't believe that he had ever talked to Beardsley. Yet that night Beardsley had been exceptionally cordial, going out of his way to be friendly, considerate, buying Nathan one beer after the next. Nathan had met him at The Old Crow, a shack of a bar at the edge of town. He introduced himself as Mr. Beardsley, never offering a first name, so Nathan was forced to use the more formal title, even though Beardsley comfortably referred to him as Nathan.

Mr. Beardsley had said that he was a private detective. He had come to the island to "take care of a little business," but decided to spend the summer, Orcas being such a beautiful place and all, and he needed some time away from everything that was going on. But Beardsley didn't strike Nathan as a nature-loving sort of guy. Nathan had the sense that Beardsley's reasons for being there were far more sinister, but Nathan asked no questions.

Nathan wasn't sure how they had gotten started talking about his problems that night, but before he knew it, he had told Beardsley about his family, his financial situation, and how unfair it had all seemed.

Beardsley listened with an empathetic ear, then proposed a scheme guaranteed to improve Nathan's lot in life, and Nathan found himself agreeing with Beardsley that there was indeed a way for Nathan to balance the scales.

"Tell you what, Nathan. You get me one of your wife's business cards, and I'll take care of the rest."

"Business card?" By this point, Nathan felt very drunk.

"Yeah, I use the card to make an invitation. I set up a massage. I take photos."

Nathan felt his vision blur. "You would do that?"

"I like you, Nathan. I can tell you're a nice guy, and I want to help."

Nathan pulled out his wallet and shuffled through its contents, trying to find a business card. The room blurred, slipped sideways. He nearly fell off the barstool. Nathan doubted he could walk to his truck, let alone drive home. Finally, he pulled out a card and handed it to Beardsley.

"I'll get the pictures, Nathan—and I'll get them to you, right after the massage."

"Okay." Nathan giggled. He thought the whole plan sounded very funny. Wouldn't Jo be amused.

A shiver now ran through him. His anxiousness had settled in his stomach and he could feel his guts churn. He would be glad when this night was over, glad when he was back at home with Jo and Gabbie.

He turned now toward Beardsley. "Do you have the pictures with you?"

"Sure do." He grabbed the bag off the floor and chuckled. "Oooooweeeee, I think you're really gonna like this. There's a little bonus in there. I got a shot of the two of them in the bar. Such a sweet couple..."

"What?"

"In the bar, after the massage. They stopped up for a beer. At least she was drinking a beer. All he had was a soda, I think." He snorted. The truck rocked as his flesh jiggled.

Jo rarely talked to her clients after a massage, never wanted anything to do with them. It must be a fluke. She must have felt obligated somehow. Probably no big deal.

"Well," Beardsley announced, "I guess I've done my part. You got something for me?"

Nathan hesitated, but then he realized what the man wanted.

"Oh, money. You want your money."

"Yeah, funny thing about that." He was all smiles.

Nathan pulled an envelope out of his shirt pocket and handed it to Mr. Beardsley, who opened it and counted each bill. Jo was going to kill him. He had spent what little cash they had, and he had no idea how he was going to explain it to her.

"Three hundred. That should do it. Nice doing business with you, Nathan." With that, Beardsley puffed out of the truck and slammed the door. His silhouette nearly disappeared against the van. Then the engine roared to life, and he pulled out of his parking space and vanished into the rain.

At least Nathan was done with him. Being around Beardsley made him feel dirty, contaminated. Still, something told Nathan he wouldn't get rid of Beardsley so easily.

Nathan turned on his lights and backed out of the parking space. Then he shifted into first and eased forward, trying to see out into the foggy wet night. The parking lot was deserted, and he felt suddenly alone, afraid, like he had felt when he was growing up.

He hit the gas hard. The back tires spun against the wet asphalt and he began his ascent up the hill. He would be home soon. He would be safe and warm in his own dry house, in his own dry bed, next to Jo, the blankets pulled up to their shoulders, his arm around hers, her breath soft and sweet.

A Place Far Away

P aul crawled into his sleeping bag, the slick nylon icy against his feet and legs. It was the good kind of cold, the kind that anticipated the glow of a warming bag. There were few things he loved more than the sense of snuggling into a bag after a hard day, with his camp set up, his food stored, his firewood ready for an early-morning start. There was something about the sound of the zipper, the feel of the nylon quickly warming, the way the bag cradled him in soothing comfort, conforming to the shape of his body, the curve of his back, the spread of his shoulders. His tent—a thin shell against the elements— became a part of the landscape, like a rock, a tree, a twist in the river, a living, breathing testament to the natural order, where he was one with his surroundings, united in spirit and body.

The night was cool and clear. A light breeze lifted the scents of the forests and blew gently through the screened window near his head. He breathed deeply the fragrances—the decaying heaps of leaves and branches and needles, the dung of a thousand animals, the rot of their carcasses, composted into the forest floor, moist and raw, enriching the earth, the life of the mountains. The air was a tonic, an elixir, soothing his spirit, healing his soul.

The river gurgled and popped, steady in its melodic tones. Each current twisting along boulders, scraping the sandy bottom, braided together in an endless song, always changing, always the same. Paul drew great strength from the river, especially at night, when its comforting tones played to him, performed their magic in a symphonic hum that made him feel a part of something greater than himself, where he was but one spoke in an infinite wheel.

It all felt so powerful, so right, especially after such a long and exhausting day. It was difficult for him to grasp that only this morning he had committed himself to his new life. So much had happened: the move, quitting his job, heading to the mountains, setting up camp— and then the accident. Poor old guy. Paul hoped he was doing okay. He sure never anticipated anything like this happening, never imagined

r. h. sheldon

he would run into anyone else, let alone pull him out of the river. If they had not come along, the old guy would have been a goner, held to the bottom by his fishing boots. Nobody would have found him till the water dropped or the winter floods washed him downriver.

But they did get him out. And none too soon. Paul had to jump into the water, like jumping into a bucket of ice. He grabbed the guy around the waist and practically threw him out of the water, and the woman— Rebecca—helped him out the rest of the way. Paul was surprised by his own strength, surprised by how quickly he reacted, once he realized it wasn't some whacky vision. But vision or not, there was still a very powerful message here. Symbols were hardly limited to dreams. Every day the world was full of significant events, meaningful portents, permeating all of life. It was simply a matter of paying attention—a matter of *seeing* what you were looking at. So Paul would have to ponder all this for a while, try to grasp the significance of the older man and the younger woman, of the near drowning, of the strength of the river.

He wondered what Rebecca thought about this. There was a nervousness about her that seemed to go beyond the accident. Maybe it was the house, such a cold and lonely place, like a cave buried deep in the earth. Sure it was orderly and clean and roomy and had the best of everything. But such a large place for only two people. Kind of sad, really. It was so stark, so lonely. The only evidence he saw of people living there was the collection of Bible stories, a fat book that sat on the end table, full of heroic pictures of saints and Christian martyrs. The couple was, no doubt, attached to some kind of religion, but Paul was afraid to ask which one. Whatever it was, it wasn't a good sign. Religion had a way of turning people mean and hateful. He would take a compassionate atheist over a moral Christian any day.

One of the most striking features of the house—in fact the only striking feature—was the portrait that hung over the fireplace. The painting was dark and severe. At the center, staring out with a look of grim judgment, a man of about forty watched the room with a steadfast gaze, his eyes nearly as black as his hair, his arms crossed over his chest, a gold wedding ring shining brightly on his exposed hand. When Paul asked Rebecca about the painting, she merely shrugged and said that it was her husband's grandfather when he'd been younger, but she offered no other information.

Paul felt sorry for Rebecca. She had such sad and lonely eyes, and there was a look of surprise about her, as though always startled by her surroundings. He'd seen that look in other women. No matter how hard they tried, they never seemed able to meet the demands thrown their way. They became lost in their surroundings, like children wandering through the dense bowels of the forest, struggling to find their way out, to gain an identity, self-realization, yet the fates refused to cede even an inch of ground, as though their world would break apart should they step out of their restraints. Yes, he had seen this in many women, women like his grandmother, his aunts, his mother. And this was the kind of woman that he saw in Rebecca.

The odd thing with Rebecca, though, was how she had played in the river before the old man had fallen in. There was something childlike about her at that moment. Something wild and wonderful. He should have told her that, should have told her how beautiful she looked, how free. Instead, they talked about nothing at all, about drying clothes and the impending return of her husband. And if Paul strayed from these subjects, she appeared shocked, disapproving. And when his clothes finally dried, she scooted him out of there as quickly as she could, as though he would somehow contaminate her awesome and lonely prison.

Paul turned over on his side. The river splashed along its rocky banks. He closed his eyes and let the sound carry him along. He felt the gentle water rock him into the peaceful world of his dreams. Yet he remained always aware of the water, the sense of drifting, floating, moving.

The shore grew into a dim silhouette that gave way to the blackness of the water, and soon he found himself adrift at the center of a great ocean. The sky was a deep rich blue, almost black. He heard no sound except for the lapping of small waves against his feet, where they pressed against the bottom of the sleeping bag. He wondered where he was, how he had traveled so far. He floated for what seemed hours, rising and falling with the mild swells. And then, off in the distance, he saw a light, just a dot at first, waving gracefully in the distance. But then the light grew, until he saw that it was many lights, held together by an invisible string. Before long, he recognized the lights of a boat, shimmering like stars. The lights glistened on the water, poking the curves of the soft waves. He watched the boat draw nearer, and he could now hear the chugging of engines. Soon he identified a giant paddle wheel that propelled the boat through water, like the steamboats that ran up and down the Mississippi during the nineteenth century. The giant engine drove the wheel in endless circles as each paddle sliced the water and propelled the boat forward.

The paddleboat drew nearer. Soon it dwarfed him as it pulled alongside. The engines stopped and the night fell silent, except for the tiny waves that licked the boat's hull. The displaced water rocked him gently, like an echo, but soon he settled back into the steady rhythm of the ocean. A string of lanterns cast a dim yellow light along the deck. Their reflection shimmered in the water, a floating galaxy that waved gently in the shifting waters.

Then a voice called down from the deck. "Ahoy!" a man shouted. "Ahoy, I say." A figure approached the side of the boat and leaned over the railing. It was the man in Paul's vision, it was the face of God, still wearing the same white T-shirt, the same baseball cap.

"How are you?" he called down. His voice boomed out as though he stood at the edge of the Grand Canyon.

Paul would have thought that God would have already known how he was doing. But this was probably one of those games God liked to play.

"I'm fine," Paul said.

"What was that?"

He shouted, "I'm fine."

"Good, I'm glad," God yelled back. "You've had quite the day."

Paul had difficulty shouting as he lay on his back, zipped into his sleeping bag, but he didn't see that he had a choice. "Yes, quite the day. But it's been a good day."

"Well, don't get too comfortable," God called down. "Lots more to come."

"What do you mean?"

God looked puzzled for a moment, as though questions were unexpected. "I mean just that. Hang onto your hat!"

"Yes, but…"

"Anyway, I've got a lot of territory to cover tonight. Enjoy the ride." With that, God backed away from the railing and disappeared from Paul's view. Soon the engine roared to life, the paddles were engaged, and the boat chugged away, shrinking out of sight much quicker than it had appeared.

Paul continued to float, long after the boat was swallowed by the horizon. The night settled upon him, and he felt as though he were evaporating, expanding into the sky. He soared into the blackness of night. He became the blackness, peaceful and alone.

Alone at Last

After Paul had left, Rebecca checked each door and window to make sure they were locked. One thing Rebecca had to give Benjamin credit for, when he remodeled of the house, he had done it with security in mind. A burglar—or would-be attacker—would have a difficult time breaking in without being heard. In addition to the sturdy construction, each window had two locks and each door a dead bolt that needed a key from the inside as well as out. And if those weren't enough, Benjamin had wired the house with an elaborate alarm system that was sure to get anyone's attention.

Rebecca rarely used the alarm when she was at home. It was reserved mostly for when neither of them was around—when they were both at church or some other event that demanded they be gone at the same time. Benjamin insisted that, whenever the house was empty, the alarm be set, even though it really did nothing but make a lot of noise. Whether anyone other than the intruder would hear the alarm—much less care—was something Rebecca dared not discuss with her husband. Discussions of this sort were best left unspoken.

Once Rebecca was satisfied that the house was secure, she picked up the clothes that Paul had been wearing, touching them as little as possible, and tossed them into the washer. Then she poured in double the normal amount of soap, set the temperature to *Hot* and the wash to *Extra Soiled,* and shut the lid with a firm bang. She waited as the water raced into the machine and a small cloud of steam seeped through the edges of the lid. Then she walked into the living room and picked up the cup that Paul had used, holding the handle with the tips of two fingers. She placed the cup into the kitchen sink and squirted in a long stream of yellow dish soap and turned on the water, so hot that she could barely touch it. Steam soon rolled up from the sink as suds spilled out of the cup. She then grabbed a sponge from the counter and began to scrub the cup. She rubbed every bit of surface, inside and out, with the meticulous care of a surgeon, until the ceramic squeaked with sterility. After one final rinse, she placed the cup in the dishwasher,

r. h. sheldon

added soap, and turned it to high. The muffled spray joined the noise of running water in the sink and the pounding rhythm of the wash machine in the next room.

Then she reached over the sink and pumped out a handful of golden gel from the bottle of Dial antibacterial soap. She lathered her hands and forearms thoroughly and then shoved them beneath the running hot water. She scrubbed and rinsed until her hands felt raw, cleansed from any germs that might have rubbed off the clothes, carried into the house by her visitor. She scrubbed harder, then held them under the water until they were bright red, until they burned.

She dried her hands, tossed the towel into the washing machine, and returned to the living room, where she sat in the same chair she had sat in earlier, relieved to be finished at long last with this day. She eased back in the chair and put her feet up on a small footstool that was covered with a needlepoint she had finished earlier this year. The needlepoint was mostly navy blue and gray, with a red rose stitched across the center. She had taken up needlepoint because Benjamin thought that the foot stool he had built—a flat circle with three rectangular legs, all made of maple—needed that "feminine touch" to turn his simple rough work into a piece of comfortable furniture. He even suggested the rose; he had always liked roses, he told her. So Rebecca talked to some women at the church, bought a kit, and made the cover. When Rebecca had finished, she showed it to Benjamin, whose only comment was "not bad."

Yet Rebecca didn't mind his comment so much. A rating of *not bad* from him was actually pretty good. She had gotten used to his high expectations, and she went out of her way to keep him satisfied. She found this to be especially true when it came to his clothes. She spent hours each week washing and ironing his white shirts so they hung stiff and smooth, like white cardboard molded into the shape of his body. She starched and ironed everything, including the garments he wore beneath his other clothes. Wrinkles, hair, lint—everything removed with meticulous care. His shoes, too, had to be managed with fastidious attention, and he would often solicit her help in their care, insisting that they be cleaned and buffed to perfection—mud removed, scuffs polished out. "The shoes must be mirrors," Benjamin would preach, "windows to the soles." Then he would chuckle at his own cleverness, but no less earnest in his message.

One time, when Benjamin had an early meeting, he decided to wear a pair of shoes that had not yet been cleaned. Rather than wear one of

his many other pairs—all of which shone like a lacquered table top—
he interrupted Rebecca from her other chores and insisted that she
help out.

"But I need to make your breakfast," she protested, "and iron your
new shirt."

"I would think you'd want to help," he responded. "After all I do this
for both of us."

At such times, Rebecca wanted to toss his shoes into his face and
run out of the house. But she had learned long ago that ultimately she
would lose, that all she would accomplish was to incite an in-depth
lecture on the virtues of cooperation and pride in her work.

Rebecca sighed and placed her cup on the table next to the chair.
Thinking about Benjamin only added to her weariness. Sometimes
she felt as though she needed a long vacation, a chance to disappear
from her life. Maybe she could change her name and move to the high
desert, someplace wide and remote. She could live like the pioneers,
isolated from civilization. She could live alone, no husband, no church,
obligated to no one but herself.

She closed her eyes and imagined her little homestead. A creek ran
near her cabin, stuffed with fat trout waiting to be caught. Deer leaped
across the land. Rabbits, squirrels, possums, marmots. Maybe some elk
or antelope. Lots of birds, too. Birds everywhere. Wild and free.

She drowsed wearily. The gas from the fireplace hissed. The river
sang in muffled tones, dampened by the brick walls, lulling her to sleep.

She dreamed then. Dreamed quickly and clearly. Joseph Smith,
founder of her faith, prophet and leader, stood before her, his eyes
bright and wild. His gaze ran up her legs, followed the curve of her
hips, circled her breasts. His tongue hung out slightly, his lips moist,
glistening in the orange glow of the gas flame. Then he reached for his
crotch and grabbed his penis through his pants. She could see it was
hard, see his excitement, his lust.

"I have great plans for you," he said. "Great plans." He grinned and
then he disappeared.

Rebecca's eyes popped open and she sat up and looked around, confused by her surroundings. Slowly she recognized the white walls, the
portrait over the fireplace, the few paintings of mountains and farm-
land, the ceiling with its cedar beams, the handmade footstool that
held her tired legs.

"I need to go to bed," she said. "I can't take much more of this."

In the Heat of the Night

Benjamin sat straight up in his bed, his breath was thick and heavy. Sweat soaked his pajamas, the sheets on which he lay. His hair matted, wet. He stared into the space before him, into a distance that wasn't there. He felt hot, a fire burning within him, a tempestuous rage of desire and fear. The rain pelted the glass door to the balcony, howling through the railing, into the slit where the door was cracked open. The rain smashed against the window in waves, as though the seas had risen up and now slammed the side of the mountain. He leaped out of the bed and slid the door open. Then he stepped out onto the balcony. The wind crashed against him, broke over him like a falling wave. The water was ice. It saturated him, drenched him. No part escaped, no speck, inside or out, remained dry. He defied the icy pelts of rain, standing wild and raw, facing the ravages of the sky as though daring it to do its worst. He lifted his arms out to his side, straight out, held by the invisible cross. The water pounded him, beat him until he felt bloody, until he was swept with agony and pain. He screamed against the wind, shouting it down, a wolf crying into the night. "No! No! No, no, noooooooooooooo…"

Tuesday Afternoon

An Afternoon Stroll

Paul walked up the Index-Galena Road a short distance and then turned onto an overgrown logging road that wound up the side of the mountain, climbing out of the valley in meandering curves that twisted through the dense thicket of third-generation growth. Trees towered high above a forest floor littered with fallen trunks and branches—weakened by snow, ice, wind, and an occasional lightning strike—and a carpet of Northwest vegetation typical of the Cascades. It was here, in the heart of the forest, where tree grew upon tree, plant upon plant, that the rotting carcass of a fallen trunk became the foundation for an ecosystem of growth, metamorphosing into a bed that sustained life, fueled and nurtured its abundance. Upon such a foundation, hemlock would grow strong, fern multiply, huckleberry thrive, mushrooms swell. Every variation of green—rich, bright, vibrant—sprang from each hole, each surface, each outcrop, until the original trunk disappeared, swallowed by the roots to which it gave birth, until its existence was merely a shape, its pulp sucked into the soil, becoming the soil, the rich fertile earth, an organic compost melted into the landscape.

Paul walked with deliberate steps between the walls of green. Clouds bunched into giant piles above his head. The air was cool and felt heavy, thick, rich with the fragrance of the decaying forest floor. There had been only a sprinkle of rain so far, and that was earlier this morning. The bulk of the storm had stayed north, where rolling dark clouds stacked up in a dark queue across the horizon.

The gray skies diffused the daylight, deepening the greens of the forest. Each plant shimmered with a bright iridescence, as though the light glowed from within the plant, a million beacons glittering and twisting in the soft breeze. The colors felt alive, vivid, as though he could taste the succulent greens, savor the moist tender sprouts, absorb the color as it vibrated out into the fragrant air. The colors pierced the edges of a deeper awareness, like the colors of his mushroom-induced vision, pulsating in clear bright radiance, tiny suns, celestially tied into an endless galaxy.

Yet the colors did not evoke the same emotions he had experienced when he watched the angels dance in the ray of sunlight. His vision then was accompanied by a sense of wholeness, of purpose. Instead he felt weary, the exhaustion of his life finally catching up as he now, for the first time in months, stopped the mad pace of his existence in Seattle, enslaved by some unacknowledged agreement with a software company whose purpose for developing the products it did was no longer based on necessity or desire but on the whims of a group of mundane marketing types who lacked vision or imagination, a group entrenched in the bureaucratic loopholes that rewarded mediocrity and political savvy over substance and ingenuity. But he should have realized right from the start what he was getting into. He should have followed his instincts when they told him he could expect little more than money from a giant corporation that—like most corporations— cared little for the people who held the organization together, purchasing the loyalty of its employees in a clear legal arrangement that could be terminated at the whim of either party, regardless of circumstances, justification, or need.

Paul stopped at the edge of the road and crouched down before a small fern. The branches stretched from the center, sprouting leaves that fanned out in a V-shaped pattern. They shimmered with tiny drops of moisture, each one clean, bright, as though they had been individually bathed in the pure, sweet essence of dew. He reached toward one of the branches and ran his fingers along its spine, feeling their tender flesh, like silk against his fingers.

At moments like this, he longed to melt into the landscape, become one with the forest, where he too could dive into the waters of decay, rebirth. The cycle of wholeness, of life and death, so near, yet forever outside. He longed to know the freedom of such release, to evaporate into the natural order of life so he could feel this peace, this wholeness that always evaded him, always kept out of his grasp, except for the brief interlude that drugs might bring, that reminded him of his connection with the world around him.

Paul stroked the plant gently, as though petting a small animal. The plant shivered. A melancholy had descended upon him this morning, like the dawn mists that blanketed the valley. He no longer felt the light freedom he had experienced yesterday, when he had fled the city and set up camp. His perspective had shifted somehow, and where he had been filled with anticipation, he was now filled with dread. He felt adrift, without a purpose or direction, left with a great emptiness inside, a vessel freed of its load, drifting rudderless in the middle of the ocean. Maybe this was what his dream had been pointing out, maybe it merely reflected how alone he really was, how isolated and afraid.

Yet nothing had really changed, only his perspective. Who he was and what surrounded him were always the same, no matter what he thought about any of it. Perhaps that was why he indulged in substances whose sole purpose was to alter his mind. They allowed him to shift perspectives, to see and feel the wholeness of life rather than the fragmented images. But the manufactured shift in perspective was not without its hazards, like now, when the brief moment of lucidity had given way to the stark images of reality, without the benefit of an altered consciousness.

The pendulum kept swinging, and it was the backstrokes that always got him.

When Paul had been in his early twenties, he visited a psychic who lived in a small cabin on an isolated ranch in Colorado. She was an older woman who talked easily of her childhood visions and life as a psychic. She gave readings out of her home, by donation only, and seldom ventured from the confines of the ranch. Paul had heard about her from several people who had visited her, but had never been to see her or any other psychic for that matter.

Paul now remembered little from the reading, the usual "old soul" kinds of things, "here for a purpose," and so on. But the one image that had always stuck with him, which he was reminded of time and again, was when she said, "I see you walking down a path alone. Your steps are very firm, very sure, but you are alone. I see you always alone."

Her visions had seldom proved wrong.

Yet Paul did not always know what to do with this loneliness. At times—quite often, in fact—he was satisfied with the solitary disposition of his life. He had learned to adapt quite naturally to going to bed alone at night, to cooking dinner only for himself, to going to movies alone. Countless activities, hours and hours of time alone, time without companionship, without the chance to share, struggle, despair. But there were times when his own company was not enough, when he desperately craved the comfort of a partner, someone to hold him when his heart ached, someone to ease the constant burden of life.

No time was he more aware of this than during his breakup with Aaron, when Aaron had told him, quite simply, that it was over. Paul could not speak, could not move. But finally he got up, wandered through the house, into the guest room, where he fell into the bed, and he pulled himself into a fetal position, holding himself in to fend off the pain. But he felt shattered, his fear and loneliness complete. This hollowness within him, this deep consuming emptiness, could never be filled. And it was at this moment, as he lay in a quivering ball, that Paul longed for someone to do what Aaron could never do, to put his arms around him, to hold him with the warmth and comfort of a companion who responded only to Paul's immediate needs, nurturing the hurt little boy whose world had been suddenly shattered.

Paul still felt the pang of emptiness when he thought about Aaron, even after a year. The breakup had become a symbol of all the loss and loneliness in his life, an empty town that stood on a barren hill, dark and cold against a gray bank of clouds.

Paul stood and continued up the road. He was again reminded of the vision of the aging psychic, of his solitary walk through the forest, just like now, just like so many other times.

The clouds grew steadily darker. A cold wind dropped down from the north and chilled the sweat beneath his shirt. He should turn around, get back to the safety of his tent, where he could, if nothing else, remain dry.

Yet something drove him forward, some inexplicable need sent him up the mountain, toward a destination that, despite today's melancholy, propelled him up the rocky roadway. Each step was a laborious struggle against the lethargy that pervaded him today, his motion a response to some inner drive, an internal insistence that would not let him turn around. He plodded forward as a man whose fate was determined long ago, and he now played out his part with indifference and acceptance.

The sky let loose a loud roar of thunder. The air felt edgy, electrified. He looked up. Light flashed behind the clouds, illuminating puffs of gray, like flash bulbs behind a screen of smoke. Thunder rumbled across the horizons, a low groan, as though the sky bent from the pressure of its own weight, a shifting fault in the celestial terrain.

He walked. The air wore thick, almost soupy, and carried the dense smell of the forest, the ancient soil of rich, rotting compost. The day grew darker still, like the dark of twilight, blurring distant trees and brush. The forest settled into an eerie wall of night. The road became a sanctuary against the darkness, and he dared not leave its protection.

He knew he should return to his camp, before the inevitable downpour drenched him with icy mountain rain. Already he doubted he would get back in time. Yet something continued to urge him forward, some power within him, an unseen awareness, sending him toward the top of the mountain.

He pushed ahead. The wind swept out of the valley and up the side of the mountain. The breeze was steady now, interrupted only by short gusts of cold air followed by a moment of stillness. Then he would hear the wind blow through distant trees, a steady hum that echoed against the sides of the mountains.

He zipped up his nylon jacket and continued forward. He kept his eyes locked on the road before him. The wind whipped across his face and down his neck, like cold fingers touching his skin. Leaves blew across the road, leaped up in tiny spirals, and disappeared into the trees. The rumble of thunder became almost steady, disrupting the howling of wind in an offbeat rhythm.

Lightning flashed. A charge of static pierced the air, and the sky cracked in a loud boom. He stopped. This was insane. He must turn around. He must get back to his tent.

A figure appeared ahead of him, racing down the road, almost running. He froze. The hiker grew nearer. He realized he was seeing a woman, the woman from yesterday—Rebecca. She didn't see him at first, so intent on watching her step, on getting down the mountain. She was only a few yards away when she looked up. She stopped and let out a slight shriek. The wind gusted out of the trees and nearly knocked her down.

"It's you," she stammered.

"Nice day for a walk, huh."

"I've got to get home, before the rain—before the storm—"

"Good plan."

A moment of hesitation, awkwardness. Would they walk together? Part here?

A flash, the sky flooded with light, the air on fire. To their right, twenty feet away, a bolt of lightning slammed against the top of the trees, like the snap of a whip. Paul yelped, Rebecca gasped, and they grabbed each other and held on, like friends, like lovers. The tree split open and the top fell toward them, painfully slow, a crawl. They watched with faces frozen, feet still, their embrace as solid as a tree. Bark tumbled down around them, limbs scrambling in every direction, like knives slicing through the air. Branches brushed near their faces, stirring the air, filling it with the smell of raw cedar. The tree scattered around them, branches and twigs and slivers of bark, a cloud of debris, puffing up, out. The trunk hit with a thud, a whoosh—and was silent.

They looked around, still huddled together. They stood at the center of the ruins, the fallen monolith stretching out from their feet, the thousands of branches twisted and bent. Yet nothing had touched them. The naked side of the trunk, clear of protrusions from its rough bark, lay inches from where they stood. They had been spared. Still clutching one another, they said nothing. Suddenly, the sky burst open and dropped buckets of icy water upon their frightened bodies.

The Boys' Club

Benjamin Randall sat at a small table in the corner of the conference room, waiting for the other members to arrive. He had not attended this morning's meetings, and he hoped he wouldn't have to explain himself. Perhaps his absence hadn't been noticed. His sleep—what little he'd had—was restless, scattered, like the gusting winds that blew across the islands during the night. When he woke, he was already late, and he hadn't wanted to draw attention to himself by walking in after it started. He also wanted to stop in at the spa before he joined the group.

He picked at the plastic nametag on his shirt until he creased the corner, leaving a white line stretched across the *B* in his name. As he tried to repair the damage, Brigham Richards walked into the room and stood near Benjamin. Brigham was a big ruddy man, with a starched white shirt and gold cufflinks. His tie was silk with a red paisley design.

"We missed you this morning," he said.

Benjamin met Brigham shortly after he and Rebecca had been married, at their church in Bellevue. He viewed Brigham as a necessary evil, a man with connections, power.

"I wasn't feeling well this morning."

"I bet."

Benjamin looked down at his nametag. "What do you mean?"

Brigham spoke softly, almost whispering. "Word has it, you might have been a little less than discreet last night. That perhaps you and a little redhead were practicing the Old Testament with a little more, ah, fortitude than might be advised, given the fact that you're at a sanctioned gathering and you're still on probation."

"She wasn't a redhead. It was more strawberry blond."

"I don't think that the color is the issue…"

"And all I did was get a massage!"

"A massage? You did that too? I'm surprised at you, Benjamin. I always assumed you had better judgment than that."

Benjamin leaped to his feet. "What do you mean? All I did was accept their gift, followed what I thought was right."

"And this *gift,* as you call it, included going into the lounge?"

"But I just...I, ah..."

"Hey, what you do on your own time is fine with me. And in all likelihood, no one here would care. But the fact that you were so public about it, the fact that you were in a bar...and now you tell me you got a massage as well." Brigham shook his head. "That shows poor judgment. And a lack of discretion. I'm surprised, Benjamin. Very surprised."

Benjamin stepped nearer to Brigham. "Listen. She gave me the massage, and I bought her a beer. That's it."

"Think about what you're saying. You let a *woman* give you a massage? Then you bought her a *beer?* Are you crazy—what could you have been thinking of?"

"I wasn't thinking anything. When I got the invitation, I went to the spa. I didn't know what to do. I didn't know it would be a woman."

"What invitation?"

"The one for the massage. The one that said I had received a free massage, a gift. I just assumed that it was one more gift, like the basket of fruit, the bathrobe."

"You got a bathrobe?"

"With my initials."

"Wow."

Benjamin continued. "So I figured this was one more gift, that I would insult them if I didn't accept it."

Brigham shook his head. "Let me get this straight. You receive some kind of *coupon* for a free massage and assume that our hosts arranged it for you. That doesn't make sense. They would never have done something like that, especially since there was a reception last night to welcome new members like yourself. And even if you did make such an unfortunate error, did you have to drag her to a bar, where anyone could see you?"

Benjamin hesitated and his voice dropped. "I didn't *drag* her. I was just trying to thank her."

"You know as well as I do how the Church views this kind of thing. The appearance of evil, and all that. They're going to be watching you very closely. Very closely indeed. I'll stick up for you as much as I can, but the truth is, it might already be too late."

With this, Brigham spun his bulky body around and walked across the conference room to the hallway, where the restrooms were located.

Benjamin listened as the door squeaked open and then slammed shut. He stood for a moment before returning to his seat. Yesterday he would have been devastated by such a turn of events. Yesterday he would have been mortified to learn that his actions were being questioned. Yesterday he would not have found himself in this situation.

He picked at his nametag again. His thoughts turned from his fragile standing within the organization to Jo, the massage therapist who had precipitated these events. After he got out of bed this morning, he went to the spa to find out when she would be in next. He had hoped to schedule another massage with her, perhaps get the opportunity to talk to her more, get to know her better. He was fascinated by her life, her personality—her body. He couldn't erase from his mind the vision of her thick mass of hair, the strong freckled thighs, the firm touch of her hands. Throughout the night, while tossing and twisting, he thought of little but her, fantasized about her hair brushing against his back, across his chest. He wanted to bury his face in her thighs, wrap his arms around her wide hips. He dreamed of her face, clean and bright, healthy and confident. This woman weakened him. She frightened him. Intimidated him.

On his way to the spa, he had walked along the water. The fog had been thick and he could see only a few steps in front of him. He had welcomed the cold damp air across his face, was glad for the cover, the invisibility. He wanted to be seen by no one, especially by other members of the Council. They could never be allowed to suspect that he, a married man, was trying to make contact with a married, non-Mormon woman. A massage therapist, no less. They must not know of his intent. But what was his intent? What did he hope to gain by all this? He had never found himself in a situation like this before, had never felt so out of control. And now he risked discovery, his future. What in the world for?

Earlier, when Benjamin had entered the spa, a customer had stood at the counter, purchasing a bottle of scented oil. Benjamin browsed the shelves full of useless items. He picked up bottles of scented oils, sniffed bars of soap, held shirts up to his chest. Periodically, he would glance around the store to ensure that no one he knew was present. When the customer finally left, he strolled up to the counter, trying to act as nonchalant as possible. It reminded him of the first time he bought condoms, at a drug store near his high school, something a good Mormon boy should never have been doing.

The sales clerk behind the counter had scrambled platinum hair, wore a pink halter-top, and was evenly tanned across her smooth, toned body. She glanced up indifferently from her magazine and asked Benjamin what he wanted.

"I, ah, would like to schedule massage…make an appointment…"

"When?"

"Um, any time would do fine. Yes, any time."

"Do you mean right now? Later today? Tomorrow?" She glanced at a full-page ad for perfume. A sleek, dark woman, dressed in all black, extolled the virtues of the fragrance. The clerk lifted the magazine and sniffed the page. The bug-spray aroma drifted toward Benjamin. He turned his head.

"Well, I, ah, I was hoping to schedule a massage with Jo. So whenever she's available…"

The woman put down the magazine.

"Jo?"

"Yes. I received a massage from her yesterday. I was hoping…"

"Jo can't"

"She can't?"

"She was in a car accident last night. Rolled her car, I heard."

A wave of panic rolled through him. "What happened? Is she all right?"

"Not sure what's going on. They flew her out last night, down to Seattle, Westside I believe. We don't have many details and don't know when she'll be back, or if. Would you like to schedule an appointment with someone else?"

Benjamin said nothing and backed away from the counter. He turned and hurried out of the store and stumbled back up the hill to his room, where he sat in front of the sliding glass doors and stared into the fog as it lifted off the water and revealed the smooth surface of the bay.

He looked at the water now, from his chair in the conference room. It was still dark and gray, and the skies looked ready to let loose another downpour. He listened to the whine of the pipes as water rushed toward the toilet that Brigham had no doubt just flushed. Benjamin did not want to talk to him or anyone else. Yet he knew that he had to play it his best. He had to present himself with the smooth, polished demeanor that had gotten him this far. He had years of experience at this, years of keeping his emotions under cover, his thoughts secret, his reactions neutral. Always the consummate professional, betraying

r. h. sheldon

nothing, letting others see only what he wanted them to see. He had been careless with Brigham, let him see more than he should have. But now he would be more wary, now he would maintain control.

Benjamin would have to gather all his strength and draw on his experience to pull him through. Despite his evening, despite his lack of sleep, despite the news of Jo's accident, he must focus on nothing else right now but this meeting. He must portray strength and control without demeaning himself, the others in the room, or the organization as a whole. Yet his conversation with Brigham had caught him off guard. He hadn't realized that last night's gathering was for the new recruits, and he should have known that they would never have given a gift like a massage, at least not so publicly. And it was bad luck that he was seen in the lounge, but it was a deed done, and his only recourse was to accept that fact and move on. And because Brigham now knew about the massage, Benjamin knew that it wouldn't be long before the others were made aware of this fact. Brigham didn't get to where he was by accident. Every situation was an opportunity to him, just as it was to Benjamin. So Benjamin needed to diffuse the situation as quickly as possible, to expose himself before he could be exposed by others, and try to turn the situation to his favor.

Brigham returned to the conference room as other members began to arrive. Benjamin felt rejuvenated. The prospect of swaying the crowds—exercising his political prowess—awakened in him a sense of self-assurance and strength that, rather than being diminished by the prospects of being ridiculed and ousted, rose to glorious heights and shone out like a lighthouse on a dark and rocky shore.

Few of the men said anything as they took their seats around the room. Their hostility was subtle, wrapped in their averted eyes and hushed voices. Good. Benjamin liked it this way. People who fell so easily into this mob mentality, who reacted to the barometric readings rather than the actual weather, were easier to sway. These crowd mentalities, responding to emotion and fear, could be implanted with thoughts far easier than a group of men who carefully considered answers, who questioned their own motives and actions.

Once everyone was seated, Benjamin stepped to the front of the room and looked around at the men who sat in front of him, trying to engage eye contact with as many as possible.

"Excuse me," he began. "Gentlemen, please, I have something to say." Benjamin's tone was smooth, even, like a train riding steady along a straight, flat track.

"I stand before you to ask your forgiveness. I have made an error in judgment and, as a result, have behaved in a manner inappropriate for a member of the Church and a member of this Council. I do not wish to make excuses for my behavior, nor do I believe that what I have done can be easily justified and dismissed as a simple miscalculation; however, I do wish to explain my behavior and provide each of you with the details of yesterday's actions and then ask you to judge for yourselves how this matter should be handled.

"Yesterday evening, shortly before dinner, I received an invitation—a gift—for a massage at the resort's spa. The invitation stated that an appointment had been scheduled for me for that evening and that all I needed to do was to show up at the spa.

"Here is where I made my first mistake. I assumed, based on the previous generosity of our noble benefactors, that this was a gift from the men who had invited me to join this great organization. I admit, I was a little taken aback by the nature of the gift, but in my enthusiasm to seem appreciative of all the great attentions I've received and in my failure to think clearly about the circumstances and to consider the implications of such a gift, I went to the spa at the appointed time."

Benjamin scanned the room slowly, always meeting the stares of the audience head on. He could see the surprise on many of their faces at the news of the massage, but no one seemed to find this information particularly noteworthy. He had to reveal the facts carefully. He must appear apologetic without seeming weak or contrite.

"Because I had never received a massage before, I had no idea what to expect. I had, up until this point, imagined a massage as little more than a thump on the back by some overgrown towel boy in a gray sweatshirt and sweatpants." He could see by their expressions that their preconceptions had been the same. "It was then a woman walked in, an employee of the spa, and announced that she would be giving me the massage." A few of the men gasped. "I resisted this idea at first. I felt, as all of you no doubt do, that it would be inappropriate to accept a massage from a woman—and rightly so. However, because of my earlier assumption regarding the origins of the gift, I mistakenly assumed that to refuse the massage would be an insult to our hosts. I can only say now that such a grave misjudgment on my part is no excuse.

"So, without belaboring the details of the massage, I will say only this, that I allowed this woman to provide me with the massage, but it was at all times completely professional. I remained fully clothed and in no way did any impropriety occur. The massage was quick, me-

r. h. sheldon

chanical, and, if the truth be known, an uninteresting test of endurance and patience. I guarantee, it is not an experience I would repeat under these or any other circumstances. I will say no more about this, other than to reiterate my wish that I had used better judgment in the first place.

"When the massage was finished, I felt a little awkward about the situation because I was not sure whether I was supposed to tip her or give her feedback or what. I wanted to be polite and considerate to her position. At this time, I offered to buy her a soda or something. Mistake number two." He paused here, looking around the room to measure reactions. He had their interest, every one. They watched and waited, anxious to hear more. "She suggested upstairs in the Orcas room. When I agreed to this, I did not realize that the Orcas room was the resort's lounge, and I had not expected her to order a beer.

"But what was done was done. I sat with her for a short period of time and then we went our respective ways. I returned to my room. By then I was already feeling a little fatigued and ready to call it a day. I have been fighting a bit of a cold, and I think that it had finally caught up with me, which is why I retired early yesterday evening and did not make it to this morning's meetings.

"As I have said, I do not offer this information as an excuse for my behavior. However, I do feel that all of you deserve an explanation for my not being here last night and this morning. I hold all of you in too high a regard not to have provided you with the truth. I realize that I have acted in a way not befitting a man in my position, and I can only ask that you forgive me for my lack of judgment in this entire matter. I am at the mercy of the Council and its board, and will abide willingly by any decisions that they see necessary to make. Thank you very much for your time."

Benjamin smiled to his audience. Not a smug smile or a complacent smile, but a smile that generated warmth, patience, understanding. A smile he had practiced over and over since he was a young boy.

Singing in the Rain

Rebecca pushed open the door to the house, stepped inside, and disabled the alarm. Water dripped from her head and shoulders and arms. Her clothes, soaked and muddy, stuck to her skin like wet paper towels.

"Come in," she said through chattering teeth. "Come in, come in." She motioned for Paul to step inside. The rain cascaded off the roof in sheets that slapped against the concrete sidewalk leading up to the door.

Paul leaped through the doorway and landed in a small puddle where Rebecca had first stood. Muddy drops splashed against both of them, splattered the door, but she didn't care. More water and dirt made little difference at this point, not after their descent off the mountain, a stumbling, half-panicked run that ended at the Randalls' doorstep.

"I can't believe I'm in your house again, soaked, frozen…" He looked down at himself, the floor. "Sorry about the mess."

Rebecca waived away his comment. "That's the least of my worries. I just want to get warm and dry." She pulled off her jacket and hung it on a hook near the door. Large drops fell to the floor. Then she pulled off her boots and hopped onto a dry part of the tile. "Get your coat and shoes off and wait here. I'll get some towels and some dry clothes."

She darted through the kitchen and into the laundry room, where she pulled off her clothes and dried herself with a giant green bath towel. Her flesh was a mass of goose bumps, and even her bones felt like ice. She wrapped the towel around her shivering body and leapt up the back stairway to her bedroom and put on a white terry bathrobe. She grabbed her husband's robe—also white terry cloth—and carried it downstairs, along with another towel.

"Here you go," she said. "Dry yourself off and put this on. I'll be in the kitchen while you're changing. Let me know when you're finished." She handed him the robe and towel and then left the room, without waiting for a reply.

r. h. sheldon

In the kitchen, she stood by the sink and wrapped her arms around herself. The dry robe and the run upstairs had helped some, but the warmth was slow to work its way in.

After the lightning had struck and the tree had fallen, they had stood and stared at the tree, at the branches that had scattered all around them. Another foot in either direction, they would have been struck by a limb or, worse yet, the falling trunk. A few inches had made the difference between life and death. During all this, they had held onto each other out of instinct, as though some survival mechanism had kicked in and this was the only way they would make it. Holding each other like that had seemed so natural, so spontaneous that she didn't question it, didn't even think about it, at least not at the time. And after that, when they realized that they needed to get off the mountain as quickly as possible, when, without speaking, they both recognized the potential for another strike and the risk of hypothermia in this icy, unrelenting rain, they fled down the mountain together. If one stumbled, the other was there with a supporting hand. Their welfare had been tied together, their survival dependent on them acting as a unit. Without question, without thought, without words, they scurried down the mountain together, united in a single cause.

And now he was back in her house, once more wet and cold. This man, this unconventional heathen, a stranger, a misfit, alone with her in her home. But now it didn't seem so bad, not as bad as last night, and many of her concerns seemed silly, unrealistic.

Yet she knew, too, that it wasn't as simple as all that. She was still alone in the house with a strange man. She might not be afraid for her safety, but she certainly was concerned that someone would find out, that someone would drop by or see them or learn of what had happened. *The appearance of evil.* Always a concern. Always a reality.

"Here I am."

Paul seemed to come out of nowhere. Rebecca let out a muffled gasp, which sounded more like a squeak, like a rubber sole scuffing the kitchen tile.

He stood before her in Benjamin's robe, the sleeves too short, his skinny legs exposed. But he was now dry and looked a lot warmer, and Rebecca was glad for this, grateful that they had both made it down safely.

"I wasn't sure what to do with the wet clothes, and I didn't want to carry them around with me and drip all over everything."

Rebecca was surprised by this. Her husband would have never been so thoughtful. He would have left them on the floor, not giving them a second thought. Fortunately, he was so meticulous about his appearance he'd never have let himself get into a situation like this. He would never have been out walking with the sky looking like it did, with clouds hanging low and thick, threatening to pour at any time. It many ways, it was strange that he insisted they live in the mountains, away from any towns or subdivisions. He didn't seem to like the mountains, didn't hike or camp and spend time in the forests. And their house and property, with its expansive lawn and paved driveway, could easily have sat in any plush suburb outside Seattle. But he insisted that this had always been his dream, that the great Cascades had beckoned him, beseeched him to nest in their graceful and majestic folds.

She figured it had more to do with his grandfather than anything else. Although he never said as much, she suspected that his grandfather had been the only person who Benjamin had looked up to, who he had felt any sort of respect toward. Perhaps he had been the only person who Benjamin had ever loved.

Rebecca pointed toward the doorway and said, "Just leave them in the hallway. I'll get them in a minute."

"Just leave them there?

She smiled. "I'm used to cleaning up."

"But I'd like to help. I mean, you shouldn't have to clean up after me—especially after taking care of me last night."

"It's not a big deal, really. Why don't you go into the living room and start the fire. You remember how to turn it on?"

"Sure do." He began to leave, then stopped. "Thanks for all your help."

He walked out of the kitchen. She could hear the muffled whoosh of igniting gas.

She walked across the cold tile and pushed the door partially open. "Would you like some hot chocolate?"

"If you're making some anyway, that is, if you don't mind…"

"I don't mind. Make yourself comfortable. This won't take long."

She pulled out a pan and filled it with milk and placed it on the gas range and turned the burner on low. Then she reached into the lower cabinet and pulled out the bag of Oreo cookies. As the milk was heating, she went out to the front hall, picked up the wet clothes, and carried them to the laundry room, where she dropped them into the washing machine. Since she was going to all this effort anyway, it would be little trouble to run them through the wash. Besides, she didn't want to fill her dryer with the sandy mud.

She expertly added soap, closed the lid, set the dial. She returned to the kitchen and placed the cookies on a plate, added chocolate to the milk, and filled the mugs. One habit followed by the next. A lifetime of washing clothes, cooking, and cleaning. The mechanics of a household mastered through years of repetition, habit, resignation. Even as a little girl, when chores were divvied up among the children, she had to help in the house, to assist her mother in those *womanly* tasks that she'd inherit regardless of desire or interest. While the boys were out on the land, digging holes, fixing fences, hunting rabbits, she was stuck inside, yearning for a boy's life, wishing the Heavenly Father could intervene and save her from this drudgery, from her destiny as a homemaker.

But she had stopped saying those prayers long ago, accepting her fate as wife—and all the chores and obligations that went with it. After all, it was part of God's plan, part of His will. She must accept her role joyfully, proudly, and find peace in the knowledge that she was doing what was right and natural, that she was living a life that could be held up as an ideal to all women. Except, of course, that she had no children. After years of trying, she and Benjamin had given up all hope that she would bear their offspring, no longer even speaking about children to one another. She tried to bring up the subject of adoption once, but Benjamin shut her down so quickly she never broached the topic again. Yet despite her childless condition, she tried to be an exemplary Mormon wife, a woman who sought only to abide by the teachings of the Church and live in obedience to God, to the teachings in the Book of Mormon, and to her husband. Life was simple, really. Do what she was told, behave as she was instructed to behave. There were really no choices, no great moral decisions that had to be made. The rules were clear, the roles defined, the lines drawn. And as long as she didn't think about it too much, as long as she didn't allow her imagination to sweep her away to her retreat in the desert, she was okay.

Rebecca sighed and picked up the tray of hot chocolate and cookies. She was surprised to find herself glad that Paul was there. It was nice having someone around who had nothing to do with her life, someone who didn't remind her of her duties and obligations. He was so different from anyone she had ever known, so unlike her husband, the men of the church. She knew what he was, of course, but if she didn't think about it too much, pretended that he was like any other non-Mormon who she might meet, she could forget, at least for a while, that he was one of *those* men, one of those homosexuals who used to stay in the campground, before the state had the good sense to shut it down.

She stepped into the living room. "Here we go," she announced.

Paul looked up from the book he was reading. Rebecca could see the picture of Angel Moroni in full glossy color.

"Interesting book."

"It belongs to my sister's children. She likes to encourage them to read. And to take interest in the Church."

"What church is that?"

"The Church of Latter Day Saints."

"Mormons?"

"Yes."

Paul closed the book and placed it back on the table. His action seemed to finalize their discussion on the subject, which suited Rebecca perfectly. She preferred not to go into her beliefs any more than necessary. She realized that this would have been considered a perfect opportunity to bear testimony, yet the idea of going into these discussions, of trying to persuade Paul to believe as she believed, was much more than she could handle at this point, and she was sure it would do little good. Paul seemed like the type who could not be easily talked into something he didn't believe. He would be a hard sell, and in all likelihood it would be a futile effort. Besides, she felt like taking a break from the whole thing, a little respite from the ongoing reminders of her life.

They sat quietly and sipped their hot chocolate and listened to the hiss of the fire, the spray of rain against the windows. Periodically, a gust of wind slammed against the side of the house, rattling the windows and hurling giant drops against the glass.

"I don't know why I even went up there this afternoon," Paul said. "I felt like I was being driven, being pushed up the mountain."

She looked at him with wide eyes. "How strange. I was feeling the same way. Even when I saw the weather getting bad, I continued on up. How stupid could I be?"

"No more stupid than me. I did the same thing." He smiled. "And was I surprised when I saw you. I figured I was the only one crazy enough to be up there."

She giggled. "Well, now you know."

"I do indeed." Paul turned toward the window. "I wonder what's in the forecast."

Rebecca looked outside. "According to the weather report, the rain should have missed us and we should be seeing clear skies by late afternoon, early evening."

"Maybe there's still hope."

"Perhaps, but I don't envy you camping right now. I can't imagine how you could have stayed dry throughout all this."

"Modern camping equipment. Nothing like it. I'm sure my tent is dry. I've been out in worse weather than this, not much worse, but pretty bad. Besides, these summer storms usually don't last too long. This will probably blow over and it will be a clear, wonderful night. Like last night. How'd you sleep, anyway?"

This question surprised her. Asking about her sleep seemed a little too personal, even if the intent was innocent. It probably wasn't that big a deal, but it still made her uneasy.

"Um, it was okay. I'm not used to being alone in the house, so…"

"You were alone? I thought your husband was due home."

Rebecca looked around nervously, avoiding eye contact, like a little girl caught with her fingers in the cookie jar. "Yes, well, I, ah, expected him home last night, but he ended up staying an extra night in the San Juan Islands. He's at some kind of conference there, so, ah, now I'm not sure exactly what his schedule is."

"The San Juan Islands. Wow, it's so beautiful up there. I haven't been that way in a while, but I love it there. It's one of my favorite places in the Northwest. Have you ever been up there?"

Rebecca was grateful for the change in subject. She was such a lousy liar, convinced that anyone could see right through her, even for the most minor stretches of the truth. Maybe Paul had realized she had made up the story and recognized her discomfort and now changed the subject just to make it easier on her. It wouldn't surprise her if he had. He seemed the kind of person to do something like that.

"No, I haven't," she answered. "I hear it's very nice."

"Amazing there. Like nowhere else you've ever been. I'm surprised you didn't go up with him. You could have hiked around or something while he was in his meetings."

"Go with him? The subject never really came up. He takes these sorts of trips so rarely, and I never even thought about going along." What she didn't say was how much she had looked forward to having the time to herself.

"Too bad. You'd have loved it up there. What kind of work does your husband do?"

Rebecca felt embarrassed by the question. She never thought much about his work, and most her contacts were through the Church, and they usually knew what Benjamin did. It was rare for someone to ask her so directly about his business. "He's into real estate."

"Real estate? No wonder you can afford this big house." He grinned.

She held out the plate of cookies. "Would you like another?"

"Oh, here I go again. I was going to try so hard to eat really healthy food, and yet…how can I resist such temptation, especially Oreos. Besides, after yet another day of somewhat extraordinary events, I think I deserve another." He smiled and took a cookie. "As you can see, I'm the master of rationalization."

Rebecca was a little put off by this. She didn't consider cookies a bad food, just an extravagance. Sure, a person shouldn't overindulge in food like this, but it was hardly the end of the world to have one now and again. This obsession with health food seemed a lot unhealthier than eating a cookie once in a while.

"I like a treat like this now and again. Sometimes I think it's the only thing that gets me through the day." She hadn't meant to say that. She hadn't even realized she felt that way.

"You're right about that, and it's probably not a problem for you. But I tend to be pretty compulsive when it comes to certain kinds of food. Like these cookies. If I brought a bag of these home, I wouldn't be satisfied until I had eaten every one, convinced that, as long as they existed, as long as they were in my possession, I was obligated to finish them off. Even if I tried putting them away, I would think about them sitting in the cupboard, calling out to me, telling me to eat every one, until there was nothing left but a few crumbs. I just can't have things like this sitting around. So I try not to. I try to avoid them because I'm so weak willed." He smiled. "And now, that said, I think I'll have another cookie."

He reached over to the plate and grabbed two more. His smile was wide and deep, like a stream of sunlight in the dark bowels of the forest. "Anyway," he continued, "I try not to be too good too much of the time. It throws everything off balance. Everything in moderation, I always say."

Rebecca turned toward the fire and watched it absently. "We inherited this house," she said, almost in a whisper, "from Benjamin's grandfather. When he died, he left everything to us…to Benjamin…"

Paul waited for a moment. "How long have you lived here?"

"Lived here?"

"Yeah, when did you move in?"

"Let me see…" She looked out the window. She didn't like to venture into these sorts of memories, into thoughts about their lives together. She continued softly, "After his grandfather died, Benjamin had a lot of work done, took down the trees, put in the lawn…must be about ten years now."

She hadn't realized that it had been that long. Ten years of her life spent up here.

Rebecca stood. "I need to check the laundry. It should be about ready to throw into the dryer."

"Sounds good."

Rebecca walked through the kitchen and into the laundry room. She pulled the clothes out of the washer, tossed them into the dryer, and turned it on. Then she went into the kitchen and opened the freezer. Paul would probably want something, and she hated to send him out of here hungry. She reached in and pulled out a plastic container of chicken noodle soup. She set it in the sink and looked out the window. The rain had eased, and it was now just a light mist and the sky was not nearly as dark. It looked like the storm might be moving off after all.

When she returned to the living room, she found Paul asleep on the chair, his legs stretched out in front of him and his chin tucked into his chest. In this light he looked so young and innocent, despite his scraggly beard and tangled hair. His breath was deep, heavy. She felt a sudden warmth for him, and a little sadness. He seemed to be searching for something, looking for meaning in a life that had held none. He carried within him a resignation she rarely saw except in some of the older people in her ward. The life he had chosen must be a difficult one, and probably not a very healthy one. He sparked in her a certain motherly response, despite his age and what he was doing with his life and who he was. She wasn't used to these feelings. People in the Church were usually well cared for, and she had little opportunity to meet anyone outside of it, let alone help them in any way. Yet Paul wasn't really seeking her help. His clothes were wet and he needed to get dry and warm, but he wasn't asking anything from her and didn't seem to be looking for a handout. But his presence struck some chord within her, a chord that caused in her a need to nurture, to protect. And she believed that, despite who he was and what he did, he was really a nice person, a good person, just someone who had been a little misguided.

Rebecca sat down quietly. She was feeling a little sleepy herself, and a nap was sounding very pleasant. She eased back into her chair and put her feet up, closing her eyes and letting her mind fold into the soft drowsy feeling of the room and the fire and the gray afternoon. She drifted into the moan of the wind, the clouds as they sailed across the heavens. And then she looked up, and the sky seemed to open. A crack of light slammed against the ground in an explosion of thunder. The earth rumbled, groaned. And there before her, filling the heaven with his ethereal image, Joseph Smith pointed down to the earth, toward where she stood. His voice boomed, shook, filled the sky like thunder. "And now," he shouted, "you are together. Now the two of you will do my bidding. Now you will know the true will of God!" And his face became hideous, his voice a thunderous boom that dug deep into her heart.

She opened her eyes and screamed, looking wildly toward the ceiling with eyes full of terror. And she saw, off to her side, that Paul stared toward her, his eyes wide with fear, his breath short gasps. And she knew, with the clarity of a visionary, that Paul had seen exactly what she had seen, that Paul had seen the face of God.

The Road to Recovery

Jo lay in her hospital bed, the back raised so she could sit up, her reddish blond hair a mass of tangles against the white pillowcases, white sheets, and white hospital gown. She held a mirror and studied her face. It didn't look as bad as she expected—a few scratches, the area around her right eye a little discolored and puffy. The biggest thing was the bump on her forehead, high up near the hairline. She must have really whacked herself a good one.

Nathan sat in a chair next to her bed, holding her hand, looking up at her face and then turning away. He would repeat this several times, and then rest his sight on the pale green walls or the gray tile.

A television hung from the wall near the foot of the bed. The screen cast a bluish glow across the room, although the sound was turned down.

"It's not as bad as it looks, really. In fact, except for a few aches and pains, I'm feeling pretty good."

His face was filled with anguish, as though he were the one who had been in the accident. He responded in a soft voice. "Then why are they keeping you here?"

She replied in a loud mocking whisper. "You don't have to talk like someone's died. This isn't a morgue." And then she continued in her regular voice. "They're keeping me for observation, because I wasn't quite myself for a couple hours and I have this bump on my head. Everything else is fine. They'll do another CT scan this afternoon to make sure my brain is still in there, and if everything's okay, they'll release me."

"I know but…"

"But nothing. Don't worry so much. I'll be up and about before you know it."

She squeezed his hand. He tried to smile but she could see how strained it was. He was really upset about all this, way beyond what he should be. She could see the guilt and remorse he felt, even if he tried to cover it. It was the same look he had when he lost his last job, that look of a kid getting expelled from school for smoking in the john. Typical man, she was the one hurt, but he was the one who needed comforting. Still, his gloominess was kind of touching. It confirmed how much he did love her, how much he cared, even if he did have trouble showing it some of the time.

He tried to look at her. "If anything were to happen to you…"

"Nothing is going to happen. Now let's change the subject. How's our little baby doing?"

Nathan pointed toward the window. "She's out in the truck, feeling abandoned and unloved. She wanted to come up here with me, but I had to put my foot down. You know how she can be."

"Why don't you take her to a park around here or down to the lake. She's probably ready for a good run."

"But I don't want to leave you…"

"Don't be so dramatic. I'll be fine. Besides, they're going to be coming for me before long to take pictures of my brain, and that could take a while. And I won't know anything for a while after that. So even if I were to be released today, it will be much later, and I strongly suspect that it won't be till tomorrow morning. Now go, and give her a hug for me."

"I don't know, maybe I should…"

"Go."

He smiled slightly. "Okay, boss. I should know better than to argue with you. I'll be back in a couple hours."

He kissed the hand he had been holding and then let go. He stood, bent over the bed, and kissed her forehead with a gentle touch. "I love you. I'll be back soon."

After he left, she grabbed the control for the bed and lowered it to a flat position. The movement reminded her of how banged up she was. She felt as though she had pulled just about every muscle in her body. Luckily they had given her a couple painkillers, which were working great, unless she moved too quickly.

At this point, she was more concerned about the bills than her injuries. Her insurance would cover most of it, but it had a huge deductible that would eat up what little they had saved plus some. In addition, her car didn't carry collision, which meant she'd get nothing for it, and she wouldn't be able to work until she was healed. This wasn't good at all, especially with Nathan not working. How would they pay their mortgage? Buy food?

She didn't want to discuss any of this with Nathan. He was already too upset. Still, they were going to have to face this together. But not just yet, not until she felt a little stronger. Besides, everything would work out; it always did, though things had never looked as bleak as they did now.

She clicked off the television and closed her eyes, ready for a nap. Just then, a voice bellowed across the room, announcing that it was time to head down to Radiology. She opened her eyes. A large sturdy woman, dressed in a green uniform, stood before her.

"Sorry, honey, I didn't realize you were sleeping."

"No problem. I just shut my eyes." She grabbed the controls for the bed and raised it to a sitting position, her stiff muscles fighting each movement.

The woman helped her out of bed and into a wheelchair and took her down to where she was to receive a CT scan. She was placed in what appeared to be a sort of waiting room. There were lots of chairs, but only one other patient was present, also in a wheelchair. He was an older man, short, stocky, a head full of dull gray hair and a few days of white stubble. His face was pale, almost ashen, and his eyes were watery and a bit cloudy. He reminded her a bit of her dad or any of the other old guys that lived in the last rural strongholds of the Northwest. All of them a little weatherworn, a little ornery, surviving by their wits and whiskey. The kind of men she was most comfortable with. A dying breed to be sure.

"Hi," she said from across the room. "I'd get up, but…" She smiled.

He grinned back at her. "Hello to you. How are you feeling?"

"Better than I did last night. But I got to tell you, those painkillers do amazing things."

"I wasn't so lucky. I didn't hurt myself enough, not like you, not like rolling a car."

This caught her off guard. "How did you know?"

"I was in the ER when they brought you in. The next bed. I recognized your hair." He chuckled. "I was there when you announced your arrival."

"You mean when I yelled?"

"Yeah. You got their attention in a hurry."

"I have my ways."

"I bet you do," he said and snickered.

Just like the others. A dirty old man. She loved this guy.

A Romp in the Park

Gabbie jumped out of the truck and ran in circles around Nathan. She slid back and forth between his legs and finally leaped up to try to lick his nose. Nathan pulled a grimy tennis ball from his pocket, tossed it above his head, and caught it with an exaggerated sweep of his hand to ensure Gabbie's interest, which, considering her frenzied reaction, was no more than a formality that he performed in part out of habit but mostly out of enjoyment at seeing Gabbie's unbridled enthusiasm. If only he could approach life with such enthusiasm and lack of restraint.

Gabbie hopped in tiny circles, rolled over several times, and then jumped up and tried to grab the ball out of Nathan's hand. He threw it toward a stand of trees at the other end of the grassy knoll, where a sign announced quite clearly that leash laws and scoop laws must be obeyed. Nathan thought little of these kinds of pronouncements and considered the notion of leashing Gabbie an abomination against himself, the dog, and the natural order of the universe. He hated the endless assignment of rules and regulations that intruded on all of their lives, though most people seemed more than happy to accept the growing infringement on their freedom.

Gabbie ran out from the trees with the ball in her mouth. She pranced proudly around Nathan, anxious to continue the game but reluctant to give up the ball.

"Give," Nathan commanded. She dropped the ball in his hand, drenching his fingers with her drool.

He tossed it towards the trees. She ran after it, her wild instinct immersed in the hunt.

Nathan walked over to a large oak and sat with his back against the trunk. He watched Gabbie sniff frantically through the twisted branches of a dense clump of rhododendrons. The Arboretum, a curving slice of land that emptied into Lake Washington, was stocked with a variety of indigenous and non-native plants that thrived in the moist temperate climate of the Northwest. One section of the Arboretum—the part where Nathan now sat—was known as Rhododendron Grove. It contained an amazing assortment of rhododendrons that each spring sprouted a rainbow of large fleshy flowers and turned the grove into a spectacle of red, yellow, blue, pink, green, and orange. Nathan had been here only once before, when the flowers were in full bloom. His parents had brought him and his brother to the Arboretum for a Sunday outing. During their visit, his mother had pulled out a plant identification book and dutifully recited the names of each species. His father would hum in agreement each time he recognized a name. His brother stood by and listened with a practiced and polite curiosity. Nathan looked around in wonder, disregarding his mother's recitations. He focused on the essence of each plant, feeling the beauty that emanated from the delicate petals. He could not hide his enthusiasm, caught in the vivid color of rapturous light, the sweet fragrance of damp grass, moist soil, the sounds of birds chattering, the wind dancing in the high branches. And as he stood there on that misty day, full of wonder, his brother whispered so that only Nathan could hear, "You little faggot, you."

Nathan tried to shrug off the memory of his brother, but an uneasiness remained. His brother reminded Nathan of what a mess he had made of his own life, and soon he slipped into a melancholy full of regret. He should never have agreed to Beardsley's plan, never have drunk so much. If it weren't for Nathan, Jo might not have been driving during the storm—and probably would never have gone over that embankment. It was his fault, all of it. How could he tell her what had happened? How could he reveal that he had involved her in this awful plot?

Gabbie ran up to the tree and dropped a wet muddy ball into Nathan's lap.

"Gabbie," he moaned.

She grinned happily, her tail spinning.

He tossed the ball off to his left, down the gentle slope toward a stand of Douglas fir. He raised his head and looked up through the husky branches of the oak. The sky opened to streaks of blue. Most of the heavier clouds had moved east, toward the Cascades. Now only a thin smoky layer filtered out the sun. Blue splotches of sky grew steadily as winds whisked the remaining clouds toward the mountains.

When he was a small boy, clouds were a source of fantasy, magic carpets that would deliver him from the pretenses of his parents and arrogance of his brother. But it had been many years since Nathan felt any magic in his life. Hope and fantasy had been replaced by the drudgery of survival, the day-to-day limitations of life, like a slow-moving storm, erasing light from the sky, until the land grew cold and dark and survivors like him shuffled wearily on the frozen earth.

Jo was the only ray of light on this bleak landscape. When they had first met, she had sought him out with an aggressive straightforward intent, with an honesty that he could not have believed in anyone but her. They had met at the Old Crow. A typical Saturday night, the air blue with cigarette smoke, country music rattling on the jukebox. He had come in for a beer, sat off in the corner. Jo stood at the bar with her friends. They drank shots of tequila and laughed and teased the bartender. It all seemed so natural, so easy. There was something genuine about her, a fullness of expression that was infectious, joyful—her bursts of laughter, the shock of reddish blond hair, her full hearty body.

Nathan had watched her for several minutes before losing himself in thoughts of gloom and loneliness. A woman like that would never go for someone like him. He was well aware of his own dark moods, of his attitude toward other people, of their attitude toward him. He could almost envision the dark cloud that hung over him, spreading gloom like a fog descending on the icy landscape.

Long before he had met Jo, when he was still a teenager living at home, he had overheard his parents talking about him.

"He can be so intense," his mom had said. "I wonder where that comes from."

His dad answered softly, "Probably just a phase."

"Maybe, but his brother has never been that way. It just doesn't make sense."

"No it doesn't."

Nathan never overheard anything more said about him. He didn't know whether it was because they never spoke about him or because he never caught their conversation. It didn't matter, though, because once he heard them he considered for the first time how other people might perceive him. It made him recognize how standoffish his classmates were, how few friends he had. Nathan didn't care for most people, so he thought little about how they felt toward him, until now, when he realized that even his parents were put off by his behavior.

But Jo was the first person ever to break through that shell, as though she were able to reach inside of him and pull out something that he had not known existed, a sense of relationship that had lain dormant for as long as he could remember. Even that first night, at the bar, she touched in him something no one else had. She walked up to

r. h. sheldon

his table and sat down, not saying anything at first, just looking at him and grinning.

Finally she spoke. "I know you better than you think."

He said nothing.

"I saw you looking at me. I saw you considering the possibilities." She stood up and laughed. "I have a feeling we'll be seeing lots of each other." With that, she returned to her friends at the bar.

Her predictions proved accurate. And Nathan was always thankful she had persisted against his standoffishness, that she penetrated his walls. She was the best thing that ever happened to him. Yet as much as he cherished Jo, as grateful as he was to have her in his life, her presence always made him feel slightly inadequate, as though he could never live up to whatever it was she saw in him. He was always screwing up, wasting money, arguing with co-workers, losing jobs, yet Jo stuck in there, put up with all his shit. And maybe that's why he had agreed to this crazy scheme. Maybe he had thought that he could somehow prove his worth to her, prove that he could do his part in building their lives together, show her that he really was worthy of having her. Or maybe he just shouldn't have drunk so much beer.

But none of that mattered now. He had destroyed the pictures when he got home last night and he would never say anything to anyone about them. He would find a job, whatever it was, and work as much as he could. He didn't care if he had to wash dishes. The only thing that mattered was that he redeem himself to Jo, to himself.

He stood. Gabbie bounced up beside him, ball in mouth, tail wagging. She looked past Nathan, off toward the road. Her tail stopped and she dropped the ball. She stood very still and growled a low rumble.

"What is it, girl?" Nathan looked over his shoulder and drew in a sharp breath.

Mr. Beardsley walked toward him, waddling like a little troll. He panted and grunted with each step. His hair was slicked back with sweat, his Hawaiian shirt pasted to his skin. He wore the kind of smile one would expect when walking into a used car dealership.

"Nathan," Beardsley gasped, "so good to see you."

Tuesday Evening

Homeward Bound

Stanley looked out the window of Nathan's pickup. The Skykomish River caught the silver blue of a twilight sky as water wound lazily along the gentle slope of the valley floor. He and Nathan headed up Highway 2, toward Index. Nathan had said few words since agreeing to Jo's suggestion that he drive Stanley home after his release from the hospital. He couldn't tell what Nathan thought of the whole thing, but he suspected Jo was a hard one to get to change her mind, once she got set on an idea. Yet despite Jo's insistence, Stanley hated to rely on someone like this, hated to put anyone out, but the prospects of finding his way home that evening were pretty grim, and he didn't like the notion of staying in some strange hotel. Still, when Jo had suggested the idea, he had protested with a gruff dismissal, having no intention of making someone he hardly knew drive all that distance out of his way.

He'd been sitting in Jo's room when she decided that Nathan should take him home. After their visit in Radiology—which lasted over an hour because of a mix up in schedules—they had returned to their rooms. Shortly thereafter, Jo called his room and invited him up for a visit, "considering we're both waiting for those stupid doctors to let us know what's going on." Stanley had chuckled and agreed to find his way there. He convinced one of the nurses to have someone wheel him up to her room, where he sat next to Jo's bed and talked about how much things had changed around the Northwest.

It was there that Jo had insisted that Nathan give Stanley a ride. "Listen," she said, "I'm stuck here for another night, and if I don't find something for Nathan to do, he'll sit here with his mopey face worrying about whether I'm going to drop dead. You'd be doing me a big favor."

Stanley laughed. Everything Jo said made him laugh.

When Nathan showed up, they were making fun of the nurse who had just come in to give Jo something for her pain. After the nurse left, Jo said, "The pills are great, but that nurse is something out of a Halloween movie."

Stanley didn't know what a Halloween movie was, but he had his suspicions. And he had a few of his own suggestions, his favorite being the Bride of Frankenstein.

When Nathan walked in, he didn't seem to notice Stanley—or he simply didn't care. Nathan was probably used to Jo having visitors all the time. She seemed the type to always be surrounded by friends, the kind who drew people to her. Nathan approached the bed and picked up her hand, but avoided looking directly at her.

Before he said anything, Jo told him about her plan for Nathan to give Stanley a ride home. Nathan grew more concerned, but she seemed not to notice. "Listen, I'm really beat, and these drugs they're giving me only make me want to sleep. Take him home. It will give you something to do and give me a chance to sleep. And Gabbie will love it. She can bark at the cows." Nathan shrugged in agreement. "Hey, so I haven't introduced you. Nathan, meet Stanley. He almost drowned yesterday."

Stanley chuckled. "Yeah, but the river didn't want this tired old carcass."

"Hide's too tough."

"I don't know what to say to that—some pretty young lady talking about my hide. Not sure my old heart can take it."

Jo pretended to frown, which made the puffiness around her eye more pronounced and the bruise on her forehead darker. Nathan looked as though he had just been stabbed. She smiled. "See what I mean about Gloomy Gus here?"

Stanley could see Nathan's discomfort. There was more going on here than just the accident. Nathan acted as if he carried the world's burdens on his shoulders. Stanley decided that it was time to leave, let them have some privacy. He said good-bye and wheeled himself out of her room. When he was in the hall, he checked to see if anyone was looking and then stood up. His legs felt weak, a little sore, but not a lot different than usual. He sure as hell could use a drink.

He wobbled back to his room, where he waited for someone to tell him it was okay to go home. By the time a doctor showed up, he had dressed and put on his boots, which were still damp from yesterday's dump in the river.

And now, sitting in Nathan's truck, Stanley watched the silvery currents out the window. The meadow was calm in the late summer day. The sun had slid beneath the horizon, but a pink glow brushed the tips of the mountains and the few wisps of clouds that floated high above the peaks. He found comfort in the long summer days, the warmth of the air, the crystal skies. Not many summer days left for him, and any one could be the last. His heart was a time bomb; the doctors had confirmed that. But he had managed to put off the inevitable just a little longer, and maybe dying in the summer would be good—his last thoughts the golden days of light and warmth. A fine way to remember his home.

Nathan coughed, pulling Stanley from his reverie. "Not much farther," he told Nathan. "My truck is up past Index, where I left it."

Nathan grunted.

"Thanks for doing this. It saves me a hell of a lot of trouble."

Nathan said nothing. His jaw tightened, his face seemed to quiver. They drove in silence, the wheels humming against the warm pavement, slicing the evening's stillness.

Then Nathan mumbled something, so quietly that Stanley wasn't sure he spoke.

"What was that?"

"My brother..."

"Your brother?"

"Yeah. He lives up here, outside Index."

Stanley looked at Nathan, surprised to hear him speak so many words. "What's his name?"

"Benjamin. Benjamin Randall. He's a land developer up here." Nathan whispered, almost with apology.

Stanley knew Randall. He had been instrumental in the sale of Stanley's ranch, which had no doubt profited Randall a great deal. But Stanley saw no reason to go into all that, and was about to tell Nathan that he didn't know his brother when Nathan did something that Stanley would never have expected. Nathan began to cry, like a wounded animal, like a man whose life had no place to go.

Stanley said nothing. He hadn't seen anyone cry in years.

Timing Is Everything

Jo lay in the hospital bed, using the remote control to flip through channels. She didn't care what she watched, as long as it wasn't a commercial. The last dose of painkillers had made her dopier than ever, and all she could do was lie there and try to rest. She wanted to sleep, but the drug made her feel a little edgy, at the same time making her groggy, so she opted for the television, which was its own sort of narcotic.

She was glad Nathan took Stanley home. She doubted she could have taken Nathan's pathetic stare the entire time he was there. Besides, she wanted to make sure Stanley made it home safely. She felt sorry for him, living alone like that up in Gold Bar. He didn't have anyone to call to come pick him up, take care of him. She planned to visit him as soon as she got out, before they headed back to the islands, just to make sure he was okay. Nobody should have to grow old alone, especially a sweet guy like that.

Jo shifted on her bed, moving her stiff body slowly. She'd be glad when the doctor showed up so she would have a better idea of what was going on, when she might get out of there. In the meantime, the only thing she could do was rest, and try not to worry too much about how this would all work out. If only Nathan could find some work, something he could stick at long enough so they could get caught up on bills, maybe get ahead a bit.

She flipped through the channels, trying to avoid the onslaught of ads and their promises of white smiles, sweet-smelling armpits, washboard abs, sexy cars, spotless carpets, and hamburgers made your way. She switched off the TV and closed her eyes. She tried to relax, letting her mind drift into fantasies about lottery winnings, rich relatives, and unexpected inheritances. Slowly she felt her body ease, the stiff muscles relax. She indulged in her dreamlike fantasies of a husband who was happy with his life, contented with his surroundings, directed toward self-fulfilling goals. She imagined living with Nathan and Gabbie in a large home on the beach, overlooking the water. They would have a boat and a hot tub and a large workshop. Nathan would build furniture from wood, his designs graceful yet sturdy. She would have a large garden, filled with herbs and vegetables and berries. At night they would sit quietly and read, invite friends over for dinner. Nathan would be entertaining, friendly.

"How we doing today?"

She opened her eyes. A woman in a white coat—apparently a doctor—hovered near the side of her bed.

"Been better."

The woman flashed a professional and brief show of teeth. "I'm Dr. Hendrickson. I've been looking over the results of your tests." She referred to a folder filled with paper. "That bump on your head doesn't appear too serious, and the rest of your tests all came back fine, so your internal organs seem to be intact." She flipped through the notes. "Hmmm, this is interesting..."

Jo moved the bed into the upright position. She felt her stomach twist into a knot.

The doctor continued. "If I had known..."

"Known?"

"The pregnancy...if I had know you were pregnant, we would have moved you to Prenatal—"

"Pregnant?"

The doctor nodded.

"But how could that...when did they...who—" Jo tried to sit up.

Dr. Hendrickson looked up from the chart. "It appears that the techs checked to see whether you were pregnant when you received you're first CT scan. According to their results, you're going to have a baby."

"A baby? But I can't be pregnant."

"You can. And you are."

"But that's impossible. I thought Nat couldn't..."

"We better run more tests, just to make sure the baby is okay."

"But..." Jo didn't know what to say, how to feel.

"Did you have any questions?" The doctor tapped her fingers against the folder.

"I, ah, I'm not sure, I mean—" She tried to concentrate but couldn't formulate any clear thoughts. "It's all so sudden...How? How did this happen?" She felt as though she'd been dropped in the middle of the ocean.

"You can probably answer that better than anyone," Dr. Hendrickson answered. "But the good news is that everything seems fine. Although now that I see this we better back off on the painkillers. I want to make sure everything stays fine."

She began to turn, ready to leave.

Jo struggled for the right words, her mind ablaze with confused thoughts and unformulated questions. "But what now?" she blurted. "What do I do now?"

"Do? I think that's something you need to discuss with your husband. In the meantime, we'll take you up to Prenatal. We should be monitoring you—and the baby—a little closer. To be on the safe side."

"A baby…"

"For now, just try to relax. We'll get you moved and all settled."

"It's just that…I, ah…"

"Let's just rest for now. After we get you resettled, one of the doctors will have a chat with you." Dr. Hendrickson exited the room.

Jo stared out the door. Pregnant? How could that be? They were told long ago Nathan couldn't have kids. Or perhaps they said it was very unlikely. Something genetic, they said.

She didn't move. She couldn't move. How could they have a baby now, with everything else going on?

Nathan, she thought. Nat, I need you. Please come get me.

A Bend in the Road

Nathan sat on a rock, down by the river. Stanley sat next to him, drinking from a bottle of George Dickel. He passed the bottle to Nathan. Nathan took a long drink, feeling the burn in his belly. The heat spread to his arms, his legs.

"That's where I was when I fell, below those rapids." Stanley pointed with a stubby, gray finger. An unlit cigarette dangled from the corner of his mouth.

Gabbie explored the rocks below them, her body little more than a gray outline against the water.

"Must have been pretty fuckin' cold."

"Must have been. Happened too fast to remember much. All I could think about was losing my flask. The rest is blank."

"Yeah," Nathan said, "pretty fuckin' cold." He took another swig.

"Just about did myself in on that one. Guess a couple folks happened to see me. Pulled me out. I don't recall that, though. Don't know who they are." He chuckled. "I'm not sure whether to thank them or curse them."

Nathan tried to smile, but the effort was too great, so he watched the water, the long dark currents, the gray edges of rock.

Cool air drifted into the valley. It felt soothing against his flushed face. The sky was clear. A few stars already appeared to the east. He should return to the city, before it got too late to visit Jo, but it felt good to be sitting here, and he wasn't in a hurry to get back to the traffic, the congestion, the people, the noise. Every time he went into Seattle it was worse. All he wanted was to get Jo and go home.

But being with Stanley wasn't so bad. Nathan didn't like most people, but Stanley he did. He could see why Jo had taken to him like she had. She had a way with these old codgers, and they always fell in love with her.

Still, Nathan was pretty embarrassed by the whole thing—to have cried like that. He never cried, never allowed himself to feel the kind of despair that had suddenly overwhelmed him, as though life itself hung in critical balance and all options pointed to pain and destruction. He could see no way out of the mess he had created. And when Stanley had mentioned that he needed to pick up his truck and that it was parked near Index, Nathan was reminded of his brother, of his bitterness toward him, of his own lack of work, of the stupid plot. And suddenly a dam had cracked and his fear and guilt and anguish burst forth in uncontrollable sobs, like a flash flood, erasing the familiar landscape that had held his emotions in check. And then his weeping turned into uncontrollable ravings about how much he hated his brother, how Benjamin had managed to inherit all their grandfather's money, what a bastard he had been all their lives.

Nathan had then told Stanley about the letter he had received from his parents, saying that Benjamin would be visiting Orcas Island, about meeting Beardsley in the bar, about getting drunk, about giving Beardsley the business card, about the massage, about the pictures.

"I've really fucked up, really fucked up big time." Nathan almost panted. He felt desperate, out of control.

Stanley pulled a bit of tobacco out of his mouth and wiped it on his pants. "You know, Nathan, I think you need a drink. There's a liquor store in Sultan. Let's stop there."

Stanley didn't ask any questions. After they stopped at the store, they opened the bottle and started to drink, continuing their trip to Index. When they drove past his brother's house, Nathan pointed and said, "That's it. You can barely see it through the trees."

"Looks like a lot of upkeep," Stanley replied.

They drove to Stanley's truck. Nathan pulled over and they walked down toward the river and each sat on a rock, where they continued to drink the whiskey.

Nathan now handed the bottle back to Stanley.

"I was just wondering," Stanley said between drinks, "why can't you forget the whole thing? You got the pictures. Got rid of them. No harm done."

Nathan shook his head wearily.

"This afternoon…that asshole, Beardsley—found me when I was out with Gabbie. He must have seen me at the hospital, followed me to the park."

The dog, hearing her name, scrambled up the rocks. She stood for a few seconds, her ears up, her head cocked sideways, and then decided it was a false alarm and climbed back down toward the river, where she disappeared against the black backdrop.

Stanley said, "This Beardsley guy, he's got a copy of the pictures."

"Of course."

"And he plans to go forward with this little scheme of his."

Nathan nodded.

"And if you don't help, he'll tell Jo what you did—show her the pictures, and maybe your brother."

Nathan buried his face in his hands. "Oh, Christ, yes. What have I done?" He pleaded. "What am I going to do?" He felt near tears, the dam again ready to burst.

Stanley flicked a sliver of tobacco off his finger. "Looks like you have two choices—go along with Beardsley or tell Jo."

Nathan shook his head. "There's one more."

"One more?"

"One more option."

"What's that?"

"Kill the bastard."

Stanley took a long drink of whiskey. "I suppose you could do that, but it might be easier to tell Jo."

"It would be easier to murder the son-of-a-bitch." Stanley had no idea what Jo could be like when she got riled. "Besides, what with this accident and bills and everything, she doesn't need any more stress."

Stanley grinned. "You're afraid of her, aren't you?"

"Terrified."

Stanley pushed against the rock and stood up slowly. His knees popped and he groaned softly. "Why don't we head over to my house. You can call Jo and check in on how she's doing, let her know that you got the old man home safely."

Nathan followed Stanley up to the road. Gabbie leaped up the rocks and danced around Nathan until he opened the back of the pickup. She jumped in and Nathan slammed the tailgate shut. The bang of steel echoed into the trees, like the blast of a shotgun.

He climbed into his truck and watched Stanley shuffle toward his own pickup, his shoulders hunched forward, his steps slow, heavy. He seemed much older than Nathan had realized, his body far more worn. He possessed a tiredness that went beyond just his body, as if his spirit too were worn and he had lived long enough for one lifetime.

When Nathan looked at Stanley and then thought about his own life, he realized how selfish he had been, whining about his own problems, laying his burden on Stanley. The old guy had plenty to contend with. Just staying alive was a fulltime job. Nathan was resolved that, when he reached Stanley's house, he would call Jo and then head back to Seattle. He would say no more about his own troubles.

Nathan followed Stanley's pickup to his house in Gold Bar. Stanley lived just a few blocks off the highway, on a small treeless lot with neighbors in back and on either side. The house was short and squat and in the pale light of the street lamp appeared to be a washed-out yellow. The trim around the doors and windows, the eaves, the screen door, and the few wooden steps were all painted the same yellow, like a dried up lemon. Even the mailbox was the same sickly color.

Nathan parked right behind Stanley. He climbed out of the truck and started to walk toward the house. Gabbie barked three times. She always barked three times when she was left behind in the truck. She had somehow determined that three was the magic number. Sometimes it worked. Sometimes not.

Nathan turned back. "Sorry, girl. But you need to hang out here."

She yelped in protest.

"Bring her in," Stanley called out. "It's fine by me."

"Yeah, but she's been in the river and is probably wet."

"I was in the river too. Want me to wait out here as well? Bring her in."

Nathan opened the back of the truck. "You win again." Gabbie leapt out, walked past Nathan, and hopped up the yellow steps, where she waited for Stanley to let her in.

Stanley chuckled. "Women always know what they want."

"Reminds me of my wife."

Stanley grinned.

Nathan followed Gabbie and Stanley—in that order—into the house. The front door opened into a small living room with dingy white walls, gray indoor-outdoor carpet, worn where a path led from the front door to what appeared to be the kitchen, a gray sofa, whose arms were slightly frayed, and a fifties-style set of walnut end tables and coffee table. On the end table nearest the corner, a blue porcelain lamp with an ivory shade, tilted slightly, glowed with a pale yellow light that cast dark shadows into the other corners and beneath the furniture. In contrast to this setting, like pieces in some offbeat art exhibit in a downtown Seattle gallery, sat an overstuffed, cushiony, black-leather recliner and a sleek wide-screen television that towered opposite the chair, devouring the short piece of wall and half the window. Nathan could smell the chair's leather. No doubt Stanley spent a good deal of time sitting there.

r. h. sheldon

Stanley pointed to the phone beneath the lamp. "Go 'head, give her a call. She'll be happy to hear from you."

Nathan pulled a slip of paper out of his jeans as he stepped over to the phone. Gabbie followed him past the chair. She stopped to sniff an ashtray that sat on the floor next to the chair. It was filled with half-chewed cigarettes and slivers of tobacco. "No, Gabbie." She lifted her head, flashed an impatient look at Nathan, and disappeared into the kitchen. Stanley followed her in. Nathan could hear him mumbling to her—something about water—and then he heard a cupboard being opened, the clang of dishes, and the flow of running water. That Stanley, despite the gruff exterior, was a soft touch.

Nathan dialed the number at the hospital. A man at the switchboard answered the phone. Nathan asked to be connected to Jo's room. He was put on hold for a minute, after which the operator came back on. "I'm sorry, but she's no longer in her room."

"What?"

"She's changing rooms. I guess they're right in the middle of the move."

"She's being moved? Why?"

The operator sighed. "I don't know. Perhaps you could call back in a little while, when she's resettled."

"I can't call back. I'll be driving in and won't be near a phone."

"You could call from a pay phone."

Nathan gripped the receiver tighter. "Listen, can you at least tell me where they're moving her to."

"I really don't know, not until she's—"

"Just check!"

"Hold on." Nathan was put on hold once more. After several minutes the operator returned. "The nurse where your wife was thinks she was moved to Intensive Care, but she's not sure."

"Intensive care? But why? I don't understand. What's going on there?" Nathan was nearly panting. He felt his chest tighten and his breathing grow shallow.

"I'm sorry," the operator said coolly, "but I don't have any more information than that. You'll have to call back when she's settled. Then we'll know which nursing station we can contact."

Before Nathan could reply, the operator hung up. "Fuckin' hospital!" He slammed down the receiver.

Stanley returned to the living room. Gabbie followed. Suddenly they were best buddies.

dancing the river lightly

"Trouble?" Stanley asked.

"They're moving her to Intensive Care. That's all I know." He looked around the room, as though uncertain where he was. "I got to go. Come on, Gabbie."

"Yeah, you better get down there. Thanks for the ride."

Nathan only partially listened. He opened the side door and let Gabbie jump up front with him. Without looking back at Stanley, he pulled out of the driveway and raced back toward the highway. The moon had lifted above the mountains and cast an eerie glow across the valley.

r. h. sheldon

Returning to the Scene

Nathan raced down Highway 2 into Monroe and then followed 522 to Interstate 405. He took this south to Highway 520, crossed the Evergreen Floating Bridge, and exited at Lake Washington Boulevard. The road wound through the Arboretum, past where he had taken Gabbie earlier that day. He thought of Beardsley briefly, but was too concerned about Jo to worry about anything else. There would be plenty of time for dealing with him later.

Throughout the journey, Gabbie lay quietly next to him, her head resting on his lap. Nathan would stroke her fur, scratch behind her ears, murmur soft cooing words like "You're a good girl, aren't you?" or "You're the best dog ever, huh Gabbie girl," all spoken absently, out of affectionate habit, the touch and words providing him with an inexplicit reassurance.

When he was a kid, his family had a dog, a small Australian Shepherd mix that had wandered into their yard one winter. Despite his mother's protest, he and Benjamin had convinced his parents to let them keep the dog. The boys vowed to care for her, feed her, take her for walks. Their parents relented and the dog was allowed to stay. Nathan was convinced that, had Benjamin not taken an interest, the dog would have been shipped off.

Benjamin insisted that they call the dog Ruth, no doubt hoping that the biblical connection would please his grandfather. Benjamin was never one to miss an opportunity. At first, Benjamin shared in the responsibilities of taking care of Ruth. But after a couple weeks, he lost interest. The dog became a source of irritation. He complained about the muddy paws, the dog hair on his clothes, the added strain on his schedule. Their parents, never excited about the prospects of having a stray animal in their house, tended to side with Benjamin. So Nathan took on all the chores associated with the dog. He walked with Ruth to the park, played with her in the yard, made sure she was fed each morning and night. He even scooped up dog shit every day to ensure that no one could complain about him or the dog. As a result of all the care and attention, Ruth grew to love Nathan more than any other member of the family. Every afternoon Ruth anxiously awaited Nathan's return from school. She would greet Nathan with unbridled enthusiasm after any absence, from ten minutes to ten hours. Although she was happy when others arrived home, Nathan had become the center of her universe, which was more than Benjamin could endure. He began to complain more vehemently about the dog, suggesting that it had been a mistake to take her in. He cited articles about dog diseases, the germs they carried, the liability incurred should they bite someone. As in most other household matters, Nathan found himself opposing forces too great for him to withstand, and it wasn't long until his parents announced that the dog would be going to live with their cousins out in the country. No amount of pleading on Nathan's part could change their minds, and one morning, when his dad was driving over to eastern Washington on business, he took the dog with him and dropped her off, and that was the last Nathan saw of Ruth.

Nathan now pulled into the hospital parking lot. Gabbie lifted her head to see whether anything was happening that should concern her. Satisfied that she was not needed, she lay her head back down and closed her eyes. Nathan sped across the lot and parked at the far end, near a thin stand of trees. Sensing that the car had stopped, Gabbie pushed herself up and waited to see where Nathan planned to take her. "Sorry, Gabbie," he said gently as he climbed out of the truck, "but this time you've got to stay." When Nathan closed the door, she barked three times. He could well imagine the gloomy look she was giving him, her sad eyes, dark and lonely, following him as he walked away, her head dropping lower with each step. He did not deserve such loyalty. He did not deserve it from Gabbie or Jo.

He stood before the grim façade of the hospital entrance, its imposing face studded with mythic creatures cast in gray concrete, stained with city grime, bits crumbling from the sharp edges. A sea of black asphalt flowed out from the stone footings, like lava seeping out of a rocky cliff. He walked through the door. The inside was bright and shiny, the floors polished, the Formica counter a glassy sheen. The white walls glowed with a fresh coat of paint. He thought he could detect the faint smell of enamel beneath the layers of antiseptic and bleach.

He stepped toward the reception desk. An efficient-looking clerk—an ancient woman with an air of a wealthy socialite who saw it her civic duty to serve the less fortunate—stared at Nathan for several seconds, as though appraising how worthy he was to receive her services. "May I help you?"

He felt immediately intimidated by this woman, despite her tiny stature, her soft voice. He was convinced that her assessment of him had revealed his darkest secrets, that she witnessed his deceit, his guilt. She waited for Nathan to answer. He leaned up against the counter, then pulled back, as though he might contaminate the pure mirrored surface.

"I, uh, I'm looking for my wife."

The receptionist held her posture rigid. When she spoke she barely moved her thin lips. "Is she a patient here?"

"Yes, she's a patient. She was in a car accident."

The woman seemed indifferent to the circumstance of Jo's admittance. "Who is she?" the woman asked.

"My wife!"

The woman spoke slowly. "I mean, what is your wife's name?"

"Jo. Jo McTavish."

"Could you spell that please."

"M-C-T-A-V-I-S-H."

She entered the name into the terminal. The keyboard seemed an extension of her fingers, her life energy flowing down her arm, through the keys, the wires, illuminating the monitor.

The woman sighed. "She's checked out."

"Checked out? But that can't be."

"According to our records, she left this evening." The receptionist watched the screen. Nothing else existed.

"But I just called here a little while ago, not much more than an hour or so. They told me she was being moved—maybe to Intensive Care."

"Who told you?"

"The guy on the phone. I don't know who he was. He said they were moving her, but he didn't have the new room member yet. He suggested I call back."

"Did you?"

"Did I what?"

"Call back."

"No! I came here instead."

This was just the kind of crap Nathan hated, this bureaucratic bullshit where no one had any idea what anyone else was doing and they didn't care about anything but their own little jobs.

The receptionist studied Nathan for a moment, perhaps trying to discern whether he was lying. Then her sense of responsibility seemed to click in, and she began typing away.

"Hmmm," she murmured.

"What?"

"If you could take a seat, I need to check this a little further."

Nathan felt frustrated, angry. "But what does that mean? What are you going to check?"

The woman would not be deterred. "Please, take a seat. I'll let you know what I find out." With that, she stood and disappeared through the door behind her.

Nathan sat in a hard plastic chair against the wall. The room was large, well lit and sparsely furnished. Plastic chairs, like the one in which he sat, lined the walls, each a dusty gray-green, cold and hard, as though meant to discourage anyone from lingering. The walls, void of artwork or decoration, were white oceans that disappeared down long hallways, mysterious passages of forbidden knowledge, held in arrogant distance to keep the uninitiated out of the holy ranks.

Nathan sat alone in the reception area. It was after eleven o'clock, and visiting hours were long over. No doubt the emergency room had its assortment of casualties, but that was on the other side of the hospital. Here it was quiet, with few voices and little noise. It reminded him of when he was a teenager and he would have to sit in the waiting room of his psychologist's office. His parents had decided, when he was 15, that he might need some help. The older he grew, the more solitary he became, the more an outsider. His parents feared that this antisocial behavior was a poor reflection on their family and their ability as parents. Nathan had become an embarrassment, and it was time to bring in a professional.

The psychologist—a woman whose name Nathan had long ago forgotten—had been as cool and detached as the walls of the waiting room, void of expression, free of emotion. She would stare at him with a sort of noncommittal gaze, always evaluating him, always measuring him against some invisible standard that Nathan would never live up to.

"Tell me, Nathan," she would say, "tell me what you're thinking about."

Nathan would shrug.

"I can't help you if you don't talk to me. You want me to help you, don't you?"

Nathan didn't answer. The psychologist smiled a careful smile, a practiced smile. Benjamin smiled this way when they were with their grandfather—or anyone else who Benjamin wanted to impress. Nathan shivered, which the doctor seemed to note.

"How are things at home, Nathan? Is everything okay?"

He said nothing. He stared at the wall, at a painting of a sailboat, anchored in a quiet harbor, the water still, the sky streaked with pink wisps of high clouds.

"Okay," she said with forced patience, "let's start someplace easier." She rested her elbows on her desk and clasped her hands, leaning forward in a manner that she perhaps thought was friendly, intimate. She smiled again. "How old are you, Nathan? How old did you say you are?" She smiled.

Nathan glanced over at her. "I thought you had that information already."

"Well, yes, it's probably here somewhere, I just thought—"

"Fifteen."

She hesitated. "Tell me, Nathan, does it bother you having people ask you questions?"

He shrugged. "Depends."

"On?"

"On how stupid the questions are."

Nathan now looked over to the receptionist's desk. The white-haired woman had returned. Nathan walked to the desk, his guts twisting in fear.

She gazed at him for a moment, in an absent sort of way, as though trying to remember who he was. Finally she said, "We can't find her."

"What?"

"We can't find her." She seemed perturbed at having to repeat herself.

"What do you mean, you can't find her?"

She sat down. "Well," she said, "it seems that your wife has disappeared."

Into the Night

J o followed the arrows painted on the floor as they wound through several corridors and down a flight of stairs. The tile felt cold against the bottom of her feet, but it was a distant cold, an awareness that acknowledged the icy surface but failed to translate it into physical discomfort, as though she stood outside her body, watching her bare feet slap the frigid surface. It was like that for all her body, for all the aches and stiffness from her accident. She knew that something was there, that something had happened to her, but she could only imagine that the discomfort had existed, a fleeting memory losing focus, becoming unreal. Logic told her that she should feel stiff and sore, but she did not.

She saw the door at the bottom of the stairs. Above it an exit sign, with large red letters, glowing prominently against a bright backlight. She pushed open the door.

The night was cool, clear. The breeze danced with her gown, slipping its fingers up the loose hem, the opening along the back. She had not tied the gown and was glad for the air's caress along her full hips, her buttocks, up the smooth flesh on her back. She looked down at her forearms, her shins. Her skin glowed in the pale light of the parking lot, like a white sail on a moonlit night.

She walked down several concrete steps and onto the expanse of asphalt. The surface felt hard, gritty against her feet. It was not uncomfortable, simply different. She didn't know where she was going, what she was doing. She wasn't even sure why she decided to leave. She had been lying on the gurney, waiting for her new room. There had evidently been some confusion as to where she was supposed to go. She had heard the nurses discuss one of the other patients. One man said, "But the mother's not dead yet," which was followed by several members of the staff whispering in frantic tones. Meanwhile, she lay there on the gurney, the medication making her groggy, indifferent to what was going on around her. Whatever they had given her earlier had really kicked in, and she now felt less anxious, unconcerned about the future.

She didn't know how long she had lain there on the gurney, but at one point she had fallen into a sort of dream state, a detached awareness, somewhere between wakefulness and sleep, a place calm and serene. She wondered if this was what death felt like. If it was, then it wasn't such a bad thing, certainly nothing to fear. She remained aware of her surroundings, the glare of lights, the beeps of the machines, the efficient paces of the staff. She observed them as though she were incorporeal, as though she herself could not be seen.

A woman walked up the hallway and stood next to her. She stood over six feet tall, with thick bones and a strong healthy body. She wore a dark business suit and had white hair that fell to her shoulders in thick flowing waves, flowing in stark contrast to the dark skin of her face. Jo couldn't tell her age—maybe forty, maybe sixty, maybe more, but there was a presence about her that went beyond age, a strong confidence that emanated vigor and self-assurance.

She looked down at Jo and smiled. "I've been watching you." Her voice was low and melodic.

Jo said nothing.

The woman placed her hand on the top of Jo's head. Warmth poured from the woman's fingers, a soft current of heat, penetrating her skin, her bones, spreading softly down through her body, as though her blood was warmed by her touch and it circulated gently through her veins. But it was more than just heat. It was the feeling of light, a pure essence of energy. The stiffness in her body seemed to melt away, to dissolve and flow into the heat.

After a minute, the woman removed her hand from Jo's head and placed it on her shoulder. Her touch felt comforting, accepting.

"You're one of my special ones." The woman bent down and kissed her forehead, near the place where it was bruised.

Jo felt as though she glowed, a warm current of energy easing through her, like a low-level flow of electricity. She felt a remarkable sense of comfort, tranquil and clear, each cell in her body vibrating in a harmonious pitch. She drew in long deep breaths, no longer feeling the stiffness in her back or her sides. Her lungs felt whole, renewed. She thought about Nathan, about their finances, and none of that seemed a problem now. She wondered how she could have been so concerned, how she had failed to realized that things always had a way of working out. She didn't need to worry about work, about her car, about Nathan finding a job. And she didn't have to be concerned about being pregnant. She felt wonderful, better than she had in a long time. The baby would be fine.

The woman spoke in a whisper. "Go to the mountains. Go and learn." She touched Jo on the forehead, as though bestowing a blessing, and then walked away in slow, deliberate steps

Jo decided that she too should be on her way. She no longer needed hospitals and doctors. She felt renewed and was ready to get the hell out of here.

She crawled off the gurney. The earlier pain and stiffness were gone. She felt light, free. The staff still discussed her predicament. They exchanged heated whispers as she slipped out of the unit, down the hall, toward the stairs. And now she stood outside, feeling the night slip its cool tentacles into her gown. Her nipples grew hard, her skin erupted into a sea of goose flesh. She felt invigorated, alive. She gulped in the air, delighting in the heavy smells of the night, the hint of ocean, the fumes of car engines, diesel exhaust, the oily black top of the parking lot.

She walked away from the building, not really choosing a direction, interested only in distancing herself from the hospital, as though the building itself had been the cause of her problems, a monolith of her struggles, her injuries, her pain. The parking lot felt rough and uneven against her feet. Tiny pebbles cut into her calloused soles, the edges of her toes. She noted the feelings with interest, nothing more.

At the edge of the parking lot, she reached an embankment that fell steeply before her. Below the thick brush of greenery, Interstate 5 stretched north and south along the foot of the hill. Even at this late hour, it was filled with cars and trucks racing along the corridor, like bullets fired toward an unseen target. Tires hummed against the roadway, disrupted only by the belch of semis as they roared through their gears. Beyond the interstate the towering buildings of downtown glittered like oblong Christmas trees against the dark waters of Puget Sound. A ferry sparkled as it floated across the black currents.

Jo walked along the perimeter of the parking lot, drawing a large circle around the hospital. The building seemed to emanate a sort of magnetic force whose only purpose was to draw her back in, ensnare her once more into its system of pills and tubes and wires. Remaining outside the magnetic field was her only hope of escaping the powerful draw.

She continued to walk until she had gone about halfway around the building, and then she saw it—Nathan's truck. She knew she was searching for something, knew that her salvation waited her, but she hadn't been sure what form it would take. Her step quickened, becoming expectant, buoyant. When she neared the truck, Gabbie popped up against the window. The dog grinned excitedly, her tail flopping against the seat and dashboard and rear window.

"Gabbie!" Jo screamed. "Hey baby. Hi sweetie. How's my little girl?"

Jo tried to open the door, but it was locked. She looked absently for her keys, fumbled with the window, pulled again on the handle. She reached her fingers through the small opening in the window, and Gabbie licked them as hard and fast as she could. Jo held her hand there until her finger were drenched, and then she pulled them out. "Sorry baby," she said, "but I can't help you now."

Jo walked to the back of the truck. Gabbie barked her obligatory three barks as Jo opened the camper shell and tailgate and crawled into the back. She closed the doors and then lay on the blanket that was normally Gabbie's domain. It smelled of wet dog and was full of fur and grit and made Jo happier than all the sterile sheets and adjustable beds and clean pillows that the hospital could offer. Gabbie let out a slight whimper. Jo tapped on the window of the truck's cab to reassure the dog, and then lay her head down on the blanket, the distant hum of the interstate the only sound in the night.

Home on the Range

Stanley eased into the soft folds of his leather chair as air gushed out of the cushions in a muffled whoosh. The leather crinkled and stretched and cradled his stubby body. The exhaustion of the day—of the last couple days—settled upon him like a layer of dust on a piece of old furniture.

He reached to the floor to grab the remote. It sat next to the ashtray, where half-chewed cigarettes lay in a small pile, the paper stained with tobacco and spit. He aimed the remote at the TV. Suddenly his heart fluttered, skipped several beats. A brief spasm of panic, his breath short, strained. And then it was over, a reminder, nothing more. His heart resumed its awkward rhythm. His breathing slowed.

It wouldn't be long now, he thought. Not long at all.

He didn't mind so much. The thought of dying had been with him a lot lately. It waited like an answer—to a question never asked. It waited with patience and fortitude, standing aside as long as necessary, but never any longer—no, not one moment too long. He had grown accustomed to its presence, almost welcoming it, knowing that what was inevitable might best be dealt with sooner rather than being put off, before it was too late, before he had lost all control, all dignity. Yet he didn't think that his fate necessarily implied some great release from this life or guaranteed peace and tranquility. At the same time, he didn't hold expectations of hell and damnation. He couldn't imagine an eternity locked up in some satanic prison with bars made from the fires of eternal suffering. Rather, he saw death as divine indifference, a passing from one phase to the next, having little consequence to much of anything, except perhaps to those left behind, and in his case, that wasn't much of an issue. And even if it were, they too must ultimately succumb to the inevitable.

He once more aimed the remote at the giant television. The screen snapped to life, filling the room with a blue haze and the tinny voice of an adolescent superstar trying to sell a juice-flavored bottle of iced tea. Stanley wasn't sure what had prompted him to the buy the television.

He was never one who had to have the latest gadgets, and with his foggy eyes and diminished hearing, quality played little role in his choice. He supposed that he could justify his purchase *because* of his sight, that the larger screen would make it easier to see and put less of a strain on his eyes. But he knew that this wasn't the reason, although he was never comfortable thinking about the real motivation for his purchase. For Stanley, television brought with it companionship. Even when he was busy doing chores around the house—washing up his few dishes, making coffee, sweeping the kitchen floor—the TV was blaring in the other room. As soon as he got up in the morning, he would stumble out of bed, pick up the remote, and click it on. And on it would stay, until he left the house—or until he went to bed. Sometimes he would leave it on when he went to the store or took off to go fishing, just so there was noise when he got home, so he wouldn't walk into the house and feel its emptiness. Perhaps the larger television filled up more of the hole, took away more of the loneliness.

Yet Stanley had not turned on the television when Nathan and Gabbie had been there. They had been his first guests in his house in several years, not counting the occasional delivery, like when the TV arrived or the new hot water heater had to be installed, or when he had to face the unexpected—and unwanted—advances of community church members who were convinced that Stanley's soul needed saving and they were the holy representatives who could make it happen. It rarely took more than a few gruff retorts, many of which contained graphic suggestions for what the visitors could do with their religious propaganda, to repel the righteous intruders from his home.

The last real houseguest was about three years ago. An old buddy from when they used to log timber up toward Stevens Pass. Hershel Whitaker was his name, a big guy, hands like sledgehammers. Fought a lot, drank even more. He was a few years younger than Stanley, strong as an ox. He could push a log around that would normally take three guys to move. He had called Stanley from Monroe, passing through town with his grandson, who agreed to drop Hershel off at Stanley's house for a couple hours. Stanley wasn't ready for the sight of Hershel, for the decrepit old man who hobbled up his front steps, bent and twisted, like the carcass of a fallen tree. His hearing was nearly gone, his voice weak and thin. He shook with a constant tremor that made Stanley want to grab him and hold him still. They talked a bit about old times, not so much reminiscing, as much as trying to remind each other of what had happened, to somehow fit the details in with their own vague recollection of events.

That's when Stanley knew, when he accepted that he had lived too long, grown too old. Age was like a disease. Years spent denying the inevitable, then the anger, resentment, and finally acceptance, an appreciation almost of the deterioration, the fading away from life into the indifferent halls of death.

By the time Hershel had left, Stanley was ready for the break from his old friend. Even a short two-hour visit was too much. They had quickly run out of things to say, and the last hour consisted mostly of awkward attempts at keeping the conversations going. Both men were relieved when Stanley had turned on the television and they could settle happily into the screen's oblivion.

Stanley had not owned the big screen TV when Hershel had visited. He bought it this past winter, when cold temperatures, rainy skies, and few hours of daylight could easily justify the added luxury. It had become his one companion, a predictable noise that filled the void, yet somehow a constant reminder of what he had become, where he was heading. It seemed odd now to realize that he had not even thought about the television when Nathan and Gabbie were there. The house hadn't seemed so empty, despite all that was going on with Nathan, and how short a time Stanley had known him.

Poor Nathan. He was like so many other men of his age. He had no appreciation for what life offered him. So caught up in his own problems that he failed to recognize what he did have—a home, a wonderful wife. Some day he'd regret having wasted so much time feeling sorry for himself. He'd wish over and over again that he hadn't screwed away his life. Once he got too old to do anything, when opportunity had withered up and society pushed him out to the edge, sacrificing him to the next generation, would he realize that it was too late, would he understand what all old people came to understand—that he had all the chances he was going to get and now it was someone else's turn.

Stanley pressed one of the buttons on the remote repeatedly until the channel landed on the PBS station out of Seattle. He watched half-heartedly as the narrator chronicled the trail followed by Mormon pioneers as they fled the persecution of the Midwest to seek out a land to call their own, where they could worship freely, carry out the traditions established by their assassinated leader, Joseph Smith, and indulge in their God-given right to sexual experimentation. Upon Smith's martyrdom, the saints, as the founding members liked to refer to themselves, decided that the central United States, which at that time bordered the western frontiers, no longer fit the needs of their political and sovereign ambitions, not to mention the fact that few were interested in following the fatal path of their leader, so they headed west, leaving behind their belief that Independence, Missouri, was destined to become the Mormon Mecca amidst a sea of sinners and nonbelievers. A few had held onto Joseph Smith's vision of utopia, including his wife and sons, and had headed to Independence to keep the dream alive, but the many and powerful went west, turning a rocky barren desert into fields filled with grain, orchards filled with fruit, cities filled with the faithful. An American success story, complete with struggle, despair, disappointment, violence, politics, sex, and death. It would have made a perfect miniseries.

Stanley clicked off the television and stared at the blank screen. The silence closed in on him in a cold rush. He was reminded of the river, of stepping into the dark pool. He could feel the shock of cold water, the pressure against his face, his separation from the rest of the world. An icy grave, harsh and indifferent.

It was just a matter of time.

A Late Night Snack

Mr. Beardsley sat in his 1980 Chevy van. He had a clear view of the front door of the hospital, where Nathan had entered a couple hours earlier. He was having fun with this one, with the whole situation, and what a gold mine it had turned out to be. The brother, Benjamin, was an uptight Mormon with plenty of money and plenty to lose. Nathan was this spineless loser who could be coerced into anything. Nathan would do all the work and Beardsley would sit back and collect what was his due. The pieces were in place, just a few minor details to attend to. And the added bonus to all this was the accident. It had been perfect—there's no way Nathan would back out now and risk having his wife find out what he'd been up to. If she discovered that the massage had been a set-up, she'd want to nail his ass for sure. And if that wasn't enough to keep Nathan interested, Beardsley had other ways of convincing him.

Beardsley grabbed a donut out of a bag on the seat next to him and shoved it into his mouth. He then leaned over and picked up a bottle of tequila and took a long swig to wash down the pieces, all the while watching the hospital door. He knew Nathan would have to come out of there eventually, but he wasn't sure how long it would take. He didn't want to lose track of him for such a long time again. Beardsley had no idea where Nathan had disappeared to. After he saw Nathan at the park, Beardsley stopped for some lunch and then headed back to the hospital, and Nathan's truck was gone.

Beardsley had followed Nathan to the park earlier to see where he was going and decided that it was as good a time and place as any to confront Nathan. And talking to Nathan at the park reduced the risk that he and Beardsley would be seen together by someone that Jo and Nathan knew. Besides, showing up at the park caught Nathan so off-guard that he didn't know what hit him, which was an advantage that Beardsley wanted to keep.

After he had returned from lunch, Beardsley waited, figuring Nathan would be back at any time. He hadn't expected to sit there for so many hours. He had even driven around the parking lot and the near-by streets to make certain Nathan hadn't slipped in. But he knew it was just a matter of time, knew that with his wife still in there, he'd have to show up eventually. And Beardsley was ready to wait. He would have sat there all night and into the next day if necessary. He could relieve himself in the bushes, run inside to take a shit, and never be too far out of range. And this case was one worth waiting for. A few hours of sitting was an easy sacrifice considering the rewards that waited.

Beardsley had been close to these kinds of rewards before, like the time in Portland when he caught the wealthy husband of a client in the arms of an underage hooker. That could have been worth a lot to him too, had not the old geezer dropped dead right there on the dance floor. A massive coronary—he was dead in seconds. The scandal erupted before Beardsley could profit by this unseemly union. But Beardsley had made a few scores in his time, enough to ensure a somewhat secure financial future. He had always gambled on the basic evil in people's lives. He knew that if he pushed hard enough, dug deeply enough, he could uncover the one secret that the individual would pay anything to protect. And more times than not, the wealthier the victims, the darker and dirtier their little secrets. Sure, Beardsley had profited well by all these secrets, but he still hoped for the big score, the one that would set him up for the rest of his life.

And Benjamin Randall could be just the ticket. The little that Beardsley found out so far confirmed what he had suspected—that Randall was loaded. He had inherited a bundle from his grandfather, and Nathan saw none of it. Between his money—along with some very shrewd investments—and his land development, Benjamin had enough for all of them. Hell, Beardsley might even share some of the profits with Nathan, if all worked out as planned. That loser could use a boost now that his wife was laid up and couldn't support him. And Beardsley was convinced he could get plenty from Benjamin. With almost anyone else, the pictures of the massage and of them in the lounge would have meant almost nothing, but to a well-positioned Mormon businessman whose reputation was worth a small fortune in itself, a massage by a member of the opposite sex, with him wearing only his boxers, was enough to cast the kind of doubt that the Mormon business community would be only too happy to jump at. After all, Mormons, like everyone else, were political animals and as such saw life in terms of gaining power for themselves and destroying anyone of power around them.

Beardsley's father had been a man of that sort. A shrewd business-man who owned a sheet metal company in Chicago. He ruled his employees like a tyrant, holding them and the rest of the world in disdain, convinced that he and his son were of superior stock, dropped into a world that failed to recognize their innate talents and sensibilities. Father, like son, saw the world in terms of opportunity. No deal was too shady, no scheme too underhanded. He greased palms, bribed officials, and, when necessary, blackmailed those who stood in his way, resorting to any means available to increase profits and squelch his competition. Beardsley had been slowly indoctrinated into the family business, learning to rule with an iron fist, to maintain two sets of books, to wash money, to bribe and coerce. Yet before he could inherit the reins and taste the sweet sense of complete power, his father fell victim to a government sting operation that virtually closed up shop and sent his dad to prison.

Apparently the bookkeeper, a squeaky little man who Beardsley, Sr. had thought too insignificant to be of any consequence, had been coerced by the FBI to participate in exposing the corruption and tax evasion that had kept the business—and Beardsley, Sr.—quite prosperous. But Beardsley's father made enough enemies throughout the years to turn the trial into a media circus with local politicians and business-men—many of whom had had dealings with Beardsley, Sr.—scream-ing for the severest penalty possible. By then, Beardsley, Jr. had been a part of the business for several years, entrenched enough into the shaky dealings that the only way for him to avoid prosecution was to testify against his father and plead guilty to a misdemeanor charge of withholding evidence. After the sentencing, his father turned to him and said, "If you would have done anything else, I would have disowned you." And then he was led away to his cell at the Cook County jail, until his transfer to Joliet.

But Beardsley, Jr. had not come out of all this empty handed. Although the business was ruined—any assets having been confiscated by the IRS—he still had access to what his father termed the "dirty files," a set of records that provided enough information to convince a few of the old timers to keep Beardsley supplied with a steady income, at least for a while.

It wasn't long afterwards that Beardsley's father died, the result of a freak accident in the prison's kitchen that left him nearly decapitated beneath one of the massive stoves. And the politicians—most of whom were already old and sick—steadily died off, leaving Beardsley with little cash, few contacts, fewer friends, none really, and a feeling that Chicago might not be the safest place any more. He headed to the Northwest, carrying with him the only skills he had ever learned: extortion, coercion, blackmail.

He now pulled a long draw off the bottle. The door of the hospital opened and Nathan stepped out into the cool night. Now that Beardsley had seen both men, he could recognize the family resemblance, although Nathan didn't stand as tall as his brother, didn't walk as proudly.

Beardsley climbed out of the car. "Hello, Nathan," he said. "Long day, huh?"

Nathan looked at him absently, indifferently.

This wasn't the reaction he had expected. He wanted surprise, anger, fear. Any emotion that showed where Nathan stood. "You've been busy today," Beardsley persisted. "Where did you take off to earlier? Out joyriding?"

Nathan looked at Beardsley as though recognizing him for the first time. "Oh, it's you. I can't talk right now." He rushed across the parking lot, toward his pickup.

Beardsley followed him to the truck. "Hey, sport, wait up. I want to talk to you." Nathan was in the truck with the engine running by the time Beardsley caught up with him. "Look here, where you off to?" Gabbie climbed toward the window and growled, but Nathan pushed her back.

"Get away from my truck," he yelled through the slit in the window. Then he shifted into gear. The truck lurched forward. Gabbie yelped several times.

Beardsley watched the truck speed away. "Fine," he snarled, "if that's the way you want it, that's the way we'll play it. But let me tell you, you loser, I'm going to make your life a living hell."

The Journey Home

B enjamin took the last ferry from Orcas Island to Anacortes. The two-day meeting of the Council ended with a dinner and reception in the upstairs of the resort's main building. After his speech this afternoon, the members of the Council seemed more receptive than ever. They greeted him with smiles, handshakes, and an occasional pat on the back. Even the reserved members of the Council board, with their staunch civility and grim forbearance, reached out welcoming hands to their newest member, ensuring Benjamin's place in the upper echelons of the Mormon business community. They no doubt saw in him the qualities of leadership, persuasiveness, and public humility that made him an asset to their exclusive organization. Benjamin knew inherently the importance of always behaving properly and always practicing the faith, and in all likelihood the majority of the members acted according to the letter of the Church laws, but Benjamin was convinced that, more important to the Council leaders, was the ability to lead men, to act with shrewd, decisive, political acumen, to land always on your feet, no matter how great the heights from which you tumble.

Throughout the evening, Benjamin spoke with Mormon businessmen from around the country, each a man of influence in his own right. But the members of the Council board all resided in Salt Lake, where their ties to the LDS stretched across bright marble corridors like golden threads that tied together Church leaders and board members in a giant web of secret meetings, hidden agendas, and far-reaching plans. Benjamin's entry into the hallowed corridors brought with it passageway into rooms from which he, along with most everyone else, had always been excluded.

Many of the Council members had left Orcas Island after the evening's festivities. Benjamin had originally planned to stay the night, but decided he was too excited about the day's events to sleep, so he returned to the room, packed, and loaded the car. He reached the ferry as the last few cars were boarding.

The ferry steered through the calm island waters. The sky had cleared and the moon slipped out from behind the black silhouette of mountains. The shoreline was dotted with dim yellow lights that reflected on the water like floating stars.

Benjamin leaned against a railing and stared at the dark currents as they slipped by the boat. A trail of white foam, luminescent in the bright light of the moon, stretched behind the boat and disappeared into the darkness.

He felt the tiredness catch up at last, as though the events of the last two days—with their high degree of excitement and anxiety—fell into the water and drifted away into the deep currents that curled around the islands. The night was surprisingly warm, for being on the Sound, and the ocean air, filled with the odors of salt and fish, was disturbed only by the passage of the ferry as it worked its way toward Anacortes. The air felt soft on his face, a gentle reminder of reality, helping to put into perspective the almost surreal events of the last two days. Even the boat's giant engines, with their rhythmic chugging and steady rumble, served as a sort of grounding that diffused this trip's excitement.

Benjamin examined the events of the last two days, trying to look at what happened through impartial eyes. Sure he had to perform some damage control, but overall he believed that, in the end, he had won over the Council and earned himself a place of prominence, if not immediately, sometime in the not-too-distant future. But then he thought about the reasons for his actions, why it had been necessary to turn the tide that had shifted against him in the first place. Jo. A lot of trouble, that one.

He tried not to think too much about her, about the problems she had caused, about how she might have proven to be the end of his career, yet the thought of her was enough to fan those still glowing embers. He felt the arousal in his jeans, the movement of his shaft as it snaked through the folds of his boxer shorts. He hadn't felt this kind of excitement for anyone in years, not since he first met Rebecca, when all he wanted was to penetrate that virginal wall, conquer and subdue, guarantee that she belonged to him and to no one else. Rebecca seemed so beautiful to him then. A wholesome, healthy girl who was unlike any of the girls he had known in high school or college. With her sparkling eyes and shiny blonde hair, she represented everything he thought he wanted. A woman who would be a good mother and faithful wife. But the passion had faded quickly, soon after they were married, and being with her had become nothing more than an obligation, a way to fit neatly into Mormon culture.

Rebecca and Jo. So different from one another. Jo could never be conquered, he knew that instinctively. Perhaps that explained his craving. She was the unattainable goal that he could barely resist, against his better judgment, despite the risk to his future.

It was just as well she landed in the hospital, out of his line of sight. Better to remove the temptation than have to face it again.

He stood on the ferry deck a little longer, waiting for his desire to subside. The last thing he wanted was to walk back into the cabin with his excitement still apparent. He forced his thoughts to his business, to land deals he was working on, to his life at home, to his wife. Thoughts of Rebecca were usually enough to turn the tides of passion. Now when they had sex, it was just a form of release, a letting loose of the inevitable explosion that failed to produce anything but a few grunts and groans, the dutiful wife performing as expected—even if without enthusiasm—and the responsible husband fulfilling his destiny, exercising his God-given right to rule his life and the life of his wife in a manner that best suited his own needs, as they had been outlined by the Church and its ever-evolving traditions. And if God had not denied him children, had not burdened him with a barren wife, he would rule their children with the same right.

Benjamin returned to the cabin—with its bright fluorescent lights and chatter from the other passengers—and sat in a corner near the front of the boat. He leaned against the window and waited out the remainder of the trip in a semi-conscious state that eased into the rhythm of the chugging engines. He would forget about Jo, forget about that whole incident, and think only about the future, *his* future, the successes and power that would be his. Nothing could stop him now.

When the ferry finally approached Anacortes, Benjamin returned to his car and waited as the boat slipped into its dock with a gentle thump against the giant wood pylons. Soon drivers started their engines and the parade off the ferry began. Benjamin eased his car forward—over the ramp, past the waiting area and terminal, and out on the highway, where the string of cars flooded the deserted road in a long line of lights and exhaust.

Benjamin had a couple hours of driving ahead, but once he got past the initial spurt of cars that emptied off the ferry, the roads would be relatively quiet. He drove through Anacortes and hooked up to Highway 20, where he headed east to Interstate 5 and then south to Highway 2. The road was dry, free from traffic, and the night clear. He listened to talk radio, some AM station out of Seattle. Listeners called in to voice their opinions on topics that ranged from welfare to socialized medicine to public housing. The callers, for the most part, were fed up with their tax dollars paying the way for everyone else. All welfare did was create a bunch of lazy people who kept having babies and refused to be responsible for their own lives. Benjamin agreed that public assistance had gotten out of hand and didn't work, but not for the reasons that most of the callers did. His reasoning was more philosophic—or religious-based, as it were. He saw prosperity as God's reward to the faithful. Those who resided in poverty, those who needed society's help to survive, were not living according to God's law. With proper faith, strong conviction, and a steadfast adherence to God's teachings, they would be able to pull themselves out of the mire in which they had allowed themselves to sink. Welfare perpetuated sinfulness, faithlessness, and godlessness.

But then Benjamin had a strange thought, a kind of thought that he would never have entertained in the past. It seeped into his consciousness like water soaking into the ground. As he drove up Highway 2, climbing out of Monroe toward Index, he began to wonder what Jo would think about all this. What exactly would her opinions have been?

He pondered this notion for several minutes, convinced that she would have views quite different from his own. When he finally realized the direction his thinking had taken, he cut his thoughts short, blocking out any further considerations of her or her ideas. Enough was enough. He turned up the volume, letting the radio blast out any unwelcome thoughts.

The drive through Sultan, Startup, and Gold Bar was uneventful, despite the tinny sound of the voice of the talk show host. When Benjamin reached the Index-Galena road, he turned off the radio and completed the last couple miles in silence. Soon he was pulling into his driveway, relieved that he was finally home. That's when he saw all the lights on inside the house. Damn that Rebecca. Had she no respect for how hard he worked, how much it cost to keep that place going?

He climbed out of the car, slammed the door, and marched toward the house. When he walked inside, the bright glare momentarily blinded him. Not only had she left everything on, she had turned each dimmer switch to its maximum power, turning the walls into landscapes of white glare.

Benjamin stomped through the hallway and past the kitchen and into the living room, stopping suddenly at the sight before him. There, on the chair next to the fire, Rebecca slept with her feet on the footrest, wrapped in her bathrobe and holding her arms tightly against her chest. And sitting across from her, also asleep next to the fire, was a scraggly looking man, a man Benjamin had never met before. And the man wore Benjamin's robe!

"What the hell is going on?"

Late Tuesday/Early Wednesday

Lost in Space

Nathan pulled out of the parking lot and hit the gas. The engine whined in a loud screech that pierced the deserted side streets around the hospital. He could feel the engine wind tighter and tighter, like the inside of his guts, taut, knotted, thick with the tension of the night. He wanted to keep moving, keep the pedal floored, the gear shifted low, until the engine blew, pieces flying in a thousand directions, an explosion of rods and pistons and burning chunks of engine block.

He had no idea where Jo might have gone. The staff at the hospital had merely said that she had disappeared. No one saw her leave. No one considered her mobile enough to have been able to slip out of there as she had. Nathan never asked why they had moved her, but he was sure that if he had questioned them, he would not have received a straight answer. Everyone seemed little concerned at Jo's disappearance, as though events like this occurred all the time. Perhaps they did, or perhaps they had been coached by attorneys never to reveal anything, never to say too much, never to supply too many answers. Still, he should have asked what was going on, why Jo had been moved.

Nathan tried not to think anymore about Jo's condition. He wanted to push that thought down deep, along with any of the other problems he didn't want to deal with right now, such as the whole blackmail idea and Beardsley and the car accident. Now he must focus on finding Jo.

Nathan lifted his foot from the pedal and allowed the car to slow to a crawl. If he were going to find her, he couldn't do so at fifty miles per hour. He opened the window. The night was quiet. The only movement was the cool breeze that drifted through the window. At this point, Gabbie would have normally tried to crawl over his lap to stick her head out the window, but she remained intent on looking out the back. Nathan shrugged off her behavior as merely one more aspect of an already quirky night.

He didn't know exactly how he should be looking for Jo. Would she be walking? Curled up on someone's front lawn? At a local tavern drinking beer with the neighbors? With Jo, anything was possible, and it wouldn't surprise him if she simply decided that she no longer wanted to deal with the hospital bullshit and had to get out of there. Who knows what they had done to her—or what they had said. Whatever it was, she probably made up her mind that enough was enough and it was time to leave.

Whenever Jo made a decision to do something, she followed through to the end, no matter how big or small the task. Just like when she had met him, deciding at that instant that he was the one she wanted. She made up her mind and never looked back, despite how difficult he could be, despite his walls, his uncertainty, his fear. He never knew what she saw in him, why she treated him as well as she did. He felt like such a loser, like the biggest failure alive.

Nathan turned onto another side street and pulled up to the curb. Gabbie continued to stare at the truck bed. Nathan tried to imagine what Jo might have done once she left the hospital. The most logical choice would have been for her to wait for him somewhere near the parking lot or front entrance. He tried to picture her standing there at the door, looking for the truck to arrive. Then he realized that she would still be wearing the hospital gown. Even Jo wouldn't have ventured too far dressed like that, yet if she had decided she wanted to get away from the hospital, she wouldn't have hung around inside. So the most likely place for her would have been the parking lot or out near the front of the building, where there were grassy strips she could lie on. As odd as it might have seemed for someone to be sitting outside at night in a gown, it would not have seemed too far fetched if it were on hospital grounds. The more he thought about it, the more he decided that it simply wouldn't have made any sense for Jo to have wandered too far. In fact, what didn't make sense is how he jumped into the truck and took off like some fool dog in heat.

But then Nathan remembered Beardsley. That asshole might still be around the parking lot, and the last thing Nathan wanted to deal with was Beardsley while he was looking for Jo, or any other time for that matter. Even worse would be if Beardsley approached Jo. That pig better stay the hell out of his way.

Nathan started the engine. The truck shuddered as the exhaust coughed and gasped. The engine turned over briefly and then fell silent. He sat for a couple seconds, grinding his teeth. His stomach felt as though acid seeped through the lining. He tried the ignition once more. The engine groaned halfheartedly, as a muffled clunk shook the truck, and then the starter squealed in a high-pitched whir that ended with an abrupt crack that sounded is if it had snapped off. Nathan slammed his hands against the steering wheel. "Goddamn it! Goddamn this fucking truck! Goddamn this fucking night!" There was nothing he could do now. He knew he would have to let the truck sit for at least ten minutes before it would start. He jerked the key out of the ignition and climbed out. "Come on, Gabbie, maybe you can be of some help." Gabbie stared at the back window and didn't move. "Gabbie, come here!" She barked. "Gabbie!"

She crept out of the truck, acting as though she had been caught digging through the garbage or chewing up one of his shoes. She tried to make herself as small as possible.

"I don't know what's come over you, but you're acting weirder than ever. Come on, now, let's go find your mom."

Hearing the phrase *your mom,* she started wagging her tail, her eyes shining with anticipation. Then she rushed to the back of the truck and stood on the bumper with her front paws, ready to leap inside.

"I swear, you're getting nuttier by the minute. Now let's go." He slammed the door shut and began walking toward the hospital. Gabbie barked, but he didn't respond. Before long, he heard the snap of toenails against concrete and the approach of the heavy panting. When she arrived next to him, she bounced up and down and leaped around him in circles, as though she had not seen him in a week.

"Gabbie, I don't know who's crazier—you or me."

They walked the few blocks to the hospital. The streets were deserted. Large oak trees lined both sides, and little light penetrated the thick ceiling of leaves. The only sound was the occasional distant siren and the steady hum of the interstate. Even this far away—with all these trees and buildings—it was still there. How could people stand it? How could they live like this—every day the noise, the crowds, the choking deadly air?

Nathan and Gabbie reached the front of the hospital. The parking lot was in back, and he had always used the entrance on that side of the building. The façade he now looked at was even more imposing. He had the sense of standing before a palace of sorts, or a Gothic cathedral. The building's face—with its long shadows and diffused lines—had a stately look, something official and sanctioned. It was a place of power and strength, designed to impose a governing will on the peons who dared to seek out its services. He could just make out the silhouettes of statues on either side of the doors, larger than life, grotesque in the dull light. A thin strip of lawn spread beneath the façade, just past the sidewalk. A line of Chinese elm trees lay in a perfect row down the center of the grassy strip.

Nathan walked along the sidewalk, feeling the weight of the heavy brown stone of the building on his tired back. Even Gabbie seemed to feel the hospital's grim exterior. Her gait seemed less excited, less full of the enthusiasm that usually kept her leaping from spot to spot as she bounced alongside Nathan.

"It's okay, girl," he whispered, striking a somehow respectful tone before the great façade.

Nathan watched for any unusual shapes in the grass, up against the building, in the crevices along the wall. He investigated each shadow with a subdued anticipation, thinking perhaps he could make out the shape of a body, a twist of a leg, an outreached arm, only to discover an empty space, where shadows intersected, where night became lost into night.

Gabbie sniffed faithfully at the edges of grass and along the sidewalk, stopping only a moment from one scent to the next, a child let loose in a candy store, trying to decide which flavor was the most enticing, which shape the most interesting—a world too vast to comprehend but one to be searched with determination and fortitude, known solely through the intricacies of taste and smell.

Gabbie was the first to see the dark outline curled up under the tree. She sniffed at the figure for several seconds until a dull groan wound out of the darkness, followed by a stifled motion. Nathan bounded over to where the dog stood, her ears cocked and her head tilted to one side. As soon as Nathan reached the dark shape, he could smell the alcohol that oozed from the semi-conscious vagrant, a sickly stench that seeped from the pores, floated on the breath like a poisonous gas erupted from a busted line. He could just make out a large bulk wrapped around the trunk of the tree—a beached whale on a starless night.

Nathan stepped back and called Gabbie. Suddenly a voice grumbled out of the shadow, a rough voice, deep and low. "What the hell's going on? How the hell am I supposed to get any sleep?" His words were slurred, full of anger, bitterness.

Gabbie growled, her teeth glowing in the dim light. Nathan recognized the voice, he recognized the puffed up arrogance, the foul disgust in the man's speech. Even in his drunken state—with words wrapped in sleep, slurred with intoxication—Beardsley spoke with the same biting tone as he had before, his voice shooting through the clear night,

r. h. sheldon

like the backfire of a truck, a rich mixture that burned out of the exhaust in a loud explosion of foul gas and black filthy smoke.

Beardsley rolled upright, then grabbed onto the tree and pulled himself up and let out a chuckle and said, "I figured you'd be back."

Nathan fled down the sidewalk toward the end of the hospital. Gabbie followed dutifully as they circled the building. He knew that Beardsley could never keep up with them if they continued to move quickly enough, especially as drunk as he was. He'd probably pass out again as soon as he took his first step.

Nathan decided to search the greenbelt area along the edge of the parking lot. Perhaps Jo wandered into the trees and then fell asleep atop a fallen log. If she were out there, Gabbie would find her. Nathan looked down at Gabbie. "Okay, girl, go find your mom." He pointed into the trees, at which point, Gabbie bounded into the brush. Branches snapped, leaves rustled. Periodically, Nathan would call out Jo's name. The dog would stop moving for a moment and then continue the search.

Nathan looked around the lot. The only movement was off at the other end, where a man walked his dog. Perhaps he had seen Jo. When Nathan was finished there, he would ask him. Nathan turned back to the trees. The steady rhythm of the interstate filtered through the foliage, in between the sounds of Gabbie's search.

"Looking for someone?" Beardsley stood next to him, his breath hot and sticky with liquor.

"Go away!"

Beardsley swayed. "Now listen here, bud…"

"No, you listen to me. Get lost!"

Beardsley stepped toward Nathan. "Why you sorry excuse for a man—" Suddenly he tripped forward, his pointed finger catching Nathan in the face. Without warning, Gabbie leaped out from the trees, ran around Nathan, and knocked Beardsley off to the side. He tried to right himself, but couldn't stop the inevitable tumble down into the greenbelt, which was steep enough to make recovery nearly impossible, especially in the dark, especially considering how much alcohol he must have consumed. He slid out of sight, a comical look of horror on his face as he disappeared into the bushes. Then from the depths of shrubbery erupted several vivid exclamations that focused primarily on the worthlessness of dogs, the deplorability of pets, and the evil disposition of all animals. Next came an outpour of several brief epitaphs that included "goddamn motherfucker" and "goddamn son-of-a-bitch" and "goddamn cocksucker." Although each statement lacked subtlety, it nevertheless made clear reference to God.

Gabbie and Nathan listened as the heavenly oaths slowly died down and were replaced by a few grunts and groans. Nathan crouched down toward Gabbie. "Good girl," he said as he hugged her neck and pet her head. "That should keep him busy for a while. With any luck, he'll get lost in there. Now let's go find your mom."

In the Heat of the Night

Benjamin stood before Rebecca and Paul, waiting for an explanation, but they both sat frozen, open-mouthed, dazed. He could feel the rage rise within him, the blood surging to his head, pounding against his temples. His peripheral vision blurred, and only Rebecca was in focus, her image like glass. Each detail a crystal of light cut against this foggy backdrop.

She stood slowly and tried to speak, but the words fell out in an undecipherable mutter, no doubt the lie being formulated as soon as she opened her mouth. He hated her then, an all-consuming hatred, a hatred unlike he had ever known against anyone. Even more than his pathetic excuse for a brother.

Rebecca tried to speak, "Oh, Benjamin, this has been too strange, you won't believe…" She looked at the floor. "A vision," she stuttered, "we saw, I mean, after the storm—"

Benjamin just stared.

She persisted, "We were nearly struck by lightning…Oh, Benjamin, it was awful—" She seemed near to tears.

Benjamin lifted his arm, as though he were about to strike her with the back of his hand. Paul stood, took a step and then froze, fear wiped across his face, his body trembling. Benjamin snarled at him and told him to mind his own business. But he lowered his hand, sucking in a deep breath.

Rebecca stepped toward him. "Benjamin," she pleaded, "it has all been unbelievable…"

Benjamin had to get out of there. "Don't come near me," he snarled through gritted teeth. "Don't ever come near me again!" He glared at Paul, then at Rebecca. This was all *her* fault. She should never have let this happen.

"Please listen," Rebecca sobbed, "it's not at all what it seems."

Benjamin felt nothing but disgust.

"I'll let you and your boyfriend alone now."

Paul spoke for the first time. "But it's not, I mean, we're not—It's not what it looks like—really, you couldn't be more wrong..."

Benjamin stared at Paul with a fierce gaze. Paul said nothing more. Benjamin spun around and stormed out of the house. He jumped into his Explorer, started the engine, slammed the car into gear, and shoved the gas pedal into the floor. Tires spun against the asphalt as he squealed out of the driveway. He could see nothing but the spread of the headlights before him. Anger filtered his vision into a tunnel, the rage a bloody wall that propelled him forward. He reached the highway and swerved into the westbound lane, without heeding the stop sign or looking for oncoming traffic. He pushed forward like a drill boring into a black wall, driving his car faster, sliding into each curve at speeds nearly out of control.

A car appeared on the highway ahead. He approached quickly, nearing the rear bumper, until the red lights were only a few feet away. The car slowed steadily. Benjamin swerved into the left lane and punched the accelerator, passing the car in seconds. The driver beeped his horn. Benjamin watched the headlights shrink in his rearview mirror.

He raced down the highway, until he reached Gold Bar. He thought he saw a car parked up on the right, mostly hidden by stretch of trees. He slowed down to near the speed limit, just in case a cop waited for the opportunity to write a ticket.

He thought again about Rebecca and what he saw at the house. He felt nothing but disgust for her, this woman to whom he had given so much, who the minute he leaves town seduces the first man who comes along, just as she had seduced him, just as she had tricked him into marrying her.

He continued west on Highway 2 toward Monroe, where he picked up Highway 522 and headed into Woodinville. There he caught Interstate 405 south to Highway 520 and crossed Lake Washington into Seattle. He headed south on Interstate 5 past the downtown area. The lights from the tall downtown buildings shimmered in the late night hours.

He moved over into the right lane, toward the exit that he would take to his condo. As he was about to turn onto James Street, he glanced up to his left, where Westside Hospital sat prominently along the edge of First Hill. With little consideration, he turned left rather than right and climbed the hill to the hospital. When he reached Westside, he parked in front of the building and walked toward the entrance. He couldn't explain why he decided to come up here or what he planned to do once he went inside. He pushed open the massive glass doors and followed the signs and arrows to the reception area, where he was met by a stuffy prune of a woman who greeted him curtly and with a somewhat annoyed look.

Benjamin was about to ask for information regarding Jo, when he realized that he didn't know her last name. Then he remembered that he had one of her business cards. He pulled it out of his wallet and read, "Joanne McTavish, Licensed Massage Therapist." The card displayed the name of Richards Resort. For a brief moment, he was taken back to his massage from the other night. A smile slipped across his lips, and then was gone. He looked at the card again and realized that it was printed on the same type of thick ivory paper as had been his invitation for the massage, the invitation that he had mistakenly assumed had been a gift from the Council board. The business card was also printed with the same brown ink and it included the name of Richards Resort. And like the invitation, the "R" in Richards was the same large exaggerated R. However, from what he recalled from seeing the Richards logo on everything else at the resort, the logo used was quite different from the card and invitation. He thought this odd, and realized that he had never thought again about who might have given him the invitation, since it wasn't the Council or the resort. And considering that he and Jo had never met, it wasn't likely that she had arranged it. Still, anything was possible.

Benjamin decided to put this aside for now and consider it more carefully when he was clearheaded. He then asked the receptionist about Jo McTavish.

"It's past visiting hours," she said.

"I realize that."

The woman succumbed to Benjamin's unabashed stare. "Well, let me check." She looked at her terminal for a minute, then mumbled something inaudible. Finally, she said, "I thought I recognized that name. Her husband was in here earlier this evening looking for her. It seems that she has disappeared."

Benjamin looked at the receptionist for a moment and then walked out of the hospital. He stood before his car, wondering what could have become of Jo. He decided to stroll around the hospital, clear his head a little, perhaps bring some order to this muddled night. Though he was confused by what he had seen at the house, he was as equally confused about why he had sought out Jo, and what all these events meant to who he was and his position in the community.

He walked across the massive parking lot, which was empty of all but a few cars and a green van, all beat up and rusty. He noticed a man walking his dog on the grass near the edge of the lot, along the strip of grass. The man stood near a street lamp and Benjamin could see that the dog was a white poodle, well groomed with pink ribbons in its ears. The man held the leash in one hand and a plastic bag in the other. He watched Benjamin suspiciously, with an accusing sort of glare, partially steeped in fear.

Benjamin shrugged him off and walked toward the front of the hospital. He climbed into his car and drove to his downtown condo, parked in the underground parking lot, and took an elevator to the twenty-third floor. He sat in front of the television, but didn't turn it on. What a day, he thought. What a day.

Now I Lay Me Down To Sleep

Paul wound through the overgrown trail toward his tent, his path lit only by the splotches of light cast by the moon. He stumbled over unseen rocks and twisted branches and the bowing trunks of young vine maples. Had he been less weary and not so overtaken by the emotional exhaustion of the last two days, he would have been better able to maneuver past these hidden obstacles, even with only the light of the moon sifting through the canopy above. In fact, on a night like this, with the moon so bright and full, he would have found wonder in its magical light, in the way it touched the earth, its delicate breath caressing the ground. But tonight, even the shimmering power could not lighten his heavy mood, and he trod awkwardly through the trees, thinking only of his tent and sleeping bag.

After several more stumbles and twists, he reached the campsite and unzipped the front flap of his tent. The sound of the plastic zipper, as it snapped around its oval track, was a great relief after the walk back from Rebecca's house. As close as she lived to the campground, the trip seemed to take forever, and the scratches on his face from the unseen branches and the lump on his forehead where he had banged into a tree served only to remind him of how glad he was to finally be here.

He climbed inside the tent, kicked off his shoes, and zipped up the tent flap. After pulling off his coat, sweatshirt, and pants, he eased into the bed. The nylon warmed quickly, and he felt the tension begin to fall from his body. He eased into his weariness, letting it draw him into the deep currents of drowsiness and relaxation. Another extraordinary day, one unexpected moment after the next. He hoped that tomorrow would be less eventful. He could use a break—and the last thing he wanted was any more encounters with Rebecca's husband. The look in his eyes—when he thought Rebecca had been cheating on him—was about as mean and angry as he had ever seen in anyone. Paul had been sure that Benjamin was about to perform some horrific act, and it had scared the shit out of him, but then Benjamin stormed out of the house in a childish fit. Doors banged, feet stomped. And he was gone, like a squall that lays ruin in seconds and then moves on.

After Benjamin had left, Rebecca said nothing. She stood there, starring at the door, her eyes wide with terror, her mouth hanging open, as though she had been struck dumb, which, given the unusual events of the day, seemed quite possible.

After a minute, Rebecca turned to Paul and shouted, "This is all your fault!"

Paul was speechless, almost numb by yet one more bizarre event. Any protest would seem as ludicrous as her accusation.

"How could you just stand there? How could you have such total disregard for our lives—for who we are?"

Paul felt like a child, rebuked for some adolescent misdeed. He felt embarrassed, self-conscious, and standing there, wrapped in Benjamin's ill-fitting robe, made matters only worse.

"I'm sorry," he stammered. "I should have—"

"I think you had better leave," she shouted.

"Yes," he returned, "yes—ah, if I could get my clothes—"

She turned formally and disappeared through the kitchen door. He could hear the snap of the dryer door when she pulled it open. Soon she reappeared with an armful of his clothes and dropped it on the chair where he had been sitting.

She announced sternly, "I'll wait upstairs while you get dressed. Please let yourself out."

She marched out of the room. He grabbed his clothes and dressed quickly. Then let himself out, into the dark cool night.

Paul now lay in his sleeping bag, relieved to be away from that house and all their problems. Tomorrow he would focus on other things—on his own life. He would avoid Rebecca and her house and her husband. Perhaps he should move on—set up camp somewhere else. He wouldn't be surprised if she called the state to complain about him being there. The way she acted this evening, anything was possible.

Perhaps this was just as well. Perhaps he needed a little nudging to move him along, to set him off on his journey into the mountains, as had been his original intent. Yet the thought of going into the woods, by himself, to isolate himself even more, to create an even greater separation from the rest of the world, filled him with sadness, as though the loneliness he had tried to ignore had finally caught up. He had spent the last year doing what he could to fend off that loneliness, distracting himself with work, with the city, sometimes with drugs, but it was always there, like a lion watching its prey, until the right moment, when the inevitable conquest would be made.

It was too bad that everything had gotten so crazy at Rebecca's house. He had felt a certain camaraderie with her—two lost souls searching for a way out. But she had returned to her shell and would not likely be sticking her head out for a long time. And now he was alone, more alone than ever. He felt rootless and uncertain and terribly afraid.

He thought about his vision when he had still been in Seattle. He thought about his dreams, the voice of the river. They had all been the same man, the same benevolent spirit, the same gentle loving God. And even the vision he had tonight, the vision he and Rebecca shared, looked like the same God. But tonight it was different. Tonight God had filled Paul with terror, rocking his world with that hideous threatening voice, those powerful vengeful eyes. And afterwards, when he tried to speak to Rebecca about what they had witnessed, she gasped in fear, muttering the name of Joseph Smith. He wanted to ask what she meant, what she saw, but she seemed too upset to talk about it, so they watched the fireplace, neither of them speaking, or speaking about something else, until the evening had passed and they had both fallen asleep, only to be woken by Benjamin.

Paul now tried to quiet his mind. He listened to the river washing over the rocks. If only he could be that river. If only he could feel its strength, know its flow, share its purpose. If only he could have some sense of his own life.

Waking the Dead

Jo opened her eyes slowly, groggily, confused by her surroundings, the movement of the vehicle. She sensed the familiarity of the truck bed, the camper shell, the gritty dog blanket, full of hair, clumps of dirt. Snippets of the past several hours came into a dull focus, lying in the hospital room, being moved, meeting that white-haired woman who wore the business suit. Strange how much better she made Jo feel. She must have come by when the painkillers were at their peak.

Jo could use some of those drugs now. Her entire body felt stiff and achy. Then she remembered the pronouncement that she was pregnant, that the accident might have risked the baby, that the reason she had been moved was to monitor her and the baby's condition. She should get back to the hospital and not take any more risks.

She tried to raise herself up on her elbow, but it hurt to move and she dropped back down. A series of barks erupted from behind her, over her head. Gabbie no doubt saw her move and now wanted to climb into the back of the truck. Jo could then hear Nathan try to settle her down. She could picture Gabbie leaping around and barking, while Nathan tried to drive with one arm and control the dog with the other. "Gabbie, no," he would shout, and then she would sit still for a few seconds before bounding up as enthusiastically as ever, torn between her desire to please Nathan and her yearning to check out whatever it was that interested her at the time, which in this case was Jo.

Jo smiled. She always teased Nathan when he tried to be stern like that, because she knew that deep down he was a big pushover, as gentle and caring as a man could be.

She tried to push herself up once more. She was ready to get out of the truck, let Nathan know where she was, what was going on.

Once up on her elbows, she rolled over on her side. She felt as if she had been a punching bag. She took a deep breath and reached her arm up, trying to stretch as little as possible, until she could touch the window of the cab. She knocked on the glass, four times, and then fell back to the truck bed.

The truck stopped suddenly. Jo slid toward the front of the bed and slammed her head against the metal wall. Pain cracked inside her skull, and she reached up to grab her head. Gabbie barked, nearly hysterical, as she bounced around in the front seat and rocked the trucked.

Jo heard—and felt—the door open and then slam shut. In a second, the door to the camper shell flew open. Nathan reached in and flicked on the overhead light.

"Jo!" he shouted.

She looked toward the back of the truck. The camper shell framed his head, his face heavy with shadow. Still, she could make out the confused look, the sense of relief, the underlying concern. Perhaps she was sensing this more than seeing it, but either way, she knew she was right. She could feel his emotions before he could. She was always able to read him, always able to see beyond his quirky, uneasy behavior.

"Jo," he said again, almost in a whisper, a request.

"Hi Nat." She spoke nonchalantly, trying not to move too much. "What's up?" She knew her casualness would drive him crazy, but she couldn't resist.

He pulled down the tailgate and started to move toward her, then stopped. She couldn't tell what his intent was, whether he planned to climb in or try to help her out. He probably wasn't sure himself.

"You're not trying to take advantage of me, are you?" She smiled.

When he finally realized what she had meant, he recoiled in horror. "No, I wouldn't—I mean, not in the shape you're in…that is, you know, the way you're feeling and all…

Jo laughed. "Help me out of here."

He grabbed her hand and started to pull.

"Easy!"

He let go. She fell back with a thump. "Ouch!"

"I'm sorry…I was just trying to—"

"It's okay, Nathan. I'm still a bit sore. We'll go real slow. Just let me steer."

He grabbed her hand again and gently helped her along. The process was slow, but eventually she was standing.

"Better hang onto me," she said. "Still feeling a bit lightheaded. Those painkillers gave me one hell of a ride."

He said nothing, waiting loyally until she was ready to make a move.

"Now, let me see my baby but don't let her jump up on me."

Nathan looked toward the front of the pickup, then back at Jo. "Why don't you stand here by the truck," he suggested. "That way you can hold on."

They maneuvered the few steps to the back corner, near the tailgate. She grabbed the shell and looked around. They were parked in front of the hospital.

Nathan walked to the cab and opened the door. Gabbie bounced out and leaped up on him. Then she saw Jo. Nathan grabbed her by the collar in mid jump, reigning her in with great effort, and walked her over to Jo. She howled and wagged her tail as she pulled him along.

"Baby girl!" Jo yelled.

Gabbie was about to explode and Nathan could barely keep her at bay. Jo reached out and pat her head. Gabbie licked her hand and arm. Jo could smell her hot breath, her thick oily coat, fragrances as sweet and welcomed as a spring day in the forests—pure, unadulterated dog.

Gabbie tried desperately to free herself from Nathan's grip, but Nathan held firm, his hand and arm straining from the constant pressure.

Jo pet the dog's head tenderly, in between licks. Gabbie began to settle down, seeming to accept that Jo had not abandoned her forever. Nathan too appeared a little more relaxed and eased up his hold, although he continued to maintain a steady grip.

Jo continued to pet the dog's head as she spoke to Nathan, "I suppose you're wondering how I happen to be out here in the truck."

"Yeah, well, out here in the truck, out of the hospital, the middle of the night...and, ah, in your hospital gown..."

She looked down at the pale blue and white gown. No wonder her backside felt so cold. "Ah, yes, well..." She smiled sheepishly. "You know, the best I can come up with is, *It must have been the drugs.*" Nathan smiled for the first time. "Anyway," she continued, "all I remember is there was some confusion about the rooms—and I was lying there on the bed or cot or gurney or whatever they call it, and then this woman came along wearing a power suit and told me I was going to be fine, and then I was walking out here." She sighed, the weariness catching up. "It was all like a dream, really, and when I saw the truck, I climbed in. How long have I been out here?"

Nathan considered this for a moment. "Probably an hour, maybe more."

The excitement started to mount once more in Gabbie, and Nathan instinctively pulled back on her collar.

r. h. sheldon

A police car sped past them and turned at the corner, racing toward the back of the hospital, its lights flashing, but no sirens.

"I'm cold," she said, "and I need to get back inside." She looked down at her feet. "Goddamn it! I don't even have shoes on."

Nathan looked down. Guilt spread across his face.

"Come on, Gabbie," he said. "Time to go back in the truck."

Gabbie looked at him accusingly.

"Go on, honey," Jo said as she pat the dog's head and rubbed her chin. "Go with Daddy."

The ills of the entire world having suddenly befallen her, she slunk away with Nathan toward the front of the truck. Nathan put her inside and returned. The dog barked three times.

"Okay," she said, "let's head back in."

"But what about your feet?"

"What about them?"

"They're bare. I mean, don't you want shoes or something?"

"Got any?"

"Well, no, not really, I mean—wait, you can have mine. Wear my shoes!"

Jo laughed. "That won't be necessary, dear. Just help me back in. I'll be fine. My feet are the least of my worries."

"What am I thinking! I brought clothes for you, they're in here, in the truck—and shoes."

"I'll be okay, really. Just help me inside."

Nathan dutifully led Jo toward the hospital. After they got inside, Nathan stopped and turned to her. "I was kind of wondering, Jo, why they moved you in the first place—I mean, I thought you would be getting out soon."

Jo studied him for a moment, wishing there was some way to prepare him for this. And then she said in a voice as calm and steady and unconcerned as possible, "Oh, didn't I tell you? I'm pregnant."

The Scene of the Crime

Detective Charlotte Rosenberg joined the Seattle Police Department right out of college, just after she received a degree in Criminal Justice from Washington State University, and after twenty years of walking beats, riding in squad cars, straddling bicycles, and moving through the ranks into the role of detective, she at long last found herself in the department's Homicide division, the place she had set her sights on when she first enlisted as a rookie all those years ago. In some ways, she found it hard to believe that so many years had passed, but if she stepped back and took a good look at herself, she could see how that idealistic novice had been transformed by the realities of life into someone who was now a bit more haggard, a lot more jaded, and mistrusting of nearly everyone she met, whether co-workers, people on the street, or those she encountered in her personal life.

Yet despite this transformation, Detective Rosenberg was, above all else, a cop, and all the challenges she faced to get to where she was now—the sexism, the homophobia, and the occasional anti-Semitism, which would pop up at the most unpredictable moments—made her even more solid in her identity as a police officer. Rather than be deterred by these challenges, she gathered strength in them, pushed even harder, succeeded against hopeless odds. And now she accepted her well-earned position with a certain grace and dignity, having achieved the respect of most of those around her and considered by many in the department to be one of the best—and certainly one not to mess with. Detective Rosenberg, the thorough, the tenacious, the unabated, was the one everyone could count on to get the job done.

She now stood in the parking lot in back of Westside Hospital interviewing the only witness to what might have been a crime. The evening had grown cool, calm, uneventful, except for the body that lay down in the trees.

"If you would, Mr. Williamson, tell me again what you saw—and try to be as specific as possible."

"Like I said, Fluffy and I were out for a walk—I usually take him out one last time before I go to bed." Patrick Williamson spoke with a sort of wheeze, his breath labored. "My wife usually goes to bed earlier than me, so I'm the one who takes Fluffy out for his last trip." He looked down at Fluffy, who lay curled up at his feet. Williamson held the leash loosely in his right hand.

"And do you usually come this way?"

"Nearly every night, unless it's too rainy or cold or something. Then we just go out in the yard. But Fluffy likes her nightly walks. Otherwise he gets restless, wants to go out too early, even before my wife wakes up. So I usually take him out sometime between midnight and twelve-thirty."

"And tonight?"

"Tonight?

"What time did you leave the house tonight?"

"Hmmm. I'd say about twelve-fifteen. Or pretty close to there. Usually takes us only a couple minutes to get back to this side of the hospital, depending on how often Fluffy wants to stop. But he's usually pretty anxious to get back here, where all the trees are. That's what he did tonight. Before we even left the house, I could tell that this is where he'd want to head. He had that excited look about him, you know how dogs get, their eyes all sparkling and they kind of bounce around."

Charlotte wasn't very familiar with how dogs looked when they were excited. She had never had a dog, not as a child or an adult. And she didn't want to know about Williamson's home life or the antics of his animal. She had the sense that, if given the chance, he would provide her with a complete rundown on his daily routine, which, no doubt, centered on Fluffy.

"Okay, Mr. Williamson, you're out walking your dog…"

"Fluffy."

"Fluffy."

"Yes, we don't like to call him a d-o-g in front of him. He's a little defensive about that."

Great. She could just imagine the field day a defense attorney would have with this witness. "Okay, then, so you're out walking Fluffy. You're back here, in this parking lot. You come here most nights, about this time. Is that correct?"

"Yes, that's right. Fluffy likes the trees and bushes, along the edge there." He pointed toward the direction where the body still lay.

Charlotte continued. "But tonight is different. Tonight you see something."

"Yes, detective. We were over there on the strip of grass, when I saw the two men."

"Can you describe them?

"One was a big guy, short, but real big around. Kind of sloppy looking, but it was hard to tell too much with where the streetlight was. Still I could tell how big he was, and how short. Pretty darn short, at least compared to the other guy. And the big guy wore a Hawaiian shirt. And the other guy, like I said, he was taller, thinner. Had dark hair, dark features, but I couldn't see him all that good from where I stood."

"And what did they do?"

"The tall thin guy, he was standing alone, then the other guy, the big one, walked up to him."

"And did you hear anything?"

"Just the taller guy yelling, but I don't know what he was saying."

"And then what happened?"

"Me and Fluffy got out of there right away, walked up the side of the hospital, out of sight from them. Thought it might not be safe."

Charlotte looked around the parking lot, trying to envision what happened. There were two squad cars on scene, plus her unmarked car. Someone from the Examiner's office would be arriving any minute. The officers from the cruisers were searching for anything that might provide information about the deceased. The beams of their flashlights peered out haphazardly from between cars and behind bushes. She pointed toward the trees, where police tape marked off an area at the edge about ten feet wide. "And you say that they stood over there, by the edge of the lot, near the trees."

"That's right. That's where they were standing before we walked to the side there, to get away from them."

She surveyed the scene once more. He was probably about thirty yards away, maybe more. Not very reliable testimony at this point.

"Okay, Mr. Williamson. Did you notice anything else before you left. Any other people around? Cars?

"I didn't see anyone else, but I remember that van there. I noticed it when we first arrived 'cause it's so beat up and dilapidated. There were a few other cars scattered around the lot, but I don't recall any details about them."

"So you can't tell me if the cars that are here now are the same ones that were there before, or whether any cars were moved, except for the van?"

"That's right, detective."

"Did you hear any cars leave when you were over on the side?"

"Not that I remember."

Charlotte knew that, even if a car had left, Williamson wouldn't have necessarily seen or heard it. Cars could get in and out of the lot on the other side of the building, so there was no way of knowing what might have been there.

Williamson waited for the next question. His breath hissed out like a radiator with a slow leak. "Just a few more questions, Mr. Williamson, and then you can head on home."

"No problem," he said. "Kind of exciting, really. Nothing like this ever happens to me. It's not every day you find someone lying there dead like that."

"No, it's not," she responded. But the truth was, dead people were found all the time. Some died of natural causes, some by accident, and the rest? Well, that's why she had a job.

"Mr. Williamson," Charlotte continued, "after you walked your dog—I mean, Fluffy—along the side of the building, you returned to the parking lot. Is that correct?"

"Yes, it is. I didn't want to go back, but Fluffy was insistent."

"About how long were you gone from the lot?"

Williamson considered this for a moment. "I'd say about ten minutes."

"Ten minutes? That seems a long time just to stand around out here. You sure it was that long?"

Williamson looked at her accusingly. "I wouldn't have said it if I didn't think that's how long it was."

"Okay. Ten minutes. And then you returned. What did you see then?"

"In the parking lot?"

"Yes, back here, when you returned."

"Nothing."

"Nothing?"

"That's right. Nothing. It was quiet. Both men were gone."

"Okay, Mr. Williamson," Charlotte said, "you return to the parking lot, the two men are gone, you didn't hear any cars leave, but you can't be sure any cars came or went when you were on the side of the hospital. Is that correct?"

Williamson looked around the parking lot, as though trying to verify whether he had the facts correct. "Yeah, that's right."

"And then what happened?"

"Well, Fluffy still had it in his head to go down to the trees, like he usually does."

"So you came to this area."

"Yeah, we did. And I let Fluffy—that is…"

"Go on."

Williamson looked at the ground. "Well, I, um, let him off the leash. I know we're not supposed to, but I figured it would be okay. I mean, it being so late and no one around. There's really not a lot a places I can take Fluffy to let him run around, and so I figured…well, anyway, I probably shouldn't have done that, I mean, I won't do it again, I just thought—"

"It's okay, Mr. Williamson." Charlotte tried not to smile. She knew how paranoid people would be around the police, and she didn't want to do or say anything that would discourage him. She remembered one time when she was interviewing a witness and the woman lied about where she was parked, which turned out to be a significant factor in the case. It all had to do with her parking illegally in a handicapped spot. As a result of her trying to protect herself, the DA was inclined to dismiss her testimony because of the proximity of where she had reported to have been parked. But when Charlotte learned the facts, all the pieces came together in a way that explained what the witness had seen and how her testimony could be used to convict the man who had assaulted another man in the parking lot.

Yet even when someone wasn't trying to hide something, Charlotte had learned over the years that no witness was a hundred percent reliable and that all witnesses usually saw or heard something that they had failed to report—whether the information had slipped their minds or whether the had intentionally changed or omitted the information. The trick when interviewing someone was to get at the hidden, forgotten details, while not intimidating or frightening or making the witness angry.

Charlotte had little doubt that Williamson's confession about his unleashed dog was the extent of his guilt, yet she was confident that he must have heard or seen something that he hadn't yet told her, whether or not he realized it, which is why she questioned him again, making him repeat the information he had already told her. In that way, she could look for inconsistencies, pick at the details that didn't make sense, and help him to solidify his story.

"Let's see if I got this right, Mr. Williamson. You and Fluffy walked over here and you then let Fluffy off the leash. Correct?"

"That's right, detective. And then he immediately ran down into the trees, just over the edge there." He pointed toward the trees, right near the spot where the body still lay.

"And then what happened?"

"That's when Fluffy starts to bark, which is not like him. He's usually so quiet, hardly ever barks when someone comes to the door."

"Not much of a watch dog, huh?"

Williamson shot her a sour look. "We think of Fluffy as a companion, as part of the family."

"Yes, of course." Charlotte couldn't wait for this night to be over. "But tonight he barked."

"He sure as hell did—oops, sorry, sure as heck did. Barked like I never heard him. Didn't you, Fluffy?" Williamson looked down. The dog failed to respond.

Charlotte persisted. "And what did you do then?"

"I tried calling him back, but he would have none of that. He just kept barking and barking. So I climbed down there. Luckily I had my little flashlight on my keychain." He lifted the keychain to show her the light. "My wife gave it to me last Christmas. Comes in handy sometimes, though I never expected to be using it for something like this."

"So you go down to see what Fluffy is barking about. And you use your little flashlight to see. Is that right?"

"Yep, sure is. At first I couldn't figure out what I was seeing. The flashlight's not the brightest and there's all those bushes down there and everything."

"But then you did figure it out. You knew what you were looking at."

Just then, one of the police officers walked over to where Charlotte and Williamson stood. "Excuse me, Detective Rosenberg," he said.

Charlotte hated to be interrupted when she was interviewing a witness—unless it was of the utmost importance. She studied him for a moment. A kid, probably just graduated from the academy. His nametag said "Sullivan."

"This better be important, Officer Sullivan."

"Yes, ma'am, excuse me, but I think it is."

"Go on."

"I believe we've identified the victim—at least it looks like a match. The van, it was unlocked. We found a wallet. The driver's license matches the victim."

Charlotte turned to Williamson. "Excuse me," she said, "can you give me a minute. And if you would, please wait right here. Don't walk around or disturb anything. I'll be right back."

"Of course," he replied. She could see the excitement in his eyes. She would have no problem keeping him around as long as she needed to. The only problem might be to get him to leave when she was finished with him.

Charlotte accompanied Officer Sullivan to the van. "Okay," she said, "what do you got?"

Sullivan shifted his weight from one foot to the other. This was probably the first fatality he had worked.

"As I said, the van was unlocked, and his wallet was inside. The picture and description on the driver's license matched the guy on the hill, so I'm pretty sure it's him."

"We can't be sure of anything until the Examiner's office has a look. Until then, the best we can do is work on the obvious assumptions."

"Yes, detective."

"Anything else?"

"Yeah, well, not sure if this means anything, but you should check out the inside of this. It's full of all sorts of electronics, computer and video equipment, that sort of thing."

The side door of the van was already opened. Charlotte leaned inside. The interior looked like a command post, or some kind of video production studio. She could see two computers—one laptop and one tower—a monitor, two printers, a small television, speakers, two VCRs, a video camera, and a couple other items she couldn't identify. The floor was covered with wires that connected all the equipment together. The guy was into something, that's for sure, but she had no idea what.

As she surveyed the scene, she could detect the faint odor of alcohol. Instinctively, she looked for a bottle, which she found lying on the floor next to the front seat. Cuervo Gold, her liquor of choice.

"Rosenberg, my favorite detective."

Charlotte pulled her head out of the van and turned around.

"Kelly, what are you doing here?" The last thing she wanted to see was a reporter, especially Michael Kelly. He had a nose for scandal and had caused no end of grief for the department.

"Heard you were having a little fun tonight. What have you got?"

"Not much at this point, but if something turns up, I'll be sure to give you a call."

"Yeah, I bet you will."

Just then, a second officer climbed up from the greenbelt and walked toward Charlotte. He wore rubber gloves and carried a letter-size manila envelope, which he held by the corner. "We found this by the body."

Charlotte pulled a white handkerchief out of her pocket and used it take the envelope. The name Benjamin Randall was printed across the front in letters that looked as though they could have been written by an eight-year-old child. She carefully lifted the flap and then tilted the envelope enough to allow several photos to slide out most of the way.

"That's him!"

The shout erupted from just over her shoulder.

Charlotte spun around. Williamson stood next to Officer Sullivan, holding Fluffy in his arms. And next to him stood the reporter.

"Kelly, you need to wait on the other side of the lot. There's still an investigation going on."

"Oh come on, detective."

She turned to Officer Sullivan. "Would you please escort him away from this area."

"Alright, alright, I'm moving. But I want to talk to this guy when you're done." Kelly pointed to Williamson. Charlotte knew there was little she could do to prevent the meeting, but at least he was out of the way.

Charlotte turned to Williamson. "You were saying?"

"That's the man I saw. The one in the parking lot."

Charlotte held the pictures up to the streetlight. "You recognize him?"

"That's the guy I saw, over on the strip of grass."

"After you came back here?" This information didn't fit with what he had told her so far. "But you said you didn't see anyone after you returned."

"I forgot about seeing him again. It was right after I called the police. I was waiting for you to show up, there on the grass, opposite the edge where I found...the, um, deceased."

"And that's when you saw this man, while you were waiting for us to arrive?"

"That's right, detective. I forgot all about it. That's why I didn't say anything, not till now, not till I recognized him from the picture. We were standing over there, on the grass, and he walked right by me. And then I heard the sirens."

"And is this the same man you saw earlier, the one arguing with the deceased?"

"Yes, I think so. It's hard to be sure, but I think so. Same size, dark features. It had to be him!"

"Now Mr. Williamson, think hard. Is there anything else that might have slipped your mind? Any other detail."

"No, detective, that's it. I swear. That's the honest truth."

Charlotte never believed anyone who told her that.

Wednesday Morning

Back in the Saddle

Stanley woke before the first light, maybe about four-thirty. He climbed out of bed, peed, boiled water for a cup of instant coffee, washed up a few dishes, and then plopped in his leather chair, where he watched the news and chewed about six cigarettes. Then he started flipping through channels, one of his favorite pastimes, till he caught the phrase *Westside Hospital*. He stopped flipping.

According to the anchorwoman, the body of an unidentified man had been found in the trees outside the hospital, and investigators believed foul play was involved. The newscast quickly switched to discussions of weather, traffic conditions, and sports. He scanned several other Seattle channels, but came up with nothing.

Stanley shifted in his chair. His thoughts turned to Nathan and Jo, the way Nathan stormed out of here, the look of lunacy in his eyes.

Young men and their tempers. Never a good mix.

Stanley flipped through channels till seven-thirty, until he grew too restless to sit. He pushed himself out of the chair and pulled on his boots and limped out to his truck. Since no pressing engagements awaited him—and really, few events these days he considered pressing—he would head back to the river and search for the gear he dropped when he took his icy swim.

Most of all, he wanted to find his flask. The rod and reel would certainly cost more to replace, and he would have a tough time finding another George Dickel baseball cap, but the flask had belonged to his dad, one of the few reminders of the old man. He didn't have many things that had belonged to him, and he wasn't much for hanging onto mementos, but the flask was different somehow. His dad always had it with him when they went fishing or were out hunting or even when they were just working around the ranch, and when Stanley thought of the flask, he thought about his dad—the way he used to slip it out of his jacket, the sun glinting on the tarnished silver, the sideways look when he drank.

Stanley parked his truck and walked toward the head of the trail into the old campground. It was only eight, and although the sun came up early this time of year, the shadows still fell long and heavy in the dense forest. He reached a beaten-up footbridge made of wood and held up by two cedar logs that spanned a slow-moving stream. Rusty chicken wire covered the surface to provide traction.

He stepped onto the bridge. The logs bowed under his weight, each step releasing a creak that reminded him of his own tired and dilapidated body.

Once across, he continued along the trail toward the river. He had no intention of following the same path he had taken the other day. He wasn't concerned so much with hurting himself or taking another plunge as he was with creating more trouble for himself—or anyone else that happened along.

He picked his way carefully along the overgrown path, his greatest risks the occasional thorny blackberry or low hanging vine maple—or perhaps crossing back over the rickety old bridge.

Soon he could hear the steady wash of the river. He continued forward until he was nearly upon it, but then he saw the tent and stopped. He had not seen a tent by the river in several years. It was pitched near the edge of the high bank, overlooking the spot close to where Stanley had fallen into the water, and sitting about ten feet from the tent, where a small fire blazed warmly in the cool morning air, was a man looking absently at the flames. Before Stanley could react, the stranger looked up and smiled, making it even more difficult for Stanley to escape unseen. Worse still, he'd have to endure the inevitable pleasantries that went with these types of encounters. He should have stayed home.

The man leaped to his feet. A look of recognition crossed his face. "It's you!"

Stanley didn't know how to respond.

The man walked up to Stanley, smiling broadly and reaching out a hand.

"You're the one who fell into the water, right? The other day, over there, that was you, wasn't it?" He took Stanley's hand and shook it.

Stanley felt stripped, exposed, as though a part of him had been lost and turned over to strangers. It reminded him of when he was a boy, when his friends would play practical jokes on him, the way he felt when he realized he was the butt of their jokes.

"I'm Stanley," he said, not knowing what else he should say.

"I'm Paul. Paul Kazinski. Am I glad to meet you. And I'm even more glad you're alright." He continued to pump Stanley's hand.

"Nice to meet you." He pulled back his arm.

"Please, please, come by the fire. Sit down. I want to hear what happened." Paul hesitated. "I mean, if that's okay with you—if you wouldn't mind."

Stanley followed him to the campsite. Normally he would have made some type of excuse to get out of there, sidestep the invitation and move onto a more isolated area. But his resistance was low and he wanted to search around this part of the river, so he didn't see a lot of alternatives. Besides, this guy seemed so glad to see him that Stanley hated to disappoint him. And it wasn't like he had any other place he needed to rush off to.

Stanley moved toward a log that lay by the fire. He eyed it suspiciously, trying to assess its stability, his own ability to balance himself, and the likelihood he'd be able to stand back up once he got down. Unfortunately, the log was his best option.

He lowered himself carefully, feeling the tension in his knees, his hips. His joints creaked, popped, squeezed against the aches and stiffness, like rusted hinges being forced opened for the first time in years.

Paul watched him settle on his perch, which made Stanley feel even more awkward about his limitations, about his struggle to perform common tasks that were once so easy. Still, much to Paul's credit, he didn't say anything, didn't offer assistance or condolences or jokes. Now if only Stanley could avoid any mention of his dip in the river, but he supposed that was unavoidable, given the eager look on Paul's face.

Stanley settled into his seat. The pressure eased off his knees and hips and migrated to his lower back. He shifted his weight, repositioned his frame, let out a half-conscious grunt, then he looked over to Paul and, with a forced grin, said, "Well, son, what exactly did happen here the other day?"

So Paul told him. He told him about seeing Stanley by the river, about hearing the splash, about watching him go under. And then Paul—along with the help of a nearby neighbor who had also seen what happened—jumped into the river and pulled Stanley out.

"You don't remember anything?" Paul asked.

Stanley shook his head. "Not much. Got a vague recollection of falling. Next thing I know, I wake up in the ambulance, and here I am."

"But you must be doing okay, I mean, here you are, out walking and everything, just like it never happened."

Paul smiled, a sort of silly grin, no doubt pleased by his rescue attempt. Yet Stanley thought it was more than just that. His near giddiness was a genuine response to seeing Stanley there, to seeing him alive and up and walking.

"Yeah, I'm okay, I guess. I mean, all the doctors could tell me was that I'm old." He grinned as he pulled a cigarette out of his pocket and stuck it in the corner of his mouth.

"I'm sure glad you're alright. We were really worried about you."

Now came the point that Stanley dreaded the most. "I supposed I owe you my thanks. That must not of been easy for you, pulling me out like that…"

Suddenly it was Paul who acted embarrassed. "Please don't…really, I mean, it was just instinct. I didn't have time to think about it…please, forget about that."

Stanley looked at Paul for a moment, trying to decide if this was real or if he was just acting modest. But Paul looked uneasy. Despite his appearance—that tall, lean frame and that bushy beard and intense eyes—Paul was definitely uncomfortable. Not one who liked the limelight.

"How 'bout this," Stanley offered, "you don't bring it up, and I won't bring it up. You know I'm grateful, I know you're glad I'm okay."

"Fair enough," Paul said. He seemed visibly relieved.

Stanley pulled a bit of tobacco out from between his lips. "So what they hell brings you here anyway?"

"Brings me here?"

"Yeah. You up from the city? Out here on vacation? You must have been here before—not many people know about this place."

Paul hesitated. "I'm from Seattle. Decided to take a break from my life down there. Guess you could say I ran away from home."

"You did, eh?" Stanley chuckled. "That's not a bad idea, not a bad idea at all."

"Yeah, well it was long overdue. I figure there's no problem so big that you can't run from it.

"Agreed. And if I had something to drink, I'd toast that sentiment."

"I'm afraid all I have to offer is some water or tea."

"Thanks, but I was thinking of something with a bit more of a kick." Stanley smiled.

"Hmmm…" Paul looked around thoughtfully. "Seems to me…" He stood up and turned slowly. Then, with a quick movement, he reached

r. h. sheldon

beneath a small orange tarp and pulled out the flask that Stanley had lost the other day.

"You found it!"

"I did indeed. Down by the rocks, down where you...near the river." He handed the flask to Stanley.

"This does indeed deserve a toast." But before he took a drink, he cradled the flask in his hand and studied the dull, tarnished surface. The original design—swirling lines etched into the front and back— were barely visible after years of handling, and what lines did exist were hardly more than dark scratches that disappeared into pools of diffused gray silver.

He unscrewed the cap and lifted the flask to his lips, tilting it back just enough to feel the sting of liquor on his tongue. He relished the feel of that first burn, the way it seemed to jolt him awake, stiffen his resolve to face one more day. There was a purity about it, a cleansing, almost a ritual, a ritual delivered as much by the flask as by the liquor within it, tying together all that had occurred, all that was his life. He looked at the flask again, as though he looked in a mirror, seeing himself in the dull and tarnished finish, feeling dented, scratched, beaten up—fading into the dark gray pools of worn silver.

Stanley held up the flask and, with a quick gesture, offered Paul a drink.

"No way," Paul said, "it would destroy me drinking anything this early. I can barely handle tea on an empty stomach."

"Yeah, it's still pretty early, even for me, but I figure, what the hell, what am I saving myself for anyway."

Paul grinned. "I thought you were supposed to be setting an example for us younger guys."

"Who says you're younger? I'm only twenty-nine—and the last twenty have been hell."

They both laughed.

Stanley scanned the woods, glanced out toward the river, the glimmering spread of water. Few rays actually penetrated the thick canopy, but down by the river, the sun shone brightly, sparkling on the surface in a playful dance of light. It would be a glorious day—bright, sunny, warm—the kind of day that made the mountains such an extraordinary place to be, the kind of day that could shine hope into the bleakest of lives. Perhaps if he were a little younger, a littler healthier, he too could share in this feeling, yet days like this, with all their promise, all their beauty, lay in the domain of the young, and at best, all he could hope for was a brief glimpse into the brightness and warmth, a vicarious sense of connectedness, a limbo for souls such as his own.

He looked back at Paul. "So tell me, son, you didn't happen to find my rod and reel when you were down by the river, did you? I imagine it went flying out of my hands, although I couldn't tell you what direction it might have gone."

Paul shook his head. "Sure didn't. But I wasn't really looking around. Just happened to find the flask when I was getting water yesterday."

"Too bad. But I suppose that would have been too much to hope for. Still, you made my day, and I'm grateful to you."

"No problem at all. In fact, I'd be glad to look for your pole." He leaped up before Stanley could protest. "I'll be right back," Paul said. "Make yourself at home."

Paul scrambled down the bank and disappeared down by the edge of the water. Then he reappeared by the area where the river wound away from the bank. Paul was sure-footed and purposeful, moving as though he'd spent all his life climbing on rocks, walking near rivers.

Stanley decided that he had better stand up before he got so stiff he'd never be able to move, glued permanently to the log, or worse still, falling off into a heap on the ground, mummified by his atrophied joints and muscles.

He sat upright and planted his feet squarely in front of him. He knew that this would take a bit of effort because he was so low to the ground, and enough stiffness and soreness had already set in that he was afraid that, should he fall, he'd never be able to get up.

He pulled the stump of cigarette from between his lips and tossed it in the fire as he spit out the remaining slivers of tobacco. He drew in a deep breath and pushed himself up and forward, shifting his weight to his legs as he lifted off the log. The muscles in his thighs squeezed hard, the strain almost unbearable. He could feel his heart beat faster, his pulse echo in his temples. He felt flushed and lightheaded. He strained forward, teetering on his wobbly legs. Then he felt himself reach a critical balance, where one wrong move would send him sprawling down to the ground.

He had passed the point of no return. He could only move forward and up or tumble down into the rocky soil. He staggered, struggled. His weight shifted toward the fire. He struggled against the pull, trying to force himself upright. He gasped for breath, feeling the pressure in his lungs, his face. He stepped off to his left, checking his fall, then pushed himself upright, wobbling nervously, like a top about to expire, and then, with one last gasp, he straightened himself up, standing perfectly still until he was certain that he had made it, that he had survived yet one more struggle to maintain control.

He remained stationary until his breath slowed and the pounding of his heart eased. His legs felt sore, his knees stiff, but standing felt good, and a few steps would help the sluggish blood in his legs pump back up to the rest of his body.

He took small steps toward the bank and looked down toward the river. Paul stood holding the fishing pole. He was talking to a woman, blond hair, some gray, a little older than Paul, and not bad looking. There was a nervousness about her, a look of apology, embarrassment, their conversation serious.

Then Paul turned toward the bank, saw Stanley, and waved. The woman, too, waved with a self-conscious gesture. Stanley nodded and stepped back, not wanting to endure the stares of strangers.

After several minutes, Paul and the woman climbed up to the campsite. Paul burst out, "Stanley, this is Rebecca. Rebecca, Stanley." He smiled broadly. "Rebecca was also there the other day—by the river…"

Stanley was afraid of that. Another person with insight into what he himself could not remember. Still, he should try to be friendly. "Rebecca," he said, "it's nice to meet you."

"I'm glad you're doing okay. I was worried about you."

"Guess I wasn't about to be done in by a little cold water."

She winced. "No, I guess not. But you're okay, right? I mean, how are you doing now? How are you feeling?"

"I suppose about as good as someone my age can feel."

"If you need anything, if there's something I can do for you…"

"No, no," Stanley chuckled. "I'm fine. You've already done enough. Really."

"I mean it, though, if there's anything at all…" Her words trailed off.

Stanley shook his head.

"What about breakfast?" she asked.

"Breakfast?"

"Have you eaten?"

"Well, no, but I usually don't…"

"Great. I'll make you breakfast."

"Oh, no, thanks, I couldn't—"

"I came over here to ask Paul if he'd like some breakfast."

Paul's face brightened. "You did?"

Rebecca smiled shyly. "Yes. I thought maybe...I just thought you might like a good hot breakfast."

Paul said, "Is Stanley going to join us?"

"I couldn't, really..."

"Of course he's joining us." Rebecca beamed.

"Great," Paul said, without waiting for a response from Stanley.

"Okay," Stanley grumbled. "Where to?"

Paul and Rebecca both smiled, their faces as radiant as the cherubic glow of a host of angels.

Breakfast at Rebecca's

Rebecca scurried around the kitchen, pulling out everything she would need to make breakfast—eggs, potatoes, bacon, pancake mix, cream, butter. She piled the food on the counter, next to several mixing bowls and the pancake griddle. Then she picked out the utensils —wooden spoons, spatula, pancake turner, and a few tablespoons and forks—and lay them next to everything else. She moved with professional control, her hair pulled back into a ponytail. She wore a pale green apron.

Paul and Stanley had not yet arrived. She had returned by way of the river, but Paul planned to accompany Stanley in his truck so Stanley would have it nearby when he was ready to leave. Paul could also direct Stanley to the house, although its location would have been easy enough to describe—just turn into the first driveway on the right. But she had left all that to Paul, knowing he could get here. After all, because of her he had to find his way home in the dark last night. She felt queasy just thinking about it, about the way she had lashed out at him, kicked him out of the house. It wasn't his fault that Benjamin showed up, that he behaved as he had behaved. But she was so surprised by all of it, so disturbed, that she wasn't thinking about what she should do. She just reacted. Too bad she couldn't do that with Benjamin, rather than some innocent stranger.

Maybe *stranger* wasn't exactly the right word. Sure, they had known each other for only a short time, but they had been through so much together—pulling Stanley out of the river, getting caught in the storm, almost getting struck by lightning, and then all that weird stuff that happened last night. She had been so upset by Benjamin showing up, by the way he stormed out, that she hadn't thought about her dream, or whatever it was, and the way Paul had woken up at the same time, as if he saw what she saw, as if he too saw Joseph Smith. It was all so strange.

But taking it out on Paul had hardly been fair. That's why she went looking for him this morning, to apologize for the way she had behaved. And when she found him, he seemed as friendly as ever. He had even apologized for having overstayed his welcome, for having put her in such an awkward position, and she would have protested his apologies, except that he was so excited about Stanley being there that she had little opportunity to make it clear that she was at fault, not him. Still, she was relieved to learn that Stanley was okay, and meeting him there, hearing him talk, made the events of the last couple days seem less terrible. And that, along with finding Paul friendly—and receiving what she preferred to think of as a sort of round-about forgiveness—lightened her morning, despite all that had happened, despite how things were going with Benjamin.

And it's not as though she hadn't tried to make things right with Benjamin. She had called him at the condo first thing this morning. She had figured this was where he had stormed off to last night, and she had been right.

When he had answered the phone, his voice was tired and gravelly, and he gave a vague, noncommittal "Hello."

"Benjamin, it's me…I wanted to make sure, ah, I was just checking that you're okay." Her voice wobbled and her throat felt tight.

She could hear his breath. A heavy sigh. "It's a little late for you to be worrying about my welfare, don't you think?"

"Benjamin, you know that's not—"

"Listen, I'm very tired. I don't know why you called so early."

She squeezed the phone tighter. "But you're usually up by now."

"Yeah, well last night I didn't get much sleep. I wonder why that is." His words plunged into her with unerring precision.

"Benjamin—if you would just let me explain…"

"Explain what? What is there to explain?"

"About last night, about all that happened while you were gone."

"I don't want your explanations."

"But—"

"Listen, Jo, I'm not about to sit here and—"

"Jo?"

"What?" He sounded like a string on a piano pulled too tight.

"You said 'Jo.' You said, 'Listen, Jo.'"

"I did not."

"You did, Benjamin. You said, 'Listen, Jo.'"

"I said 'Rebecca,' and you know it."

"No, you said—"

"I know what I said. And I said 'Rebecca.' I said, 'Listen, Rebecca.' You know that. You know that's what I said."

r. h. sheldon

Her hands shook. "Okay, Benjamin, I must have been mistaken. I just thought…"

"Why would I say Jo, anyway? Why would I use that name? Don't you think I know who you are? Don't you think I know your name?" He nearly shouted.

"Yes, dear…yes, Benjamin. You're right. I must have been mistaken. I'm sorry."

"I mean, I know who you are, after all. Who better than me?"

She drew in a deep breath. "Yes, Benjamin, you're right. I'm sorry. It was silly of me."

"You bet it was. Damn silly. I've never heard anything so ridiculous. I can't believe you sometimes."

"You're right, Benjamin. Of course you're right. But I want to explain about last night. I want to tell you about what's been happening."

She was met with silence.

"Benjamin?"

"I'm going back to bed. I need to sleep."

"But what about—"

"If I get a chance, I'll call you later."

"But when are you coming home?"

"I don't know. A day or two. Maybe more. I have a lot of work to do down here."

"Benjamin—"

"I'm going back to bed." With that, he hung up.

Rebecca held the phone, listening to the whispered hum of a disconnected line, which was soon interrupted by loud beeps and then a recorded voice suggesting that she hang up.

She stared at the wall in front of her. The phone conversation had been like a dream, and she wondered whether it had occurred at all. She had certainly heard his anger before, but she had never felt him cut her off so completely. And that whole thing with him saying Jo. She was convinced that she had heard him correctly, and yet it seemed so important to him to prove that he had said no such thing. But that was so typical of Benjamin, always having to be right, always above anything that could be perceived as criticism.

Rebecca wondered what Benjamin was going to do, when he would call, when he would be home. She felt the frustration begin to mount, as though she were a well slowly filling with water. She had done nothing to deserve such treatment. For him to assume the worst, to not wait for an explanation, was a far greater crime than anything she had done.

As far as she was concerned, it was about time for Benjamin to start living up to the standards he imposed on everyone else.

⛈

Rebecca mixed the pancake batter in a medium-sized stainless steel bowl. She folded in the last egg and beat it gently into the rest of the ingredients. The trick to good pancakes, she found, was to mix the batter just enough, but not too much. For some reason, if the batter was whipped up too much, the pancakes turned out chewy, flat.

A pound of bacon sizzled in a large cast iron frying pan and filled the air with its sweet greasy smell of hickory and maple. In another pan, the potatoes browned evenly in hot oil. She grabbed a metal spoon and deftly tumbled them about the oil.

She grabbed another bowl and the carton of eggs. She picked out one, cracked it open on the edge of the bowl, and dropped in the contents. She repeated the process with five more eggs. Then she reached across the counter and grabbed a container of shredded Parmesan cheese and sprinkled it into the eggs. Next she picked up a small plastic cutting board, which held a pile of diced green onions, and brushed them into the bowl. She then took a carton of cream and poured some in with the eggs. Satisfied that her mixture was now complete, she whipped the ingredients together until the eggs felt smooth and frothy.

She was about to drizzle a few drops of water on the griddle to see whether it was hot enough when she heard a knock on the front door. She rushed out of the kitchen into the front entry and opened the door. Paul stood grinning while Stanley waited off to the side, looking a bit tired and apprehensive. Stanley's truck was parked in the driveway.

"Come in, come in." Rebecca felt enormously relieved to have the company.

Paul stood aside, waiting for Stanley to go in. The old man shuffled through the door. Paul followed.

Stanley looked around, acting noticeably awkward. "Should I take off my shoes?" he asked.

Rebecca looked down at his feet. "Your shoes? Oh no, don't worry about those."

Paul said, "Me too?"

Rebecca smiled. "You too."

Paul closed the door. "It smells great in here, Rebecca."

"I hope you're both hungry. I've got lots of food cooking."

"You've got to quit spoiling me like this."

"Well, if you'd rather not eat…"

Paul grinned. "I meant *after* we've had breakfast."

"I see," she said lightly. "But speaking of food, I need to get back to the kitchen before it all burns up. Let's go in there. We can visit while I cook."

Stanley and Paul followed her into the kitchen. She rushed to the stove and turned down the heat under the bacon.

"Have a seat," she said, pointing to the table. "We'll eat in here."

Stanley walked over to the table and sat down. Once he was situated in the corner, he seemed more relaxed. The table was at the far end of the kitchen, surrounded by large windows that looked toward the garden and campground in one direction and the driveway in the other. It was hard to believe that only a couple days earlier she had ventured into the campground, that she had helped pull Stanley out of the water. So much had happened since then—way too much too absorb—and all because she had decided to take a walk into the woods. To go where she had never dared go before. She wondered what it all meant, how she now found herself making breakfast for two men who just a few days ago she had never met.

"Nice place you have here," Stanley said. "And nice of you to be making breakfast like this."

"I'm glad to do it. I'm glad you both could join me."

Stanley chuckled. "Didn't look like I had much choice."

Rebecca feigned a mock sternness. "No, you didn't. Nobody messes with me."

Stanley whistled a low sort of hoot. "No ma'am," he said, "I bet they don't."

"You learn fast," Paul said.

"Years of practice."

Rebecca returned her attentions to the food.

"Hey, Rebecca," Paul said.

"Hey, Paul," she replied.

"Is there anything I can do to help?"

She looked around for a moment, unaccustomed to being offered a hand with her work. "Hmmm, let me see," she said. "I suppose you could set the table."

"I better just sit back here, out of the way," Stanley said. "I know better than to interfere."

Rebecca gave Stanley her stern look again. "I've heard that line before."

"And you'll probably hear it again."

Rebecca smiled. She thought Stanley was sweet and kind of funny.

She turned toward Paul and directed him to the dishes, glasses, and silverware, which he dutifully set out on the table. He placed everything in three neat settings. Forks to the left, knives and spoons to the right. He even folded the napkins and placed them atop the plates. As she watched him, she thought, he must be gay, which made her smile, not only because she had thought of something funny, but because she would never have had a thought like this before.

When Paul finished setting the table, he sat down across from Stanley. Rebecca stirred the potatoes, turned the bacon, added the eggs to a third frying pan, and ladled out several pancakes on the griddle. The smells and sounds of cooking food, the bright day outside, the visitors at her table, all made her feel warmer somehow, almost satisfied.

"So, Stanley," Rebecca said. "I should have asked you whether there was anything you didn't like—any food you wouldn't want to eat."

"No, ma'am," Stanley answered. "Anything you put out is okay by me."

"Hey," Paul protested, "how come you didn't ask me?"

Rebecca laughed. "You haven't turned down anything yet."

"Yeah, well…"

Stanley eased back into his chair. "Really, Rebecca, anything you make is fine."

"Me too," Paul added.

"I didn't ask you," she chided.

"I know." He pretended to pout.

Stanley chuckled. "I can hardly blame you, son. Who could refuse such gracious hospitality?"

"It wouldn't be easy," Paul agreed.

"Especially coming from such a pretty young lady."

"Hear, hear," Paul added.

Rebecca turned away. She could feel her face and scalp flush. Yet she didn't mind it, really. Coming from an old man and a, well, coming from Paul, she knew it was meant good-naturedly. And it was kind of flattering at that.

She turned her focus back to the food as she grilled more hot cakes and stirred the eggs one last time. Then she scooped everything out into serving dishes and placed the food on the table. Steam curled up from the plates and bowls. Before she sat down, she put out orange juice and apple juice, butter, and a pitcher of water. She was about to sit down, then realized she had forgotten the syrup. She hurried over to the stove and pulled a bottle out of a steaming pan of water and returned to the table and sat down.

"Okay, boys, dig in."

While Rebecca was handing the eggs to Stanley, she looked out the window. A car was pulling up behind Stanley's truck, green, nondescript, a large, four-door sedan.

"I wonder who that is," Rebecca said. Stanley and Paul turned toward the window as a very professional-looking woman—maybe in her early forties—climbed out and walked toward the front door.

"Go ahead and eat."

She left the kitchen and headed toward the hallway, reaching the front door just as the visitor knocked. Rebecca pulled open the door, and the woman jerked back.

"That was quick," the woman said.

Rebecca smiled. "I was in the kitchen and saw you coming."

The woman hesitated, staring at Rebecca as though she recognized her. "I'm sorry to bother you," she said, quickly gaining her composure. "Is this the Randall residence?"

"Yes, it is. May I help you?"

"I hope so." She took a small step forward as she pulled a wallet out of her jacket pocket. "I'm Detective Rosenberg. Detective Charlotte Rosenberg—from the Seattle Police Department."

Rebecca stared at the badge, not at all certain she was ready for another surprise.

And Baby Makes Three

"Are you sure you're up for this drive?" Nathan asked. "Are you sure this is what you want to do?" He glanced over Gabbie's head at Jo, who was squeezed up against the door so there was room for the dog.

"I'm sure, Nathan. Besides, look at what a beautiful day it is. A ride to the mountains is just the thing."

He opted to change the subject. "We could have put her in back," he said and nodded toward Gabbie. She looked back up at him accusingly and leaned up closer to Jo.

"Leave our little girl in back? No way. We're getting reacquainted."

"You weren't separated *that* long," Nathan knew this was one more argument he'd lose. "I think it's a conspiracy, that's what I think, that you two are out to get me. Girls against the poor defenseless boy. I'm surprised you're not making *me* ride in back."

"That could be arranged." Jo patted her stomach. "With any luck, we'll have a girl—then you better really look out."

Nathan groaned. "I'm a lost cause."

Nathan felt a little better this morning. Finding Jo and having her be okay had lifted his spirits, despite their ordeal in the hospital. After they had returned from Jo's ride in the back of the truck, the people at Admissions acted as though they had never heard of her. Jo's file had fallen through an electronic black hole, her record put on hold indefinitely, and no one seemed to be able to figure out what to do about either her file or her. As a result, Jo and Nathan waited in the admitting room for several hours, until she finally announced, "I'm starving," so they headed out for some breakfast and to let Gabbie out of the truck. When they returned to the hospital, the snafu had still not been cleared up, a new staff member sat at the desk, and Jo had to explain once more what was going on. After two more hours of waiting, Jo said, "We're leaving," which they did. They went to the Arboretum, spread a blanket on the grass, and took a nap. Afterwards Jo said, "I think we should go for a ride to the mountains and see how Stanley is doing," which, despite Nathan's protests, was now what they were doing.

r. h. sheldon

They traveled up Highway 2, following the same route Nathan had followed yesterday, when he had driven Stanley to his truck up by Index, up by his brother's house. What an odd coincidence that was. To think that Nathan should end up in this area, after what he had tried to do to Benjamin, seemed very strange indeed. But all he cared about was putting it all behind him. Of course, he would have to tell Jo about what he had done, and the sooner the better, and he knew she was going to be really pissed—and he hated the prospect of being the target of her anger, especially when he deserved it—but he knew too that the sooner he told her the better. But not yet, not quite yet—he wanted just a little more time to muster the courage he would need to face the inevitable storm.

Now he planned simply to enjoy the morning, to indulge her desire to come up here. But then they would need to get home. He had to start taking responsibility for his life, their lives, start pulling himself together. It would take a lot to drag them out of the hole they were in, but now that Jo was pregnant, now that her car was wrecked and her ability to work would be impeded in the immediate future by her bruised body—and later by her pregnant body—he had no choice but to do whatever it took to bring in the money. He didn't care if he had to work two jobs. If that's what it took, that's what he'd do. He'd make things right for them. He'd prove to her yet that he deserved to have her in his life.

When they reached Gold Bar, he turned off the highway and onto the street that Stanley lived on. Gabbie immediately popped up her head and stared intently out the window.

Jo said, "Someone acts like she knows where we're going."

"She fell in love with Stanley. He doted on her totally. She, of course, took full advantage of it."

"That's my girl," Jo said, as she patted Gabbie on the head.

When they reached Stanley's house, Nathan pulled into the driveway. "He's not here. His truck is gone."

Gabbie shifted excitedly from leg to leg.

"Where do you suppose he is?"

"Let's go up river to where he likes to fish. That's where we went yesterday, to pick up his truck. He said he might head up there this morning to see if he could find his gear."

"Is that where he fell in the other day?"

"Around there. It was getting pretty dark when we arrived, so we just sat out by the river."

"You sat by the river? You and Stanley?"

"Yeah, we just hung out and talked for a while."

Nathan tried not to glance over at Jo. He knew she was looking at him, but he didn't want to give himself away. The thought of talking to Stanley last night had reminded him of how he had cried and of his confession by the river, and suddenly he felt overwhelmed with guilt.

He put the truck in reverse and turned toward the back window, avoiding eye contact with Jo. She could read him so well that if he looked at her just then, it would be all over.

As he started to back out of the driveway, Gabbie grew more anxious and began to whine. "Sorry, girl," Nathan said, "but he's not home." He tried to keep his voice steady, grateful for the diversion.

"So how far we going?" Jo asked.

"I'd guess about ten miles. We follow the Skykomish River, until it splits, and then head up the North Fork, just past Index"

"Index?"

"The town. It sits in the valley, by the river, just as we're getting into the mountains."

"I forgot about that…" She spoke with a soft voice, as though waking from a dream. Nathan glanced over at her. "That's what she said, to come up to the mountains."

"Who said?"

"A woman in the hospital. I don't know who she was."

"She told you to come up here?"

"She told me to go to the mountains. This was after you and Stanley left, right after they moved me and I was waiting for a bed. A woman came up to me, an older woman, I think. There was something stately about her, almost regal. She told me I should go up to the mountains. I'd forgotten all about that. I was just thinking it would be nice to check in on Stanley before we headed home."

Nathan figured she'd been dreaming, but he went along with her anyway. "And why did she tell you to come up here?"

"I don't know."

They sped along the highway as it wound up into the mountains. The sky was clear, the sun bright, the air crisp, the forests lush and green. The road made a long sweeping curve to the right along the side of a mountain. The river flowed off on the left, and they could see it periodically through the trees. As they continued to curve around, Mount Index appeared in front of them, its jagged peaks a sharp contrast against the crystal blue skies.

"I haven't been this way in years," Jo said. "I forgot how incredible it is up here."

"It's pretty amazing. We came up here when we were kids. My grandfather used to own land up here."

"I can't believe how close we suddenly are to these mountains. They're so massive. I just want to run up one of these slopes."

Nathan smiled. "You bet, honey. I'll pull over and let you out. We'll wait down here."

"Bastard." She reached over and punched him lightly on the shoulder. Gabbie lifted her head, then lay it back down on Jo's lap. Everything back to normal.

When they reached the Index-Galena Road, Nathan turned left and followed it toward where he and Stanley had parked last night. They passed the bridge that went into the town, drove past several houses, and bored through a tunnel of trees. Nathan looked straight ahead as they passed his brother's house, until he reached the place where he had hoped to see Stanley's truck. Gabbie leaped to attention, her tail wagging, her ears up, eyes alert.

"Well," Nathan said, "I don't see his truck anywhere. Maybe he's already been here, or maybe he'll show up. Either way, seems a good time to stretch our legs, let Gabbie run around."

"Sounds like a plan."

Gabbie leaped out of the truck before Nathan was all the way out, knocking him to one side.

"Gabbie!"

She ran down to the river, pretending she didn't hear him. Jo giggled.

They followed Gabbie down to the water and sat on a couple of good-sized rocks. The river splashed loudly at their feet.

Jo watched Nathan for a moment, as though she saw something he didn't know was there. He pretended that he didn't notice.

"Okay, Nathan," she said, "what's been going on? What are you afraid to tell me?"

He looked at her with surprise, started to protest, but stopped. Then he spouted out, "I, ah, I…I," and stopped again.

She said nothing.

"I've screwed up," he finally said, "screwed up big time." Then he waited, not sure what he waited for. Jo waited as well, but he knew what she waited for, she waited for him to tell her everything.

"It's my brother," he said.

"Your brother?"

"Yes, my brother. Him and everything else."

And so he told her. Told her what he had never told her before, told her about his brother, about his parents, about being raised a Mormon, about how Benjamin inherited his grandfather's land and money, about how Nathan had received nothing. And then he told her about Beardsley, about the massage, about the pictures. And she listened intently, never saying a word, until he had said it all, until no words were left for him to mutter, no apologies unspoken. And when he had finished, he sat there waiting, waiting for her to say something, for her to do something. She stared at the river for the longest time. And then, with a heavy sigh and a slight movement of her head, she looked at him and said, "Well, I'll be damned."

A Step Backwards

Jo said nothing else for a moment, then jumped to her feet. "I'm going for a walk."

She began to climb the rocks up toward the road. Gabbie leapt after Jo, wagging her tail excitedly.

"Call her, Nathan. I want to be alone for a little."

Nathan whistled. Gabbie stopped and looked back and forth between Nathan and Jo.

"Go on," Jo said. Gabbie climbed down the rocks toward Nathan. Once the dog was down there, Jo turned away and headed up toward the truck.

The road was much quieter than down by the river and grew quieter still as it wound away from the water. She walked on the left shoulder, staring at nothing in particular. The forest grew thick on either side, the river a low rumble. Easier to think, in the hush of trees, away from Nathan, away from everything.

She wasn't sure how to react to his news. She supposed she should be angry. She had good reason to be angry—to be used in that way, an unwitting accomplice in this scheme—yet there was something humorous about the whole thing, about Nathan being drunk, going along with this plan, forgetting about it by the next morning. His involvement was so contrary to who he was, so opposed to the way he had always behaved, had always thought, that the whole thing seemed ludicrous, like a contrived plot out of a cheap mystery novel or something you'd see on daytime soaps. She didn't know whether she should laugh or cry, whether to yell at him or buy him a beer.

Part of her felt sorry for Nathan. Poor guy, never seemed to do anything right. He was so desperate to be successful in her eyes, to prove his worth to her, that he always ended up making things worse. And now he does this. She could hardly believe that he went along with such a cockamamie plan, even if he was drunk. That Beardsley must have been one hell of a smooth talker. She remembered seeing him, during the massage and after in the lounge, but she never suspected that he was anything other than some befuddled tourist with a brand new video camera.

What was the most interesting about all this was that it was Nathan's brother she had massaged. A man she had never met. A man she knew almost nothing about. When Benjamin had shown up at the spa the other day, his name had meant nothing. Nathan had not used Randall in years. When they had married, he had insisted that he take her name—McTavish—that he felt no pride in being a Randall and felt no inclination to carry on the family name. And even then, he said little else about his family. Today was the first time he said anything about his brother living in Index. And what made this even more intriguing was how taken with her Benjamin had been. She wondered what Nathan would think if he learned of Benjamin's little infatuation.

But that wasn't really the concern at this point. She figured she had two problems to contend with: how angry she should be at Nathan and how much damage he had done. With regard to the first matter, she simply wasn't sure. Of course what he had done was stupid. What could he have possibly been thinking of? Was he so drunk he lost all sense? Certainly that must have been the case. Yet she knew that even in his intoxicated condition he had done it out of love for her, no matter how misguided his intentions. But despite his intentions, what he had done was stupid, immature, and it could end up causing them a great deal of trouble. And if she thought about him sitting there, too drunk to think, agreeing to Beardsley's plan, she wanted to hit him over the head with a two-by-four. It was time for them to have a long talk about what they both needed and wanted, and where they were going from here. Of course, with the baby coming, their immediate futures were mapped out for them. They needed money and would have to do whatever it took to get it, that is, whatever it took short of blackmail.

Which brought her to the second problem—what damage might have been done. Nathan's big concern had been that this Beardsley guy would say something to her about Nathan's involvement in their scheme. But based on what Nathan had told her about Beardsley, she doubted her knowing would be enough to prevent him from going forward with this plan—and using Nathan in the process. All Beardsley would have to do is threaten to implicate Nathan in the scheme, figure out a way to let the police know what Nathan had been up to, without jeopardizing himself.

Jo stopped walking and heaved a deep sigh. The irony in all this was the fact that a simple massage and beer could have so many ramifications. Based on her limited knowledge of Mormons and her encounter with Benjamin, she had no doubt he would be mortified if those pictures and videos were made public. Benjamin Randall was an ambitious man, a man who took great pride in his reputation and standing in the community. If he were suddenly seen lying in just his underwear on a massage table, being rubbed by a woman, and then out with that woman in a hotel lounge, his reputation would be forever tarnished—at least in his eyes and perhaps the eyes of his peers and community—and what would by most standards be seen as inconsequential, would be to him a source of eternal shame and embarrassment.

Jo turned and started walking back toward where Nathan waited. It was clear that, regardless of what else was going on, taking care of this mess with Beardsley had to be their top priority; otherwise it would hang over them like a gathering storm. She supposed Nathan could simply deny all involvement, but she suspected Beardsley would be prepared for that outcome and had already figured out a way to ensure Nathan's cooperation. She might be mistaken in this, but they couldn't take the chance.

She strolled along slowly, only partially aware of her surroundings. And then she came to a small opening in the trees, where the sun streamed down with warm bright rays. She looked up and stared at the light, feeling the heat on her face, a warm glow that seeped into her bones and made her body glow. And that's when the idea came to her, pouring out of the light like a divine revelation. She stopped, letting her thoughts sort themselves out.

She then stepped forward lightly, until she was in sight of the truck. Gabbie, who stood near the tailgate, saw Jo and ran toward her in a bounding ball of fur.

"There's my baby," Jo called.

Gabbie nearly collided with Jo, her tail spinning, her mouth pulled up in a grin. She circled several times. Jo tried to pet her moving head and back, but the dog whipped around too quickly. Finally, she settled down and the two of them walked to the truck, Gabbie taking a dozen steps for every one of Jo's.

Nathan leaned against the cab, waiting for the pronouncement. Jo could see the apprehension on his face, the tight nervousness.

"Come on," she said, not betraying any emotions.

"Where we going?"

"To see your brother."

"My brother?"

"Yeah, I figured that since we're in the neighborhood, we should pay a visit."

"My brother?"

Jo grinned. "Come on, baby, get in the truck."

Gabbie leaped into the cab and Jo slid in next to her. Nathan stood next to her door as though trying to figure out what just happened.

"Let's go, dear. Might as well get this over with."

"Why are we doing this?" he asked. "Why do we have to go see Benjamin?"

"We need to find out what he knows, that's all. Find out if your Beardsley friend has talked to your brother."

Nathan winced. "And then what?"

"Depends on whether or not Beardsley has approached him."

"If he has?"

"Then we tell Benjamin we just found out about the photos. That's why we came to visit him."

Nathan shifted from one leg to the other. "I'm not sure I follow."

"We tell Benjamin that we found out he was going to be on Orcas and I wanted to meet him. You resisted the idea, but I was *persuasive*." She smiled. "You know how I can be…"

He nodded with a serious look.

Jo continued, "So you got Beardsley to help arrange the massage, you know, print the invitation, slip it under Benjamin's door, all so I could meet your brother under the guise of the massage. We tell him that I had not met Beardsley and had no idea of what he was up to, not till last night."

"Last night?"

"Yeah, when Beardsley told you about the photos and his plan to blackmail your brother."

"Oh, I get it."

"And we tell your brother that when we found out about it, we decided to tell him as soon as possible—after we told Beardsley that we wouldn't go along with it."

Nathan seemed to consider Jo's ideas. "Okay," he finally said. "It's a bit of a stretch, but still plausible, especially considering how estranged Benjamin and I have been over the years. But what if Beardsley hasn't talked to my brother?"

"That's simple. We tell Benjamin that we were in the neighborhood. I say that I didn't realize who he was until I talked to you and mentioned his name—then it all came together."

"And what if he asks about the invitation, about how come he received a massage?"

Jo had not considered this. The invitation could present a problem. She considered this for a while, and then said, "I suppose I could tell him that the resort does that sometimes for special guests."

"Think he'll buy it?"

"I don't know, he's your brother. But if he doesn't, we'll resort to the first story. I'll just say I was too embarrassed to admit it."

"And what about Beardsley? What do I say to him?"

"First, we talk to him together, so he knows that I'm aware of what's going on—but we never admit any sort of complicity. We tell him that we did it so I could meet Benjamin, that we had no idea he would try to blackmail your brother, and that if he goes through with this, we'll go to the police."

"Okay," Nathan said slowly. "Okay. This all sounds reasonable. I'm not sure how Beardsley will react, but it's worth a shot. At this point, what do we have to lose?"

He closed Jo's door, but stood there, looking nowhere in particular, the heaviness he felt apparent on his face. He finally walked to the driver's side and slid into the cab, squeezing up next to Gabbie. "Come on, girl, give me just a little room." She reluctantly scooted toward Jo.

He sat for a moment, looking ahead, then finally turned toward Jo. "Why are you doing this?" he asked. "Why are you sticking by me?" A sense of defeat had settled upon him.

She watched him for a few seconds, feeling his anguish, his sense of loss. And then she said, "Nathan, do you know why I fell in love with you? Why I still love you?"

He stared out the window.

"I fell in love with you because you were not like the others. You didn't try to smooth talk me. You didn't try to dazzle me with a lot of macho bullshit. Do you understand?"

He looked at her, his face taut, his eyes nervous. "No," he said, almost a whisper. "I don't understand."

"Listen, Nathan, I didn't want to be with some overgrown adolescent, self-centered, egotistical jock who defined himself by his maleness, by some masculine prowess that was forever jostling for position, seeking bigger and better, climbing some invisible mountain so he could always be at the top, always prove himself superior to anyone else."

Nathan said nothing.

"I didn't want someone like your brother! I wanted you—for who you are, not what I thought you could be. I wanted your realness, your humaneness. I wanted you because you could see and feel and touch. Because you could look at a sunset and be brought to tears. Because you could watch the ocean and get lost in its vastness. From the moment I met you, I knew you were different from the others. I knew that in you I could find something in myself I was losing. I knew that you had a soul, a spirit as great as these mountains. And by damn, I'm not going to let go of that!"

She reached over and touched his face, wiping away the tear on his cheek.

"Now let's go see your brother," she said. "Let's go give the bastard some hell."

Filling in the Pieces

Detective Charlotte Rosenberg pulled out of the driveway, glancing one last time at Rebecca Randall, who still stood in front of her house, a look of wonderment hanging on her face. Charlotte had seen that look before—on spouses, lovers, when they first discovered their significant others might have lives they knew nothing about. More times than not, another man or woman was involved, maybe several, and those left at home found themselves victims of deceptions and lies that might have been going on for years. And Rebecca Randall might very well be one of those women—the look on her face when she saw the pictures, with her husband receiving the massage, sitting in the lounge with this unidentified woman—feeling betrayed, shocked by what she saw, in total disbelief.

"But he's a good Mormon husband," she had told the detective. "A faithful member of the Church, a hard worker, a leader in the community. There must be some mistake."

All Charlotte could tell Mrs. Randall was that they didn't know anything definite yet. They found these pictures in the possession of a man who had been found dead, and they needed to talk to her husband. Until then, Charlotte could draw no conclusions.

She pulled onto the Index-Galena Road. As she was speeding up, she noticed a vehicle in her rear-view mirror, turning into the Randall driveway, an old pickup, light blue, like one of those small Toyota or Datsun trucks. She knew it wasn't Benjamin Randall's car. Mrs. Randall had told her he drove a white Ford Explorer. She doubted the visitor concerned her, but if her years of experience taught her anything, it was to remain suspicious of everyone, even people driving old blue pickups.

Despite her curiosity, she needed to get back to Seattle and find Benjamin Randall. The reaction of Mrs. Randall made her want to question him even more. An upstanding Mormon businessman, with a fair amount of money from what Charlotte could tell, would go a long way to protect his reputation, so the more Charlotte could find out about him, the better, and the place to start was with Randall himself.

She sped toward the highway. She'd make a few calls en route to try to discover whether Randall was at the Seattle condo, his office in Monroe, or somewhere else. Mrs. Randall had provided both numbers, but wasn't sure herself where Benjamin might have been right at that moment. She had spoken to her husband earlier that morning—only briefly—but had not heard from him since, and wasn't expecting him home that day.

Charlotte could see that Mrs. Randall had been uneasy talking about him. Perhaps the two had recently argued or things were not quite right at home. Charlotte was also aware that Mrs. Randall had guests in her house this morning—the detective could see them through the kitchen window—and now at least one more person was arriving. Of course, none of this meant anything by itself, but all details should be considered and carefully sifted through for clues.

Charlotte returned to her conversation with Mrs. Randall. There wasn't a lot there, really, just a confirmation that the man in the pictures was indeed the Benjamin she was looking for, and he had been in Seattle the night before.

"Mrs. Randall," Charlotte had asked, "do you recall what time Mr. Randall left here for Seattle?"

Rebecca had hesitated. "I'd guess about eleven-thirty, maybe a little earlier…"

"That's pretty late."

"He had—he wanted to get down there. I think he had some work to get done this morning—in the city."

"Did he say anything before he left, where he might be going?"

Again she hesitated. "No, I mean, I just assumed he was heading down to the condo."

Charlotte didn't push her too hard. She didn't want Mrs. Randall to feel so uncomfortable she'd close up completely. No doubt, Charlotte would have to come back to talk to her another time.

Charlotte said, "So he left here around eleven-thirty last night, and you spoke to him early this morning at the condo. Is that correct?"

"Yes, that's right. I woke him up. He wasn't happy—he was still asleep."

"And did he say when he would be back up here?"

"No—no, not really, only that he might be there for—I'm not sure. He'll probably call later and let me know…" Her hands shook, her lower lip pulled into her mouth.

The detective tried to move the interview in a different direction. "Mrs. Randall, you said that Mr. Randall had to work in the city this morning. Is that correct?"

"Yes, that's what he told me this morning."

"Does he have an office down there?"

"No, his office is in Monroe, but often he needs to run down to Seattle on business."

"He must go back and forth a lot."

Rebecca nodded. "He drives all over the place. If it's not Seattle, it's Everett or Olympia or somewhere east of the mountains."

"That must be tough, living way out here like this and having to drive so far all the time."

"Benjamin doesn't seem to mind it. He says he likes to drive. Helps him clear his head."

"And what about you?"

Rebecca looked surprised. "Me?"

"Yes, Mrs. Randall, I was wondering what you thought about it. How you liked living way out here." Charlotte wasn't sure what had prompted her to ask this. She supposed that she could justify it as being part of her job to understand the personal lives of the people involved in a crime, even though in this case there was no conclusive evidence that a crime had been committed—just some suspicious circumstances. And really, at this point, all she really needed to do was talk to Benjamin Randall. For all she knew, he had never met Beardsley and had never seen the pictures. Yet she was curious about Rebecca Randall, had felt a need to learn more about her.

Mrs. Randall answered slowly, "It's alright, I guess. I mean, I'm used to living in the country, and I have everything I need…I suppose sometimes it gets a little…but it's okay."

Rebecca reminded Charlotte of a lot of other women she had met, women who had suppressed their own feelings and desires for so long that they were barely capable of even hinting at them, let alone speak about them outright. Any discussions that focused too much on their own circumstances tended to be steered into other directions, toward inane talk of housekeeping, children, fashion, or memorable shopping bargains. Yet there was something different about Rebecca Randall, something that churned beneath the surface, as though she possessed a depth she intentionally kept hidden, a spark of insight and intelligence she dare not expose to anyone, even herself. Charlotte could see it in her piercing blue eyes, in the way she watched and listened, the manner in which she considered what was being said, what was being asked.

Charlotte decided to change the subject. "Mrs. Randall, does the name Beardsley mean anything to you?"

Rebecca looked at her blankly. "Beardsley?" She shook her head. "No, I don't think so."

"I have only one more question, Mrs. Randall, or rather, a request, and then I'll let you get back to your guests."

"My guests?"

"Yes," Charlotte said as she pointed toward the kitchen window.

Rebecca turned around. "Oh dear, I had forgotten…"

Charlotte reached into her pocket and pulled out a business card. "I just wanted to give you this." She handed the card to Rebecca. "If you talk to your husband, will you please give him my name and number and ask him to call me? It would be a big help."

Rebecca took the card. "Of course, I will. As soon as I hear from him."

Charlotte turned onto Highway 2 and headed toward Seattle. She figured it was just a matter of time before she talked to Benjamin Randall. Now that she had positively identified him and determined where he lived, the rest would fall into place.

It had been relatively easy to identify Randall. All she had to do was match the photographs to the picture and description used on his driver's license. Given that his name had been on the envelope, she simply had to look for those individuals with some variation of his name. Of course, it was always possible he had been from out of state or that the name on the envelope had not been the person in the pictures or the one seen in the parking lot, but the best approach was always to look in the most obvious places first. In most cases, this was where the solution lay.

Charlotte used her cell phone to check her messages. She then called the Randall condo. No answer. Next she dialed his Monroe office. A woman answered in a pleasant, friendly voice.

"Good morning," she sang. "You've reached the office of Benjamin Randall. This is Mandy. May I help you?"

"Is Benjamin Randall in?"

"No, ma'am. I don't expect him in the office today."

"Do you expect him tomorrow?"

"I'm not sure," she bubbled. "He's out of town, at a conference."

"A conference?"

"Yes, ma'am. Is there something I can help you with?"

Her perkiness made Charlotte want to vomit. "This is Detective Charlotte Rosenberg from the Seattle Police Department. I'm investigating a case and had a few questions I wanted to ask Mr. Randall. Do you know how I can reach him?"

"Can you hold just a sec?" Charlotte could hear the shuffling of papers. "Here we go," the receptionist said, pleased with her own resourcefulness. "He's staying at Richards Resort on Orcas Island. He'll be there through today, but I don't know when he'll be checking out or when he'll actually be getting back into town."

"If you hear from him, will you give him my name and number and ask him to call me?"

"I sure will," she chirped.

Charlotte supplied the information and hung up, relieved she didn't have to listen to that cheerfulness any longer.

She called Information and requested the number to Richards Resort, and was automatically connected. She asked the man who answered the phone if she could be connected to Benjamin Randall's room. She didn't expect him to be there, but it might help to confirm his whereabouts.

The man on the phone told her that Randall had already checked out.

"Do you know when he checked out?" she asked.

"I'm sorry, but I can't give out that information."

Charlotte identified herself. This sometimes worked, but sometimes didn't. In this case, it didn't. The man said, "I'm sorry, but I still can't give out that information, not without seeing proper identification."

Charlotte thanked him and hung up. She could hardly blame him. Still, it would have made her life easier. Now she would have to have someone at her office call the sheriff's office on Orcas Island and get someone from there to check this out for her. In the meantime, she'd return to her office in Seattle and see whether the Medical Examiner's office had turned up anything else.

The phone call to the resort did at least establish that Randall had been there. Yet Charlotte wasn't certain how Randall's visit to Orcas Island might fit into everything else that was going on. She felt fairly confident that Rebecca Randall had been telling the truth when she said that Benjamin left the house around eleven-thirty last night, but Charlotte had not asked where he had been prior to that. Perhaps Mrs. Randall's discomfort had something to do with the Orcas Island trip. Maybe he had gotten home not too much earlier and she hadn't wanted him to leave so soon, or perhaps he had surprised her by returning home early from his trip and she didn't like that. Or maybe she had been with him on the trip.

Whatever had taken place, it was pointless trying to guess. One thing at a time. Gather all the information, and then draw her conclusions.

She placed the cell phone on the seat next to her and eased back. As she cruised down the highway, she looked around for the first time. The Skykomish Valley had flattened into wide lush fields of grass. Horses and cattle grazed lazily. On the far side of the fields, the land swept up into steep slopes covered with trees. The sun shone brightly before her.

Charlotte had not been up here in a long time, not since she broke up with Lucy several years ago. They used to camp up here, not far from the town of Index. She had forgotten how beautiful it was up here, how much she enjoyed their getaways, how much she missed Lucy, her partner of eight years.

Charlotte had dated few times since then, and never did she date anyone more than once. Most women were uncomfortable with the idea of her being a cop, and she met few who could deal with her un-predictable hours, her commitment to her work, and her intense per-sonality. Most of the interesting women she met were already attached or straight, and the last thing she needed was to get involved with any-one in either situation.

Yet she knew she wanted something more in her life. She could feel the lack of companionship, intimacy. Her years as a cop had brought out a certain cynical bitterness, and although she loved her job, thrived on it, she yearned for someone who could turn her away from her work, who could help her regain her humanity.

The road curved up around a small hill and emptied into the town of Monroe. No doubt she would have to come back this way, either to see Benjamin Randall in his office or in his home. And she might need to talk to Rebecca Randall again.

The thought of seeing Mrs. Randall sent a small jolt of excitement through her. She didn't recognize at first what this excitement was about, but as she pictured Mrs. Randall standing outside of her house, her hair pulled back, her eyes bright and welcoming, Charlotte felt a sense of warmth that brought a smile to her face.

This is ridiculous, she thought. Rebecca Randall is part of an investigation. She's as straight as a ruler, married to a man who might be implicated in a crime, and who knew whether she was involved as well. Charlotte reminded herself that she was a professional, that she had a job to do and that job came first. But the image of Rebecca crept back into her thoughts, the fine blond hair, the thin strands of gray, the soft lines on her face. There was a kindness about her, a gentleness, and Charlotte knew that, more than anything else, these were the things she needed.

A Second Chance

Benjamin had tried to fall back to sleep after Rebecca's phone call, but had little luck. He mostly lay there, tossing from side to side, in much the same way he had spent most of the night. In fact, it hadn't been until shortly before the call that any sort of real sleep had taken hold, making Rebecca's interruption all that more unwelcomed.

And now he sat there, staring absently at the television, too tired to work, too keyed up to get any more sleep. The events of the last thirty-six hours were, at the very least, extraordinary, and he wasn't certain he could handle any more challenges. Right now, all he could do was try to sort out everything that had happened—getting the massage from Jo, meeting with the Council, arriving home last night, coming into the city, going to the hospital—and then, if there were any actions to be taken, he would take them.

He realized that, before he could do anything else, he would have to deal with the situation with Rebecca. When he had arrived home last night and found the two of them sitting there—in bathrobes—he nearly exploded. He had never felt so angry, so out of control, yet something inside of him drove him out of there, made him leave before he did anything he might regret the rest of his life. Still, there was something else in him that could have torn the two into pieces, and even now, if he dwelled too long on what might have taken place between them, the anger surged through him, like a boiler burning too hot and ready to explode.

But at least now he could step back a little, consider the situation, and if he applied a little logic to what he had witnessed, he could begin to entertain the notion that Rebecca's guilt lay in her poor judgment and not in her infidelity. Despite his frustrations with her, he had to admit she had always been a faithful wife, unerringly loyal. Still, little could excuse her behavior last night, and she had a great deal to explain when he got back there.

Benjamin decided to head home this morning. There was no way he was going to get any work done, and the sooner he took care of the

r. h. sheldon

situation with Rebecca, the better. The last thing he needed was for people to think there was trouble at home. Any impression of strife between him and his wife could have a direct impact on his standing in the Church and in the Council. It was bad enough that Rebecca was unable to produce children. He had to protect the main thing that he had going for him at home—a supportive, dutiful wife.

Benjamin showered, shaved, flossed, brushed his teeth, applied deodorant, and dressed in a clean pair of slacks and a shirt. The ritual of his morning ablutions helped to revive him and make the trip home seem less daunting. He threw his dirty clothes into his overnight bag and headed down to the garage. In five minutes, he was on the freeway, speeding toward home.

The drive toward Index was fairly routine. The worst of the morning rush hour was over, and once he crossed Lake Washington and was heading north Interstate 405, he was traveling opposite the main flow of traffic. He turned on the radio and listened halfheartedly to the news, but mostly he was thinking about Rebecca and what he had seen the night before. He tried to imagine the possible explanations that she might provide, but he simply didn't have enough information. He had no idea who the man was who'd been sitting there, and didn't know why they wore robes. He had no choice now but to wait to hear what she had to say. Whatever excuse she came up with, it had better be good.

As he drove through Monroe, he resisted the temptation to stop by his office. He didn't even plan to call in this morning, not until he got a few things resolved at home—and after he got some rest. For once, work could wait.

He followed Highway 2 toward Index. He must have driven this road a thousand times over the years. He had watched the development cut slowly into the valley, at a rate not nearly as fast as he had hoped, but fast enough to earn him a good deal of money from a variety of real estate transactions and land development.

Even so, a part of him was a bit sad to see how the area had changed. When he was a boy coming up here with his family, there was a lot less traffic and a lot fewer homes and businesses. Back then, even Monroe seemed the middle of nowhere, but now it was packed with strip malls, fast-food restaurants, gas stations, convenience stores, grocery stores, departments stores, traffic lights, stop signs, and an endless number of cars.

He and his family would drive up here to see his grandfather, his dad's father. No one in the family got along with the old man. A shrewd, unyielding businessman, he ruled the world around him with confidence and precision, controlling every situation until the day he died.

Benjamin had worshipped his grandfather, and growing up, he wanted nothing more than to be like him. Benjamin showed him a respect that was sincere in both affection as well as admiration. While the rest of the family saw time at Grandfather's house as a painful obligation, which was difficult to hide from the astute patriarch, Benjamin looked forward to the visits with great anticipation, an attitude not lost on the old man, and he too looked forward to Benjamin's visits. The grandfather came to trust Benjamin above all other family members. He was the one who taught Benjamin about business and investments, who encouraged him to go to college, and who paid for his education. Everyone in the family knew that Benjamin was Grandfather's favorite, and although they were generally relieved to have the burden lifted off of them, with regard to having to spend time with the old man, they were at the same time a bit envious of how Benjamin was able to reach his grandfather in a way no one had ever been able to do.

After Benjamin's grandfather had died and the will had been read, the envy had turned into a deep-seated resentment. Benjamin had inherited the land, the house, and the bulk of the estate, with only a relatively small portion provided to the rest of the family, each share with the provision that the recipient must be a participating member of the Church. Otherwise, that money would be donated to the LDS, and the potential recipient left out in the cold.

Everyone in the family qualified for their small share except Nathan, who told Benjamin that he and his grandfather and the Church could go fuck themselves. That was the last time Benjamin had heard from his brother.

But for Benjamin, the death of his grandfather meant more than a generous inheritance. On his grandfather's passing, Benjamin had felt the pain of loneliness and loss for the first time in his life. He had married Rebecca a few years earlier and had already made several shrewd land investments. His future looked bright, his prospects unlimited. Yet he had come to rely on his grandfather for a type of support and encouragement that he could get from no one else. His grandfather had been the rock in his life on which he could always hold steadfast, always look to for solidity and direction. His grandfather's death had shaken his world to the core, leaving a hole in his life that had never been filled.

Benjamin headed up the Index-Galena Road and followed it up to his driveway. He turned in and moved slowly toward the house, suddenly reluctant to be home. Then he saw the pickups, two of them, neither of which he recognized and both of which were in poor enough condition to make him seriously doubt the character of their drivers.

Benjamin stopped the Explorer near the trucks and jumped out. Now what was she up to? Every time she thinks he's not going to be around, she has a party!

He rushed up to the house and threw open the front door. Standing before him at the end of the entryway, with looks of surprise on all their faces, a small group congregated as though they were at a church social. Benjamin could hardly believe what he saw. Next to Rebecca stood his brother, Nathaniel, and next to Nathaniel stood Jo, the massage therapist he had met on Orcas Island. And across from Jo was the man from last night.

Benjamin stammered, "What the…" He looked from face to face, not sure what to think, how to react. "But what are you—" He turned to Rebecca. "What's going on…why are they…" He seemed incapable of forming a complete sentence.

Rebecca watched him for a moment. He could not quite describe the look on her face. It wasn't one of guilt or concern. And it no longer held any sort of surprise. Perhaps it was slight wonderment, mixed in with a bit of resignation and determination. He had never seen her look like this before, and he wasn't sure he liked it.

Finally Rebecca said, "Perhaps we should all go into the living room and sit down. I think we have some catching up to do."

Rebecca headed out and the rest followed, leaving Benjamin to wonder what had just happened.

"Come on, Benjamin," Rebecca called. "I think you'll want to hear this."

Wednesday Late Morning/
Early Afternoon

Those Darn Straight Folks

Paul wasn't certain what to do. Stay or leave. He didn't want to simply take off and leave Stanley, after insisting that Stanley join them, yet now that Benjamin had arrived, Paul was anxious to get out of there. He recalled vividly how Benjamin had erupted when he showed up at the house the night before, and that was not a scene he wanted repeated. Besides, Stanley evidently knew the couple that had just arrived, so he'd probably be fine if Paul left.

Yet Paul couldn't help but be curious about what was going on, as confusing as it all seemed—something about a massage, some photographs, a man found dead in Seattle, and Benjamin involved. This might be too good to miss.

Paul looked around the group. He wasn't the only one ill at ease. Rebecca watched the others as though waiting for a sign to direct her into action. Nathan shifted from leg to leg, not looking at anyone. Jo grabbed Stanley's arm and winked at him. He smiled back. Benjamin continued to stare at Nathan and Jo, as though trying to put the pieces together. Finally, Rebecca ushered them into the living room, including Benjamin, who seemed a bit put out by her taking control. No doubt he was quite unaccustomed to being *ushered*. Paul thought this would be a good time to leave, despite his curiosity. Besides, he could see that the wind was picking up and it was growing darker. He wanted to secure his campsite in case a storm blew in.

The change in weather surprised him. Just a little while ago, when he and Stanley had been sitting in the kitchen and Rebecca stood outside talking to her visitor, it was clear and calm. Of course, he was looking more at the visitor than at the sky. As soon as he saw her, he knew she was family, a full-fledged dyke who, if he were not mistaken, had a bit of an eye for Rebecca. He could be wrong, of course, not knowing the woman and watching her through the window like that, but Paul's intuition about these things was often correct, and he figured why not, if he were a lesbian, he'd find Rebecca quite attractive. Perhaps there was a closeted little Mormon dyke in there. Wouldn't that be fun.

"I wonder who that is?" Paul had said to Stanley.

"Never seen her before. Looks kind of mean to me."

Paul turned in his seat and shrugged. "Maybe," he said, and then stood up. "Think I'll rinse off some of these dirty dishes." He grabbed their plates.

"You're just trying to make me look bad."

"Me? Never."

"I might just get up and help. What do you think of that?"

"Okay." Paul sat down.

"In a minute, that is. I'll help in a minute."

Stanley started to pull a cigarette out of his pocket, then seemed to think better of it and stuck it back in.

Paul smiled and stood. "Okay, you jump in whenever you're ready." He carried the plates over to the sink, then returned to the table and grabbed dirty glasses and silverware and carried them over as well. He scraped and rinsed whatever dirty dishes, utensils, silverware, bowls, or pans that he could find and stacked them in the sink. He put food into the refrigerator, closed containers, straightened the counter, and wiped surfaces.

"You can come and do my house next," Stanley said.

"Only if you cook me dinner."

"Knew there'd be a catch."

Paul forged ahead on his cleaning mission. He wiped off the sides of cabinets, scrubbed stains off the stove, picked up dirt off the floor. This was nothing unusual for him, jumping in like this. He preferred keeping busy in unfamiliar situations. It helped to hide some of the discomfort he felt when he was around people he didn't know well. Stanley seemed like a nice guy and all, yet he was still a stranger. And really, even he and Rebecca didn't know each other that well, although what he did know he liked, despite the way she treated him the previous evening. So when he was around people like this, especially when there were more than one at a time—even though Rebecca was outside—he would sometimes feel overwhelmed, on the outside somehow, as though the others shared secrets he'd never be privy too.

Paul rinsed out the sponge and set it down by the sink. He looked over at Stanley. "Rebecca still out there talking to her visitor?"

"Yeah, no telling how long she's going to be tied up."

"I wonder if we should politely excuse ourselves."

"I was wondering the same thing. Maybe we should, let Rebecca off the hook."

r. h. sheldon

"Not much else I can do, anyway. But it's a shame to let all that food sit there, getting cold like that."

Stanley surveyed the table. "We better get out before she tries to feed us any more." He feigned a type of horror.

Paul was intrigued by the expressions on Stanley's face. He seemed capable of displaying the subtlest of looks. A slight movement of an eyebrow, a twitch of a lip, a glint in his eye, all revealing the playful, sharp mind inside. He had a certain mischievous impish quality, yet all the time maintaining his gruff exterior.

Paul always appreciated people who operated on more than one level, those with interior lives deeper and more expansive than what they showed on the outside, or at least what was readily apparent. Paul had found that it was often easy to miss the signs, to make assumptions about people without really looking inside. He was often surprised to find life where he might have thought that no life existed. Perhaps he would have perceived Rebecca as one of those lifeless ones if he hadn't met her under such extraordinary circumstances. He knew from the way he had seen her standing in the water, celebrating the sheer joy of the river, that she was a woman who possessed an interior life as vast as the Cascades. Yet if he had met her under normal circumstances, if he had met the good Mormon wife, maybe he wouldn't have seen the real Rebecca, wouldn't have felt the slumbering giant who longed to be wild and free and alive.

What an interesting few days, Paul thought.

Stanley began to stand up, leaning heavily against the table. He groaned and creaked and popped and turned red. "Okay," he said, gulping for air, "let's do it."

Just as they exited the kitchen, the front door opened and Rebecca entered.

"I'm so sorry," she said. "I didn't realize I was out there so long—all of this happening—" she stopped. "I need to talk to Benjamin—" She looked around. "What a day. What a week. Maybe we should go—" She stopped again. "Perhaps we could..." She looked toward the kitchen door. "Did you eat? Did you get enough breakfast?"

Stanley laid his hand over his belly and puffed out his cheeks to show how full he was. Paul was about to speak when there was a knock at the front door.

Rebecca gasped. "Now what?"

She spun around and hurried through the front hall. Paul could hear her pull open the front door and say, "May I help you?" He thought he detected at least two visitors talking, a man and a woman, but he couldn't understand what they were saying. At one point, Rebecca said, "It's you, the one in the pictures." Then more muffled voices, and Rebecca said, "Come in, come in, we can talk about it in here." And soon she and her guests appeared.

Rebecca said in a breathless voice, "Stanley, Paul, this is my brother-in-law, Nathan, and…I'm sorry, I didn't get your name—"

The woman said in a loud voice, "Stanley!" She rushed over to Stanley and hugged him and kissed him on the cheek. She had a small bruise by her eye and a bump on her forehead.

Stanley responded with a sort of delighted embarrassment, "Jo. Nathan." He grinned.

Jo hugged him again. "So what are you doing here? How you feeling? We came looking for you this morning. Gabbie can't wait to see you."

Rebecca stood with her mouth open.

Stanley chuckled. "How's that girl of yours doing, anyway? You're not still mistreating her, are you?"

Jo pointed a thumb at Nathan. "He is," she said. "Wanted to make her ride in back."

Nathan stepped up and shook Stanley's hand. "There's no defending yourself against Jo or Gabbie. You know how they are."

"I better stay out of this."

Paul could see how comfortable the three of them were around each other, as though they had known each other for a long time.

Rebecca said, "Your name is *Jo?*"

Jo smiled. "Yes, it is."

"That's the name Benjamin used. He said he didn't, but he did… this morning. He called me Jo by mistake…and then there were the photos." She spoke absently, as though thinking out loud.

"Yeah," Nathan said, "the photos, you mentioned those when we arrived."

"Yes, the photos. That's right. The ones the detective showed me. Detective Charlotte Rosenberg. From the Seattle Police Department."

Nathan stepped slightly toward Rebecca, his faces full of concern. Jo leaned forward. Even Stanley grew more attentive.

Rebecca said, "The detective was here right before you arrived. She had pictures of you and Benjamin, you were giving him a massage—" Paul could hear the discomfort in her voice.

"Yes, those were from the other day," Jo said. "I gave Benjamin a massage on Orcas Island. I'm a massage therapist at the resort where he was staying, but…but I didn't know about the pictures, I mean, not then…I didn't know that someone was taking pictures. But it was just a massage—at the spa where I work."

Stanley looked at Nathan as though asking a question. Nathan gave a quick nod, and Stanley seemed to relax.

Paul was sure he wasn't hearing the entire story, but he was so confused by everything he didn't know what to think. Whatever was happening, he had the feeling that Rebecca knew little more than he did.

Nathan said, "But why was the detective here? Why was she bringing you these photos?"

Paul could hear the strain in his voice.

Rebecca stared at him for a moment. "She said somebody died and these pictures were in his car. She said Benjamin's name was on the envelope that contained the pictures. She was trying to find Benjamin, and she asked me if I knew who the woman was—" She looked at Jo. "Who you were."

The front door flew open and Benjamin stomped in and marched through the hallway. When he saw everyone, he stopped dead, looking from face to face, a stunned glaze in his eyes.

Paul wasn't certain how afraid he should feel. After Benjamin's fierce display last night, Paul felt anything but safe. Yet Paul suspected that with everything else going on and with all those other people there, Benjamin would perhaps be too preoccupied to focus entirely on Paul's presence. Still, he would remain wary.

But all that aside, he needed to get back to the campsite, though he had to admit, it was all pretty damn intriguing. And now that the two brothers were together, Paul could see how similar they were in appearance. Both had the same dark features, the same intense eyes. And both of them very handsome men. Paul wouldn't mind at all being a sandwich between these two.

Before he had time to indulge too deeply into his fantasies, Rebecca announced that they should all sit down and figure out what's going on. She spoke with authority, control, and everyone else seemed happy to have some direction, except Benjamin, who appeared taken aback and still very much stunned by what was going on.

And that's when Paul decided to take off.

"Rebecca, I better get going. I left some stuff out at my campsite…"

"No, please stay." She seemed to be pleading. Paul said nothing, but followed the others toward the fireplace, waiting to see what would happen next.

If nothing else, Paul thought, this should be interesting.

A Family Reunion

Benjamin followed the others into the living room and sat in the chair near the far wall. He glanced out the window toward the river. The wind had picked up and thick clouds were spilling into the valley. He was surprised by this sudden change of weather. It had seemed perfect during his drive up.

Benjamin turned back toward the others. Nathaniel, Jo, and the old guy—who he recognized from somewhere—sat on the couch. Jo squeezed between the two men, her face a bit puffy and discolored. It was odd seeing Nathaniel here, after so many years without one word exchanged between them. And it was odder still that he should be married to Jo. Benjamin didn't know what to make of that, but it seemed too unlikely a coincidence that she should have given him the massage on Orcas Island.

He continued his scan of the room. The other man, the one from last night, sat in the chair near the far end of the couch, opposite from where Benjamin sat. He wondered if the stranger had been there all night, and wondered what Rebecca would have to say about all this. She sat near the fireplace, on the little stool he had built in his shop, unfazed by Benjamin's discomfort or the chaos that now surrounded them. Perhaps it was just shock.

The wind gusted against the house. He glanced outside, saw the trees bend and shake. The sky was growing darker still. Paul looked toward the window nearest him, concern wrapped across his face.

The phone rang. Rebecca jumped up and ran into the kitchen. In a few seconds, she came out with a puzzled look. "That was the detective. But the phone went dead before I could hear what she wanted."

"The detective?" Benjamin felt as though he were drowning.

Rebecca sat down, turned toward him. "I don't think you know everyone here. Well, you know Nathan, of course, and I take it you met his wife, Jo, when you were on your business trip."

Benjamin stared at Rebecca. What did she know, what did she think?

Rebecca continued, "And you met Paul last night briefly."

What was this game she was playing? How could she be so casual about last night?

"Paul and I were the ones who pulled Stanley," she pointed to the old man, "out of the river, which is how I met both of them."

Stanley said, "I don't remember that, of course. You might say I was out cold." He chuckled and Jo grabbed his hand and smiled at him. "But I remember you," Stanley said to Benjamin. "You were one of the developers who bought my ranch."

"Really?" Rebecca said.

"Yeah, we've had dealings before, but that's been a while."

That's why Benjamin recognized Stanley. Beautiful piece of property, which Benjamin obtained for a very reasonable price through some clever legal maneuvering. Benjamin knew what Stanley was thinking, that they had cheated him somehow. But it was strictly business, and it was a long time ago. And it wasn't as though Stanley didn't get anything for the ranch. The old man had made a tidy sum, in fact, a lot more than he'd be able to spend in what little time he had left.

Rebecca didn't say anything about the business deal, but instead looked toward Stanley and Jo and said, "But I don't understand how you two know each other."

Jo said, "We met in the hospital. Yesterday. Stanley started flirting with me."

Stanley protested, "I did not. I was merely admiring that fine hospital gown you were wearing."

"It *was* rather fetching," Jo replied. "Anyway, Stanley wooed me."

"It's been a long time since I wooed anyone. I think you just have a thing for old men."

"You're right, of course, look who I married."

Stanley and Jo laughed briefly. Nathaniel smiled, but Benjamin could see that he was too uneasy to join in the fun.

Rebecca said, "You were in the hospital as well? I hope everything's all right."

"I'm doing fine. I got banged up a bit in the car accident." She turned toward Benjamin. "That happened right after I gave you the massage. Maybe I shouldn't have let you buy me a beer."

Benjamin couldn't believe she brought that up, right here in front of his wife, in front of everyone else. He wanted to say something, try to defend himself.

He looked at Rebecca, but she watched Jo, smiling slightly, acting almost amused, and then she said, "To think, Benjamin getting a massage, and by his sister-in-law, no less." Rebecca acted completely unperturbed, as if she didn't comprehend any of the implications of what happened. She continued, "But I wish I had known it was you, Jo, when I saw those pictures."

"Pictures?" A desperate feeling welled up in Benjamin. He slid forward in his chair, about to stand, but thought better of it and just stayed at the edge.

"Yes, the ones the detective showed me."

"Yeah," Nathaniel said, "you started to tell us about that. You said someone died, that he had the pictures with him." Nathaniel looked as though he was about to be sick.

"That's right," Rebecca said.

"But she didn't say who it was, what happened?"

"No, Nathan, she mostly was looking for Benjamin, wanted to talk to him."

Benjamin stammered. "Pictures? Detectives? What's going on? Why didn't you tell me about this?"

The others looked at Benjamin as though they'd forgotten he was there.

Rebecca said, "A detective from the Seattle Police Department stopped by here a little while ago, looking for you." She hesitated. "A man died in Seattle. He had an envelope with your name on it and with pictures inside."

Benjamin shifted uneasily. "Pictures? Of me?"

"Of you and Jo. She was giving you a massage. Then you were in a lounge."

"But how…how could that be?" He could feel the blood drain from his face.

Jo leaned forward. "I'm guessing it was that chubby tourist who interrupted the massage. Remember? We also saw him wandering around the lounge."

Benjamin nodded.

Jo seemed to choose her words carefully. "And remember he was carrying a video camera, kind of walking in circles?"

He nodded again. He felt his guts twist tighter.

"Anyway, he made pictures of you and me."

Benjamin felt the panic rise. "But how? Why?" He wanted to scream.

Nathaniel grew even more uneasy, Jo more alert. Even Stanley acted more attentive, as though his large ears perked up, like an old dog stirred from his afternoon nap.

It was apparent that Jo and Nathaniel knew something, that each considered what to say next. It was also apparent that Rebecca was as much in the dark as Benjamin. Except for the visit by the detective, she knew nothing. She sat with a look of expectation, uncertainty. Paul displayed a mixture of curiosity and restlessness, as though he wanted to know what was going on but would have at the same time preferred to be far away.

Finally, Nathaniel said, "I'm afraid that it's—"

"—that it's my fault," Jo said.

Nathaniel looked at her. "What?"

"I might as well tell him."

"But I don't—"

"Benjamin," Jo said in a stern voice, while giving Nathaniel a look that strongly suggested he shut up, "I was the one who brought all this on."

Benjamin said, "Brought what on? I still don't understand."

"If you would let me explain." Her tone reminded Benjamin of how she sounded when he had met her two nights ago, condescending, confident, putting him in his place with an ease that seemed designed to leave him feeling off-guard.

"I'm sorry," he said, "I was trying to…" He stopped. Rebecca glanced at him. Could she see how intimidated Jo made him feel? He felt exposed to her and everyone else in the room. And he hated it.

Jo continued, "Nathan received a letter from your parents that mentioned you would be on Orcas Island. I decided I wanted to meet you, but Nathan didn't think it was a good idea." Nathaniel began to protest, but Jo ignored him. "So I suggested we arrange the massage. That way, I could meet my brother-in-law, but not create any family tension."

"So you knew who I was when you gave me the massage?"

Jo hesitated. "Yes, I knew."

"And the guy who took the pictures? You knew him too?"

Nathaniel nearly jumped out of his seat. "No," he said, "she didn't know him, I did. I met him on Orcas. He helped set up the massage. Made the invitation. Delivered it to your room."

"But it was my idea," Jo added quickly. "I insisted that Nathan help set it up. I never thought any harm would come of it. It all seemed just a bit of fun."

r. h. sheldon

Benjamin considered what they were telling him. He could well believe she could come up with something like this and convince Nathaniel to go along with it, but he had a hard time accepting that she knew who he was when she gave him the massage. Something didn't sound quite right, but he had no way of proving it, at least not yet. In the meantime, he would go along with their story, pretend he believed them.

Benjamin finally said, "So who's this guy who took these pictures?"

Nathaniel answered. "His name is Beardsley. I don't know his first name..."

Rebecca looked startled. "Beardsley? Did you say *Beardsley?*"

They all turned toward her.

"I think that's the name the detective said. I think that's who she asked me about."

"You mean he was the one who died?" Nathaniel's eyes grew wide, afraid.

Rebecca thought about this. "No, she didn't say he died, at least I don't think she did." She sighed. "Now if I could only remember..."

"Try, Rebecca," Benjamin said.

"I *am* trying, Benjamin." She closed her eyes for a moment. When she opened them, she said, "No, that's not what she said. Near the end of the interview, she asked me whether I knew a Mr. Beardsley. I said I didn't, and that's all she said about it."

Jo said, "We didn't know anything about the photos, Benjamin, not until..."

"Last night," Nathaniel said. "Not until I saw him at the hospital and he showed me the pictures and told me what he had in mind."

"But Nathan would have nothing to do with it," Jo added.

"What he had in mind?" Benjamin stood and paced nervously around the chair.

"I was too busy looking for Jo to be bothered with Beardsley. Besides, he was too drunk to take seriously. I figured that once he sobered up, he'd go away."

"And really," Jo said, "who would have thought that giving someone a massage would be a big deal. People get massages all the time."

Everyone was silent. The wind howled. Rain blew against the window.

After a minute, Paul asked the question all of them were no doubt wondering. "So the guy who died could have been Beardsley, right?"

No one said anything at first, and then Rebecca spoke. "She didn't say it was Beardsley. She didn't say it wasn't. She didn't say much of anything about the dead man, only that he died and that he had the pictures with him. And she asked for Benjamin. I assumed because his name was on the envelope."

Benjamin felt the tension in his back, his neck. He sat back down and said, "Did she ask anything else?"

"She asked if that was you in the pictures, and if I knew who the woman was." She glanced over at Jo.

"And that was it?"

Rebecca started to nod, then stopped. "Oh, yeah, there was one other thing. She asked about where you were last night, what time you left the house?"

"She asked where I was? That doesn't make sense. What did you tell her?" He felt ready to explode.

"I told her the truth, that you left here about eleven-thirty and that I talked to you at the condo this morning.

"And that's all?" He looked at her, then Paul, then back at her.

"Yes, Benjamin, that was all I told her. I didn't tell her how you jumped to unfair conclusions, how you blew up, how you stormed out of here in a fit of anger."

He felt attacked, without friends, allies. "That's not what I meant. I only wanted…" What was the point? He could never talk to her about anything.

A flash of lightning lit up the room. Thunder rocked the house. Hail shot out of the sky and pounded the roof and walls and spit against the window like the rapid fire of a machine gun.

"Gabbie!" Jo yelled.

Rebecca and Paul both said, "What?"

"Gabbie, our dog. She's in the car. She'll be terrified." She turned to Nathaniel. "We should get out of here, before it gets any worse."

Stanley said, "I should probably get going too. You can come over to my house. Bring Gabbie with you."

Another explosion of thunder. The house seemed to jump on its foundation.

"No one is going anywhere in this weather," Rebecca announced. "Nathan, run out to the car and get your dog and bring her in."

Jo and Nathaniel both protested, but Rebecca stopped them short. Nathaniel ran out of the room. Benjamin could hear the front door open, the howling of the wind, the pelting of hail. "Jesus!" Nathaniel bellowed.

Benjamin glared at Rebecca. He couldn't believe she told them to bring their dog in here. She knew how much he hated dogs. Then, to make matters worse, she turned to the others and said, "Would any of you like hot chocolate?"

The front door flew open. The storm echoed through the house.

"Christ almighty," Nathaniel yelled. "It's unbelievable out there." The door slammed shut. "Gabbie, wait! Come back here. Let me wipe you off."

After a minute, the dog leapt into the living room, her tail wagging, her mouth in a grin. Nathaniel followed behind her, wiping water off his head and arms. "I've never seen it rain as hard as that. It's amazing." He tossed the towel back in the hallway.

When Gabbie spotted Jo, she raced across the room and howled excitedly.

"How's my baby?" Jo said and pulled Gabbie's head into her lap and started rubbing it.

Benjamin watched, but said nothing. Animals belonged outside, and the intrusion of one in his home was as disquieting as having his brother suddenly appear. And watching the dog with her head in Jo's lap heightened the insanity even more. He was reminded of lying on the table, her thighs inches from his face, the sense of excitement that propelled him into the situation he now found himself. And Jo seemed oblivious to the effect she had on him. They all seemed oblivious, except perhaps Rebecca, who had caught him watching Jo. She acted as if she hadn't, yet she had a look in her eyes that suggested perfect understanding.

Gabbie lifted her head and looked at Stanley, noticing him for the first time. She barked happily and scooted toward him. She sat up and placed her paws on his legs, then began to lick his face.

"Gabbie, get down!" Nathaniel called.

Gabbie ignored him.

Stanley grinned as he rubbed her neck. "It's okay, Nathan," he said, "women always behave like this around me."

The others smiled, except Benjamin, who found this kind of talk—and the whole scene—appalling.

Jo said, "Looks like our girl has got herself a boyfriend."

"I told you," Nathaniel said. "She fell in love immediately."

Rebecca glanced around the room. "Look how dark it's gotten." She stood and walked from lamp to lamp, turning each one on. Gabbie leapt up and began following her. "Now there's a good girl," Rebecca said and pet her head. Gabbie wagged her tail enthusiastically.

Just when Rebecca—along with Gabbie—were about to go into the kitchen, another bolt of lightning exploded outside. The thunder was immediate, letting out a roar that shook the house with a brutal force. The lights flickered and died. Gabbie ran back to Jo, her tail between her legs. The house seemed darker than ever, and the light from outside was more the light of evening than the middle of the afternoon.

"Oh dear," Rebecca said.

Benjamin rose. "That was close. I better see what damage there might have been."

"And I better pull out the candles and flashlights."

Suddenly there was a loud banging at the door, rapid, heavy, like the sound of a battering ram.

"Now what?" Benjamin yelled, and he and Rebecca raced toward the front hall.

Matters of Life and Death

When Charlotte had been pulling into Monroe, after leaving the Randall's home, her cell phone rang. She hit the talk button. "Hello, Gavin," she said and pulled into a parking lot so she could write down what he said. After she parked, she glanced toward the east and saw a concentration of dark clouds.

"And how's my favorite lesbo cop?"

"Just dandy," Charlotte answered, "and how's that little faggot husband of yours?"

"Pissy. I wouldn't put out last night, so he punished me by not talking when we got up. It was the most peaceful morning I've had in months."

"Time for separate vacations."

"You're telling me. We can't even agree on that. All he wants to do is go to queer playlands—Palm Springs, Key West, P-Town. Me, I prefer a break from the scene."

"Maybe I can beat some sense in him."

"Oh, baby, I love when you talk butch like that."

"It's how I get what I want from you."

Charlotte had met Gavin when she first made detective. He worked in the Medical Examiner's office. From the start, they had each other figured out and soon developed a bond that helped them survive the sense of alienation they felt working in their respective fields. When she was still with Lucy, the two of them would often spend time with Gavin and his partner, Curtis, going to movies, dining out, taking hikes. One time the four of them went camping up near Index. Charlotte and Lucy split wood, built fires, and hauled water. Gavin and Curtis cooked the meals, washed the dishes, and supplied the music. The perfect arrangement, one they had laughed about for years afterwards, until Charlotte and Lucy split up—and Charlotte made it known to Gavin that she preferred not to talk about her relationship or the past.

Charlotte now asked Gavin, "So what've you got for me?"

"Other than my undying love and devotion?"

"Yeah, other than that."

"Well, not a whole lot, I'm afraid. Guy's name was Francis Michael Beardsley, originally from Chicago, but he's lived all over the Northwest. Called himself a private detective—he was even licensed—but looks like his specialty was more along the lines of extortion and blackmail."

"Sounds like a charming fellow."

"Reminds me of the guy I dated before Curtis."

"What else you got?"

"He'd been dead only a short time when we found him, hour tops. Hit in the head with something hard, like a rock—or his head hit the rock. Hard to say."

Charlotte jotted down a few notes. "Find the object?"

"Not yet, but we're going back shortly, take advantage of the daylight."

"So maybe he fell, maybe he was hit."

"That's about it, except that he had a fair amount of alcohol on board."

She wrote "alcohol," circled it, and then said, "So we have a drunk who might have fallen or might have been hit. We know he'd been arguing with someone in the parking lot before his *accident*. And we know the time of death coincides with Williamson's account. We just don't know whether we have a crime."

"We have the photos."

"Yes, those photos, and if I ever find Randall, I might get some answers about them." She tried to assess the information she had just heard. There simply wasn't enough to go on. "Anything else?"

"Animal hair."

"Animal hair?"

"Yeah, maybe dog hair. A few strands, on his clothes."

She pondered this. "Well, there was the Williamson's dog. A white poodle."

"It wasn't the poodle. We found his prints near Beardsley, but none of the dog's hair on him. There was another pair of dog prints close by, but nowhere near the body. And the only other footprints down there belonged to Beardsley and the witness."

"Which means he was near another dog—or animal—but not down there."

"That's right."

"He could have picked those up anywhere," she said absently. "What color are they?"

"A kind of yellowish, some an off-white. We'll check into this further and see what we come up with."

"Okay, Gavin, thanks. This at least is a start, but even if Randall is somehow involved, I suspect we have little here that we can prove. Randall's a hotshot land developer, and the DA's not about to touch this without something a lot more conclusive. Christ, we don't even know if we have a crime. I hate this type of case."

"I like to think of it as a challenge."

"Okay, Pollyanna, you do that."

"Please, Ms. Rosenberg, I've asked you not to address me by my drag name when I'm at work."

"On that note, I'm out of here."

"Bye, my darling."

"Bye, Gavin. Give Curtis a hug."

She hung up and looked through her notes for the Randall number, and then she called their house. Rebecca answered in a hurried voice. "Hello."

"Mrs. Randall?"

"Yes," she said rapidly.

"This is Detective Rosenberg again. I had one more question."

The phone snapped and hissed. Rebecca said something, but Charlotte couldn't understand what it was. She proceeded anyway. "Do you and your husband have a dog?"

Again the answer faded into static.

Charlotte tried again. "Mrs. Randall. Have you heard from your husband yet?"

The phone buzzed, hissed. "He's right here," she said. "He just got home."

Charlotte wasn't sure whether she would be heard, but said in a loud voice, "I'll be right there."

The line went dead.

The Tempest

Charlotte turned onto the Index-Galena Road and headed toward the Randall home. The sky in front of her looked almost too ferocious to continue. Yet she didn't want to pass up the opportunity to talk to Benjamin Randall directly, and if she could catch him at home—where he might be less likely to be distracted by work or anything else—so much the better. Besides, how bad could the storm get?

A gust of wind slammed against the car and let loose a torrent of rain. She flipped on the wipers, but they did little good against the fierce downpour. She crept forward. A bolt of lightning seared the air. Off to her left, the churning river swelled against its rocky banks.

She should turn around, or at the very least park until the storm had subsided, but she couldn't see any place safe enough to stop. Besides, she wasn't about to let a little storm slow her down.

The rain and wind worsened the closer she got to the Randall home. Limbs fell, blew across the road, littering her path with branches and leaves. Icy pellets pounded her car. The sky flashed with light. An endless thunderous roar echoed across the valley. She drove through deep puddles, her knuckles white, her teeth clenched. She hated these storms, hated the way they slowed her down, hated the way she felt attacked, as though she were the reason for them.

She drove further. Lightning shot through the air in a bolt of white light, snapping against a giant cedar twenty yards ahead. The tree exploded in a fountain of sparks. She slammed on the brakes. The shattered trunk teetered on its foundation, then fell toward the ground, hitting in a roar of broken branches and cracking limbs and leaving only a cloud of smoke.

She jumped out of the car. In seconds, the icy rain had soaked her clothes, as hail pounded her head and shoulders. She ran to the downed cedar. It had fallen directly across the road, blocking her access to Randall's as well as Randall's access to civilization. Even in this weather, she could smell burnt wood. She raced to the other side of the road, toward

r. h. sheldon

the top of the tree, to see whether there might be any way around, but as she got closer, she could see that it had fallen into a creek, directly on a beaver dam. Water now gushed through the dam, flowed beneath the log, ran along the edge of the road, and raced across a low spot in the pavement several feet behind her car, a spot deep enough to prevent her from driving in that direction as well.

She headed back toward the car to radio for help. When she was only a few yards away, lightning struck the roof and exploded in a wave of sparks that blew out the tires and erupted in a wall of steam from beneath the car. She fell flat on her back and could hear nothing but a loud ringing. She waited for the noise to subside, her clothes soaked beyond redemption, then pushed herself upright and walked slowly to the car. The rain washed away the steam quickly, and she could see the dark singe mark on the roof. When she was near enough, she touched the door carefully to see whether it was hot, but was surprised by how cool it actually felt. Still, she was very cautious when opening the door.

The inside of the car looked fairly normal, except for the dashboard. All the displays were discolored and the microphone wire melted. When she tried to turn the key in the ignition, nothing moved. She switched on the headlights, but they didn't work. She slammed the door closed. Her only option was to head to the Randall house.

Charlotte hobbled toward the fallen tree. She felt cold, dizzy. The rain poured in unrelenting sheets, mixed with large chunks of hail that pounded her head and face and body. Her shirt stuck to her skin like a layer of ice, and the wind pushed her so hard she was afraid she would topple over. She struggled over the tree. A limb snagged at her legs and ripped her pants. Blood seeped from the exposed skin, mixed with the rain. She climbed down the other side of the trunk. As she touched the ground, she slipped and fell forward and rolled across the pavement. She tore her sleeve and was covered with small rocks and sand and leafy debris.

Hail continued to pound her head and her shoulders. She held up her hands as a shield, but got little relief. The wind gusted, knocked her sideways, into a tangle of blackberry bushes. Her face and arms grew bloody from the scratches, diluted by the pouring water. She tried to stand, but the tangled thorns and blasting wind made movement all but impossible. She sucked in a deep breath and pushed herself out of the snarled branches, crawling back onto the road. She struggled to her feet, but didn't know how long she could keep herself upright.

Lightning struck again. Twenty yards away. Maybe closer. An alder exploded. For an instant, the top of the tree hovered in place, then fell in slow motion in the direction opposite from where she stood, clamoring against the trunks of other trees, ripping off branches, splintering wood. She felt even more lightheaded, her equilibrium out of whack, her ears ringing worse than ever. She gasped for breath. Her shivering grew more violent, her chattering teeth ready to crack inside her numb and icy face.

There was something strange about this storm. Stranger than most. She seemed to fight against a formidable enemy, an unseen foe, as though every time she exerted effort, her enemy exerted more. She was reminded of her childhood lessons in Hebrew school, of stories about a vengeful God, suffering believers, faithful martyrs. Out of all these stories, the one that stuck with her the most was the story of Job. Despite the interpretations and explanations, she could never grasp why God would let all these terrible things happen to Job simply because Satan had issued a challenge. Here was this righteous man, a true believer, a really good guy, and God lets Satan strip Job of his wealth, afflict him with disease, kill his seven sons, all so God could prove a point. Why?

A light flashed above her and she looked up. In the blinding rain, all she could see was the vague outline of blowing trees. Another flash gave way to the low haze of clouds and then to something more, a vague image, a face looking down upon her, a face from childhood memories, from books and lessons, from the countless pictures she had seen, dancing among the clouds, like the face of Job, gazing upon her battered body, his mane of white hair and long snowy beard wrapped in the clouds, swirling around in the stormy winds. And then he was gone.

She tried to wipe her eyes, blinked repeatedly, but she saw only rain and hail and the bending trunks of giant trees. Whatever she had witnessed, whatever she had imagined, was gone, as though it had never existed, like a flash of lightning, quick, unreal, uncertain, and now all she saw was what she would expect to see. And she realized how exhausted she must be, how depleted. She wanted to drop to the ground, to give in to the storm, quit the struggle. But she drove herself forward.

She stumbled onto the Randall driveway, gasping for air, for warmth, for the strength to continue. When she saw the Randall house, she pushed on with her last bit of strength. The wind whipped fiercely off the river. Branches fell from trees, hit against her head, her shoulders. She waved at them weakly, as though she tried to drive away a swarm

r. h. sheldon

of flies, but even that she could not maintain as she stumbled forward, up to the front entrance. With her last bit of strength, she banged on the door, over and over. Suddenly it popped open, and there stood Rebecca and Benjamin. Rebecca waved her in. Charlotte stumbled into the front hall, stood for a moment, shivering, dripping, looking around absently. She felt dizzy, sick, ready to faint. Then she dropped to the floor in a heap of soaked clothes and water and mud and blood.

Riding Out the Storm

After the power failed, Paul rose from his chair and stood by the window to the left of the fireplace. The sky was thick with dark gray clouds, lit up only by the occasional flash. The rain fell so heavily it was like looking through a waterfall, and he could barely make out the trees rocking and bending, as if the piercing howl were not enough to tell him exactly how bad it was. He leaned closer to the window and tried to see the river. It was nearly impossible to make out, despite its proximity to the house. But he still caught enough of the raging current to see it was rising quickly.

And then he heard the pounding on the front door. Rebecca and Benjamin ran to hallway. The sound of rain and wind grew louder. Rebecca yelled out something, but the storm washed out most of her voice. Then he heard the front door slam shut and Rebecca shout his name.

Paul ran toward the hallway, but it was dark and at first he couldn't register what he was seeing. Then he realized someone sat on the floor, between Rebecca and Benjamin.

"Jesus," he said. "What next?" He wondered how many more surprises he could take.

Rebecca spoke frantically. "It's the detective, Charlotte Rosenberg."

"She's pretty banged up," Benjamin said, "full of scratches, bruises—and she's soaked."

The detective tried to speak, but she breathed too hard and shivered too much for her words to be understood.

Paul hesitated only a moment. "Let's get her by the fire and get her dry. Benjamin, how about we help her into the living room. Rebecca, would you grab some blankets and towels."

Rebecca ran into the kitchen. Paul and Benjamin helped Charlotte stand up and then got on either side so she could drape her arms around their shoulders. Her skin felt wet, icy, her arms smeared with blood and mud. Paul's clothes soaked up the water, the chill passing quickly from her body to his. They walked her into the living room and helped to support her as they she stood on the tile in front of the fireplace.

Rebecca entered with an armful of towels and blankets.

Paul said to the detective, "We've got to get these clothes off you and get you dry."

"Why don't you let Jo and me help her," Rebecca said.

Paul felt relieved, but then felt guilty by this sense of relief. Still, he wouldn't argue with Rebecca.

Rebecca said, "Do you feel strong enough to stand on your own?"

The detective nodded weakly.

Paul and Benjamin let go as Jo and Rebecca stood nearby to make sure she could stand. Paul and the other men stood over by the hallway, keeping a discrete distance.

A shiver ran through Paul. Even from that brief exposure to the wet and cold, he felt chilled. The detective must be frozen to the core. He knew exactly what that felt like.

The women worked deliberately and quickly to undress and dry Charlotte. Occasionally, Paul would catch a glimmer of white pasty skin and her shaking body. Rebecca piled the wet clothes off to the side, on the tile near the fireplace. Jo set a holster and gun next to the clothes, leaning them carefully against Charlotte's boots.

Rebecca wrapped a blanket around Charlotte, then she and Jo helped her to the couch. Rebecca insisted that she lay back and rest. Charlotte tried to resist, but had almost no strength.

The men returned to the main part of the room.

"How's she look?" Benjamin asked.

Jo said, "A lot better now that we have her cleaned up a bit. Some cuts and bruises, but I don't see anything too serious."

Rebecca added several more blankets, tucking them up around her chin.

Charlotte whispered, "You're an angel…"

Rebecca smiled. "I just know what it's like to be cold and wet." She glanced at Paul.

Even with the blankets, Charlotte still shivered. "Benjamin," Paul said, "any way to crank up the heat on the fireplace?"

Paul wasn't sure how Benjamin would react to a request from him, but Benjamin seemed to welcome the distraction. "Yeah," he said, "there's a valve under here." He bent down at the foot of the hearth and turned a dial. The flame brightened the room a little. Paul welcomed the heat and the light.

"How you doing?" Rebecca asked.

"I'm okay." Her voice was thick, raspy. "Must have been overcome with exhaustion, but I'm already feeling better."

"You know," Benjamin said, "we can still use the stove. Maybe we can make something hot for her to drink."

Charlotte started to protest, but Rebecca paid little heed and said, "How about some broth? I've got bouillon in there." Rebecca turned to the others. "If you could keep an eye on our patient, I'll go make some up. Paul, could you help me in the kitchen?"

Paul was about to reply, when Benjamin said, "I can help."

Rebecca snapped her head around. "Really?"

He looked down. "Yeah, come on. We should get some candles and flashlights while we're in there."

"Okay," Rebecca said, her voice skeptical. And then to the others, she said, "We'll be right back."

They disappeared into the kitchen. Gabbie followed. Benjamin looked as though he were about to say something to the dog, but held back. It was obvious to Paul that Benjamin wasn't a big fan of dogs. He avoided touching the animal, avoided letting any part of her touch him.

Paul moved closer to Charlotte. He wasn't sure what to do at this point, so he asked the only thing he could think of. "You think you're okay? Did you take any falls, get hit with anything?"

"I took lots of falls and got hit with everything the wind could throw at me…" She smiled. "But I'm fine, just a little worn out."

Nathan said in a low voice, "Hey Jo, maybe you and I can wring out these clothes and hang them up so they start drying." He never looked in Charlotte's direction.

Jo said, "Perhaps Rebecca's got something we can hang these on. Otherwise they'll take forever to dry."

Nathan grabbed a towel and laid it on the floor, then the two piled the wet clothes on top of it.

"What about this?" Jo asked, as she held up the gun and holster.

Charlotte sat up in panic.

Jo, seemingly unperturbed, grabbed another towel, wrapped it around the firearm, and handed it to Charlotte. "You'll probably be more comfortable having this with you," she said. "Careful though, it's pretty wet." Jo then handed Charlotte her a wallet. The detective seemed to relax.

Jo scooped up the clothes and she and Nathan headed into the kitchen. Paul could hear them talking to Rebecca and Benjamin. Paul then realized that Stanley, who had been standing off to the side, now pushed around a towel with his feet, trying to soak up the water left from the clothes.

"That's quite the technique you've developed," Paul said.

Stanley didn't look up, but Paul could still see a slight grin on his face. "Years of practice," he said. "Started about the time my knees gave out."

"And how do you pick up the towel once you've finished?"

"Watch this."

He grabbed the poker from next to the fireplace, which must have been there for show because it served no purpose in maintaining the fire, and hooked the towel. He held it over the hearth, shook the poker slightly, and dropped the towel into a neat pile, where he could easily retrieve it.

"I think we've witnessed a master," Paul said.

"I'll say," Charlotte added, smiling slightly. "Maybe you could come clean my house."

"You couldn't afford me," Stanley said and sat down in the chair at the end of the couch, the one to the left of the fireplace, near where Paul stood.

Paul looked toward Charlotte. "I'm Paul," he said, "and this is Stanley. He's today's entertainment."

She smiled. "I'm Detective—I'm Charlotte."

"Well, Charlotte, it's nice to meet you, even under such weird circumstances."

"Yes, weird indeed. That's quite the storm."

Stanley shook his head. "Never seen anything like it, and I've lived up here all my life."

Despite the continuous rain and wind, Paul had forgotten about the storm and with this reminder, realized how loud it had gotten and how they all had to speak up to be heard. "Yeah," he said, "it's amazing."

Paul walked back to the window and watched the river through the rain-smeared glass. "The river's getting terribly high." He felt the tension settle in his guts. The skies, if anything, seemed darker than ever. He hated to think about what was happening to his campsite. Who knew what he would find when he got back. If he got back. He had committed one of the cardinal sins of camping—leaving his tent wide open, his sleeping bag hanging out to air, and his supplies uncovered.

Sure that he would not be gone long and the weather would hold, he had left everything exposed to one of the worst storms he had ever seen. What a mess he would find when he returned.

"Stanley," Paul said as he turned away from the window, "what do you think we can expect here? How bad do you suppose it will get?"

Stanley first looked at Paul and then at Charlotte. "Bad," he finally said. "Real bad."

Wednesday Afternoon

A Call to Order

Stanley eased back in the chair, closed his eyes for a moment. Sopping up the floor left him feeling lightheaded. Even now, he felt more tired than usual and had a bit of indigestion. He supposed he could shrug it off to all that had gone on, that perhaps the last few days were catching up with him. And maybe the indigestion was nothing more than a reaction to the enormous breakfast, a meal far larger than anything he'd eaten in years. All this, combined with the freakish weather, was probably enough to explain the heartburn and dizziness.

Despite these rationalizations, he was far from convinced that all he needed was a good night's sleep and a couple antacids. And even if these explanations did prove sufficient, there was nothing he could do at this point but sit here, listening to the wind howl, to the rain beat against the windows and side of the house.

Paul still stood at the window, trying to watch the river, his face full of concern. Charlotte sat upright and pushed herself out of the couch, the blanket wrapped around her shoulders.

Paul said to her, "Bet you weren't expecting this today."

She gave a weak smile. "All in the line of duty, I suppose. But I'm sure glad to be in here."

"I don't think any of us would want to be out there right now, not even Stanley."

Stanley didn't feel up to interacting right now, but forced an answer. "You can believe that, although I wouldn't at all mind it if I was camped out at home right now, taking a nice long nap."

Paul smiled. "It's nap time already? I missed my cue."

Stanley wanted nothing more than to shut his eyes and drop into a deep long sleep. Talking had made the tiredness worse and the heartburn more severe.

Nathan and Jo appeared from the kitchen, followed by Gabbie. Nathan carried one of those folding clothes racks, and Jo carried a load of wet clothes in one arm and a load of dry clothes in the other. Nathan set up the rack near the fireplace, with Gabbie watching intently.

Jo handed the dry clothes to Charlotte and said, "Rebecca dug these up for you."

Charlotte reached a hand out from beneath the blanket and took the clothes. "Thank you," she said. "This will be much better."

"I bet," Jo replied. "With Stanley around here, you don't want to take any chances."

Stanley smiled, but said nothing.

"You okay?" Jo asked. "You look a little pale, even in this light."

He waved his hand dismissively. "I'm fine. Just a little tired, is all." He felt anything but fine.

A bolt of lightning struck nearby, and thunder rocked the house. Gabbie laid her ears back and scooted up next to Stanley and leaned against his legs.

"It's okay, girl," he said and pet her head. "Just a little thunder." A wave of nausea spread through his guts.

Jo and Nathan hung up the wet clothes on the rack. Charlotte disappeared into the bathroom and soon returned wearing blue sweat pants and a large white hooded sweatshirt with BYU printed on it. Stanley assumed that she wore her holster and gun beneath the sweatshirt, but it was too big to tell.

Just then Rebecca came out of the kitchen carrying an oil lamp and a cup of what must of have been the broth. The light cast a white glow across her face, making her look almost divine. Benjamin followed her out carrying two more lamps and a flashlight stuck under his arm. He was all business.

Rebecca handed the cup to Charlotte. "You're up," she said, "looking a lot better than before."

"Thanks," Charlotte replied as she took the cup. "Thanks to all of you. I feel much better."

Although Charlotte's statement was addressed to everyone in the room, Stanley noticed that she looked only at Rebecca. He wondered why the detective had taken such a keen interest in their hostess.

The wind slammed against the house and rattled the windows and shook their frames.

"The river's still rising," Paul said, almost to himself.

Rebecca looked around the room. She placed a lamp on the mantle. Benjamin placed the other two lamps on the end tables at either side of the couch.

"Why don't we all sit down and get our bearings," Rebecca announced. "We're not going anywhere for a while, and now seems a good time to clear up a few things."

Benjamin looked at Rebecca with surprise, but seemed to resign himself to go along. Paul was the least interested in joining the discussion. His focus was on the rising water, as it damn well should be. Stanley wondered how soon the others would catch onto the seriousness of the situation. All he wanted was to get home and get to bed. He felt worse by the minute.

"Come on, Paul," Rebecca said. "Come and join us. The river isn't going anywhere."

"But it's almost out of its banks."

"Don't worry," Benjamin said. "It's gotten high before, and we're sitting up above everything else. We'll be okay."

Benjamin hadn't even looked outside.

Paul said nothing, but turned away from the window and sat down on the floor, between Stanley and the fireplace.

Rebecca sat on the couch, with Benjamin on one side and Charlotte on the other. Jo sat in the chair opposite Stanley, and Nathan sat on the floor in front of her, with his back up against the chair. Everyone seemed to be taking stock of Charlotte's presence for the first time. Nathan and Jo looked uneasy, restless, especially Nathan, who kept glancing over at Charlotte but never looking directly at her. Benjamin also appeared apprehensive, but Benjamin appeared apprehensive about so many things it was difficult to tell whether this was one of them. One moment he would be staring at the detective, then at his wife, then Jo, and then Paul. Rebecca acted the least affected of all, her concern being that of a mother hen rather than someone being questioned by the police. And Paul sat fidgeting, tugging at his beard, biting a nail, continually glancing out the window.

Rebecca turned toward Charlotte. "Okay, detective, perhaps we can start with you. Maybe you can tell us what brings you here, what brings you back, especially in such nasty weather."

"Are you sure you want to talk about this now? Wouldn't you rather wait till we could have some privacy?" She spoke to both Rebecca and Benjamin, but looked mainly at Rebecca.

Stanley watched Benjamin to see how he would react. He seemed to consider the question, weigh the pros and cons. Always the professional.

Finally Benjamin said, "No, let's get on with it. I want to know what this is all about."

"Okay then. It's about some pictures that were found, pictures of you and of...I'm sorry, I never learned your name."

"Jo."

Stanley wondered when it was that Charlotte had realized that it was Jo who had been in the pictures. Despite the circumstances, she had never given herself away, never betrayed what she might have been observing, thinking.

Benjamin said, "You mean the pictures of me getting a massage?"

"Did you know about those pictures?"

"I just learned about them."

Charlotte said nothing. The wind howled, blew rain against the windows, but the lightning seemed to have subsided somewhat. Then Stanley realized he had not heard any hail in a while.

Charlotte continued. "Mr. Randall, were you in Seattle last night?"

"Yes."

Benjamin gave no more information than he wanted to give.

"And did you stop anywhere else?"

Benjamin hesitated. "Why yes, I did. I stopped at Westside Hospital.

Rebecca looked up sharply. "You did?"

Benjamin spoke in a quiet voice. "Yes, I did...I had heard about Jo's accident, had heard that she was at Westside, so I decided to check in on how she was doing..."

Stanley couldn't tell whether Benjamin was talking to Rebecca or Charlotte. He looked at neither of them, but instead focused on some point near his feet.

Charlotte said to Jo, "You were in the hospital?"

"Well, ah, sort of..." She smiled.

"I don't understand."

Jo glanced over at Stanley and then down at Nathan. Her eyes twinkled in the light of the fire. Stanley thought she looked especially enticing.

She said, "It seems I decided to take a stroll last night. I mean, I was in the hospital all right, because of a car wreck the night before, and I was doing okay and they were moving me to another room and while I was waiting for the bed, I guess I just sort of decided to leave...and ended up in the back of our truck." She patted Nathan on the head.

"So you were there too?" Charlotte asked Nathan.

Stanley could see his discomfort as he nodded. And then Nathan said, "I was looking for Jo...I ah, I didn't know she was in the back of the truck."

Jo grinned. "I was trying to keep an eye on you." She seemed to be the only one enjoying herself.

"Before I go any further, I suppose I should check if anyone else was down at the hospital last night."

"Not last night," Stanley said. "It was more like afternoon."

Charlotte looked over at him. "You were down there as well?"

"Not last night."

"I know, but…"

"I nearly drowned. These guys pulled me out." He nodded first toward Rebecca and then at Paul.

"Pulled you out?"

"Of the river. That's where I nearly drowned. That's why I was at the hospital."

"Hmmm," Charlotte murmured. "Well, I'm glad you're okay."

"Not sure the doctors would agree." He grinned, then stopped. His heartburn flared. Too much talking. Too many people.

"So Paul and Rebecca, you pulled Stanley out of the river, right?" They both nodded.

"Were either of you down at the hospital recently."

"Nope," Paul answered as he shook his head.

"I wasn't there either," Rebecca added. "We were up here last night."

Stanley said, "Me too. After Nathan dropped me off…"

"Nathan?"

Stanley pointed to Nathan. "Yeah, he brought me home." Exactly where he wanted to be.

Charlotte said to Nathan, "Was this before you were looking for Jo last night?"

"Yes."

Benjamin leaned forward. "So detective, what's this all about? What difference does it make if we were down by the hospital?"

"A great deal of difference. That's where we found the pictures, and that's where we found the body of Francis Beardsley, dead from a blow to the head."

Rebecca gasped, and Jo shook her head in disbelief. Nathan was the most surprised and looked almost sick to his stomach, while Benjamin remained still. Stanley couldn't tell what conclusions Charlotte might be drawing.

Charlotte continued. "We also have a witness who saw Beardsley arguing with another man in the parking lot. The witness identified this man as Mr. Randall.

Benjamin protested. "But I didn't know Beardsley, and I didn't argue with anyone in the parking lot."

"And you didn't learn about the pictures till today?"

"Not until I got home."

"And how did you learn about them?"

Stanley didn't like where this was leading. The detective was sure to discover Nathan's involvement. What a mess Nathan had made for himself. Stanley wished that there were something he could do or say to lead the detective off her trail, but he was feeling too tired and lightheaded to think of anything. If he were not sitting, he might have fainted. He looked down and saw that Gabbie watched him intently, her eyes bright and alert, her ears pointed forward. She stood up.

Stanley felt perspiration on his forehead, sickness in his stomach. His left hand began to tingle, and his arm went numb. A sharp pain stabbed through his chest and radiated down to his elbow. He tried to catch his breath, but the pain was too great. The others watched him, their faces wide with fear. They spoke, but he understood nothing. Everything blurred, their words, their faces. Only Gabbie remained clear, but the rest of the room grew dark and a loud buzzing filled his head and before long even Gabbie disappeared. And then the pain softened, eased, and he felt himself expand out of himself, and darkness washed over him like the cool waters of a slow-moving river, wiping away the last of the discomfort and disease and pain.

r. h. sheldon

No Place Like Home

Rebecca jumped up from the couch. "Stanley!" She raced to his chair, her insides a rush of panic and fear.

Charlotte grabbed his arm and felt for a pulse and checked to see whether he was breathing. "He's still alive," she said, "but just barely."

"We need to get him to the hospital," Benjamin said.

"Of course we do," Charlotte answered. "But how? A huge tree is blocking the road, and by now more might have fallen."

This was the second time in three days that Rebecca had seen Stanley near death, but this time it was worse. His skin was a sort of ashen gray, and it felt cool and sweaty. His head lay back into the chair, and his mouth hung partially open, his lips tinted blue around the edges, saliva dripping from the corner of his mouth.

Jo knelt down in front of Stanley and laid her hand on his leg. "Any way to call for an ambulance?"

Rebecca answered, "The phone wasn't working earlier, but let me check again." She ran into the kitchen and picked up the receiver. Nothing. She rushed back to the living room and announced, "Still dead," immediately regretting her choice of words.

"My cell phone won't work here," Benjamin said.

Charlotte added, "And I dropped mine out there somewhere, in the storm."

Paul said, "What about a radio? You got one in the car?"

"Everything's fried. All the electronics. Lightning."

Paul said, "Maybe we should get him on the couch, make sure he's comfortable."

"Okay," Charlotte said, "but we should prop his back up a bit, sort of in a semi-sitting position, but not quite so extreme."

Rebecca grabbed a blanket, folded it into a rectangle, and placed it on one side of the couch. Then they each grabbed a part of Stanley and started to carry him over. They moved awkwardly, trying to keep from bumping into each other and stepping on each other's feet, each taking turns shouting commands.

"Careful!"

"Not that way!"

"Watch his head!"

"Someone grab his feet!"

"The other way!"

"Make sure he can breathe!"

"Keep him warm!"

After much effort, they positioned him on the couch and covered him with a blanket. Rebecca watched his chest to make sure he was still breathing. He barely moved. And then everyone started talking again.

"Should we raise his legs?"

"No, they should be lower."

"I think they're supposed to be flat."

"But not his head."

"That goes back."

"No, forward."

"What about another blanket."

Finally, Charlotte took control. "Let's leave his legs flat for now, position his head back just a bit, so his airway remains open. And we've got to keep him warm."

Rebecca followed her directions, grateful that someone seemed to know what to do.

Paul announced, "I'm going for help."

Rebecca turned toward him. "You can't go out there."

"Someone's got to."

Rebecca didn't know what to say. He was right, of course, but she hated the idea of someone going out there, especially Paul.

"I'll go with you," Benjamin said.

"Benjamin!" Rebecca wanted to cry.

"No, Benjamin," Nathan said. "I'll go with him."

Benjamin answered, "I know this area better than anyone."

Nathan protested. "But you're needed here. This is your house. If something goes wrong, you'll know what the options are." He stepped toward the hallway. Benjamin followed.

"Nathan, this isn't the time to—"

"Listen, Benjamin, the rain is still pouring, the river is rising. You're needed here."

Rebecca moved toward them, "Benjamin, he's right. You've got to stay."

Nathan said softly, "You do, Benjamin. It's best if I go." Benjamin stepped back toward Rebecca.

"Wait," Paul said. "I can go alone. I know my way around here."

"No one is going out there alone." Rebecca was surprised by the force of her own voice.

Nathan stated, "That's settled then."

"Not quite!" Jo yelled. "If you're going, so am I."

He turned toward her. "No you're not."

"Yes, I am."

"Listen, Jo, for once do it my way."

"I'm not letting you go out there without me."

"You have to. You have to stay with Gabbie."

"She'll be fine here."

"No she won't and you know it, and we can't have her out in this storm. Besides, it's not just you I'm thinking of." He looked at her stomach.

She also looked down. "Oh, that's right," she said. "Still…"

Rebecca realized what they were talking about. "You're pregnant!"

"Yeah," Jo said. "I'd forgotten, but I'm feeling fine."

"You can't leave," Rebecca said, "not in your condition, not after the accident. Besides, we might need the extra hands here to help take care of Stanley." Rebecca could see how upset Jo was and gently took her arm. "They'll be okay. The storm's not quite as bad. It's not even hailing now."

Nathan said, "Okay, Paul, we better get going."

"Yeah, the sooner the better."

Paul and Nathan moved quickly. Nathan stopped only long enough to kiss Jo good-bye, scratch Gabbie behind the ears, and assure both of them that he would return as soon as possible.

Paul opened the front door. The sound of wind and rain echoed even louder throughout the house. Rebecca called out to him to be careful. She wanted to say more. She wanted to run over and hug him, but all she managed was a weak smile. She tried to convince herself that he would be okay, that they would all be okay, but when the door closed and the house grew quieter, all she could feel was fear and a deep sense of doom that left her wanting to run to her bed and bury herself beneath the pillows.

She returned to the couch. Charlotte had remained with Stanley, watching him like a mother would a sick child.

"How's he doing?" she asked.

Charlotte replied, "About the same."

Benjamin stepped up next to Rebecca. "Listen, dear," he said in a soft voice, almost tender, "I was thinking that we should be prepared for the worst."

"Worst? Could it get any worse?"

He sighed. "I was thinking about the river, about what could happen."

"You mean if it keeps raining?"

"Yeah," he said. "I've never seen it like this before."

"But earlier you said we'd be okay."

"The house will be okay, but if we have to get out of here…"

Jo asked, "Do you think it will get up over its banks?"

"It's happened before," Benjamin said. "I remember my grandfather talking about it. He said the house was always alright because it sits up like it does, but we could be surrounded by water."

"Like a moat," Charlotte said.

"Exactly."

"How deep did it get then? Did your grandfather say?"

"Too deep to get out. That's all he said."

"And too fast, no doubt," Jo added.

Rebecca shifted nervously. This was the last thing she wanted to hear. Even when the Snake River flooded, they would never need to be scared, and they would not have been so totally cut off. For the first time since moving to the house, she realized just how much she hated it here.

"What do you propose we do?" she asked.

"Just be prepared," he answered. "I want to gather up some tarps, get a board ready, in case we have to get out of here, in case we have to move Stanley. I thought I'd run out to the shop, get what we need, and bring it back here."

Rebecca could no longer focus. "Okay," she said, "but don't be long."

"Why don't I go with you," Jo said, "in case you need a hand. I'll go nuts just standing around here waiting."

"I'll be fine," Benjamin replied. "It shouldn't take me long at all."

"I'm sure you'll be fine. I wasn't asking that."

"I know, I just thought…you shouldn't be out there."

"We're just going across the driveway. I think I can handle that."

"But it's just a board, some tarp. It's not necessary—"

"Relax, Benjamin, if nothing else you might need me to hold the flashlight."

"But—"

"And I'll let you do all the lifting."

Rebecca noticed a tinge of challenge in Jo's voice. Not quite sarcasm, but something else, more like she was mocking him. And he acted almost intimidated by her.

Rebecca said, "Just be careful, Jo. If it's too bad, you should both come right back."

They headed toward the front door. Gabbie followed. Rebecca could tell that Benjamin wasn't pleased, but she wasn't sure whether it was because Jo was going along, Gabbie, or both.

The three exited the house.

Charlotte had stayed near the couch, where Stanley lay. She sat in a chair next to him, one brought in from the dining room. Periodically she checked his pulse, all the time watching him breathe.

"Still the same?" Rebecca asked.

"Yeah. His pulse is weak, his breath shallow, but he's hanging in there. He's a tough old bird."

"Sure is," Rebecca said. "And how are you doing?"

Charlotte looked up in surprise. "I'm fine. I can't believe how wiped out I was, but I'm fine—thanks to you."

Rebecca looked away. "You were pretty exhausted when you showed up. I'm amazed you made it."

"I can't believe I made it either. That wind was unbelievable. Never seen anything like it. And the hail made it all the worse. And the lightning, as though it was out to get me."

"This is the most terrible storm I've ever seen. But the hail has stopped, thankfully, and the wind doesn't seem to be as bad."

"No, it doesn't."

Rebecca was glad for the confirmation. She kept thinking of Paul and Nathan out in this weather.

Charlotte said, "You're pretty worried about them, aren't you?"

Rebecca bit her lower lip. "I just want them to be alright. I want everyone…" She glanced at Stanley. "I want everyone to be alright."

She felt tears well up in her eyes. One streaked down her cheek. She couldn't recall how long it had been since she had cried.

Charlotte stood up and led Rebecca to her chair. "You sit down," she said. "You look like you could use a break."

Rebecca felt the warmth of Charlotte's hand on her arm. It was strong, yet comforting. There was something maternal about it, something protective, and something more.

"I'm sorry, detective…Charlotte, I just…I don't know…it's just that the last few days—and now. It's been too much. I wish I could be stronger." She sniffled.

"There's all kinds of strength," Charlotte said and stared straight into Rebecca's eyes.

Rebecca felt the blood rush to her face. She said, almost mumbling, "I'm glad you're here. It makes me feel better somehow." She took Charlotte's hand and squeezed it, but let go quickly, suddenly realizing how inappropriate that might seem. She would never show that kind of affection to the women in her church, let alone someone she had met only today, no matter how extraordinary a day it was.

Charlotte said nothing.

"I just met Paul, a couple days ago, when we pulled Stanley out of the river." Rebecca wasn't sure why she brought this up. Perhaps she needed to talk to someone, to just say something about everything that's been going on. "He's such a nice guy, very kind, understanding. I haven't met many men like him—" She stopped, feeling horrified by what she just said. "I don't mean that we…that there's anything like *that* going on. I mean, we're just friends, that's all. He's not like that, he's, ah, he's—"

"Is he gay?"

Rebecca looked up, startled. "But how did you…how did you know?" Rebecca was surprised to hear Charlotte say the word *gay*. She made it sound so normal.

Charlotte smiled slightly. "Just had a feeling, that's all."

"Anyway, he's a nice guy. I like him. I don't care if he is…I just like him."

"You're right, he is a nice man, and you two have been through a lot together in a short time. And I like him too, even though I haven't known him that long."

Rebecca felt relieved. She was glad that Charlotte liked Paul. She was happy that something seemed right about the last few days. She felt herself relax slightly and was glad that she had a little time to gather her thoughts, get a bit grounded.

Stanley sighed. Charlotte moved in closer to the couch, and nearer to Rebecca. She held Stanley's wrist and felt for a pulse, and the watched him carefully to make sure he was still breathing.

"Seems about the same," she said.

Rebecca closed her eyes and prayed for the strength she would need to continue, for the safety of Paul and Nathan, for Stanley's return to health. Yet she no longer knew whom she prayed to, whether her prayers meant anything at all. She felt uncertain, afraid, the confusion washing over her like a mixed-up dream, where none of the pieces fit, none of the players made sense. She longed for normality, for her life of rules and structure, for a time when surprises were few and change as rare as a hot day in the Cascade Mountains. She wondered how much longer she could endure this.

When she opened her eyes, she discovered that Charlotte was watching her.

"Guess I'm more worn out than I realized," Rebecca said.

"It will be fine," Charlotte said, her voice low and soft. "It will all be fine."

Out of Bounds

Jo followed Benjamin out toward the large workshop, with Gabbie at her heels. The rain fell like breaking waves in the strong wind. She tried not to think about Nathan and Paul, but that only made it worse.

"This must be what a hurricane is like," Jo shouted as a gust of wind knocked her sideways.

"I'm glad it's eased up some," Benjamin yelled back.

She grabbed his arm and checked to make sure that Gabbie was close by, and together they forged their way through the biting rain, until they reached the workshop.

"In all my years, I've never seen anything like this," he said as he tried to catch his breath. His head was soaked, his dark hair pasted to his scalp as though it had been waxed into place. Water dripped down his face, onto his shirt. She thought he looked kind of cute standing there, like a little boy.

She reached over and wiped a strand of hair from his forehead. "There, maybe that will keep the water from dripping in your eyes."

He stepped back. "I, um, better find those tarps." He scurried off toward the back of the shop.

She didn't know why she had done that. She had acted without thinking, as absently as she would have done it to Nathan.

"Wait," she said, "you're going to need some light." She pulled the flashlight out of her pocket and followed him deeper into the building. Gabbie scurried along behind her.

The back of the workshop was dark, the air cool, damp, like the inside of a cave. The rain pelted the roof, filling the room with confused, sputtering echoes. The only light was the narrow beam of the flashlight.

"Where should I aim this, chief?" She spoke as lightly as possible.

"Beneath the bench," Benjamin said. "I think there are some tarps down there."

Jo obliged by aiming the light just to the left of where he stood. A deep shelf spanned the width of the bench, its contents stacked neatly

r. h. sheldon

against the back wall. Jo could make out cans of paint, thinner, turpentine, brushes, rollers, and a pile of canvas drop cloths.

"You must do a lot of painting," she remarked.

"That's Rebecca. Seems like she's always got some project going." Jo could hear the strain in his voice.

Jo moved the light further to the left. The beam landed on several neatly folded blue plastic tarps. "There," she said.

Benjamin crouched down and reached beneath the workbench. Jo leaned to one side to provide him more light. She rubbed up against Gabbie and could feel her wet fur through her pant leg. Benjamin pulled out the tarps and set them on the floor next to Jo's feet. She could hear Gabbie sniffing at them, her nose rubbing against the plastic.

"Now," he said, "if you could point that a little more to the left…" She moved the beam. "There it is." He grabbed a large plastic container that was marked "Bungee Cords" and pulled it out, placing it next to the tarps. "Now all we need is a board."

He stood, his face only inches from hers. She could barely make out his features in the dark, but could feel his breath on her, smell the dampness of his skin, his shirt.

He didn't move, and at first she wasn't sure whether he knew he was that close. Then she felt his hand brush up against her arm, so soft she couldn't tell whether it had been intentional.

She felt nervous and didn't want things to grow any more awkward than they already were, yet something in her hesitated, made her not want to lose the close proximity of his warm, solid form. Finally she said, "So, where are those boards?" She aimed the flashlight at the far wall.

He stepped back. "Uh, they're over there…" He moved in the direction of the wall.

"What exactly did you have in mind?"

"What?"

She hurried to clarify herself. "With the boards, I mean…what do you have in mind to do with them?"

"Oh, the boards…yes…I was thinking we'd find something big enough for Stanley, maybe a piece of plywood."

The wind screeched in a high-pitched whistle. Jo scanned the wall with her flashlight. Off to the left, in the corner, sat a mammoth power mower, parked neatly up against the back of the building. To the right, suspended in a straight row, hung a number of garden tools—rakes, shovels, a hoe—and further to the right, stacked in precise angles against the side of the building, sat an assortment of two-by-fours and two-by-sixes. Next came several half-inch planks, followed by a number of small pieces of plywood, none of which would be very useful.

Jo looked a little more to the right. "How about that door?" She shone the light directly on an old door that looked beaten up and weathered.

"That's the door to a shed I used to have on the property."

"It would be perfect. We could pull off the hardware, and the door would be ready if we need it."

"If we need it," he repeated.

"Do you think we will?"

"Will what?"

"Need it…do you think we'll need to carry Stanley out of here?" For a moment, she had forgotten why they were out there, forgotten how bad things had gotten, how Nathan and Paul were out there going for help, how Stanley lay on the couch.

Benjamin stepped toward her. "I'm not sure. I don't know how much worse it will get…but the more prepared we are, the better."

She said nothing.

"Are you okay?" His words seemed to fall out of the air.

"I'm fine." She took a small step back and knocked into Gabbie. The dog yelped. Jo turned toward her. "I'm sorry, baby, I didn't mean to knock into you." She reached down and patted her on the head. When she stood, Benjamin was right there, closer than before.

"Jo…" She could hear the desperation.

"What is it, Benjamin?" She kept her tone even, calm. She was afraid of what might be coming and didn't want to give it a chance to be spoken.

"I only thought…"

"Why don't we gather up everything and head back to the house. We can talk in there." She turned and headed back toward the tarps. "I'll get these and you can get the door. Wait there and I'll come and hold the light."

She reached down for the tarps and bungee cords. Gabbie stuck her nose in her face and licked her nose. "Good girl." Jo had to smile. Dogs always had a way of neutralizing a situation.

She stood up, her arms hugging the tarps. The flashlight beam danced on the ceiling. Then she felt a hand on her arm and gasped.

"Sorry. I thought you might need some help."

"You startled me, that's all. I thought you were over there." He still held her arm.

"Jo…" He spoke as though he were afraid to say her name.

"What!"

"I just—"

She waited for him to finish. He grabbed her other arm, reaching around the bundle of tarps, and pulled her toward him. The plastic crinkled and air whooshed out the edges. Gabbie barked.

"Benjamin!"

He leaned in and kissed her awkwardly on the mouth. His lips felt hard, dry, and he didn't press fully against her lips, but instead caught the edge, landing part way on her cheek. She pushed him away.

"What are you doing?" She laughed halfheartedly.

He stepped back, letting go of her arms. "I thought, I thought…I only—"

"Let's just get back to the house."

He didn't move. "But I thought you, I mean, the way you acted, the massage, the beer—coming out here, brushing the hair from my face… you seemed so…so…"

"Benjamin, you can't think—"

The wind let out a painful moan and rattled the side of the workshop. As though on signal, the sky let loose another downpour and pelted the building with rain so hard it seemed that the roof would cave in. Gabbie whined and squeezed up next to Jo.

"Come on," she cried, "we need to get back to the house."

The Call of the Wild

Nathan reached behind the seat for the two nylon jackets. Rain bombarded the roof of the truck and the part of his body that stuck out of the cab, his lower back turning to ice. He pulled himself out of the truck and handed one of the jackets to Paul. The rain soaked his head, ran down his neck.

"That's Jo's," he said in a loud voice. "It's pretty big on her. It should help some."

"I'm not sure anything will help." He slipped on the jacket and pulled up the hood.

"Which way?"

Paul pointed to the end of the driveway.

The rain wasn't as heavy as before, and even the wind had died down some. Still, it was coming down pretty hard, probably worse than most storms he had been around. Never had he seen so much water fall in so short a time, and it was still coming.

He glanced back. He could barely make out the river, but could still tell that it swelled in its banks, ready to brim over, moving fast, an uncontrollable rage. The wind howled above their heads, bending the tops of trees. Branches littered the ground, a number of small trees.

He tightened the hood. All he could hear was the slap of raindrops against the nylon. Icy water ran down his face, soaked the lower part of his jeans. Already he felt the cold seep into his bones, freezing his legs, his nose, his hands. Thank God it had quit hailing.

Paul moved quickly toward the road, and Nathan had to work hard to keep up with him. With visibility so bad, they could not risk losing sight of each other. What would normally have been an easy walk into town had turned into a hazardous venture into the unknown. There was no telling how many trees would be down, how high the river would get. And they'd have to be on guard for power lines—those already down or those about to fall. Christ, even lightning was still possible.

They reached the end of the driveway and turned right toward town. A thick carpet of branches covered the road. Fallen trees filled in the spaces. The worse was the giant cedar that blocked the detective's car. If it had hit her, she wouldn't be with them now. It could take days to get the road cleared.

They climbed over the cedar. Broken limbs stuck out from the trunk like knives, sharpened by the winds and unrelenting rain. Just what he needed, to be taken out a downed tree. Yet if something should happen to him, either here or anywhere else, he had only himself to blame. His foolhardy schemes are what brought them here. They should be back at their own home, enjoying the fire, listening to music, staying warm, dry, and most of all, safe.

But now wasn't the time to be delving into this type of thinking. He must stay focused, get to town safely, find help.

Nathan followed Paul over the tangle of broken limbs and slick bark. Just as he stepped on the high point of the trunk, he slipped on a patch of moss and twisted backwards. Paul grabbed his arm just before he was about to fall.

"Thanks," he shouted, but he wasn't sure Paul could hear him.

They climbed down the trunk and stood before the detective's car, now nearly covered by fallen debris. Behind the car, running over the road in a sweeping arc, a overflowing creek made driving out impossible, even if the tree could be moved.

Paul moved nearer to Nathan and yelled, "I'm not sure how low the road dips here, but we have no choice but to cross it."

"It's running pretty fast," Nathan shouted.

"I know."

Nathan agreed they had no other option. The creek probably emptied into the main river, and crossing it here was as good a place as any.

A gust lifted the rain into a rolling wave that washed over them. The chill blew right through Nathan, sucking out what little warmth he had left. "Come on," he said, "let's do it. It won't get any easier."

"Agreed."

Paul led the way, taking slow steps into the current. Nathan followed close behind him. The icy flow closed in on his legs. Soon he was up to his knees, then his thighs. With each step, the current become stronger, pulling him off to the side, and he could barely step without fear of tumbling over. He got to the point where he had to shuffle forward, rather than take steps. He wanted to keep both feet on the ground, but his legs were already numb, and control became nearly impossible.

The stream ran about twenty feet wide, and he wasn't even half way across, but he was far enough that there would be no turning back. He could only hope that it wouldn't get any deeper. He wasn't sure he could make it if he did.

The chill turned his blood into currents of ice. The muscles in his thighs ached, tightened up. Paul was now several yards ahead of him, his jacket little more than a blue haze through the blowing rain. His height was definitely an advantage, and he seemed sure-footed and confident, much more so than Nathan felt. He wanted to catch up, but he dare not push himself faster. If he fell, he would never get up.

Paul glanced back and stopped. He struggled to hold himself upright while waiting for Nathan. Nathan pushed forward.

The road leveled out, and with any luck, would dip no lower. A strong current shoved him to one side and he stopped before losing his balance. The cold saturated his legs. He could barely make them move forward. When he finally started up again, he struggled just to remain upright. He could no longer feel the bottom of his feet.

When he got closer to Paul, Paul flashed a quick smile, then began moving forward. Nathan followed. After a few steps, he realized that the road began to rise, slowly at first, almost imperceptibly. But before long, his steps became more manageable. He would make it, he was sure of that now, and suddenly the conditions seemed a little less extreme, the cold less severe.

Paul finished quickly and turned to watch Nathan, who now walked in only a foot of water. The last several yards seemed like nothing. Paul grinned, his face a beam of sunlight. He grabbed Nathan's hand and pulled him the last few feet, a gesture more than a necessity. Nathan took the hand, grateful for the comfort, the sense of camaraderie, and smiled back at Paul.

"Wow!" Paul shouted. "That was one hell of a hike! I about froze my fucking legs off."

"I thought I was going to have to fucking swim home. Christ almighty, I've never been so cold."

Their bodies shivered, their teeth chattered, both of them grinning at still being alive.

"Come on," Paul yelled, "let's keep moving before we freeze."

Nathan laughed. "If I can still walk."

They took off once more. His legs ached, moved stiffly, his feet burning with each step. But he welcomed the pain and the sense of strong feeling. He moved forward willingly, with Paul beside him, and slowly

r. h. sheldon

the blood circulated its warmth, and movement becoming a bit easier, and even the weather didn't seem as bad.

They continued down the road toward town. Evidence of the storm lay about them in tangled heaps of green and gray. At times the road was so thick with debris that it was difficult to see the asphalt. Guided by the wall of trees on either side, they aimed for the center, watching for downed power lines and falling branches and trees. At times the wind would gust and blow the rain so hard they'd stop and turn their backs to it, hoping that nothing would come hurling down upon them.

They said little as they walked. Between the noise of the weather and the need to conserve energy, shouting became an extravagance. Instead, they communicated with looks, gestures, pointing out potential hazards, providing direction over fallen branches. Sometimes Paul would look over at Nathan and grin, a playful gesture meant to ease the tension. Nathan welcomed the relief this provided, almost a sense of fellowship. He wasn't used to entering into this sort of partnership with someone, to working so closely with another person, but the urgency of the situation, the extraordinary events, had left him no choice, and now, rather than being put off by the notion of having to coordinate his efforts with someone else, he found comfort in the idea and discovered in himself a willingness to do what it took to achieve their common goal, as though he, the individual, had somehow been submerged into something greater, a feeling he had seldom experienced, but one he now embraced.

The road twisted to the left and opened up. Paul pointed in front of them. Nathan looked through the dense rain, saw nothing at first, only more distant trees and indistinguishable horizons, but then he realized what Paul had pointed at. A hundred yards off, almost invisible in the gray air, the dim outline of a bridge poked out of the misty rain. He wondered at first if he imagined it, so surreal did it appear, but as they drew nearer, he knew that this is what they were looking for, this was the bridge that headed into the town of Index.

They quickened their pace. The road now moved toward the river and soon they were walking along its banks. The water roared violently past them, pounding against the rocks in ferocious bangs. The banks seemed incapable of holding it in much longer.

"This is the area I was most concerned about," Paul shouted. "The way the river comes screaming down here and bends around, it could take out part of the road. Might still happen."

"How much time we got?"

"No telling. But I wouldn't stand here too long."

They rushed to the bridge and started across. Below them the river churned and raged in giant waves. The wind howled through the wires of the bridge, buffeting against them and spraying them with icy rain. The storm had taken a turn for the worse. Nathan could feel the sway of the bridge. He didn't know whether it was from the river or the wind. He just wanted the hell off.

When they reached the other side, they looked around. Giant puddles carved out holes in the street, branches littered the roads, power lines snaked across ground. Not a person to be seen, not a light to be found. They headed for the tavern, hoping someone would be there. Just before they stepped inside, Nathan looked back up river, toward where the house was located. The clouds thickened, grew darker. The rain came down in streaks of gray mist. Suddenly lightning filled the sky in a flash of white light, brighter than any he had ever seen, and a hideous roar of thunder rolled down the valley, as though the earth itself were caving in.

On the Home Front

Charlotte checked Stanley's pulse. Still rapid, weak, slightly irregular, his skin cool and moist, a sort of oily, clammy feel. His face had a pale sheen, the thin strands of hair matted to his scalp. She had seen this look before in heart-attack victims and doubted he could survive much longer, not without medical intervention.

But he stilled breathed, and that was something. But it was shallow—his chest barely moved—and occasionally he would let out a long sigh. Each time he did, Charlotte watched and waited, wondering if he had taken his last breath. She didn't know what they would do if his heart stopped. To try to resuscitate someone in these circumstances—when medical help might be hours away—would do little good. It might help to thump his chest right after his heart stopped, but if they had to perform CPR for any length of time, there would be no bringing him back. And even in the unlikely event he were to survive the CPR, the damage could be immeasurable. If she were alone with him, she would probably let him go in peace, without forcing him into a system that would ultimately strip away what little dignity might remain.

Yet Charlotte realized she was no doctor and had no formal medical training, other than routine first-aid classes, so she had no right to second-guess possible outcomes. Still, things looked bad right now, and she hoped she wouldn't have to make any critical decisions. But the fact was, she had never seen CPR work on someone who didn't get immediate medical care.

Charlotte got up from her chair and tried to stretch the tightness out of her back and neck. She was alone in the room right now, except for Stanley. Rebecca was in the kitchen, and the others were still out of the house, although Benjamin and Jo should be back any time. How convenient they should be out there together, just the two of them. She wondered what Rebecca thought of the whole thing. In fact, Charlotte wondered what she herself thought about everything that was going on. After all, her intent in coming up here was to ask Benjamin about Beardsley and the photos, but when Benjamin heard he'd been identified as the one who argued with Beardsley, he acted genuinely surprised. Either he was a damn good liar, which was definitely a possibility, or he had indeed never met Beardsley. And if that had been the case, then her witness, Williamson, had been mistaken, and someone else had argued with Beardsley. Someone who looked like Benjamin?

Charlotte's thoughts turned quickly to Nathan. Williamson could have easily mistaken the two, especially at night in a dimly lit parking lot. Nathan had acted quite nervous when they talked about Beardsley and the pictures, and Nathan had been down at the hospital. But if it was Nathan, what could he and Beardsley have argued about?

And then there was Jo. Pregnant Jo who wandered out of the hospital and climbed into the back of the truck. Pregnant Jo who was the massage therapist in the photos. Pregnant Jo who was married to Nathan.

Three people, all either directly or indirectly tied to a man found dead in a strip of trees outside a Seattle hospital. All at the hospital near the time when the man had died. And all Charlotte had was a body, a bottle of tequila, a set of photos, a well equipped van, and what might prove to be an unreliable witness, but nothing to tie any of them to a crime.

She sat back down next to Stanley. Still no changes. She shifted in her seat, causing her leg to brush up against the sofa and pick up a few dog hairs. She grabbed one and twisted it in her fingers. Suddenly, she remembered what Gavin had said about the hair on Beardsley. Of course, she thought, the dog.

Rebecca returned from the kitchen, carrying a glass of water. "Thought you might like something to drink."

"Sounds great." She gulped down half the glass. She hadn't realized how thirsty she had been, and the water tasted exceptionally clean and refreshing, nothing like you'd find in the city. She placed the glass on a coaster on the end table. "Perfect, thanks."

Rebecca sat down. "Wow, what a day."

Charlotte turned slightly in her chair. "Say, Rebecca, I was wondering if you could answer a question for me."

"Sure."

"Earlier this morning, when I first showed you the photos, you said that you didn't recognize the massage therapist."

Rebecca looked uneasy. "That's right."

"So today was the first you met Jo?"

"And Nathan."

"And Nathan?"

"Yes, Nathan."

"But if I understand correctly, and I might not, considering what an odd day this has been, Nathan is your brother-in-law."

"Yes, that's right, but this is the first I've met him. And Jo. And Stanley for that matter, I mean, officially met him."

"You never met your brother-in-law before?"

"He and Benjamin hadn't seen each other in years."

"Wow, this *has* been quite the day for you."

"These have been the strangest few days of my life." She laughed nervously. "I don't even know what to think any more."

"I'm sorry. I shouldn't have brought this up. The last thing you need is to be answering a lot of questions. I promise, I'll try to stop being a cop for a while."

"I have a feeling that's something you could never do."

Charlotte knew that Rebecca meant this good-naturedly, yet even in jest, the remark hit a little too close to home. "Yeah," she said, "I guess I can be a little intense at times."

"Oh, no," Rebecca protested, "I didn't mean that at all. In fact, I admire that you're so committed to your profession, and I envy that commitment. I'm sorry, I really am…if I said anything…"

"It's not you, really, I mean, I'm sorry, I didn't mean to imply…"

They both broke out in laughter.

"Oh, dear," Rebecca said, "aren't we the pair."

"Maybe we could start over, talk about the weather…"

Rebecca looked out the window and they both laughed again.

Finally, she said, "I suppose it would be hard to find a lot of happy things to talk about right now."

"I suppose you're right."

"Besides, we haven't known each other very long. I mean, I know so little about you. After all, I only met you today as well."

"Funny thing is, I feel like I've known you longer than that."

Rebecca's eyes sparkled. A slight smile hung on her lips. "Maybe that's what all this is about. Maybe I'm getting to make new friends. You. Paul. And even Stanley…I hope Stanley."

"And perhaps Nathan and Jo?"

"Yes, them too, at least I would want that. I like them. They seem such a good couple, so right for each other, like a team, like two people working toward the same goal."

Charlotte had been thinking along the same lines, but didn't say anything. Instead, she said, "I'm glad you include me in your list of potential friends."

The front door swung open and banged against the wall. The noise of the storm filled the house, and then Jo yelled at Gabbie to wait till she dried her off.

Rebecca jumped up from the chair. "How did it go? Did you find what you needed?"

Before anyone answered, Gabbie bounded into the room and greeted Rebecca as if they were old friends. Rebecca leaned over and scratched her behind the ears and spoke to her in a quiet murmur.

Jo came in carrying the tarps and Benjamin carried the door. They both seemed hurried, distracted.

Jo said, "Where should I put this, Rebecca?"

"How about over there, near the kitchen."

Benjamin stood the door up near the hallway, against the far wall.

Jo placed the tarps on the floor and headed toward the couch. "How's he doing?"

Charlotte answered, "About the same."

Benjamin walked across the room and sat in the far chair and stared out the window. Gabbie walked to him and sniffed his hand, then headed back toward Rebecca.

Something must have happened out there, Charlotte thought. Benjamin acts like he's walking in his sleep.

Rebecca crouched down and rubbed Gabbie's head. "It's so nice having a dog around here," she said. "I've always loved dogs."

Benjamin turned toward Rebecca, his look a mix of confusion and wonder. Then he returned to the window. Rebecca didn't seem to notice, and Jo was busy watching Stanley.

The wind screamed, rain spit against the windows.

Benjamin said, "The river is spilling out of its banks."

Lightning flashed and filled the room with a bright glare. Thunder rocked the house so hard it seemed about to fall off its foundations. Gabbie barked and ran to Jo. Stanley let out a long deep sigh.

Wednesday Evening

Up, Up and Away

S tanley wasn't sure what just happened. In fact, he wasn't sure of much of anything right now. One minute the beautiful woman stood before him—her head covered with thick golden hair, her skin shimmering white and smooth, her face soft and gentle—and the next minute she was gone, disappearing in a flash of light that seemed to emanate from within her. And in her wake she left in him a sense of vast disappointment, as though in that brief moment, he was able to touch her goodness, feel her purity. And when she was gone, when a void was felt from knowing her so briefly, even though neither had spoken, he realized that she held what he had always searched for, that she was his source. Such was the essence of her power and strength.

Stanley drifted aimlessly, thinking of the angelic visitor. Having seen her like that, floating among the trees, hanging gracefully near the edge of the clouds, seemed to fit well with how strange everything else was right now. After all, how could he explain the fact that he now hovered above the Randall home, like a helium balloon floating aimlessly amid the treetops? And what made the whole thing odder still was that he could see the group of people who waited inside the house, as though walls and ceilings meant nothing. Rebecca and the detective sat near the couch. Jo lay across one of the big chairs, her legs draped over the armrest while Gabbie leaned up next to her. Benjamin sat opposite her on the other chair, staring absently out the window. And lying on the couch, looking as corpse-like as anyone he had ever seen, lay Stanley's own body, his breathing shallow, his face ashen gray.

Damn, he thought, what a grim picture I make.

Stanley wondered if he was having an out-of-body experience, like the kind people talked about on TV, where they described in vivid detail standing alongside their own bodies, looking at others in the room, floating freely through walls and ceilings. Or maybe this was more like a near-death experience. How else could he explain his angelic vision and flash of white light? Admittedly, there was no tunnel at whose end the light lingered, pulling him forward like a magnet to a piece of steel, and the light itself came and went so quickly there was barely time to think, let alone be drawn by its invisible force. And come to think of it, none of his deceased friends or relatives were present, and according to all those reports of near-death experiences, at least some of the dearly departed should have been there to greet him.

Of course, maybe *near* death was not quite the right way to look at it. *Near death* implied some sort of return, a temporary condition to be overcome. It was quite possible that this was the real thing, that Stanley was merely waiting for his body to heave its lasts gasps and then he would be flung out into the cosmos, free from the last few strings that tied him to this earthly plane.

But at this point, all this was conjecture. Until something actually happened, until some resolution pulled him one way or the other, he could do no more than hover above the house, waiting fate to deliver its final blow. He thought again of the angelic visitor, of her golden hair and radiant light, and the warmth returned, filling him with a sense of lightness, exhilaration—like a child, swinging freely beneath a giant oak, the world limited only by his imagination, free from the aches and stiffness and tiredness that condemned his body to a regimen of pain and lethargy.

Soon he felt overcome by giddiness and wanted nothing but to dance among the treetops, like a sparrow flitting lightly from branch to branch. He bounced along the trees, spun circles around their trunks, flipped over long limbs. He soared to the tips of giant cedars and lifted up to the clouds. He glided up the valley, along the edge of mountain-tops, then swooped back down to the river, sliding past rock, sand, water. He laughed and giggled and whistled and hummed and hooted and sang old songs he had forgotten he had known, and then with an effortless twist of his head, he floated to the Randall house, where he sat on the roof, smiling happily at the extraordinary world around him. And finally, with a contented sigh, he lay back on the roof, resting his head on the shingles, and fell into a peaceful sleep and melted into the glorious landscape he called home.

In the Good Ol' Summertime

The flash of light jarred Benjamin back to the present, out of the workshop, out of his kiss with Jo. He returned his attention to the room. Rebecca sat on one of the dining room chairs, with the detective perched next to her, on the edge of the couch, squeezed in between her and Stanley.

Jo sat in the chair across from him, but he dared not turn toward her, afraid that even his look would betray what had happened in the workshop. Better for him if he just pretended nothing had happened. He returned his attention to outside. The sky was quieter now, brighter, and the wind had died down. No longer did rain pelt the windows, but instead fell softly, siphoned to a mere mist. Even the river appeared less treacherous, and it seemed to him that it might have begun to recede.

Benjamin couldn't explain the sudden change in weather. All he knew was that, after the monumental flash of lightning, the storm began to let up, as though the explosion of light had blown a circuit, turning off the wind and rain. And now the house was quiet, and the moaning winds and driving rain had been replaced by the muffled wash of the river and the soft murmurs inside, as if life were suddenly normal again and they could return to the way things were—predictable, under control.

"It's easing up," Benjamin said as he glanced at Jo.

"That's what's different," Rebecca said. "I wasn't sure. After that last bolt of lightning and the horrible thunder, I was so scared I hardly noticed how quiet it had gotten."

Jo reached out and rubbed Gabbie behind the ears. "How do you like that, girl? Better than that noisy storm, isn't it."

Gabbie stood and wagged her tail.

Rebecca said, "She looks like she's grinning."

Jo flashed a proud smile. "That's her way of saying, 'I like this better. Now when do we go play?'"

"She's a pretty dog," Charlotte said. "How long you have her?"

"About five years. We got her when she was a puppy."

Charlotte watched Gabbie for several seconds, then turned back to Stanley.

"How's he holding up?" Benjamin asked.

Charlotte answered without looking up. "About the same." She hesitated. "I hope Paul and Nathan have some luck."

They all turned toward the windows. The sky had brightened still more.

"Will you look at that," Benjamin said. "I think I see a streak of blue sky."

Jo leaped up from her chair and stood next to him. Gabbie followed. "Where?" Jo asked. "Show me where."

Benjamin tried to point to what he had seen without looking at her, but she stood in such a way that he had to reach around her to show her where he meant. Did she do these things just to taunt him?

"Up there, to the left, just by the corner of the window."

He could see the freckles on her tanned legs, smell the slight sweaty odor, a raw, pure scent, sensuous, exciting. He longed to touch her legs, hold the firm thighs between his palms.

Jo glanced down at him, saw how he stared, and returned quickly to her chair. Gabbie began to follow her back but detoured to check in with Rebecca and Charlotte. Rebecca rubbed her head and scratched behind her ears. Charlotte did nothing, as though confused by the presence of a dog. She simply watched as Rebecca pampered the animal.

Gabbie then stepped back from between Rebecca and Charlotte, walked around Rebecca's chair, and returned to the couch, near where Stanley's head lay. Then she sat down and stared at him without moving.

"I wonder what she's up to," Rebecca said.

Jo shrugged. "No telling. Maybe she's waiting for a treat."

Gabbie continued to watch Stanley, and the others watched Gabbie. Benjamin wasn't all that interested in what the dog was doing, but looking at her made it easier to keep from looking at Jo. But the dog itself was just that, a dog. Benjamin could never understand what people saw in their pets. It seemed unnatural, letting an animal run around the house like that, paying it all this attention, but he wasn't about to say anything now. He'd save it for later, when everyone was gone.

Gabbie never moved from her spot, never took her eyes off Stanley. Occasionally she would lean forward, just a bit, her body poised with expectation, but then she'd relax, shifting back into her watchful pose.

Benjamin turned back toward the window. The weather continued to improve. The clouds lifted out of the valley and the air cleared, leaving not even a mist. He could see the river easily now, and although it was still high, it no longer swelled out of its banks, leaving only muddy puddles where it had washed up onto the lawn. He looked back to the couch. Gabbie held her vigilant pose.

"Mr. Randall." Charlotte's voice was like a knock on the head.

He turned toward her, careful not to look toward Jo. "Yes?" He tried to keep his voice neutral.

"Is there any way out of here, other than the main road that I came in on?"

"The road you came in on—the Index-Galena Road—does a big loop and comes out east of here, past the town of Skykomish."

Charlotte looked out one of the side windows. "And what about your driveway? Is that the only way to the road?"

"Pretty much. There are a few overgrown trails that might lead out, but after this storm, they're probably impassable. Why, what are you thinking?"

"My guess is, even with the weather improving, it's going to be impossible to get an ambulance anywhere close to here, at least not for a long time. The road might be blocked all the way to the highway."

Rebecca gasped. "Do you think it's that bad?"

Jo leaned forward. "Judging by what we saw, anything is possible."

"We'll have to carry him out," Benjamin announced.

"That's one possibility," Charlotte said. "The problem is we don't know how far we'd be carrying him, and jostling him around like that could make him worse."

Benjamin said, "But if we wait till an ambulance can get through, or at least close enough to carry him, we'll be delaying treatment and they'll *still* have to carry him out."

"Oh dear," Rebecca said and shook her head.

"You're right, Mr. Randall," Charlotte said evenly. "But the improving weather offers another possibility. We fly him out."

Jo said, "Of course, one of those medical helicopters."

"That's right."

Benjamin protested. "But how do we get it here? Where does it land?"

"I've been thinking about that. As far as landing it, you have plenty of open space out there. We scope out a spot, make sure we clear any of the bigger branches, and be ready for it. As long as the weather holds out, there should be no problem. I've seen them land in tighter spots than this. Your place is actually ideal from what I can tell."

"And what about getting them here?"

"I'm assuming that Nathan and Paul—or the people they contact—will think of it once they see that the weather is clearing. If that's not the case, the paramedics should, at the very least, have a radio."

Benjamin considered their options. The idea of carrying Stanley out of here—possibly all the way into town, or worse yet, all the way to the highway—was a pretty overwhelming prospect, so a helicopter made a lot of sense, and he had to admit, there was plenty of room to land.

"Okay," Benjamin said, "I can buy the helicopter idea, but what if Nathan, and, ah…"

"Paul," Rebecca said.

"Yes, Paul, what if Nathan and Paul don't get back here right away? What if it's dark by the time they return?"

"I'm not sure what we'll do, but I don't see any choice but to wait." Charlotte paused. "I don't think we should go out looking for them because we don't know where they finally ended up, and there's no point more of us wandering around and adding to the confusion. And we definitely don't want to start carrying Stanley out of here until they return and we know what the conditions are like out there and when emergency help will be arriving. All we can do is assume they'll find help and that they'll be back here soon."

Jo stood. "And with this weather improving so quickly, I'm sure they'll be back in no time."

"I know they will," Rebecca said.

Benjamin had to agree that the sudden improvement in weather did change things. If all went well, they could get help for Stanley and go from there. But where exactly would they be going? There was still the issue of the pictures, the dead body. And what about Jo? What was he going to do about her?

Benjamin tried not to think about any of this now. One problem at a time.

"Alright," he said, "I suppose the thing for us to do is to start clearing a landing zone."

"Great," Charlotte said. "Also, do you have any flares around?"

"Flares?"

"They might help the pilot see where to land and show him what the wind is doing."

"I think there are a couple in my car. I'll check."

Benjamin stood.

"I'll go with you," Rebecca said. "I could use some air."

"I can help too," Jo said.

Benjamin froze. "It would be better if you stayed in here to give the detective a hand if she needs it." The last thing he wanted was to be outside with Rebecca and Jo working side by side.

"You're probably right."

"We'll be fine," Rebecca said. "If one of us gets tired, you can replace us."

Gabbie suddenly leapt to her feet and stood nose-to-nose with Stanley. Her body quivered and she squeaked a soft, drawn out yelp. Then she backed off a couple inches and waited. He opened his eyes slightly, closed them, opened them again, then blinked several times. Gabbie wagged her tail and grinned.

"I must be in dog heaven." His voice was weak and crackled like a speaker with a loose wire.

Rebecca grabbed his hand. "Stanley," she said in a quivering voice.

"I feel like shit," Stanley grumbled.

Rebecca smiled. "I'm sure you do."

"And I need a drink."

"Me too," she whispered.

Road Warriors

Paul fumbled for the door of the Index Village Pub, his fingers barely able to function. In the last couple days, he had felt wetter and colder than he had in his entire life, and today was the worst yet. Every piece of clothing was soaked, even with the rain jacket—anywhere the water could seep in—up the sleeves, down the collar, in from the bottom. His jeans were pasted to his legs, wrapping him in ice. Water dripped from his hands, his face, his head, and formed a puddle where he stood. His teeth chattered so hard that he could barely hear anything else.

He walked inside, with Nathan close behind. The pub was dark, dreary. A few candles burned dully on the bar top. The bartender leaned against one of the dark wooden walls behind the bar. He was short, thin, slightly bent. Gray stubble covered his face. A lone customer sat on a stool, leaning on the bar, a glass of beer in front of him, a cigarette dangling from his lips. A wisp of smoke drifted up and spread out in a thin cloud near the dark ceiling, adding to the layers of tar that gummed up its surface. Yet the stale smells of cigarettes and beer were comforting somehow, as if this dose of reality could help ground Paul in the midst of the chaos that surrounded them.

He shook off as the water and stepped toward the bar. His shoes squeaked and he left a trail of water.

"Do you have a phone?" Paul asked. "We need an ambulance." His words felt rushed, shaky.

"Phone's out," the bartender answered. "Power and phones are out almost all the way to the highway. No cable, either. Probably won't get the game tonight." He paused. "Can't drive in or out either."

Nathan said, "You mean we can't even get out to the highway?"

"You can walk out, I suppose, but not drive. Heard there were a couple good sized trees down."

"How about Reiter Road?" Paul asked. Reiter Road was a back road—narrow and mostly dirt—that connected Index to Gold Bar.

"Heard that's worse—one part washed out."

The man sitting at the end of the bar spoke, his words slurred. "Strange thing, though, it's only bad here in town. Arrived as it was starting. It was all centered in this valley. Downriver is fine. If you can get to the highway, you should be okay."

"That's right," the bartender added. "Someone walked in from there a little while ago. Left right before you got here. Says the highway is fine. Gold Bar is fine. It's only here that things are bad."

Nathan turned to Paul. "So what do we do?"

The bartender pointed to outside. "There's a fire station down the street, past the general store. They keep an ambulance there. Maybe someone's around."

"Come on," Paul said.

They headed outside.

"Look at this," Nathan called. "It stopped raining!"

Sure enough, only a light mist fell. The wind had all but died down, and the clouds were beginning to lift.

"Amazing," Paul said. "I think the worst is over."

Paul could feel his spirits rise, and he could see that Nathan too walked with a bit more of a bounce. Even the wet clothes didn't seem so bad, the chill not as deep.

They walked to the firehouse, about a block away. Deep puddles of muddy water stretched in every direction. Long branches littered the streets, sidewalks, yards. Garbage cans knocked over, their litter strewn in all directions.

They approached the firehouse. The flagpole lay on the ground. A man in gray overalls tried to untangle the flag. By the time they reached him, the light mist had subsided and the air was clear. The sky continued to brighten, and the clouds thinned into wispy bands.

"Do you believe this weather?" the man said. "It's the weirdest thing I've ever seen."

Paul stepped toward him. "Can you help us? Our friend...we think he's had a heart attack."

The man stood quickly. He wore an emergency medical insignia and a nametag that read *Jim Carlisle*.

"Where?" he asked.

Paul replied, "Up the road, about a mile."

"At the Randall home," Nathan added. "Benjamin Randall."

"You can't drive up there," Paul said. "You can get a little way, but you'd have to walk the rest. Too many trees down."

"Damn." Jim paused. "Let me radio for backup." He ran into the station. In a few seconds, he returned. "She's on her way. We'll drive as far as we can, and walk in with what we need."

The sun broke through the thin layer of clouds and shown down on the road. The puddles glistened as steam rose up gently and disappeared into the streams of light. Paul would have loved to find a nice sunny rock and fall asleep.

"How was he when you left?" Jim asked.

"Unconscious," Nathan said. "His breathing was pretty shallow, his pulse weak."

Paul added, "And his color was bad too, real pale, his lips a little blue."

Jim shook his head. "Okay," he said, "we'll carry in what we need, including a backboard, in case we have to carry him out."

"In case?" Paul felt the panic mount. Did he mean in case he wasn't already dead?

Jim added quickly. "If the weather holds, we might be able to fly him out. From what I recall, the Randalls have a big yard, lots of room for a helicopter."

Paul felt some relief. "That's right. A lot of space."

Four people rode the ambulance the short distance from the firehouse to the first giant log lying in the road. Paul and Nathan sat in back, where it was bright and sparkling clean and smelled of antiseptic. When they stopped, Paul and Nathan climbed out. Jim and the woman who had joined them, Tina Blodgett, jumped out the front and grabbed the equipment they would need—several packs and a backboard.

"What should we take?" Nathan asked.

Jim replied, "You sure you're up to carrying anything? You guys look like you've been through a war."

Nathan and Paul looked at each other. Paul hadn't thought about his own condition, but if he looked anything like Nathan—wet, muddy, face scraped, clothes torn—he was quite the sight. They smiled at each other, like comrades who had been to battle.

"We'll manage," Paul said. "Let us help."

Paul and Nathan walked side by side, with the other two behind. Paul carried the backboard, Nathan one of the bags. They walked quickly, climbing over fallen limbs, working around deep puddles.

Nathan said, "This trip's a hell of a lot better than the first one."

"I can't believe the difference. How could it get so nice so quickly? If it wasn't for all the debris, you'd hardly know we had a storm."

"I think I might actually thaw out."

Paul grinned. "You forgot the stream."

"The stream?"

"The one by the car. You couldn't have forgotten wading in waist-deep water."

"Thanks for the reminder."

"My pleasure."

Jim called out from behind him, "How you two holding up?"

Nathan and Paul glanced back. Nathan said, "We're fine."

Paul spoke in a voice so that only Nathan could hear. "Speak for yourself."

"Lightweight."

Paul chuckled. "Truth is, I didn't realize how exhausted I felt until now."

"Me too. I can't believe having gone such a short distance could have been so hard."

"A nap would be nice right about now."

"And some food."

"And a beer."

"Especially a beer."

"I doubt we'll find one of those when we get back to the house."

Nathan laughed. "You can bet there will be no beer in the vicinity of my brother!"

Paul said nothing. Talking about the house reminded him of the seriousness of the situation, of what might be waiting when they return.

As though reading his mind, Nathan said, "I hope Stanley is alright."

"Yeah, me too."

They walked a little further, until they reached the stream. The four stood before the water. It gurgled and sputtered across the pavement, much calmer than before, much lower.

Jim said, "You didn't tell us about this."

Paul gave a mock surprised look. "I forgot."

Tina studied the pavement. "Wow, look at that water line. How high was this thing?"

"Close to our waists," Nathan said.

Paul laughed. "And moving a hell of a lot faster than it is now."

"Guess we shouldn't complain," Jim said.

Paul went first. Crossing it now was like wading through a puddle. Considering how wet he already felt, the added discomfort seemed like nothing, especially in comparison to their last crossing.

When they reached the other side, Tina asked, "Whose car?"

"The detective's," Paul answered.

"Detective?"

"Long story," Nathan said.

Paul added, "You'll meet her at the house."

One at a time they climbed over the giant cedar. Paul and Nathan went first, then helped the others with the gear. Once over, they headed toward the driveway.

Jim said, "I hope to God we can fly him out of here."

As they walked toward the house, Paul could feel the anxiety grow. He looked at Nathan. "You ready?"

"I'm not sure."

Benjamin was outside, near the side of the house, pulling a large branch across the lawn. When he saw them, he dropped the branch and darted over to the small group. Benjamin seemed genuinely glad to see them, and looked as though he were about to hug Nathan, then stopped himself.

"How's Stanley?" Paul asked.

Benjamin smiled. "He just woke up."

Paul and Nathan looked at each other. Paul shouted "Yes!" and Nathan screamed "Yahoo!" and they both laughed and hugged and shook hands and patted each other on the back. And then the front door flew open and Rebecca and Jo rushed outside and joined in the hugging and smiling and laughter. And soon Gabbie popped out and starting running and jumping and grinning and howling. Paul couldn't help but notice how Benjamin stood off to the side, saying nothing, a look of sadness on his face, and then, without a word, he signaled for the paramedics to follow him and led them into the house. But Jo and Rebecca stayed outside, asking Nathan and Paul if they were okay, telling them how glad they were that they had made it back safely, how much better Stanley seemed. And Paul felt happier than he had in a long time, glad to be back, glad to hear the Stanley had not gotten any worse, glad to be with his new-found friends. He felt like a lost child who at had found his way home.

What Goes Up...

The disappointment that Stanley felt after waking up was difficult to measure, for it was greater than any he had known throughout a lifetime of disappointments, and the prospect of facing yet more time entrapped in this tired and worn body—especially after tasting the freedom of his unencumbered spirit—was more than he could bear. And as he lay there on the couch, each breath a struggle, his limbs too weak to move, he wished only that he could close his eyes and will the cessation of his heart, freeing his spirit from the confines of this dismal existence.

He thought back to the sight of that beautiful angelic creature, to her safe and peaceful comfort, to soaring freely above the trees, along the tips of mountains, and he longed to spread his wings once more and glide up to the heavens and let go his earthly ties and return to her gentle warmth. Yet he could not say if what he had just experienced was anything but a dream, wishful thinking that projected itself so deeply into his subconscious that, at the moment he teetered on the edge of death, his mind conjured up an incredible fantasy that seemed more real than life itself. But the source of his experience mattered little. For whatever caused him to taste this remarkable freedom, he was now faced with the unpleasant reality that his life continued, and his sense of entrapment far outweighed any lingering inclinations toward survival.

Yet even now, with this disappointment weighing so heavily, he could not help but be touched by the way Rebecca held onto his hand, the way Jo wiped his forehead with a cool towel, the way Gabbie sat next to the couch, waiting for him to get up. Still, it was these very acts that reminded him that the last thing he wanted was to be a burden on anyone, to be the subject of their pity, and now he found himself at the mercy of their ministrations. And what did he have to offer them? What was there for a sickly old man to give back?

If only he could get up from here, if only he could return home and lie back in his chair, without having everyone fuss over him, and then whatever was meant to happen would happen, and he would at least have his dignity.

"Do you want to try some water?" Rebecca asked.

Talking was difficult. His throat felt rough, his mouth dry. "Not yet," he answered. Even those couple words tired him.

The sound of shouting men erupted outside, reminding him of when he was younger, when he and the boys would head out on Saturday night, when they were still too green and arrogant to know how tough life really was.

Rebecca said, "Better go check this out." She patted his hand gently before letting go.

"Me too," Jo said. "We'll be right back." She followed Rebecca, with Gabbie close behind.

Charlotte sat down where Rebecca had been sitting. "Is there anything I can get you? You need another blanket?"

He shook his head. What he needed was oxygen, lots of it. His lungs felt like as though he were slowly drowning and the act of breathing only made it worse.

More shouting erupted from outside, along with a great deal of barking. Charlotte looked toward the front door and smiled, but didn't get up.

"Weather?" Stanley asked in a crackly voice.

"It's stopped raining and the sun is starting to poke out. Looks like it's getting quite nice out there."

Stanley was glad. That storm had been a bad one, and if it had kept going like it did, there was no telling how much worse the damage would get.

Just then, Benjamin walked in, followed by two paramedics—a man and a woman. Just what he needed, more questions, more probing, more tubes, more wires, more needles. He could try to refuse, he supposed, but he doubted that Jo and Rebecca would let him. Besides, if he didn't go with the paramedics, he would be stuck here, and he couldn't do that to them. So he would have to resign himself to the inevitable in the same way he had resigned himself to being alive. With any luck, this would all be over soon.

"My name is Tina," the woman said, "and this is Jim. The first thing we need to do is to give you some oxygen and start an IV." She stood behind the couch and reached down with a plastic mask and placed it over his nose and mouth. She slipped the elastic band over his head to hold the mask in place. She then reached down and felt his pulse in his left wrist, looking at her watch as she timed his heart's rhythms. He wondered whether she could really feel anything. Then she slipped a blood pressure cuff over his arm and pumped it up. The cuff squeezed the muscle in his arm against his bone, sending a shot of pain up to his neck.

Jim stood in front of the couch, preparing the IV. He said, "You're going to feel a slight poke." Stanley felt the needle sink into his flesh, the twitch of his hand as he tried to resist the pain. The paramedic quickly taped the tube and needle in place, then laid his arm on a small board to keep his wrist from bending. Jim lifted the IV bag and adjusted the rate of the drip. "Could one of you hold this?" Benjamin stepped forward and took the bag. "Just make sure it stays at least a couple feet higher than the patient."

Jim checked the IV once more, looked at Stanley, and said, "Didn't we see you a couple days ago?"

Stanley nodded weakly.

Tina proceeded to hook Stanley up to a monitor while Jim took a hand-held radio to the other side of the room. As Tina hooked up the wires, she began asking Stanley a series of questions about his health, illness, allergies, medications, and recent problems. Whenever possible, he would nod or shake his head. Talking had already been difficult. Talking though the mask was nearly impossible. Often Tina had to lift the mask off his face to understand what he said. In between the questions, she jotted down quick notes on her clipboard.

She now turned her attention to the monitor. After adjusting a few settings, she flipped on a switch. The machine made a slight whirring sound as it ejected a strip of paper from the side. At first, Stanley watched what she did, looked for her reaction to monitor's report, but he quickly lost interest and began to feel detached from everything that was going on, as though the paramedics were working on someone else and he was slowly backing out of the room. All he wanted was to sleep, and soon he closed his eyes and Tina's voice drifted away, and then all he could hear was the muffled rush of the river, with its soothing tones, lulling him into a peaceful, deep sleep.

This Old House

B enjamin stood with his arms crossed and watched the helicopter disappear over the treetops, working its way toward Seattle. The echoes of the thumping blades trailed up the valley. He had never seen anyone flown out by helicopter before, and he had seen only few taken away by ambulance. The first time was right here, when his grandfather had to be rushed to the hospital. That was when his cancer was first diagnosed, when he received official confirmation that things were never going to get better.

Benjamin always suspected that his grandfather knew what was coming long before the doctors made their terminal pronouncements. By the time the medical community got involved, his grandfather already looked thin, pale, as though recovering from a long bout of flu. The diagnosis was no doubt a formality that the ailing elder had resisted as long as possible.

In the months prior to the fated ambulance trip, Benjamin had noticed a change in his grandfather's behavior. Although he had always been a man of business, one to attend naturally to the endless details that accompanied his enterprises, his focus had shifted to business of a more personal nature, and he began to look more scrupulously at property deeds, insurance policies, portfolios, leases, and most of all, his will. He spent long hours reviewing and modifying draft after draft, until he was satisfied with the results, until he was sure that no action could ever be taken that contradicted his wishes.

On the day the ambulance took away his grandfather, Benjamin had been at the house. Together they were working on a sales agreement that would deed a chunk of land along the highway to a group of developers who wanted to build a strip mall. It was a great location, just east of Sultan, in a spot easily accessible to tourists, locals, and the growing number of commuters who spilled over from the Seattle area. His grandfather had bought the property for practically nothing, knowing that eventually this area would turn, and he also knew that now would be the time to sell, when he could realize the greatest percentage of appreciation. Most of the prime property had already been grabbed and prices jacked up, so there would little to gain by hanging onto it, at least that is what he told Benjamin.

While reviewing the agreement's final draft, his grandfather started to speak, but his words fell off into a sort of mumble, and he began to sway, almost falling out of his seat. And for a moment he acted incoherent, unable to put his thoughts into words. Benjamin was sure he was having a stroke and grabbed the phone to call for help. His grandfather tried to stop him, but he was too weak and could barely sit upright.

When the ambulance arrived, Benjamin wanted to go with him to the hospital, but even in his distress, he was coherent enough to stop Benjamin, to insist that he stay and take care of business. Benjamin watched helplessly as the ambulance pulled off, just as he had watched the helicopter lift off and leave with Stanley. Was this the fate of all old men in this house?

Benjamin listened long and hard to the sound of the thumping helicopter, waiting for the echoes to die off, until all he could hear was the river, splashing on the other side of the house, the same place he had stood when they had taken away his grandfather.

By now, the others had returned inside. He wondered what would happen next, what they would do with all these people. And what about Jo? And the detective?

He walked toward the front door. He wanted to linger outside, enjoy the peaceful evening, the sweet smell of the forest, the chance to be alone. Funny, he had never really thought about these things before, never noticed the beauty of the trees, the graceful way they swayed in the gentle breeze, how the tips shimmered in the evening sun, before the light disappeared altogether. His had always been a life of business and money, one in which achievement and power shone above all else, where people were a commodity, time a resource, and in the midst of all this he strove to reach the top of the hierarchy, to stand above everyone and everything, regardless of the consequences.

But being outside like this, dwarfed by the trees and the mountains and a crisp blue sky, all that he had worked for, everything he had accomplished, seemed unimportant right now, his life suddenly diminished by what had always been there, and perhaps too by the events of the last few days, and by those who now gathered inside his home—the detective, Jo, his brother, Rebecca, and her late night guest. And then there was the man dead in Seattle, pictures of the massage, Stanley on his way to the hospital.

Benjamin stepped toward the front door, hesitated, drew in a deep breath. Then he entered the house.

The paramedics packed up the last of their equipment. Rebecca pulled Charlotte's clothes off the drying rack and placed them in a plastic bag. When Charlotte saw Benjamin, she walked toward him.

"Mr. Randall," she said, "I'm going to head out with the paramedics and work my way out to the highway. Given the circumstances—and the sort of day it's been—I thought it would be better to try to talk in the morning, when things have settled a bit."

Benjamin tried to focus on what she said, make sense of her words.

She continued. "I just thought it might be easier tomorrow, after everyone has had a chance to rest up. Sounds like you'll all be here anyway, so maybe we can put together the pieces at that time."

"Everyone will be here?"

Rebecca looked up as she twisted a tie around the plastic bag. "Yes, Benjamin, where else are they going to go?" She handed the bag to Charlotte.

"Thank you, that was very kind of you."

"No problem at all."

Jim grabbed the backboard. "We better get going while there's still light."

"I'm ready," Charlotte replied, as she held up the bag.

"We'll see you in the morning," Rebecca said. "And thanks for all your help today. I don't know what I would have done without you." She reached over and hugged her. Charlotte smiled warmly.

Benjamin stared. Rebecca never said anything like this, never hugged people she hardly knew. One more extraordinary event on an extraordinary day. Nothing should surprise him at this point.

Charlotte and the paramedics left with their arms full of equipment and smiles on their faces. Benjamin felt as though he had missed something, that everyone here had shared a common experience, one big event, while he had experienced something altogether different. Theirs was a connection that permeated the air, elevated their moods, inspired them to closeness, despite the grimness of events, despite the circumstances that had brought them here. Yet he wasn't part of any of it. He wallowed in the reality of events, feeling uncertain and afraid, separated from everyone else. How could something that brought them so close together make him feel so far apart, as if he were the one who did not belong, the one on the outside looking in?

Paul interrupted Benjamin's thoughts when he said, "I'm going to head to the campground to check on my stuff, before it gets any darker."

Rebecca looked concerned. "Can't you wait till morning?"

Paul grinned. "Might as well find out the worst tonight. Besides, I want to see what I can salvage."

Jo said, "Hey Nathan, why don't you go with him. I bet you-know-who could use a walk right about now." Gabbie perked up her ears. Benjamin wasn't sure what it was she recognized that might have caught her attention.

"What do you think, Paul? You up for company?"

"Sure thing, as long as the dog gets to come and it's not just you again!" His smile was wide and his face full of mischief.

"Hear that Gabbie? You've opened yet another door."

"Okay," Rebecca said, "You two—I mean, three—go, but don't dawdle. We have to figure out something to do about dinner. And bring a flashlight with you."

"Yes ma'am," they both answered.

The three rushed outside in a whirl of excitement and exaggerated good-byes and grins. When the door shut behind them, Rebecca shook her head, and Jo rolled her eyes.

"They're like little boys," Rebecca said.

"Worse," Jo added.

Their amusement and pleasure was evident, despite what they had said. He wondered how long it had been since Rebecca had been amused or pleased by anything he had done.

Rebecca said, "Jo, would you help me make up a couple beds, before it gets any darker in here."

They disappeared through the kitchen. The back stairs creaked as they worked their way up to the second floor.

The house grew quiet, more massive and empty. The sun had dropped behind the mountains and filled the valley with shadow. The room quickly chilled. Earlier, when the sun had come out, they had blown out the lamps, turned down the fire. Now evening descended rapidly and with it the cool air of night. The house would hold the heat for a while, but despite the updated windows and doors, the place was still thinly insulated and could even be a bit drafty. You wouldn't know it by the bright veneer, but the core remained untouched, and even a summer evening could feel cold and damp.

Benjamin lit the oil lamps and turned the gas in the fireplace back on, keeping it set to low. Then he sat down in the chair near the far corner and watched the fire. What would happen next? He wondered. What would life be like tomorrow?

The End of an Era

Nathan and Gabbie followed Paul out the door and into the clear calm evening. Nathan stopped and took a deep breath. The air smelled rich and delicious, and no particle of dust or pollen or pollution of any sort seemed to have survived this afternoon's torrential scrubbing.

He caught up with Paul at the end of the driveway, where Gabbie also waited, and they headed up the road, opposite the direction they had taken earlier. Gabbie bounded happily along, sometimes leaping out in front, sometimes winding between their legs, often running off into the trees to chase her invisible prey. An afternoon of stormy weather and being cooped up inside now exploded into a rush of boundless energy that could take many miles to work out.

Paul laughed. "Guess she was ready to get out."

"You might say that. Good thing she didn't play her mad dog routine inside."

The sun glowed from behind the mountains and cast giant shadows across the valley floor. The dark road, with its tunnel of trees and mounds of debris, felt surreal to Nathan, almost magical, adding to the strange quality of the last few days. The forest disappeared into layers of dark greens and grays and blacks, each tier descending into a darker shade. They didn't have much time before it would be too late to see anything.

Paul said, "We don't have far to go. I just want to get in there, check out what's left of my site, and maybe grab a couple things from my car."

Gabbie leaped up on Paul and let out a quick bark.

"Guess that's settled then," he said.

"Guess it is."

Paul glanced over at Nathan, as though he were about to say something, but thought better of it.

"What?" Nathan asked.

"I was just…I don't know—"

Nathan waited.

"It's just that I feel a little odd about staying at the house…at your brother's house."

"Me too, but I'm sure my reasons are different than yours."

"I don't mean it's anything personal, I hardly know him. And I love Rebecca, she's great."

Nathan nodded in agreement.

"It's just that last night, I mean, it was perfectly innocent and all, but your brother, he assumed that I, that we…" And Paul told him about rescuing Stanley and meeting Rebecca and her drying his clothes and about running into each other again yesterday and the lightning and ending up at the house. "And all we were doing was sitting by the fire and we both fell asleep and then Benjamin walked in…"

"Upset, was he?"

"I'll say. I thought he was going to kill someone. It didn't help that I was wearing his bathrobe."

Nathan stopped and let out a short laugh. "His robe? You were wearing his robe?"

Paul stopped too. "It's not funny," he said, but he was smiling too. "I thought he would explode."

"I bet. What did he do?"

"Got all pissy, then took off. He was out of there so fast I didn't think he'd ever come back."

"And what about Rebecca? How'd she react?"

"She just stood there for a while, looking toward the front door. Maybe she was waiting for him to come back in. But then she got upset at me and kicked me out the house."

"Rebecca?"

Gabbie looked up.

"Hard to believe, I know. And I know she felt bad about it. She came over to my tent this morning to apologize. But please don't say anything to her about it. I know it would upset her."

"I won't say anything to anyone."

Paul hesitated, then said, "You know the funny part about all this, about Benjamin blowing up like he did and storming out of there…"

Nathan waited.

"I'm gay."

Nathan began to speak, but stopped. Then he looked down at the ground. The news surprised him, made him feel uneasy, and he didn't know what to say. His uneasiness wasn't so much that he cared as it was of feeling put on the spot, as though he now had to react to the news.

He knew what Jo would say if he told her about his discomfort. She'd tell him to get over it. And the truth was, it really was no big deal with him. He thought Paul was a great guy. In fact, Paul was someone he'd feel honored to call a friend. So what was the problem? Nothing, really, no problem at all. Just surprise.

"I know that kind of silence," Paul said.

"I'm sorry, you caught me off guard, that's all. I don't know a lot of gay people."

"You know me."

"Yeah, I know..."

"And then of course there's Charlotte."

"Charlotte?"

"The detective."

"Yes, I know, but how did you..."

"Instinct."

Nathan smiled. "I heard about that."

"Anyway, I only mentioned it because of the situation, being in your brother's house, how he was last night. I didn't mean for it to sound like some sort of confession."

"I know, I just...listen, Paul, this is okay, really."

Paul was quiet for a moment, then said in a loud voice, "Whew! I thought you were going to disapprove!"

Nathan started to protest, but then saw the glint in Paul's eye. "Oh fine, make fun of me."

"If it helps, I'll try not to hold the fact that you're straight against you."

"I appreciate—"

"Only just don't go flaunting it. Or talking about it. I can't handle that."

"Okay, but—"

"And don't start any of that macho bullshit. Can't deal with that either."

"Yes, Paul, I'll—"

"And the clothes, don't start dressing like a slob just to prove something."

"May I speak?"

"Of course."

"Gay or straight, you're still an asshole."

"Thank you."

"You're welcome."

"Now perhaps we should continue before it gets so dark we'll never find our way home."

They walked.

"What about Rebecca?" Nathan asked. "Does she know?"

"Oh yeah, she knows."

"But not Benjamin."

"Not yet."

Nathan snickered. "Man, I'd love to see his face when he finds out."

"You're finding this very amusing, aren't you?"

"Very."

"Go ahead, joke. Gabbie will comfort me. Gabbie, come here girl."

Gabbie bounded toward him. Paul crouched down and scratched her head and ears. "That's my girl," he cooed. "I'd rather be with a dog than a mean ol' straight man any day."

"Me too."

They walked another few yards.

"This is it," Paul said.

They crouched down under the barrier to the campground and headed deeper into the trees, across the old wooden footbridge, and down one of the overgrown trails.

"I'm glad you know your way."

"It's not that bad. Just a few twists and turns. Just watch out for that steep drop-off to your left. Those rocks will tear you apart."

Nathan glanced toward the trees trying to see where Paul was talking about, but all he could see were shadows. Then he heard Paul's laughter.

"You just wait."

"I'll do that."

They walked.

"How'd you end up camping here, anyway?"

"Long story. The quick version—used to come camping up here. Couple days ago I got fed up with my life in Seattle. Abandoned my apartment, quit my job, drove up here, all within twenty-four hours."

"Sounds like you've had quite the week."

"As have you."

"Yeah."

They followed the trail toward the river. With each stop, the sound of rushing water grew louder. When it seemed that they must be nearly on top of it, Paul stopped.

"It's gone!"

r. h. sheldon

"What?"

"My camping gear! My campsite! It's all gone." Paul pointed to a sandy bank that broke off in front of them. "That's where it should be, right here."

"Oh man, Paul. This sucks."

Paul stared at the hole that was once his site. The river had carved out a big horseshoe in the sandy ridge. No evidence of a site or equipment remained.

Paul searched the area to see whether anything could be found. Nathan joined in, although he knew it was a lost cause. Everything would have been washed downriver, along with the bank that held it all up. Still, he continued the search, waiting for Paul to come to the same conclusion.

Finally, Paul said, "I guess that does it."

"Yeah," Nathan answered.

Paul stood for a moment, looking at the spot where his site once stood. Finally, he said, "I have some clothes in my car. Let's head over there."

They wound through the trees, back toward the road. It had grown so dark that Nathan could barely make out the trail, but Paul seemed to know where he was going. He would have suggested they use the flashlight, but he knew, as Paul no doubt did, that once they turned on the light, they would lose their night vision and be able to see only what was in the beam. The longer they waited, the better. Still, Nathan planned to stay close.

When they were almost to the road, Paul said, "It's back over here, behind this brush."

They shuffled between a couple huckleberry bushes.

"Shit!" Paul clicked on the flashlight.

It took a moment for Nathan to see what Paul was seeing. All he could make out was the trunk of a giant fir that had toppled over, no doubt another victim of today's tirade. But then he looked beneath the trunk and realized that a car lay beneath it, smashed into a blue metallic pancake, impossible to access.

Paul moved in closer and scanned the length of the car. The sides were so smashed down the wheel wells were barely visible. The side doors and windows had disappeared, and the only evidence of their existence was the broken glass sprinkled on the ground.

Paul stepped back and stared at the tree. He shined the light up and down its length. The base was only about twenty feet away. The bottom flared out into thick roots that shot out like tentacles. Paul walked toward the bottom and around to the other side. Nathan and Gabbie followed.

Paul said, "Looks like it hit more to that side."

He was right. This side of the car—the passenger's side—was a little less smashed down, the roof matching the curve of the tree trunk. Still, it would be nearly impossible to get at anything inside.

Paul crouched down toward the passenger window and pointed the light into what was left of the inside of the cab, which had been reduced to a space not much larger than a mailbox. The glove compartment had flipped open, with much of its contents intact.

"I think I can get in there," Paul said.

"Careful of the broken glass."

"If you could hold the light…" He handed it to Nathan.

Paul reached into the space and grabbed a handful of items. "There is a god," he said as he pulled out his arm.

"What did you find?"

"My wallet and checkbook. Normally I would have hidden them somewhere by my campsite, but I had forgotten to. At least that's one thing I won't have to worry about."

"Anything else in there of value?"

"Just my registration and insurance stuff. I suppose I should grab it." He reached in again, fished around, and pulled them out.

Nathan then aimed the flashlight at what was left of the trunk. "I don't think you're going to get much else out of there."

"I suppose not."

Nathan moved the light back and forth across the wreckage in case there was any way to salvage anything else. But it looked pretty hopeless.

Paul said nothing. Nathan could only guess at what he was feeling, having lost all his gear and car. That was a lot, especially given that this was his temporary home. Luckily he had a place to stay tonight, but he was no doubt wondering what to do after that.

Nathan put a hand on Paul's shoulder. "I'm sorry, Paul. If there's anything I can do to help…"

"Thanks."

"Maybe we should get back to the house."

"Yeah, not much else we can do here."

"We'll come back during the day. See if there's any way to salvage anything." Nathan tried to sound more hopeful then he was feeling.

"I doubt there is," Paul replied.

"You never know…"

They stood before the ruined car a little longer. Paul finally said, "Things could be a lot worse, I suppose."

"Yeah, could have been."

"I might have been in there."

"Don't even go there."

"Or I could have been there and not the car."

"Let's get back to the house."

"And you know what the worst thing about that would have been?"

"Paul, let's go…"

"I might now be as short as you!"

At first Nathan didn't realize that Paul was joking, and the remark confused him, but then he heard Paul's snickering, which grew louder and louder. Soon they were both laughing, a hard silly laugh, one of relief and sadness and giddiness.

"Paul," Nathan said, "you're one sick bastard."

"I know," Paul said between his cackling. "I know."

They stood there until the laughter subsided. Nathan thought he could heard Paul sniffling, but he wasn't sure, and he wasn't about to ask.

Strange Bedfellows

Rebecca lay next to Benjamin, his breathing deep, slow. She assumed he was sleeping, but couldn't be sure. They had said little to each other after the others had gone to their rooms, and he had climbed into bed before she returned to the bedroom. He didn't seem angry. *She* didn't feel angry—preoccupied would be a better way to describe it—and perhaps that's what he was feeling. So much had happened, so much to think about. Never a chance to let everything sink in. And now here they all were—Paul, Nathan, Jo, and even Gabbie—a house full of guests she had only just met. So different did her life feel since the last time she lay next to her husband.

She realized just how much a stranger he was to her. She felt closer to their guests than she did to Benjamin, especially Paul. A level of comfort had developed between the two of them that she had known with few people. Like tonight, when they were making dinner by oil lamp and candlelight, she and Paul worked side by side, as though they had been working together all their lives, no tension, no miscommunication, only cooperation and fun. Jo was like that too, easy to be with, playful. In fact, if circumstances had been different, had Stanley not been taken to the hospital, had the pictures of the massage not been found, had she and the others not been so exhausted—had Benjamin not been there—this would have been a perfectly delightful evening. The group was relaxed, good-humored, fun, all those things that had been missing in her life.

Yet Benjamin's presence wasn't that bad. He didn't seem upset with anyone, didn't act rudely, wasn't pouting about some imagined slight, yet he was definitely withdrawn, on the outside. He went along with whatever anyone suggested, helped when he was asked, responded politely when spoken too, yet he never seemed all there, as though he were incapable of participating, unable to have fun.

Rebecca felt a little sorry for him. She never considered before that the reason he held himself aloof was because he didn't know how to talk to people on a human level, didn't have any experience being a friend. On a professional level he was one of the best, and he was a well-respected member of the Church. People looked to him for guidance and strength, not only for business-related issues but also for issues related to morality and Church law. Yet the same people who looked to him for advice seldom thought of him for anything of a more fun nature. They didn't invite him on picnics or to go snowmobiling or waterskiing or down to the city for a baseball game. No one ever thought of Benjamin as someone who could have a good time. But they did respect him. They respected his intelligence, his steadfastness, his certainty, his consistency. And maybe that's what Benjamin was thinking about tonight. Maybe he realized how easy it was for the others to be together. Maybe he saw how Paul and Jo laughed and joked and teased and genuinely enjoyed each other's company. Even Nathan seemed to grow more comfortable as the night progressed, despite the history with his brother, despite the circumstance of their visit. But Benjamin always stood off to the side, visibly uncomfortable with the gathering, not knowing what to say, how to interact.

Despite Benjamin's gloominess, Rebecca enjoyed the company. She was happy to have Paul there and glad she finally got to meet Nathan and Jo. And she loved having a dog around. Being with all of them had been such an adventure, a departure from her life's doldrums. She knew she shouldn't feel that way, not with Stanley in the hospital and the police asking questions about Benjamin, but she couldn't help herself. This was the most alive she had felt in years, and she didn't know whether she could survive if life were ever to return to normal.

She tried to remember what her old life had been like—the cooking, cleaning, going to church—and was filled with a sudden sadness, as though she had fallen into a well, the darkness closing in, imprisoning her in its depths. She shuddered and pulled the covers around her neck. Benjamin did not move.

Rebecca could face the confusion and uncertainty of the last few days, but she didn't know if she could face her old life. Yet what choice did she have? What options awaited a middle-aged housewife with few skills and no experience? Was she doomed to return to the way things were, after experiencing so much, after feeling so different?

She closed her eyes and tried to imagine what form an escape might take, what force could sweep her away from the fate that awaited her. She knew that her family wasn't a solution. The last thing she could do was go running to her parents, and her brothers and sisters had their own lives. Besides, none of them would ever support her leaving Benjamin. When they looked at him, they saw the faithful husband, the good provider, and would hold her responsible for any discordance. And for the same reason, there was no one in their ward she could turn to. The members idealized Benjamin. To them, she would always be the lucky Mrs. Randall.

Her escape then would have to come from other means. But what did that mean? If she struck out on her own, she would never be able to support herself. What would she do? How would she survive? And she knew few people outside the Church, at least no one she would turn to for help. In fact, she probably knew her house guests better than almost any nonmember. And even Stanley could be included in there. And Charlotte, for that matter.

The thought of Charlotte made her feel warm inside. There was something about her that felt safe, as if the Seattle detective could provide a solution to her dilemma. But what would that solution be? And what was it Rebecca was looking for? She could hardly run away without a place to run to, and she certainly couldn't go running to Charlotte, someone she had just met, someone she hardly knew. And why would she think of Charlotte in the first place?

Her eyes popped open This was insane. She could hardly believe that she was imagining what it would be like to leave Benjamin. She couldn't leave him. She couldn't leave the house, their community. This kind of thinking was unhealthy, wrong. She should seek guidance, talk to the Bishop. She had everything she could need or want. Sure, she would have loved to have had children, but it was too late for that. Too late for a lot of things. And starting a new life was one of them!

She closed her eyes and tried to fall asleep, but she felt too wound up, too confused. If only she could quiet her mind, dull her senses. If only she could stop the parade.

She wasn't sure how long she lay there like that, whether sleep came with any permanence or whether she slipped in and out of consciousness. But her mind never rested, and the dull ache in her heart never left. At some point, she fell into a vague state of sleep—a semi-aware consciousness—and began to dream, and in her dream she was again visited by Joseph Smith, only this time his words were soft, his look kind, caring, and he touched her gently on the head, as though bestowing a blessing, and in words low and sweet, he said, "Rest, my dear, rest and take heart. For your time has come at last."

Thursday Morning/Afternoon

Connecting the Dots

Charlotte had much to tell everyone, but wasn't sure what news to give first. She supposed that she should leave police business till last. That way, if she had to switch into a more official mode, she wouldn't have to deal with the awkward repercussions that might follow. She could simply leave.

She looked around the room. Benjamin sat in the chair opposite her, and Jo, Nathan, and Rebecca sat on the couch. Paul sat on the floor, near her chair, with Gabbie lying next to him. He stroked her fur absently as he waited for Charlotte to speak. In fact, they all waited for her to speak, and like her, were no doubt wondering where she would begin.

Finally, Rebecca leaned forward, looking as though she were ready to pop out of her seat. "Tell us about Stanley. I've got to know how he's doing."

Charlotte had not wanted to start there, not with the nature of the news, but now she had no choice. And given that a direction was chosen, she thought it best to jump right in. "I visited Stanley this morning."

"How'd he look?" Jo asked.

Nathan added, "And how's he doing?"

Charlotte shook her head. She didn't want to come off sounding too pessimistic, but she knew that she couldn't hide how troubling the visit had been. "He's in Intensive Care, pretty medicated."

"Was he awake?" Paul stopped rubbing Gabbie and sat with his hand on her side.

"Sort of," Charlotte said. "He did recognize me, at least I think he did. But he couldn't speak because he had a tube…" She pointed to her own mouth, "going into his lungs to help him breathe."

Rebecca shook her head. "Poor Stanley."

Charlotte continued. "And he wasn't awake long."

Nathan took Jo's hand and said, "Were you able to find out what's going on with him?"

This was the question Charlotte dreaded the most, but she knew she had to tell them. "I spoke with one of the nurses. He was very helpful… He says that Stanley's heart has been severely damaged and several arteries are nearly blocked. He also said that, given his age and his weakened condition, it would be impossible to operate."

"What are you saying?" Rebecca sounded frantic.

Charlotte took a deep breath. "The prognosis isn't good. If they can stabilize him and get him off life support, there's a possibility that he could eventually be moved to some sort of nursing care."

Paul said, "Or hospice?"

She knew exactly what he was asking. "Stanley can't survive on his own. He'll never be able to go home."

Jo spoke in a rapid voice. "But isn't there anything we can do? Isn't there any way we could take care of him?"

Nathan joined in. "He could come live with us."

"Or I can help him," Rebecca said, "so he can be in his own house."

Charlotte sighed. She hated being in this position.

As if on cue, Paul said, "I think what Charlotte is trying to tell us is that Stanley isn't going to get better, that the best he can hope for is to be moved to a full-time facility, where he'll require round-the-clock care." He lowered his voice. "His life little more than a regimen of tubes, wires, monitors, and medication."

Charlotte nodded slowly. She was sure Paul spoke from experience. As a gay man, he had no doubt seen plenty of his friends in the same situation.

Benjamin spoke for the first time. "Does he have any relatives? Someone we can contact?"

"The nurse told me that they've located his daughter, in Oregon I believe. She's on her way."

"Then she'll be the one who will have to make any decisions," Benjamin stated. "Unless he's left explicit instructions."

Charlotte shook her head. "The hospital knows of none."

No one spoke. The house seemed exceptionally quiet. Charlotte could hear only the soft flow of the river. She wished there was something else she could say, provide them with information that would make them feel better.

Finally Jo said, "Can we at least get in to see him?"

"I don't know," Charlotte answered. "I showed them my badge, but didn't offer much explanation. They might be restricting visitors to family, but perhaps if you were to suggest that you're related…"

Jo said nothing for a moment, then whispered, "Okay."

"I'm not sure when you might want to visit," Charlotte said, "but I checked with the road crew, and they thought they would have it cleared by early afternoon—at least this far. They worked through the night to get it opened into town."

Benjamin asked, "How far were you able to drive in this morning?"

"About half way between here and the bridge." The others said nothing, so she continued. "I called the electric company. They're hoping to have power to you by tomorrow. Same thing for the phone company."

"That's not too bad," Benjamin said. "We can live with that."

Nathan turned to Jo. "We can stop and see Stanley on our way out this afternoon."

"Good," Jo said. "That sounds good."

Rebecca stared at the floor as Paul continued to pet the dog.

Charlotte needed to move onto the discussion of Beardsley and the night he was found dead. She hated to do this, but she couldn't put it off any longer. At the same time, she didn't want to create a hostile environment.

"Listen," she said, "one of the reasons I came here was to talk about Tuesday night. However, I know you're all pretty upset about Stanley, so if you'd rather wait…"

"No," Rebecca said in a surprisingly strong voice, "let's get this over with. You came all this way, the least we can do is answer your questions."

Charlotte looked at Rebecca. She liked this woman very much.

"What about the rest of you? Are you up for doing this right now?"

"It's okay by me," Paul said evenly, "but it doesn't really involve me as far as I can tell. In fact, if the rest of you would be more comfortable, I could take off."

"Well, for that matter, it doesn't involve me either," Rebecca said, "at least not directly."

Benjamin said, "It's okay with me if we answer your questions now. I would like Rebecca to stay, and I'm fine with Paul being here." Charlotte would have expected Benjamin to resist Paul's presence.

Nathan and Jo nodded in agreement, which Charlotte took as a sign to continue. "You're right, Paul, this doesn't involve you, and Rebecca this involves you only indirectly. Still, I would be glad if you both stayed."

"Okay," Paul said, "as long as Gabbie gets to stay." He flashed a smile as he scratched the dog's belly. She snuggled up closer to him.

Charlotte appreciated his warm nature right now and was grateful to have him there. And she could see that he had a calming effect on the others. Even Benjamin seemed glad that he was there. Perhaps they liked him around because he had no history with them—no marital struggles, no sibling rivalries, and he wasn't a cop.

"Okay, then, I'll get started. Just to summarize what we've discussed so far, Benjamin, Nathan, and Jo, all three of you were down at the hospital on Tuesday night and each one of you was in the parking lot."

The three nodded.

"Benjamin, you said that you did not meet or see Mr. Beardsley that night or at any other time. Is that correct?"

"Yes, that's correct."

"And you did not know about the pictures until yesterday, and you have never seen them."

"That is also correct."

At this point, she believed Benjamin. She doubted he would be foolish enough to say he had never met someone if he actually did. No matter how clandestine a meeting, there was always the possibility that someone had seen them.

Charlotte turned toward the couch. "Jo, had you ever met Mr. Beardsley?"

"Not directly."

"What do you mean?"

"I saw him wandering around at the resort. At least I'm assuming it was him."

"When did you learn about the pictures?"

Jo considered the question. "I'm not sure of the exact time, but it would have probably been very early on Wednesday…yesterday? Was that just yesterday morning?"

"Yes," Nathan said.

"Wow, I can't believe…so much has happened. Anyway, Nathan told me yesterday sometime."

"I guess that leaves you, Nathan," Charlotte said. "You evidently knew about the pictures."

"That's right." His words seemed to stick in his throat, and he acted the most nervous of anyone.

"And did you know Mr. Beardsley?"

"I did, but I didn't…I mean, I didn't know what he had in mind. He was just supposed to help set up the massage—nothing else. The pictures…I didn't…" Nathan mumbled out a few indecipherable words and then finally talked about how he had met Beardsley in a bar and how he got talking about his brother coming to town and how Jo wanted to meet him. Beardsley had offered to make up the invitation and slip it under Benjamin's door at Richards.

Charlotte looked at Jo. "You knew about this?"

She hesitated only a second. "That's right. I wanted to meet Benjamin."

"But you weren't there when Nathan worked all this out with Beardsley."

"Right, I hadn't met Beardsley."

"Then how did he take the pictures?"

"When I was giving Benjamin the massage, he just sort of wandered in, looking like a lost tourist. He was holding a video camera in his hand, looking like he was about to get some shots. I guess that's what he was doing."

"And you didn't know it was Beardsley who wandered in?

"No I didn't."

"But you did know that the person you were massaging was your brother-in-law?"

Jo glanced at Nathan and then said very carefully, "Yes, I knew it was Benjamin. It was my idea to set up the massage. I got Nathan to help me, even though he was against the idea. But I wanted to at least meet Benjamin."

Something didn't sound right. Nathan had a stranger set up a massage so Jo could meet her brother-in-law? "Why didn't you just introduce yourself or at least arrange to bump into him somehow. Surely that would have been easier than going through this elaborate setup just so you could see who he was."

"You're right, of course," Jo said. "But I thought it would be more fun this way." She smiled at Benjamin. He looked away.

"Then why use Beardsley at all? Why not just slip the invitation under the door?"

Nathan jumped in. "That was my idea. Beardsley said he had a computer and could make an invitation that looked authentic, so I gave him one of Jo's business cards." Nathan hesitated. "He also offered to slip the invitation under the door, so Benjamin wouldn't see me or Jo."

Charlotte considered this for a moment. "And when did you learn of the pictures, Nathan?"

He shifted in his chair nervously. "Tuesday night."

"You met Beardsley in the parking lot?"

Nathan answered slowly. "Yes, I was looking for Jo and he showed up."

"And you two argued?"

"He showed me the pictures, told me about his blackmail scheme. I, ah, told him I would have nothing to do with it."

Nathan looked panicky. She doubted very much that he'd pass a lie detector test. "What happened next?"

Nathan looked away. "He started to threaten me. Said I was involved whether I liked it or not."

"Then?"

"Then? Nothing really. I pretty much told him to get lost. I was more concerned about Jo at that point and Beardsley was pretty drunk. I figured he wouldn't even remember the encounter the next day."

"And where was he when you left? There in the parking lot?"

Nathan seemed relieved to hear this question. He didn't hesitate or look away. "Actually, he was down in the bushes. He fell down the little ravine there in the back of the parking lot. I think Gabbie scared him and he stumbled and fell into the bushes."

"And that was the last time you saw him?"

"Yeah, I got out of there before he climbed back up. As I said, he was real drunk, calling me names, swearing at the trees and bushes. He was still yelling when I drove off."

"So Mr. Beardsley was down in the bushes, yelling at you, calling you names, and trying to climb back up."

"That's right."

"And was that the last thing you heard when you were driving away?"

"Definitely. He was too noisy not to hear."

Charlotte believed this part of the story, and it fit with what they knew—Beardsley was drunk, no footprints were found other than his and those of the witness, and as she had learned this morning, the rock that had killed him had been found right near where the body had been. What troubled her was the story about the blackmail. Neither Nathan nor Jo were telling the truth, at least not the whole truth. Despite what they said, she doubted very much they would have gone through all that trouble just so she could meet Benjamin, and what was more doubtful was that, even if they had decided to do it, they would use Beardsley. Jo could have easily managed to come up with a gift certificate and slip it under Benjamin's door. Still, if the two of them stuck to their stories, she could not refute them, given that the only other person involved in the scheme was Beardsley and he, according to their stories, was solely responsible for any thoughts of blackmail.

Charlotte wished she could believe them. She would like nothing more than to turn in a report saying that Nathan and Jo had been playing a joke on Benjamin and Beardsley took advantage of the situation. If she didn't feel so uneasy about what she had been told, if she didn't have the sense that something was being hidden from her, she would probably be fine with saying just that. But she hated loose ends, hated things that didn't add up, and above all, she hated being lied to.

"Okay," she said, "I think that about covers it." She tried to sound as noncommittal as possible. "I might have a few more questions down the road, but I think I've gotten everything I need, at least for now."

Nathan shifted nervously. Jo smiled, glanced over at Benjamin, who looked out the window.

Rebecca leaned forward. "What happens now?"

"I turn a report in to the DA and the Medical Examiner's office does the same. If the DA's office determines that a crime has been committed, they'll follow up from there. I wish I had a better answer for you, but that's all I can tell you for now."

Benjamin stood. "Then we're done here, right? That's all you need from us?"

"There is one other thing, Mr. Randall, and this pertains specifically to you." She pulled a newspaper out of her satchel and opened it up. "I'm sorry to have to show you this, but the paper got ahold of the pictures and published a couple of them, along with a story about you and Beardsley."

Benjamin grabbed the paper and read. His face turned white and he began to shake. She had read the article earlier. "Dead Con Man Found Near Westside." The story described how the body of a known con artist had been discovered near Westside Hospital and how several photos were found with him. The paper then printed one of the photos of Benjamin lying on the massage table, wearing only his boxer shorts. Jo got off a lot easier, only her arms and body showed, although Charlotte doubted Jo would have cared much one way or the other. Next the article described how Benjamin was a prominent Northwest land developer, although it was unknown how he had been involved with the deceased or whether there was any foul play connected to his death.

Benjamin looked up at Charlotte. "But how is this possible? How did they get this information?"

"The reporter who wrote the story—he showed up at the hospital that night. I'm not sure how he got a copy of the pictures. I did notice him talking to the witness, and it wouldn't have taken him a lot of effort to gather the rest of the information."

He let the paper fall to the floor and dropped back into the chair. Rebecca grabbed the paper and read. "It's not that bad, Benjamin, really. I think it will all be forgotten in no time."

He stared at her without moving. Then he said, "Not that bad? What do you mean not that bad?" He jumped to his feet and headed toward the front door. "I'll be outside, unless the detective has any more good news." He stomped out of the house without waiting for a reply.

Rebecca handed the paper to Jo, who, along with Nathan, read the article. Jo shrugged and Nathan groaned.

Charlotte said, "Rebecca, I'm sorry it had to turn out this way. If I could have prevented it, I would have."

"I know," Rebecca said. "I know."

Charlotte stood. "Well, everyone, I must get back to the city. It was good seeing all of you again, even if under such difficult circumstances." The others stood, including Gabbie.

Paul hugged her and smiled. "Let's get a beer sometime."

"You're on."

Jo hugged her quickly.

Nathan stood for a moment, not doing anything. Finally he said, "Could I talk to you before you leave."

Jo stepped forward. "What do you need to talk to her about?"

"We'll be just a minute," he told Jo in a firm voice, and then to Charlotte said, "Come on, let's go outside."

Charlotte followed him out. She half expected Jo to follow, but she stayed inside. They walked down the driveway a little way, out of earshot of everyone else.

"I've been lying to you."

Charlotte waited.

"I knew about the pictures, knew Beardsley was going to take them."

"Go on." She felt more relieved than angry.

"It was Beardsley's idea. I was just dumb enough to go along with it."

"And what exactly did you go along with?"

Nathan told her about how he had been drinking, how he met Beardsley and complained about his brother, how Beardsley came up with the scheme, how Nathan had agreed. "I can't believe I went along with it. He said he'd help me out, get me the pictures, and I could do with them whatever I wanted. Like I said, I had been drinking a lot, and by the next day I had only a vague recollection of talking to Beardsley and didn't think about it much after that. And then on the night of the massage, Beardsley called me and told me he wanted to meet, that he had the pictures. And then he demanded that I buy them from him for a couple hundred dollars. Otherwise, he'd send them to my brother and Jo and tell them both about my involvement in the blackmail scheme. So I paid. I couldn't have my brother involved, couldn't have him know that I had helped Beardsley to set up the massage and get the photos."

Nathan sounded so frantic, she felt a little sorry for him. "What happened next?"

"I met him that night, gave him the money, and he gave me a copy of the pictures, and I went home and burned them. But then he showed up in Seattle and threatened me and said he was planning to go after Benjamin and that I had to help him, or he'd go to the police."

Charlotte believed she was finally hearing the real story. "What did you do?"

"The first time he found me, I didn't know what to say, and the next time I told him to get lost, that I wanted nothing to do with it. And then on Tuesday night, I stumbled on him again. He was passed-out drunk in the front of the hospital and Gabbie woke him up. So I hurried out of there and walked around to the back of the building, but he found me in the parking lot, and that's when we argued and that's when I told him to leave me alone and never come near me again. By that point, all I could think of was finding Jo and making sure that she was alright."

"So what you're telling me is that you got drunk one night, agreed to some silly scheme, sobered up, decided against it, and after that Beardsley kept showing up and dragging you into his plot."

Nathan nodded slowly.

"And Jo?" She didn't know about any of this?"

"Not till yesterday morning. She was only trying to protect me."

Charlotte smiled. "She does have her hands full with you, doesn't she?"

Nathan stared at the ground. "I know."

"It's not so bad, Nathan. From what I can tell, the only real crime here is on the part of Beardsley, when he made you pay money for the pictures. I'm not sure you're guilty of anything other than bad judgment."

"But what about Beardsley? The pictures? His death?"

"Given that he's the one who took the pictures and threatened you, he's the one guilty of extortion, and he's the one who got drunk and fell down and hit his head, I can't see that you have anything to worry about."

Nathan's face lit up. "So you believe that his death was an accident?"

"Definitely."

Nathan smiled. "Thank you, Charlotte, thank you very much."

"All in the line of duty."

He laughed. "I guess this hasn't been the easiest case for you."

"Certainly one of the more interesting ones."

He hesitated. "I should get back in to Jo. She'll go nuts if I don't tell her what's going on."

"You better."

Nathan started to leave, then turned back and hugged Charlotte quickly. This was the first case she had ever worked on where the suspects hugged her. She liked the change. And better still, the pieces finally fit together. As far as she was concerned, the only guilty party was now dead. True, being drunk didn't excuse Nathan from the law, but at the same time, he really had taken no action that could be construed as a criminal act, at least nothing of any significance. The only thing he could really be accused of was conspiring to take pictures of his brother and Jo without either of their knowledge, but given that he destroyed the pictures, criminal intent would be difficult to prove. The only question that remained was how she would write up her report. She supposed she should include everything Nathan told her, but what would be gained?

Charlotte wanted to say good-bye to Rebecca and headed toward the house, just as Rebecca was coming outside.

Charlotte said, "I'm sorry I had to be the bearer of such troubling news."

"It's not your fault."

"I know, but..."

"Come on, Charlotte, I'll walk you to the road."

They headed down the driveway toward the line of trees that bordered the road. Off to the right, near the side of the house, Benjamin picked up branches and piled them in the center of the lawn. He never acknowledged their presence.

"He must be pretty upset," Charlotte said.

"He must be. He never does yard work."

"That newspaper article hit him hard."

"Benjamin doesn't like surprises. I'm sure in his mind his life has been ruined."

"And you?"

"Me?"

"What about your life?"

Rebecca shrugged. "I'll have to wait to see what happens."

When they reached the end of the driveway, Charlotte stopped. A soft breeze wound through the trees, gently rocking their trunks. Light and shadow danced on the gravel. The sound of chainsaws echoed up the road.

Charlotte said, "Perhaps sometime when you're in Seattle we could go have lunch or something, I mean, after all this is behind you."

"I'd love it," Rebecca said.

Charlotte wanted to say more but felt all twisted inside. Finally she managed, "You still have my number, right?"

"I do. And you have ours."

"I wish…" She wanted to tell her how nice it would have been to spend more time together, to have met each other under better circumstances. She wanted to tell her what a remarkable woman she was, how beautiful and kind. "I wish…the road were clear. I'm still a little sore from yesterday."

Rebecca smiled. "At least the sun is shining."

Charlotte must have been staring, because Rebecca blushed and turned away.

"Okay," Charlotte said, "I better be going. Good luck out here. Good luck with everything."

Rebecca hugged her with a firm grip. She felt warm, soft, comforting. Charlotte never wanted her to let go. When Rebecca finally released her, Charlotte turned and started walking away. After she took a few steps, she looked over her shoulder and called, "We'll talk soon," and then headed toward the giant cedar that lay across the road.

The Best Laid Plans

J o began to follow Nathan and Charlotte outside, but thought better of it and returned to the couch. Obviously Nathan had made up his mind, and making a scene would do no good. All Jo could do was wait for him to finish.

She sat down and let out a long sigh. Paul was back on the floor next to Gabbie. She rolled onto her back to allow him to rub her belly. Rebecca sat next to them and scratched the dog under her chin.

Jo normally loved it when people took such an interest in Gabbie, but right now she was too keyed up thinking about Nathan and Charlotte. Jo just wanted all this behind them so they could get on with their lives. They had much to work out—money, bills, the baby. So much had happened since she found out she was pregnant she had little time to consider the implications of having a baby. To be faced with the prospects of being a parent was in itself overwhelming. Add to the mix their financial straits and it was enough to send her over the edge.

She eased back into the cushions and closed her eyes. It felt good to be still for a minute, to just sit and listen. The river flowed quietly now and was mixed with the distant sound of chainsaws. Rebecca and Paul spoke in soft tones, their comments mostly directed at Gabbie, reminding her what a sweet dog she was, how pretty, how soft her fur. Gabbie ate up every bit of attention.

Jo sat for several minutes without moving, trying not to think about anything, but the harder she tried, the more her mind filled with the images of babies and hospitals and massages and photographs and police and stormy weather. She bolted upright and leapt to her feet. Paul and Rebecca stared. Gabbie cocked her head. Jo smiled and walked toward one of the side windows to look for Nathan and Charlotte. While leaning against the glass, a voice behind her said, "Looking for someone?" She spun around and there was Nathan.

"Everything okay?"

"Everything's fine."

r. h. sheldon

She could feel herself relax. "Come over to the couch. Let's sit down."
They would talk more later.

Rebecca stood. "I'm going to try to catch Charlotte before she takes off." She sprinted outside.

Paul continued to stroke Gabbie. "So what are your plans now?"

Jo glanced at Nathan. "We haven't really discussed it, but I guess as soon as the road opens we'll take off. Stop in Seattle at the hospital and then head up to Anacortes, see if we can catch the last ferry. What do you think, Nathan?"

"Sounds like a plan. But what about you, Paul? What are you going to do?"

Jo could hear the concern in Nathan's voice. He had really taken a liking to Paul, which was a good thing. Nathan could be so standoffish at times, but the circumstances of the last few days, along with Paul himself, seemed to cut through that.

"Just what I was trying to figure out. After all, I'm sort of homeless right now. Maybe I'll get a sign and hang out on a corner in Seattle. It could say 'Homeless in Seattle'—or something as equally clever."

"How about 'Homeless sick bastard in Seattle'?"

"That works."

Jo hit Nathan on the shoulder. "You two. Neither of you are being very nice."

"Alright, alright," Nathan said. "You can drop the *in Seattle* part."

Another slap on the shoulder.

"Man, I'm going to have a bruise."

"Hit him in the head. He won't feel that."

"Enough. Both of you."

"Yes ma'am," they said in unison.

"That's better."

"So Paul, seriously, what are you going to do?"

"I thought I'd head to Seattle, call my insurance company, take care of getting the Volvo out of there, rent a car, buy some clothes…"

Jo said, "But where are you going to stay?"

"I'm sure I can stay with some friends—or maybe rent a room for a couple nights. No big deal."

Nathan sat up. "You can stay with us if you need to. We have room."

Jo sat in amazement. Then Nathan turned toward her. "Is that okay?"

"You two in the same house—oh my god, *I'll* have to move out."

"Jo!"

"Of course you can stay. Besides, Gabbie would love it."

Paul grinned. "I'd love it too, but I'll need to take care of business first, and that mostly involves Seattle."

He was right, of course, Orcas Island would be very inconvenient, but she could see Nathan was disappointed.

Jo said, "Then you'll have to come visit afterward. We'd love to have you."

"In the meantime," Nathan said, "we can drive you down to Seattle."

"Good, because that was just what I was going to ask you."

Jo added, "And maybe you'd like to stop by the hospital with us."

"I'd definitely like that. I want to check in on Stanley."

The mention of Stanley reminded Jo of her first meeting with him, having him come to her room, seeing him here at the house. Poor old guy. She hoped he wasn't suffering too much.

Nathan and Paul grew quiet. Finally, Paul said, "I'm going to see if I can snag Rebecca and head over to the campsite. I'd like a chance to visit with her before we take off—and I need to make one more sweep of the area to see if I can find any remnants of my equipment."

"Good. And Nathan and I can help clean up around here so Rebecca's not stuck with all this mess."

Paul stood and Gabbie looked up at him sadly.

"You're now getting her famous abandoned look," Nathan said. "It's one of her better ones."

"She's a pro, alright." He headed toward the door. "See you guys in a little."

Jo and Nathan sat for a moment, not saying anything. Nathan picked up the newspaper. After a couple minutes, he said, "Look at this, an article about yesterday's storm."

"What's it say?"

"Not much, really. They're calling it a supercell, some sort of intense storm center, unusual for this area, but not impossible. Says it took out power in a small area and knocked down a couple trees. That's about it."

"Nothing about the river, the flooding, the lightning?"

"Nope. Only about two lines in all."

She stood up slowly. "I'm ready for a vacation."

He followed her lead and rose from the couch. "A very very long one," he said.

Where It All began

Rebecca thought about the first time she went into the campground, just a few days earlier, when she had met Paul. She remembered how frightening it had seemed, and wondered what it was exactly she had been afraid of. And now, as she walked toward the campground with Paul, those fears seemed more than ridiculous than ever.

"So when will the three of you be leaving?" she asked Paul.

"As soon as the road is clear. And from the sound of those chainsaws, that shouldn't be much longer."

"The house is going to feel pretty empty without all of you there."

"Yeah, I bet it is. It's not every day you have a house full of stranded guests you hardly know."

Rebecca smiled. "Pretty unusual, wasn't it? After the last few days, little would surprise me."

"It's probably a good thing to have our foundations shaken once in a while. Keeps life interesting."

"That it does."

They walked. The road was littered with twigs, leaves, and branches large and small, but with the bright morning sun and clear skies and soft breeze, it didn't seems so bad and in some ways looked more like a wide trail through the forest than a road clogged with remnants of a storm.

"What a glorious morning," Paul said. "We've certainly had our mix of weather lately."

"Maybe it will settle down for a while."

"I have a feeling it will."

Rebecca glanced over at him. She could tell he was serious, and for some reason, she believed it as well, as though whatever it was that nature was trying to get out of its system, it had, and now everything would be calmer. Not just the weather, but life in general. That didn't mean it would be the same—or necessarily easy—but not quite so tumultuous.

"This is it," Paul said, "the entrance to the campground."

She followed as he crouched under the thick metal bar that blocked the old driveway.

"I haven't come through the front door before."

"That's right," Paul said, "you've always opted for the more dramatic entrances."

"I never do anything the easy way."

"I'm not sure this way is any better. As you'll see, the bridge is getting pretty rickety and the trails overgrown. Still, it's not so bad."

When they reached the bridge, she said, "It's kind of fun. I like the way it bounces when you walk."

"This is the way Stanley came yesterday morning, and he managed okay."

"Poor Stanley," she whispered.

The stream gurgled softly beneath them as their steps echoed across the water. Rebecca stopped for a moment and looked at the water, so clear she could see each rock, each twig and leaf that lay on the bottom. Upstream the water disappeared into a tunnel of green formed by the low-lying branches of vine maple.

"This is so lovely," she said, "so peaceful and serene."

Paul waited at the end of the bridge. "It is," he said, "an amazing contrast to the main river."

They wound through the trees until the trail ended.

"This is where it was," he said, "my campsite."

A chunk of the bank had been carved out by the water, as if the river had intentionally reached out and torn off a piece of land.

"Oh dear, look at this."

"Yeah, just look at it. Anyway, I wanted to search around a bit, just in case anything blew off into the trees before the site got washed away."

They searched the surrounding brush, looking into bushes, behind trees, next to fallen branches. When they found nothing, they walked down by the river and searched between the rocks and boulders lining the banks, then they returned to what had been the campsite. Rebecca waited to hear what Paul wanted to do next.

"That's it," he said. "I just needed to be sure."

"I'm so sorry, Paul."

He shrugged, not a shrug of disinterest, but one of sad acceptance. "Let's head to the car."

They walked silently through the trees and back over the wooden bridge. When they reached the smashed car, Rebecca gasped. "This is awful!"

"It was time for a new car."

"Paul, you don't mean that."

"I guess not, but it looks like I'm going to get one."

They walked around the fallen tree to the side of the car that wasn't quite as flat.

"I was thinking I might be able to pull some clothes from the back, if I can just bend back some of the trunk's lid."

"We should have brought something from the house."

"Yeah, but maybe we can make do with one of these fallen branches. I need to pry it open just a few inches."

"But how?"

"Back here, right by the rear corner. See how the lid is creased and the edge is sticking up?" The car was smashed down so low that the trunk stood a little below knee level. "If I can slip something in there, I can pry it up, just far enough to reach in."

Rebecca looked around and spotted a downed limb about three feet long and four inches in diameter.

"Perfect," he said.

He took the branch and stuck one end through the narrow opening in the trunk. He cupped his hands beneath the free end of the make-shift lever and pulled it upward. The muscles in his arms and neck tightened. He sucked in a deep breath, clenched his teeth, and pushed against the ground with his legs. He grunted. His face turned red, sweat beaded up on his forehead. The limb moved slowly, almost imperceptibly, but then the metal began to bend, like the lid of a tin can, and a gap appeared in the crushed metal. The sound of the crinkling trunk filled the air. He continued to pull up, watching the gap widen. Then the limb snapped and a piece of wood flew into the air and Paul tumbled backwards into a thicket of huckleberry.

"Damn!"

Rebecca raced toward him and helped to lift him out of the bramble. "Are you okay?"

He brushed himself off. "Just a little scratched up. I'll be fine."

She was reminded of pulling the weed out of the garden, how monstrous it had been, how she had somersaulted backwards—how long ago it all seemed.

They returned to the car. The lower part of the branch lay on the ground near the place Paul had been working. Rebecca wasn't sure where the other half had flown off to.

"Can you reach in there?" she asked.

"I think so." He struck his arm into the new opening. "I had some extra clothes in here, in this corner." He fished around for his invisible catch. "Here we go." He pulled out a pair of jeans, then reached back in, searched around some more, and retrieved a T-shirt. He continued this process until he had extracted several more T-shirts, a few pairs of underwear and socks, another pair of jeans, and a couple flannel shirts. The last time he stuck his arm in, he felt around for quite a while, reaching in as far as possible. Finally, he said, "I think that about does it." And he pulled out his arm.

Rebecca gathered up the clothes as Paul stood.

"Better than nothing," he said. "At least I can put on some clean clothes."

"I'm glad you were able to find something in there."

"Yeah, that was lucky."

Rebecca would have hardly called any of this lucky—no place to live, barely any clothes to wear, no car. "Paul, if there's anything I can do, anything you need…"

"I'll be fine, Rebecca, really. It's a bit of a hassle, no doubt, but not the end of the world."

"But this won't be cheap, replacing all this…How are you going to pay for it, what will you do?"

Paul grinned. "I'm not completely destitute. I have money in the bank. And better still, I have credit cards!"

"Don't kid around. I'm worried about you."

He smiled. "Thanks, Rebecca, I appreciate that. But I'll be okay, honest. I really do have plenty of money saved. All I was doing was working or hiding out in my apartment and not spending it on anything. I might be homeless and jobless, but I'm not broke."

Rebecca stared at him. How much she admired his thinking, his courage.

"But what about you?" he asked. "What about your life? Are you going to be okay?"

"What do you mean?" She could feel herself squirm.

"Do you remember the day we met, the day we pulled Stanley out of the river?"

"Of course I do. It wasn't *that* long ago."

He chuckled. "No, it wasn't, was it…Anyway, before all that happened, I saw you standing in the river, playing in the water, as though you were dancing, celebrating."

She felt herself blush. "You saw that? I had no idea…"

"You looked like a child. So beautiful, so graceful, so free. It was such an amazing sight that I thought I was having a vision."

"Oh, Paul, don't…"

"I remember thinking that you would be a person I would want to know, a person alive, vibrant—full of joy and spirit."

She smiled, remembering for a brief moment how wonderful that felt, but then she remembered the realities of life—her husband, her home, her responsibilities. "Life isn't like that all the time, Paul."

"Maybe not, but there's no reason it can't be like that some of the time."

She didn't respond. It was dangerous feeling the way she felt that day. It could lead only to greater dissatisfaction, greater unhappiness. "Maybe we should get back to the house," she said.

He smiled.

They began to walk. Paul wanted to take the clothes, but she wouldn't let him. She told him it was because he was too dirty, but she knew there was more to it than that. They shielded her somehow, provided protection.

They said little walking down the road. As they drew nearer to the house, the sound of chainsaws grew. Rebecca realized what an assault they were after the morning of quiet. The blocked road and lack of electricity meant no car engines, no televisions, no telephones, no radios, only the peaceful sounds of nature—the river, the wind, the birds.

"It's kind of sad." She spoke in a quiet voice, not wanting to add to the din of the chainsaws.

"How's that?"

"The noise, the disruption. They'll probably have the road cleared soon."

"I'm going to miss you, Rebecca. Getting to know you has been amazing."

"Me too, Paul. I hope we stay in touch."

"You won't be able to get rid of me."

"I'm glad."

They walked into the driveway. Benjamin and Nathan stood outside, but they were too far away for her to hear what they said or see how they might be getting along. Jo was out by the truck, cleaning out the back. Gabbie watched. When the dog saw Paul and Rebecca, she grinned and howled and wagged her tail and then ran out to greet them. Jo turned and smiled and started to walk toward them. Rebecca felt elated to have them there, to share in their lives, but her heart ached at the thought of them leaving. How would she ever face her life again?

Brotherly Love

Nathan walked out of the house and around the side where Benjamin picked up branches. He had been putting off talking to his brother, but he knew that, before he left, he would have to tell Benjamin the truth. He couldn't say for sure why he felt this way, maybe in part because Jo had become implicated in the scheme, even if her role did seem innocent enough. And maybe too he felt a little sorry for Benjamin. Nathan had always imagined his older brother had everything—career, money, success, the respect of the community—but now that Nathan had gotten a glimpse of his life, saw the sterile world in which he lived, saw the emptiness of his relationship with Rebecca, he realized how foolish he had been. Sure Benjamin had money, and plenty of it, and even if the pictures in the paper did affect his business, he no doubt had enough stashed away to live a long time in luxury. But was there anything about Benjamin's life that Nathan would really want, aside from the ability to pay his bills?

Nathan knew that the months ahead weren't going to be easy, knew that money would be tighter than ever, that he would have to take whatever job came along, but he was ready to face it, ready to do what it took to turn their lives around. And who Benjamin was and what he had accomplished and how much money he had mattered little to what lay ahead for Nathan and the choices he needed to make.

He stood for a moment by the side of the house, watching his brother as he picked up an armful of branches and stacked them carefully on the growing pile in the center of the lawn. One of the branches fell from the pile and stuck out about a foot from the mound. Benjamin picked it out from the others and placed it back on the top.

Nathan stepped forward. "Hi, Benjamin."

His brother grunted a mild greeting but continued to work.

"Listen, Benjamin, I was hoping to get a chance to talk to you before we left."

"Okay," he said as he picked up a branch.

"It's about the pictures, the whole blackmail business."

Benjamin stopped and stood up straight. He had several branches in his arms.

Nathan felt the usual twisting in his guts and shortness of breath. He continued, "I know we haven't always gotten along, I know we—"

Benjamin threw the branches on the pile. "What's this about, Nathaniel?

"I…" Benjamin walked toward him. "I knew about the pictures, the blackmail."

"Of course you knew. You already told us that Beardsley approached you that night, told you about his scheme."

"No, I…before that, I knew before that. I went along with it, gave him Jo's card, told him about you."

"You…" He stared at Nathan for several seconds. "So this wasn't just a way for Jo to meet me?"

"No, Jo didn't know anything about it."

"She didn't know who I was, didn't know she was giving a massage to her brother-in-law?" He shook his head. "I should have known something wasn't quite right about her story."

Benjamin's response confused Nathan. He expected him to be ranting by now.

"It was all a mistake on my part, Benjamin. I should never have talked to Beardsley. I told him about you, about all your money, about you coming to the island, and he came up with his little scheme. I went along with it at the time…" He hesitated. "I was drinking a lot—too much. But after that, I didn't really think about it a lot, thought it had all been forgotten and I'd never see Beardsley again, and then he called, said he had the pictures. I didn't know what to do, so I bought them from him just so I could destroy them and forget this whole mess. I wanted nothing to do with him or his scheme."

Benjamin began to pick up branches again. "So you were going to blackmail your own brother. You were going to ruin my life just so you could get a little money." Benjamin spoke calmly, evenly. There was an eerie quality about his voice. "All our lives you've never been able to take on responsibility, never been able to grow up, and then you do this, against someone in your own family. How low can one person sink?" ·

Nathan felt as though he had stepped into a deep pool of water, the weight of his sins pulling him down. "I wasn't going to go through with it." His voice was a scratchy whisper. "That's what Beardsley and I argued about. I told him to get lost, to stay away from me."

Benjamin threw a big limb onto the pile. "But it was a little late for that, wasn't it? Because the damage was already being done, my life already being ruined." His remained cool and distant. "But you washed your hands of it, so it didn't matter to you, did it?"

Nathan said nothing. What could he say? No matter how he looked at it, he was the one to blame.

"And now what happens?" Benjamin asked. "You go back to your nice little life, as if nothing had occurred, and I'm left dealing with your mess. I guess some things never change."

"I'm sorry, Benjamin. I'm truly sorry. If there were anything I could do..."

Benjamin stopped working and stared at Nathan, his face full of disdain. Finally he said in a low voice, "Jo must be very proud of you."

The words cut through Nathan like a deadly arrow. He felt like a child, wrapped in embarrassment and shame. How could he have gotten to this point? How did he now find himself suffering the condescension of his brother, enduring his spiteful malice? Too many years had these feelings of inadequacies and self-loathing lurked beneath the surface, waiting to strike, and now he was forced to endure them, because of his own ridiculous mistakes. He wanted to creep away, hide from this moment, from his brother, but there was nowhere to go, no place to run. He was stuck at the house until the road cleared, until they could drive off, never to return. And his brother just stood there, looking down upon him as he would scum in the street, with his smug feelings of moral superiority. It was the same sort of look he would give Nathan when they were younger, when Nathan would screw up in school, at home. Benjamin was always there, to condemn, to belittle. And when Nathan thought about these times, when he remembered the sense of inadequacy, the frustration, he wondered how it was that after so many years these same feelings could still exist. But he wasn't a child anymore and Benjamin couldn't control him as he once had and Nathan didn't have to take this sort of treatment, and he felt within himself a surge of power, rising from a source deep within, emerging gradually, like lava from a volcano. And it filled his body, growing higher and higher, and he looked at his brother and saw how pathetic he was, how alone and sad, and he said, "You're right, Benjamin, Jo has little to be proud of. And I too have little to be proud of. But when I look at your life, when I look at all your money and your big house and your smug attitudes of superiority, I see nothing but a pitiful, lonely man, and I'm thankful that, despite all my screw-ups, I still have such an amazing life."

Just then, Jo walked around the house and approached the two men. Gabbie bounced along after her, wagging her tail and looking all around. "The road has just about been cleared," she said. "We'll be able to leave soon."

Nathan smiled. "Great. I'm ready to get home." And he and Jo and Gabbie walked toward the house, Nathan and Jo holding hands, leaving Benjamin standing by his pile of debris.

Until We Meet Again

Paul waited outside for Jo and Nathan to gather up their few belongings. Rebecca waited with him. He could see Benjamin at the far side of the house, still collecting fallen branches. The pile in the middle of the yard had grown enormous, as though he were preparing for a giant bonfire, like the kind they used to have at high school pep rallies.

"Is he going to come over here to say good-bye?"

Rebecca glanced at Benjamin. "I don't think so. It's best just to let him alone right now."

Paul had considered going over to say good-bye, to thank him for his hospitality, but Rebecca's advice confirmed his own conclusions.

Paul changed the subject. "What about Stanley's truck? Anything we can do about that?"

Rebecca stared at it for a moment. "I hadn't really given it any thought."

"It doesn't seem fair that we're leaving you here to deal with it. Maybe when I'm back up we can move it or something."

"Don't worry about it. You have plenty to keep you busy." She was right, but he didn't want her saddled with the burden. "Besides, I'm not sure what we should do with it."

Paul thought about this. "Maybe Charlotte could help. Perhaps you could call her and see what she thinks."

Rebecca brightened. "That's a great idea."

Jo and Nathan came out of the house, with Gabbie bouncing after them. They threw their packs in the back of the truck and came up to where Rebecca and Paul stood.

Jo threw her arms around Rebecca. "It's been wonderful meeting you."

Rebecca hugged her back. "For me as well. And you have to keep me posted on the baby."

"I promise."

Then Rebecca hugged Nathan. "You too, brother-in-law. I want to hear from *all* of you."

Nathan glanced toward Benjamin. "We'll keep in touch, I promise."

Rebecca crouched down and scratched Gabbie on the head and behind the ears. "And you can come to visit any time you like."

Paul said, "You'll notice that she didn't make that offer to any of us."

Rebecca stood. "Oh, Paul, what are we going to do about you?" And they hugged each other long and hard. Paul felt as though he were saying good-bye to someone he'd known many years.

"I'll be back soon," he said, "to take care of my car. So you're not rid of me that easily."

"Good. And when you get here, we'll go for a long walk."

"Let's just hope it doesn't rain."

"Amen to that."

Paul draped his arm around her shoulder as they walked toward the truck.

Jo said, "Gabbie and I will ride in back."

Paul protested. "No, Jo, I can ride back there. I'll be fine, really."

"So will I, and I can catch up on some sleep."

"But Jo—"

"Paul," Nathan said, "best to give up right now. You won't win."

"But I just thought…"

Jo winked at Rebecca. "When are these men going to learn?"

"Paul," Rebecca said, "get in front and don't argue."

Paul squeezed her shoulder. "Yes, ma'am. I'll do as I'm told."

He jumped into the truck, closed the door, and opened the window. Jo and Gabbie climbed in the back, and Nathan closed the tailgate and the door to the camper shell, then walked around to the driver's side.

"Thanks for everything," he said.

"Yes, thank you," Jo called through the side window.

"Yeah," Paul said, "thanks for putting me up and taking such good care of me."

Rebecca waved them off, slightly embarrassed. "I was happy to have you." Her eyes glistened with tears. Paul was grateful he would be seeing her again soon. "Make sure you give my regards to Stanley," she added. "Tell him I'll be down to see him soon."

They pulled out of the driveway, with the three of them waving and Rebecca waving back. She looked so lonely standing there—and sad—and Paul wished he could do something to alleviate her loneliness.

When they were about to pass through the trees at the end of the driveway, Paul glanced toward Benjamin and saw that he just stood there, watching them ride away, but he was too far away for Paul to see his face clearly, and there was no way of knowing what he was thinking or feeling.

The Index-Galena Road was still littered with branches, leaves, and pine needles, but the closer they got to the highway, the clearer the road became, and once they were on the highway, there was no evidence of a storm.

"This is too weird," Paul said. "It's like the storm was centered right over the house."

"Pretty strange. Makes getting home sound even better."

The idea of going home was what felt strange to Paul. Even before he had given up his apartment, he had never felt quite at home. He acted more like a boarder, coming home late, leaving early. He had never really gotten settled there, never hung pictures, never unpacked all the boxes. He had moved in right after he split up with Aaron, and viewed the apartment as little more than a necessity, a place to store his possessions until he figured out what to do next. His life became his work, and his apartment a hotel room with a color TV and a queen-sized bed. He had little other furniture and what he did have were beat-up remnants he picked up at second-hand stores and yard sales. When he moved out of the house where he and Aaron had lived, he had taken few things except his clothes, some books, camping gear, and a handful of kitchen utensils. Anything of real value—photos, letters, personal files—sat in a small storage unit in Seattle, which he had not opened since moving into the apartment, not until a couple days ago.

And now he headed back to the city, his plans for a wilderness adventure thwarted, with no place to go, no direction to take. Yet he couldn't help but be pleased by the new friends he made, and he hoped he would have the opportunity to spend more time with all of them, once he figured out what he would do next, where he would go—and how he would get there. When he had left Seattle on Monday morning, he had no idea what lay in store for him. All he knew was that something had to change, and now was the time to make that change happen. He didn't care about his job, his career, his apartment, or his possessions. What he did care about was filling that deep void that had

overtaken him, an emptiness overshadowed by long hours at a meaningless job that filled his meaningless life.

"What's going on, Paul?"

"Huh?"

"Just wondering where you went off to, if you're doing okay."

"Yeah, I'm okay. Just thinking. I've got a lot to consider."

"I know that feeling."

"I bet you do."

"And I know you got a lot on your mind—the car, your camping
gear, where you're going to stay."

"It's not just that stuff—I wish it were, but it's not. I ran away from
Seattle, not wanting to look back, maybe afraid that I would chicken
out and end up back in another little apartment in the middle of the
city, working a job I hated, for people I didn't respect."

Nathan shook his head. "My worst nightmare."

"I found myself living a life I never thought I'd be living. Doing
things, saying things, feeling things—as though I was living someone
else's life, stuck in his body, everything out of control. I felt so trapped—
like I was dead, but still alive."

Nathan sighed. "I know that one all too well. I've always felt trapped
by the jobs I've had, hating every minute of them, hating the people I
worked with, the work I was doing. Sometimes I thought I'd explode."

"And how did you deal with that? How did you force yourself day in
and day out to join the ranks of the living dead?"

"I didn't. I exploded regularly. Ask Jo."

"I guess I didn't explode enough. But I do know that if I had kept
doing what I was doing, there would have been nothing left."

"So now what?"

"That's the big question, isn't it? I wish I could tell you." That was indeed the big question. The notion of slipping into the wilderness didn't
hold the same fascination as before, not after this week—and he wasn't
about to stay in Seattle. What he wanted was something new, something different, yet something that he was moving toward, working for,
not something that he was escaping.

"What about you, Nathan? What would you like to be doing?"

"Me? That's not too complicated, really. I'd have myself a big workshop, full of woodworking tools, both power and hand tools, the best
of everything, so I could do big and small projects, quality stuff only—
the finest wood, the best designs, the best construction."

"That sounds great. How come you're not doing that?"

"Money."

"Oh, that."

"Yeah, that. Takes a lot, not just equipment, space, but to carry myself through till I could build up a business. It could take several years and it seems like every time we get ahead a little, something comes up and we're broke again. Mostly it's my fault. I'm always screwing up at work, and I end up quitting or getting fired."

"Not surprising if you're always doing work you hate."

"You managed."

"At what price though?"

"Yeah, well, who needs a soul anyway?"

"Exactly my point." Paul flashed a smile. "Besides, my motivation was probably different than yours."

"How so?"

"I had first taken the job just for something to do, to make money, but slowly I got sucked in, and then about a year ago, when a relationship I was in ended, I threw myself into my work because it was the only thing I could figure out to do. And then the job just sort of took over, but all the time I was hating it, and hating myself just as much, but I stuck in there, because I didn't know what else to do."

"And now?"

"I still don't"

"So you just up and take off for the woods."

"I had a little help."

"Help?"

"Mushrooms."

"Mushrooms?"

"Of the magic variety."

Nathan looked at him briefly. "You were tripping and decided it was time to leave your apartment and your job and all your possessions and head to the mountains?"

"They were very good mushrooms."

"Oh my god. That's too wild." Nathan began to laugh. "Mushrooms! I can't believe you, Paul." He laughed harder. "Only you!"

"I didn't even tell you about the vision part."

"The vision?" He could barely speak because he was laughing so hard.

"God told me I needed a vacation."

And now Paul began to laugh and the truck filled with their roars and Gabbie barked from the back. Soon Paul's side hurt from laughing so hard, and he could feel his face turn red and his eyes water.

Nathan tried to speak but his words were garbled by the noise.

"What did you say?"

"You're nuts. You're fucking nuts."

"Sticks and stones…"

"Can I tell Jo this story? She'll die."

"I suppose, but I doubt she'll find it as funny as you do. Just because you think my life is a joke…"

"All our lives are jokes."

"Seems to me that it's my life we're laughing at."

"You've got to admit, Paul, you do provide a lot of good material."

"Is it my fault God has such a sick sense of humor?"

Nathan continued to snicker, as though replaying Paul's comments over and over in his head.

"Fine, Nathan, have your fun. Now I see why Jo wanted to ride in back."

"Come on, Paul, give me a break. You're the only homeless gay druggie I know who talks to God."

"Well, if you put it that way…"

Nathan exploded in laughter.

Paul turned in his seat and looked at Jo, who lay next to Gabbie, rubbing her head. Paul opened the windows between the cab and the camper shell. The noise of the wind filled the truck. "I wish to register a complaint about your husband," he said in a loud voice.

Jo shouted back, "What did he do now?"

"He's being abusive. Got any good ammo?"

"Ask him about the time he peed in the flower pot?"

"Jo!"

"Thanks." Paul shut the windows. "How about it, Nathan?"

"I can't believe she told you that…"

"Well?"

"No comment."

"I bet she's got lots of good stories."

"Which is why I'll do everything in my power to keep you two separated."

Paul chuckled. "Good luck."

They drove into Monroe and turned onto Highway 522. The afternoon was bright and sunny, the sky without clouds. The hum of the highway lulled Paul with its gentle rhythm and soon he was struggling to keep his eyes open. It felt good to have someone else driving, to be able to rest, to not have to worry about what was going on around him. He allowed himself to drift into the afternoon's warmth, into the soft rocking of the truck, and soon he fell into peaceful sleep that felt soothing, deep. And then Nathan said, "We're here," and he opened his eyes and realized that they were at Westside Hospital, pulling into the back parking lot. He could not believe he had slept the rest of the trip. It felt as though he had just closed his eyes, that only a couple minutes had passed, yet here they were, at the hospital, on their way to see Stanley.

Perchance to Dream

Stanley looked around the room, making sense of little. He could feel the tube going down his throat and the air pushing in and out of his lungs, but it all seemed unreal. And even the sounds in the room—the beeps, the clicks, the sighing of machines—possessed that same surreal quality, as though part of a dream that he could not quite wake from.

Despite the confusing sensations, he knew very well what was going on. He could envision the IV in his arm, the wires hooked to his chest, the monitor tracking his failing heart. He wondered how long he had been here, how many days and hours they had kept him alive. He wanted to move, to crawl off this bed, but his body held no strength, and even keeping his eyes opened proved too great a task. So he closed them and listened to the uneven beeps of the monitor and pretended that he was at home on his giant leather chair and there were no pumps or motors or clicks or whirs or tubes that forced air into his tired and failing lungs.

When he opened his eyes again, he could make out the forms of several people standing near his bed. At first he thought that the doctors and nurses were again hovering over him, perhaps laying odds on how long he would survive, but then the faces came into focus, and he saw that Jo, Nathan, and Paul had come to visit, and he felt relieved by their presence, not only because they weren't part of the medical staff, but also because he was surrounded by friends, and he was glad to have their company, even if he couldn't speak.

He felt Jo squeeze his hand and saw that she smiled at him, and then she said, "We've missed you," and he wanted to smile back, to say how glad he was to see to see her, to see all of them, but all he could do was watch—and hope that they knew.

He fought to keep his eyes open, but his lids grew heavy, and soon he drifted into a state that lay near the edge of sleep, like that space between dream and imagination. He remained aware of the wires and tubes and of his own heaviness—and of the presence of his friends—

yet felt as though a part of him floated above the earth, like a kite tethered to the ground. But the string that tied him to his anchor grew longer, and he grew indifferent to the heaviness of his body, no longer interested in looking back, in knowing what lay behind him. He soared freely, past the shadow of dreams and into the bright light of day, where he watched for the place he had called home all those years. He felt himself pulled by the draw of the mountains, not like an animal tempted into a trap, but like a voyager returning home, his sights set on the only direction that he could choose. And soon he found himself soaring up the Skykomish Valley, past familiar stands of trees and open roadway, until he reached the North Fork and flowed up the river toward his favorite fishing hole, past the Randall home and the old campground. He felt the peace of the mountains envelop him, like an old friend greeting him after years of separation, and before long he stood in the river, wearing his George Dickel baseball cap, holding his fishing pole in one hand, his flask in the other, chewing on a cigarette, the river squeezing his legs affectionately, the fish jumping around him, as though they welcomed his return. Light danced on the water, glistening brightly in the afternoon sun, and he could feel it warm him, easing the aches of his tired body, freeing him from the heaviness, the discomfort, the pain. And then he realized he was no longer alone but that standing next to him, in waders and a flannel shirt much like his own, was the angelic woman from his dreams, her face pure and bright, her golden hair waving in the soft mountain breeze. She held a fishing pole and gently cast out a line. And then she turned toward him and smiled, and he could feel the light emanate from her, and he realized that she was the source of the warmth that he now felt, that she was the one who freed him from the confines of his tired body. The breeze picked up and blew off his cap, and it landed in the water upright and floated down the river. She laughed gently and opened her arms, and he stepped toward her, drawn to her radiance, and the light sparkled brighter on the water, until there was nothing but light, and he moved without effort, without thought, drifting toward her essence, until all awareness faded away, until all he knew was the light, and he felt a gladness and peace and comfort he had never known possible. And he knew then that he was home.

Just the Two of Us

Benjamin watched them pull out of the driveway, all three of them waving to Rebecca, Rebecca standing there, waving back, until the truck disappeared. But she continued to stand there, staring down the driveway, as though she expected them to turn around.

He returned to clearing branches from the expansive lawn. Normally he would have hired a couple local kids to clean up, but right now he needed the distraction, and the exertion felt good. He could let his anger and frustration flow into his work, and maybe then he could make sense of all that had happened. Maybe if he breathed hard enough, sweated long enough, he could stop this downward spiral and see a way out of the fate that had befallen him.

He sped up his pace, loading his arms with as many branches as he could hold. The pile had grown gigantic, and he wasn't sure what he would do with it once he was finished. Maybe he would burn it. Maybe he would build a pyre to his old life, a symbol of the destruction caused by his brother.

He dumped his load onto the other branches and headed back to where he had been working.

"Benjamin."

He turned. Rebecca had called from over by the driveway and now walked toward him. He waited, panting hard, his shirt soaked with sweat.

"Benjamin, I've been calling you. Are you okay?"

"Sorry, I was distracted."

"You ready for a break? Would you like something to eat?"

"No, I'm fine."

"Want some help?"

"No."

She started to walk away, and he was about to go back to work, but then she stopped.

"Benjamin, we need to talk."

He wasn't in the mood to talk. "About what?"

"About what?" She hesitated. "About all that's happened. About what we're going to do."

"I don't see that there's a lot we can do. The damage has been done. Nathan has made sure of that."

"Nathan?"

"Didn't he tell you? Didn't my dear brother—who you seemed to like so much—mention that he was going to blackmail me, that he was part of the whole scheme?"

"He told you that?"

"Yes, he told me."

She acted almost relieved. "I was wondering if he would."

"You knew about this?"

"Jo told me, when we were making up the beds last night."

"And you didn't tell me?"

"I wanted it to come from him."

"You wanted—but what about me? What about my feelings?"

"I'm sorry, Benjamin. I just thought it would be best. Besides, he wasn't going to go through with it. Did he tell you that he changed his mind?"

"Yes, he told me!" Even she had conspired against him. "I should have him arrested, that's what I should do."

Rebecca started. "You would do that, to your own brother?"

"He was going to blackmail me!"

"But he didn't. He didn't do anything to you."

"And what about the pictures? What do you call those?"

Rebecca hesitated. "I suspect that the pictures would have been taken whether or not Nathan was involved."

"You don't know that."

"You're right, I don't. But I know that Nathan is a good person, that he was feeling desperate, confused. Yes, he made a mistake, but he realized it was wrong and didn't go through with it."

Benjamin couldn't believe that he had to defend himself. "We'll see what the courts have to say about it."

She was quiet for a moment. He could see the confusion on her face, the hurt, the anxiousness. But then she took a deep breath and said, "You would do that? You would risk the publicity? You would let the world know that your own brother hated you enough to consider blackmailing you? You would have this go on for months and months, maybe even years, just because you've been embarrassed? And in the end, what would you accomplish? Ruining his life? Ruining all their lives? Breaking up their marriage? Leaving the baby without a father? If you did it right, you could make sure they lose what's left of the little money they have. Maybe they would even lose their home. Would that satisfy you? Would that be enough to heal your wounded pride?"

He couldn't believe that she would talk to him this way. "But look what he's done to me!"

She wasn't about to back down. "What *he's* done to you? Benjamin, have you ever considered that maybe you're also to blame?"

"Me? I didn't do anything."

"That's right, you didn't do anything. Tell me, Benjamin, how many people have you cheated out of their money through your slick dealings?"

"If you're talking about my business, that has nothing to do with it."

"Doesn't it?"

"You never complained about the money."

"I didn't complain about a lot of things."

"You sound happy about the pictures."

"You know, I think I am. Maybe it's the best thing that could have happened. Maybe you won't be able to do to anyone else what you did to Stanley."

"What do you know about Stanley?"

"More than you realize."

A cool wind gusted through the trees. A shiver ran up his spine and he turned back toward Rebecca and could see that she also felt a shiver by the way she shrugged her shoulders. Then she looked around, and her face was transformed from anger to a sort of wonder, and she looked calmer, slightly distracted.

"I thought he was here," she said in a quiet voice. "I thought I would turn around and see Stanley, standing right behind me. I thought I could almost smell him, that kind of musty smell he had." She looked around again. And then she turned back toward Benjamin, and stared at him for a long time. Finally she smiled. "I'm leaving for a while, Benjamin. I'm taking a trip." Her voice was soft, almost wispy.

The sudden change confused him. "A trip? What are you talking about? Where are you going?"

"I don't know. I don't know where I'm going. I just decided this very moment, just this second."

"You can't just pick up and leave."

She smiled again, her voice calm. "I can, Benjamin, and I'm going to."

r. h. sheldon

"But how, when…"

She looked toward the sky. "Soon, I should think. Very soon."

He could see she was serious, no matter how silly it sounded. "But what about me? How could you leave now, after all that's happened?"

"Look at it this way, Benjamin, with all the extra time you'll have on your hands, you'll be able to learn how to cook and do your own laundry."

He couldn't believe she was saying these things. "You can't leave. I won't allow it."

Rebecca broke into a grin, and then began to laugh—a hard, genuine laugh, full of amusement and fun. "Oh Benjamin…" She made it sound as though he were the one being ridiculous.

"I'll cut you off. You won't get a cent from me."

She dismissed him with a flick of her wrist. "Fine," she said, "do whatever it is you need to do. In the meantime, I'd better get packing." With that, she turned and walked toward the house, her gait light and carefree, like a little girl off to play with her friends.

Benjamin never felt so confused, so betrayed. He stood for a moment, then walked toward the river and sat down on a rock near the water's edge. He felt as though he were drugged or in a bad dream. The water splashed and gurgled and washed over the rocky bed in long silvery ribbons. He had not sat down by the river in years, not since the last time he had visited his grandfather, just before he died. The old man had wanted to come outside that day and sit on the rocks next to the water, and there was no convincing him otherwise. So Benjamin helped him walk down to the rocky bank, and they sat and watched the churning water and listened to it spill over the rocks and into the deep pools.

"I never came down here enough, Benjamin, never paid much attention to what was in my own backyard."

Benjamin didn't know how to respond. His grandfather had been saying a lot of these sorts of things since returning from the hospital. Benjamin assumed it was the painkillers.

"Make me a promise, Benjamin. Promise me that when you're living in my house, you'll come sit by the river whenever you can. Promise me that, Benjamin, promise you'll do it often."

"Sit by the river?"

"Yes, I want you to come down here. Every day if you can."

"I don't understand. Just come down here and sit? But why?"

His grandfather stared at him, his look tired, almost sad. "I just want your life to be different, that's all."

"But…"

"Just promise me, Benjamin. Promise me you'll do that. Promise me you'll come sit by the water, like we're doing now, and you'll watch the river—and listen. That's all. Just watch and listen."

"Yes, sir, but I don't…"

"Make sure you do it, Benjamin. Don't forget."

Benjamin hadn't thought about that conversation in a long time, and even now he wasn't sure what his grandfather had been talking about.

He looked at the river now. The water splashed against the bank, spraying tiny drops against the rocks by his feet. Out of the corner of his eye, he noticed something floating toward him, close to the shore. He couldn't tell what it was at first, but then, as it grew nearer, he saw that it was a baseball cap, off-white and dirty. The hat floated upright, as though the air caught inside kept it afloat, like a raft turned upside down. When the cap was close enough, he grabbed it and held it in the sun to get a better look. The hat was old and worn, but only the edge that touched the water felt damp. Benjamin didn't understand how that could be possible, unless someone had just lost it, but even if that was the case, it should have been wetter. He turned it around to read the front and found a black emblem that said "George Dickel Tennessee Whisky." He placed the hat on his head and leaned back against a large rock and watched the river flow over the boulders and listened to the melodic sounds of the moving water.

Late Summer

Dear Paul—

Thanks so much for your last letter. As always, it's great hearing from you and getting an update on everything that's been going on. I loved the pictures, but I've got to tell you, I can't even tell that Jo is pregnant. And you tell her that no matter what she thinks, she doesn't look fat. In fact, she looks more beautiful than ever. I bet the baby is going to be gorgeous, just like her parents. Have they picked a name yet?

Your news about you and Nathan came as quite a surprise. When and how did you two decide to go into business together? And a wood-working shop, no less. I didn't realize that Nathan was so talented. I would love to see some of the furniture you described, especially that table. It sounds magnificent. But I still can't figure out how you fit into all this. I thought you worked with computers! When did you become a woodworker? And what about poor Jo—I can only imagine what this arrangement is like for her. You two are like kids when you're together. What's she going to do when the baby is born?

Really, though, it sounds like a wonderful idea. You seemed ready for something new, and I bet Nathan loves working with you. Together you must make quite the team (and no doubt an entertaining one). I'm anxious to see your work. I have a feeling that together you two can create some extraordinary furniture.

I appreciate you sending me the program from Stanley's service. I'm sorry I wasn't able to be there, but I needed to leave right away. I was afraid I would never have the courage again. But I was glad to learn that you made it and you met up with Jo, Nathan, and Charlotte. And I was also happy Benjamin showed up. I wasn't sure he would. Your description of the service made it sound quite lovely, and even though I couldn't be there in person, I was with all of you in spirit. I've thought about the events of that week a lot, about how I met you and Stanley and the others. In some ways, it all seems years ago, yet in other ways it feels like only yesterday that you and Stanley were sitting in my kitchen. How strange I could miss someone so much I had known such a short time. I feel lucky to have met him, just like I feel lucky knowing you. I can't wait to see you and the others in September. (Don't forget to send me directions to Orcas Island.)

I've been staying in touch with Benjamin, although not as often as he'd like. He doesn't understand how I could have left, what it is I'm looking for, and honestly, I can't say I understand either. I'm not sure when, if ever, I'll return to him or Index, but the longer I'm away, the more difficult that sounds. I'm not the same person I was before you and I met, and I know Benjamin sees this, but he doesn't know what to do about it and wants some part of his life back to what it used to be, before his world was turned upside down. And I think he's having a tough time living in that house by himself. Without work to distract him, he's home more than ever. What makes it harder is that he's never been one to make friends, and I don't think he's even going to church now, not since that newspaper printed the photographs. From what I can tell, he spends most of his time alone, hanging around the house, working in the yard, walking in the woods. He even told me he's taken to sitting by the river in the evening. I don't recall him ever sitting by the river, let alone walking through the woods.

The last time I talked to Benjamin, he said that his parents were coming to town over Labor Day weekend and that he and Nathan would be spending time with them. This might be the first time the four of them have all been together since the boys were teenagers. (That will be an interesting reunion!) So maybe Benjamin and Nathan are communicating now. I hope so. I do feel sorry for Benjamin, for how much he has lost, how much has changed, how alone he is, yet I can't be the one to help him or take care of him. It's taken me over forty years to start taking care of myself, and there's no turning back.

By the way, Charlotte updated me on the final ruling on Beardsley's death. (Did you know we've been writing?) I was relieved to learn they concluded his death was accidental and no further action would be taken. Charlotte told me there really was no evidence to prove wrongdoing and by all appearances, Beardsley fell and hit his head. I'm glad that's all behind us, although I imagine Benjamin will never fully recover from having those pictures published in the paper. The truth is, I doubt the repercussions would have been as bad as he thought, but he insists that his life has been ruined.

The funny thing is, my life has never been better. I love being here in Arizona. Every morning, before heading into the restaurant in Winslow, I walk up to a plateau near my house and watch the sun rise. The land is vast and empty and I can see for miles as the morning light spreads across the open grasslands. It's so extraordinary, and it makes me think of you, the way you got excited about the forests and the mountains. Each morning the sun touches some part in me that I've never known before, as though for a brief instant I'm part of its light. And then, once I'm fully charged, I head back down to my house and then off to work.

The restaurant where I wait tables is a lot of fun, and I absolutely love my job. It's just this greasy little diner that's dingy and worn and full of grizzly old guys just like Stanley, gruff on the outside, but with hearts of gold. I love them all and look forward each morning to waiting on them. They tease me and joke with me and flirt with me. It's like being a kid again. You'll have to come check this place out. I'll even wait on you, if you leave a decent tip!

Anyway, Paul, I should get going. I need to wash out some clothes before going to bed. But before I end this letter, I wanted to tell you about the dream I had last night. You were in it and we were walking up the side of the mountain and the sky was dark and scary, like that time we got caught up there. And then lightning struck a tree, just like before, and we grabbed onto each other. But this time, rather than it starting to pour down rain, the sky seemed to open up and a man appeared. At first I thought it was Joseph Smith, but then he seemed to change to an old guy, frumpy and unassuming, and then he sort of switched back and forth between the two and finally he became both of them at the same time, just like what will happen in a dream. He smiled at us and started chuckling, and soon this became louder and heartier, and all of a sudden he was laughing so hard it felt like the earth was shaking. And then in a flash of light he was gone, but we could still hear the echoes of his laughter bouncing around the valley, and they seemed to go on forever. And we just stood there, holding onto each other, surrounded by the endless echoes of laughter. And that's when I woke up. Isn't that a wild dream?

I hope you're well, Paul. Write me soon and tell me how everyone is doing. Give Nathan and Jo a big hug for me. And give yourself one too. And you and Nathan try not to drive Jo insane!

Love, Rebecca

P.S. Let me know when Gabbie has her puppies. I definitely want one!